MVP

A NOVEL

James Boice

Scribner

New York   London   Toronto   Sydney

SCRIBNER
1230 Avenue of the Americas
New York, NY 10020

First Scribner trade paperback edition 2007

SCRIBNER and design are trademarks of
Macmillan Library Reference USA, Inc., used under license
by Simon & Schuster, the publisher of this work.

For information about special discounts for bulk purchases,
please contact Simon & Schuster Special Sales:
1-800-456-6798 or business@simonandschuster.com

Designed by Davina Mock-Maniscalco
Text set in Aldus Roman

Manufactured in the United States of America

1   2   3   4   5   6   7   8   9   10

Library of Congress Cataloging-in-Publication Data

Boice, James, date.
MVP : a novel / James Boice. —1st Scribner trade pbk. ed.
p.   cm.
1. Basketball players—Fiction. 2. Teenagers—Fiction. 3. Murder—Fiction.
4. Rape—Fiction. I. Title.

PS3602.O45M97 2007
813'.6—dc22   2007061712

ISBN-13: 978-0-7432-9299-3
ISBN-10:   0-7432-9299-5

To my mom

Prologue

MAN CHECKS INTO A HOTEL, meets a girl, has sex with her. A man exits a plane, takes a limo to a resort hotel, lugs his bags in through the door of the lobby, then he's having sex with a stranger. A professional man—an athlete, a basketball player—meets a woman at a hotel in Las Vegas, love at first sight, and not even an hour later they are wrapped up together in the throes of passion. He is in Las Vegas in the off-season to invest in a new casino maybe and he is forbidden from having anything to do with gambling in his contract and something sparks between him and a girl in the lobby as the concierge hands him the room key and they walk up to his room together, kiss on the mouth outside his door, stumble in together, take off each other's clothes, fall into each other like two comets, and when it's over she is no longer alive and he leaves. Woman gets screwed in hotel room, man is arrested for murder. Man murders woman in hotel room. Rapes girl in hotel room then kills her. Girl paid and sent by casino owners to make him feel welcome is murdered by celebrity. Girl sleeps with celebrity, dies. The rich globe-trotting celebrity with all he desires at his fingertips—hordes of willing females in every city, comped Courvoisier, rapper friends, his biggest worry putting a ball through a hoop more times than his opponents, a contract that places a check for hundreds of thousands of dollars in his mailbox each week—rapes a twenty-one-year-old cocktail waitress until she bleeds, chokes her until she stops breathing. Girl sleeps with the second strange man in two days, bleeds a little because of the size of this second man and because both men are a bit on the rough side with her. Girl wears a skirt, he stands behind her, lifts the skirt up, she's bent over the chair, in a hotel room. A girl from the suburbs of Vegas gets a job as a Bacardi promo girl at a new casino outside downtown—off the beaten path, the manager says to her—easy money, more than waitressing, which means soon she will finally move out of her parents' house and go to L.A. or New York, somewhere cooler than Las Fucking Vegas, only to be approached by the manager after a week and told she won't be handing out free Bacardi Silver samples any more because she is being hired by the casino to work in a special position being created just for her. She is a girl who envied cheerleaders in high school and is relatively attractive she knows—long red hair, smartly applied makeup, average-sized but well-shaped boobs, good butt and abs from hours at the gym—because in high school she was unattractive and invisible—acne, freckles, baggy jeans, and hoodies that hid her. It stays with her. She has been hospitalized for anorexia three times in the last year and a half, she meets a famous professional basketball player at a hotel outside of town, all the way near Red Rock, but a more luxurious hotel than she ever imagined she'd be in, and she goes with the professional basketball player into his room consensually and he rapes her then chokes her to death.

—You gonna tuck me in tonight? he says when she approaches him at the front desk.

—Me? No.

—Don't you ever smile?

—I don't know. Yeah. I guess.

—I want to see you smile. Come on.

She smiles and he says, —Why don't you show me where my room is? I'm bad with directions.

The concierge leans over the desk and goes, —Oh it's real easy, it's—

—I got it, bud, he says. Then to the girl, —Real quick. I'm tired.
Please?

And as she rides up with him her knees buzz with validation, high.
All the miserable nights she's spent alone, every dark violent manic
thought evaporates and the ceiling of the dull dead prison of her life
pops off and stars and contrite moonbeams spill their life over her, the
hotel's museum-esque cold cleanliness bursting into warm tones of
sepia and oak as she breathes sweet scents she's never breathed before
and absently fixes her hair. As he flirts with her, teasing her about her
late work hours, she looks forward to moving into her own place soon
with all the money she's been making. In L.A. or New York dye her
hair and change her name and get into the entertainment industry or
start a magazine and have lots of people like her. And a half hour later
she is dead and he is leaving with her panties crumpled and dotted with
blood in his hand but otherwise neatly dressed, shirt tucked in, as he
closes the door behind him with a cold click.

There is sex. There is death.

He's half black and half Asian but that makes you all black, and
he's on a private plane to Las Vegas, headphones on, exaggeratedly
long frame slinkied into a great big tan leather seat like a recliner with
plenty of squirm room even for the averagely built, bottled water un-
opened on the tray, eyes closed, a colorless sky painted outside the
window—lands at nine o'clock at night. He is the winner of six consecutive scoring titles, three consecutive championships, youngest
league MVP ever, youngest to score fifty points in a game, etc. He is
born in Boston to a man who slept with a girl, grows up, becomes rich
and well-liked and heavily involved in charity work in Third World
countries, is asked whether he has any aspirations for a political career
when his playing days are over, sleeps with a girl, she dies during it,
goes to trial with the chance of them deciding to put him to death.
Born a boy, an only child in a happy family that travels the world together, because his father's a basketball player, and rich too, with only
one another to turn to, like a tribe of transients untrusting of outsiders, a clan. Parents who've been married since after high school,
their love obviously predestined, though there have been some hard
times in their marriage that their love and determination toward each
other have gotten them through and they remain faithful and dedicated to their child and very much in love and the boy benefits from
that, grows up well-adjusted. The father is African-American, though
he has never been to Africa, and his mother is Japanese-American, and

they have a boy who is American. They have credit cards with six-digit limits and a low-interest mortgage on their house, a pantry stocked to the point of booby trap, and half a dozen high-interest savings accounts for the boy's college education and braces, etc. He has thin eyes and clear diction, palish skin. He grows up without a culture thus yearning to connect with *something* and he finds this in women who want him because he's rich and famous and in optimum physical condition. He spends a few hours with one such girl who is—essentially—a prostitute in Vegas and a redhead with the whitest skin he has ever seen and it turns out that on top of having a severe eating disorder she also has a hole in her heart that doctors haven't found yet and no one knows is there but is the kind that is basically a ticking time bomb, and she dies while having sex with him and he panics and flees because if it comes out he is associating with casino owners his career could be over and his name disgraced and he'll lose his endorsements and never be voted into the Hall of Fame.

He finds himself in a hallway, alone again, and he has her panties in his pocket, and he walks without moving down the hall, heart pumping and colors vivid, praying there will be no guests in the elevator because he's sweating through his clothes and there are none and none in the lobby either as he exits the elevator smiling and waving to a janitor mopping the lobby floor who looks up and breaks into a look of recognition. And out through the automatic sliding door into the parking lot where the concierge is smoking a cigarette on one of the benches and doing something with his cell phone and the concierge hides the cigarette behind his back and says, —Everything okay, Mr. Marcus? —Yeah, fine, thanks. Nice night, eh? —Sure is. Can I get you a cab? —Please. Thank you. And he gets into the cab and tells the cabbie in a firm steady voice to take him to the bus station, finds himself on a bus, and finally it is death, and he feels a hot wave of crying rush up behind his face, covers his face, and says out loud, —Call the police. No one looks at him and he brings his knees up and curls into a ball, only four other passengers on the whole bus, possibly illegal immigrants, and he is grateful for this, and as they tear through the desert toward L.A. he never wants to leave, clenching his eyes shut. He will ride buses around the country for the rest of his life, he decides, never saying another word to anyone, change his name and get plastic surgery and speak in a new voice, and disappear on the fastest buses they make so he will never be standing still again.

PART ONE
Boy Alone

1

ONE DAY, A LIGHT.

It is opaque and weightless and is created from the back of a starless sky. It comes twirling down through the gravity-less expanses, through galaxies we'll never know, finding eventually the Milky Way, then planet Earth, its eastern hemisphere, the United States of America. It hits Boston, Massachusetts, on a Thursday night in November when there's already snow on the ground. Muddy slush is hit by Greek bus drivers who are gray-headed and have bad knees, barely missing the shivering legs of girls going home alone from discos (this is the 1970s), smoking cigarettes and hugging themselves, walking briskly, heads down and highheels clacking. Men sit at bars talking about the Colonials game. The city of Boston is alone and oblivious. The light goes to a posh apartment in The Berkshires building in the Back Bay. It buries itself into the ovaries of a Japanese woman—not much more than a girl herself, actually—as her husband, a Colonial, comes inside her after returning home from the game. Somewhere down in the street a man is yelling something.

Her husband's name is Mervin Marcus. Former army private, current professional pine jockey. They've been married two years. Their apartment is enormous and highly coveted, in a building with a surveillance camera pointed at the sidewalk and a doorman. He plays for the Colonials and tonight they played New York, the Boston Center half-empty and desolate, ever-lingering warm stench of human sweat. Both Mervin and Sue are fit and attractive and young. After a Thursday night home game, the players' routine—because Friday practice isn't until eleven—is to shower, dress, and seep out into the city's private rooms, for expensive food, comped drinks, pussy, and anxious club owners leading them through the crowd. Not Mervin though, he doesn't like to go out with them—makes him feel absorbed by the masses. He believes that to be great one has to exist alone, different and weird and even unliked, unbound by social responsibilities and uncompromised by friendship. And he'll *be* great, soon enough. Just not yet. For now he'll have to settle with watching John McNeal be the starting point guard. The reason they don't invite Mervin out is because they used to but he never goes out, always has something like he's not feeling well or he has to study film or practice free throws or hit the weights. Though the truth is most nights he goes home and argues with Sue. Like tonight, a sort-of argument because he doesn't care about the candle she bought today.

When he got home tonight after the game he wanted her to speak to him about him. He wanted her to say, —I saw you on TV.

He wanted to shrug as he undressed and go, —That? That was nothing, baby . . .

—Sure it was. At least you got a chance. I was so proud.

—You call that a chance? That wasn't no chance.

—Called my mom. Sister. Denise.

—I don't mean to be overly negative baby and I appreciate you saying that. But the towel guy could have done it. They could have gotten some dope from the stands to run around like a moron for thirty seconds and not even touch the ball while John McNeal got his ankle looked at.

—Thirty-one seconds.

—That wasn't a chance. I'm sorry baby and I really do appreciate you calling them and saying that. But that wasn't shit.

—Don't worry baby, was all he wanted his loving sexy young wife to say. —You'll get your moment.

And he wanted her to rub his shoulders and make him something to eat and sit across from him at the table with her chin in her hand, watching her husband eat.

Got out of the cab, which he took home even though the Boston Center was not even a mile away. He nodded coldly to the doorman and stood in the elevator staring back at his reflection, liking how he looked. He walked down the hall and opened the door, turning the key the wrong way first and almost kicking it in. Before he could turn and take the key back out once inside, Sue was in his face blabbing about a goddamn candle and he told her, —That's fucking great, Sue. A candle. Wow. I give a shit. Fucking amazing.

Her Asian features, her eyes like inexpressive notches, her mouth spastic.

And she stared at him, walked away and into their bedroom, slammed the door, protecting the candle in her arms like a baby. Mervin apologized, and then they screwed, tired and uni-position. He got the idea to spice it up a little by putting a finger up her butt. She told him once that she liked it and he remembered they hadn't done it in a while. At least eight months. He has a mustache. Sue had been drunk when she told him that she liked it when he put his finger up her butt and had said yes she liked it because he had asked her specifically if she liked it and she'd wanted to answer correctly so that he would be pleased. Their apartment has four rooms and wood floors. Mervin's mustache is neatly trimmed. The alley next door has a sign posted that says it is under surveillance. His hair is grown poofy and makes him look like a dandelion. Sue has the same hair. She searched his face as he had sex with her. He watched himself, dipping in and out. She wanted him to kiss her, to feel his thick jaw against hers, his tongue and heavy breath in her mouth, the stubble, dangerous but safe. She grimaced and yanked his hand away, and he felt ashamed and alone, started thinking about the taxi ride and the gray of the road in the driver's windshield, then Philadelphia (Saturday night) and their defensive schemes, which is when he shot it and got off her.

Sue and Mervin go for weeks without it, Sue not noticing but Mervin notching the wall behind the nightstand, and she likes to converse from the other side of the apartment, so most of their conversations consist of *what? huh? who now?* And in the rare circumstance when they do find themselves doing it, it's boring and cold, and he finds himself either thinking of other girls or thinking of offensive schemes. He thinks on his way downstairs to a cab waiting to take him to practice one morning, This shit has to stop. I know what I'll do. Go down to Victoria's Secret. Get her some sexy drawers. That's the problem here. Put some sexy drawers on her, that'll heat things right up. Girls love that sort of shit. Get her a couple thongs. Asian girls like her don't have much ass to work but she'd still be sexy in a thong. Sexier than she is in those damn big-ass granny panties she wears all the time.

Met in a bar in Japan when he was stationed in Nagasaki his second year in the service, as he calls it. He spoke to her slowly and loudly for the first couple of hours until she told him she not only understood English but was from Boston. They fell in love, fucked in the barracks when no one was around, and in the canteen and the shitter, after breakfast, before breakfast, during breakfast. Squeezed into his bunk when he was supposed to be asleep and she was supposed to be gone, knowing the others could hear them, but that only made it better. High school basketball star from the grit of Dorcester serving his country and becoming a man like his own father before cashing in his full-ride scholarship offer from Boston College and the English major from Emerson going at it like mad jolly elves in empty public libraries, alleyways in the city at night, feet in trash, in the bathroom at bars while angry drunk soldiers pounded on the door, closets, cars, the firing range over spent shell casings in the moonlight, three times a day sometimes, exhausted and grinning and their privates aching and useless, in love. Got married, played so well at B.C. that he quit school and declared himself a pro after two years but no one signed him. Tried out

for the Colonials as a free agent and made it only because the team
was in such a dour state at the time, with the retirement of Q____ and
T_____ and the rest of the core that had dominated for nearly two
decades. A rebuilding era. He was promptly put on the bench, where
he stayed.

And now, ever since, it's only once a month.

But some red panties will change that, Mervin thought. Small red
ones, lace, so her ass hangs out and you can almost see that little tight
coochie, yeah, and black too, a whole truckload of them, call Filene's
and tell them just dump a load on our roof from a helicopter so Sue
can go up there every morning and grab a new pair, no excuses. That's
what you do if you want your life to be the best, Mervin thought, remembering the military: take responsibility, make changes, put some
effort into things, work a little. That's the matter with people who
aren't happy, is Mervin's opinion on the matter—they don't want to
motherfucking *work*. If you're *unhappy* it's because you're too motherfucking *lazy* to do anymotherfuckingthing *about* it.

Mervin Marcus masturbates in the shower every morning. Sometimes
he stands before the bathroom mirror in the bathroom with the door
locked pretending to be shitting. Mervin watches Sue come into the
room and walk over to the oak dresser and bend down to the lowest
drawer, slightly bow-legged he's noticed, pouting in the way she does
when she's tired. As she bends down her ass beneath her sweats flat-
tens and morphs into her back, the elastic waistband of her big gray
panties, uninviting and nonsexual. Could be a *man's* ass.

An ass is an ass, he thinks.

Mervin pulls himself out of Sue and wipes himself off with Kleenex
from the box on the nightstand and lies beside her for a second, where
they both stare at the ceiling. His sperm begins swimming up her
birth canal and they stare. He goes into the living room to watch game
tape with his notepad as sperm by sperm die out, until one is left, and
it approaches the membrane skin of an ovary.

She goes into the bathroom where she knows he masturbates
nearly every morning when he's home, pretending to be going to the

bathroom. Her feet are cold on the tiles of the floor, her skin veiny and purple in the fluorescent light. She touches her belly, caressing herself where she senses something amiss, the low part right above the heavy untrimmed tuft of hair, the sounds of Mervin out in the living room talking to the tape and himself. And she cocks her head like she's listening to something far away or deep in the most lost pits of her, absently looking into her own glassed eyes in the mirror, and her lips part slightly, her thin eyebrows furrow, and she listens.

Though the season was winding down and the Colonials were making a push for the playoffs, Mervin took two weeks off to be with his boy, who looked just like him he said when the nurse first handed it to him. He said to the middle-aged white nurse with an Irish accent who seemed to pride herself on her inability to smile (plus look Mervin in the eye), —You know, people talk about babies so much you don't realize how amazing it is when it happens. This life crawls out of you. It just pops out of us.

And the nurse said, —Maybe that's why everyone talks about it so much.

With his new free time he painted the spare bedroom powder blue like how Sue wanted it and though he thought yellow or green might be better he wasn't about to argue with someone who had done what she'd done—he was in an awe of her so great that it bordered on fear, if not apprehension about having sex with her anytime soon—the image still vivid in his mind of the grotesque facts of birth, the mess he witnessed with open jaw as he held her hand, things being stretched and pulled and sea urchins popping through there—yikes.

As Mervin watched Sue give birth he made a note to himself to get her on some sort of exercise regimen starting tomorrow to help her get all that weight off.

With his new free time he assembled the crib, cursing and scrambling for lost pieces. He did the dishes for her, cooked dinner, watched her breast-feed, not a little irritated about it. He liked himself for being a good father and husband, supportive and helpful and taking some weight off her shoulders. It seemed like every week he was pushing the stroller through a department store swallowing the emasculation it sent through him every time another, childless man passed him, as Sue searched through racks of faith-strainingly small clothes—the little fucker could sure as hell grow!

That's right, that's my boy.

They sat next to each other on the couch and marveled at the being they created, confounded by the simple ease of the world and comforted by something primal and necessary, laughing from the joy of seeing their child's eyes scan the room and fat hands grasping air until the eyes, which were huge, as big as theirs, landed on them—the parents, the ones he relied on for survival and focused, twinkling. And Mervin and Sue's baby, who they named Gilbert Animal Marcus, smiled.

Mervin liked to make the comment that young Gilbert looked like someone took Sue and Mervin and mashed them together.

Sue serene in her motherhood. An easy grace to her lips that said nothing when Mervin kept shaking his head and talking to fill the silence: —It's a little PERSON. I can't believe we all start out this way. He's TINY. He's a tiny PERSON.

Gilbert changed everything and they needed space. They moved west into the contentment of Hingham, after another season of failed expectations in which the championship slipped through the Colonials' fingers, the first year with Larry Bird, aka Larry Legend, the Hick from French Lick. Bird was the savior, white, goofy, who played with your head and knew the game like he was staring at your X-rays. He arrived the season after Jerome Alvin told Mervin he was improving dramatically and would be seeing some real playing time this year, especially with how much success Julius Erving was having over in Philly, the same kind of flashy street ball that Mervin played but up till now kept Mervin on the bench.

A white kid comes in and they call him Legend? Mervin thought. But *I* was supposed to be Legend. I was supposed to be the slam-dunking, no-look-passing, behind-the-back-dribbling human highlight reel, king of the league, sitting on a pile of gold. So why do they get to be Dr. J and Larry Legend and I have to be the towel boy? They're stars, I'm on the bench. They get six million, I get one. It makes no damned *sense*.

Mervin made a pact with himself then and there to make sure that Gilbert would be everything Mervin was supposed to be but the coaches and owners (white, all of them, by the way) cheated him out of becoming. Gilbert will never be on the bench, he told himself. They'll see Gilbert and how he came from me and they'll say, We screwed up, we passed on greatness.

Told himself, *Gilbert will be a star.*

It was a massive off-white house on Oak Hill Drive, in a windy town by the water.

The thought of moving outside the city where she was born and raised, away from her friends and family and any other Asian person, made Sue ill. But she knew a good house when she saw it. She saw herself as the kind of woman who knows how to appreciate what she has. She grew up in semipoverty, waiting tables since she was eleven after school and all day on the weekends at her parents' café in Jamaica Plain, waking up when it was still dark and all her friends were sleeping happily. Sue was a girl who in high school was on the debate team and went to the football games on Friday nights with her friends from church and was an English major at Emerson College, who married the first and only boy she'd had sex with, even if her father—born in Japan and could barely speak English, who worked the grill unseen in the back at the diner—didn't speak to her for two and half years (breaking the silence only when his grandson was born) because she married a nigger.

She'd sort of technically had sex with another boy once when she was in high school. This smart Japanese boy whose parents were friends with her parents and who ended up going to Amherst and lived on the Cape she heard now.

A display of their success, this house. But, as she whispered to Mervin, after going through with the inspector, little Gilbert snoring on her shoulder, —There just doesn't seem like much to do out here.

—What're you talking about? You don't do shit.

—I do too. I worked at Houghton Mifflin.

—Answering phones. Making coffee. Look, baby, this place is within the jurisdiction of the Benny Glenn League. Know what the Benny Glenn League is? The best youth basketball league in the state. The *state*. Nothing to do . . .

* * *

The boy waited silently in the backyard facing the wall like he was about to be shot, in his pj's, snow no longer falling but a deep gust of ice-wind gnawing at his ears and nose. The sky was gray and the trees naked, the snow up to his shins and digging through the skin.

The boy sniffed a leak of clear thin snot back into his nostrils, his palms flat on the siding, studying a hard crust of bird poo right at eye level.

He wasn't crying anymore. His mouth was tight and eyebrows furrowed in a little-boy pout. And aside from involuntary shaking, he showed no signs of freezing. He was woken up at 4:30 AM, still dark, in the middle of a dream having something to do with a bag of potato chips and being alone, by somebody standing over his bed with the cool basketball sheets on it, like the wallpaper that had basketball and football and baseball and everything just about, shaking the bejeezus out of him, and when he opened his eyes and sat up and rubbed his face, squinting, he saw that he was in the presence of the greatest coolest most strongest feared man on earth, who was saying, —Get up, Animal. *Get up*, Animal . . .

—Why?

—Go out back. Put your hands on the siding. Don't move until I get back.

—But there's no school today. It's a snow day.

—Not for you. The neighbors say they saw you screwing around on the court last night.

—Nuh-uh.

—They tell me they saw you half-assing it. Throwing up circus shots. Punting the ball. Sitting on the ball. Playing with worms. Screwing around.

—But I did a hundred.

—The neighbors told me everything. They don't lie. You saying the neighbors lie?

—No, sir.

—I have the neighbors watching. I'm going to ask them, Did his hands leave that siding? They better tell me no. Not even a little? Not even to scratch his nose? They better tell me, No, Merv. He stood like that all day. Like a rock. Nothing could shake him.

Gilbert went downstairs and looked at his mother standing in the kitchen in her turquoise bathrobe next to the coffeemaker, eyes puffed by sleep, porcelain skin, so pretty, and he pulled on his waterproof boots with fur, tied them tight, slowly pulled on his new blue ski jacket, knit Philly hat with fuzzy ball, waterproof gloves. Sue stopped pouring her coffee midcup and reached over, snatched the Philly hat off his head. —But Mommmm . . .

She replaced it with a green and white Colonials hat, saying, —I don't want to hear it.

Mervin came downstairs and said, —Nuh-uh. Did I say anything about a jacket? Did I say Animal go put on your boots and jacket and gloves and go outside?

—No, sir.

—Did I say Animal I want you to stand out back in your boots and jacket?

—No, sir.

—I didn't say anything about boots and jacket. Who said anything about boots and jacket?

—No one, sir.

—Did your mother?

—No, sir.

—Sue, honey, sweetie, did you happen to mention to our son here that I said to put on his boots and jacket?

—Merv, Sue said.

—Maybe Animal's soft? Maybe Animal likes to wear his furry little boots and new pretty jacket? Do you like your beautiful pretty jacket? Do you feel cute in it? Is that the kind of man you are? A sweet cute little man? A little soft faggot who wears furry little boots and pretty blue jackets?

—No, sir.

—Then take it off.

— . . .

—I said, *Strip. Now.*

The snot frozen on his upper lip. The slow itch of waiting. Seeing what kind of shapes he could make his breath come out in.

Though he was hungry and bored and cold, he hoped that Mervin would come back and tell him he was like a pro, like Julius Erving, Gilbert's favorite. (But he'd never tell his daddy that.)

He'd come home from a road trip late at night, and Gilbert would be waiting for him in the living room. Sue would let him stay up late. And when he heard the garage door opening he'd run to the door and open it and see his daddy walking toward him, gym bag in one hand, jacket slung over his shoulder, and he'd go running out and wrap his arms around his daddy's legs and his daddy would smell like after-shave and he'd say, —Did you win, Daddy?

—Yeah, we won, Animal.

—Did you score the most points?

—The most, Animal.

—Did you dunk, Daddy?

—I dunked, Animal.

And Mervin would look away from Sue, standing in the doorway giving him a look. He'd walk into the house, dragging the small boy behind him.

The Marcuses had never met the old couple next door. Not like Boston where everybody on your block knew everything about you. Here just scattered grand homes built with pieces from the warehouse, with stone fronts and gates and long driveways and well-kept grass and built-in ponds and multicar garages, pool houses, silence. A mid-upper-class Camelot.

The next-door neighbors weren't next door—they were three hundred yards away and obscured by trees. They didn't wave in the evenings when they drove by Gilbert frantically shooting a hundred baskets in the driveway so he'd be allowed to go inside and eat.

The neighbors who Mervin had spying on him now.

The only kids Gilbert knew were Sandy who was a girl and whose mom was friends with Gilbert's mom and Brian and Lauren whose dad played basketball with Mervin. They'd drive forever to Brian and Lauren's house so Brian and Lauren could gang up on him and tell him his name was stupid and why did he look like an alien and they wouldn't let him play hide-and-seek with them. They hardly ever drove to Medfield to see Sue's friend and Sandy. Gilbert asked his mom once why there weren't any kids around here to play with and she ignored him and so he asked again and she said, —You'd get dirty . . . and turned up the TV.

* * *

What's incredible is how something as beautiful as snow, which wields almighty powers of school cancellation and sled-ability, can turn on you and become your torturer.

You can't trust anything, was the lesson Gilbert was getting out of this.

He could see his mom inside through the window. It had been only a half hour of being out here, and he was already crying. He hated himself for crying. Mervin wouldn't cry.

He wanted to lift his tender destroyed size 4 feet one at a time for air. But the neighbors were watching. He was all alone. There's nothing worse for a little boy than being all alone.

After a half hour he pissed his pants. He didn't want to do it. He held it in as long as he could, clenching every muscle. But suddenly he was pissing, the snow below him yellowing, which turned out to be good because it warmed him, his legs coming back to life.

He started banging his forehead against the wall and screaming like a girl, —Mommy! Please! I love you, Mommy, please help! MOMMY!

THWACK! THWACK!
   —MOMMMMMYYYYY!!!!
As her son thumped away at the window, Sue's ass was firmly implanted in the cushions of the couch, watching the big-screen Magnavox that wasn't so much a TV as it was a hulking portal into the future, arms folded in order to keep her robe closed, her legs stubbly and crossed in the womanly way with her right foot twitching nervously, worn-out blackened-sole blue slipper dangling from her big toe, watching the *Today* show and sipping her coffee, getting ready to get up and take a shower, when she put her mug down on a coaster on the coffee table, splashing a little. She stood up, wrapping her robe and walking into the kitchen, came back with a bottle of Pledge and a roll of paper towels and took all the cooking and home-making magazines—NO sports magazines during the season!—off the coffee table and the cork basketball coasters with basketball hoop coaster stand and remotes for TV and VCR (—These things are *bad*, baby, Mervin'd said when he came home with it. —It can tape things off TV and play movies and game tapes. And it was only six hundred dollars!) and sprayed the table down with Pledge and wiped it with

long gentle loving strokes that quickly turned frantic, paper towels tearing, grunting with force, blood rising into her face, a tit about to spill out of her robe. When she was done she let out a long breath and stood up and, clipping her robe closed at the neck and thighs with her hands, carried the Pledge and paper towels under her arms back to the kitchen, put the Pledge under the sink and the paper towels on the paper-towel holder and came back in and sat down. She took a sip of her coffee but it had gone cold. Gilbert's screaming and thwacking only got louder, and she was biting her lip, trembling as her teeth sank into her flesh, short bitten nails digging into her arms, and all Sue really needed right now was to know who was celebrating their one hundredth birthday today, finding herself shouting at the TV, —*Tell me who's fucking turning one hundred today, Willard!*

—MOMMMMYYYYY!

She turned the TV up with the remote and tried to concentrate on the segment now about baby races. But whatever Jane Pauley was saying was drowned out by the muffled screams of horror interspersed with the sound of five-year-old skull striking the aluminum siding they'd had installed just last summer.

—*MOMMY! (Thwack!) HELP ME! (Thwack!) PLEASE LET ME IN! (Thwack!) PLEE-HE-HE-(Thwack!)-HE-HE-HE-(Thwack!)-HEEEEASE! (Thwack!)*

And standing up, back firmly to the window, hands hanging at her sides and bathrobe completely untied and only barely covering her nipples, big white panties in full exposition, hair a thin drooping mess, eyes bloodshot, fists clenched and shoulders rising and falling, she went to the storage closet and came out lugging the vacuum and plugged it in, almost bending the little prong things in the process, jerking it to and fro like a dead dog, and STOMPING the foot switch, causing an eruption of noise that brought instant relief.

And Sue vacuumed, little pinpoints of perspiration gathered at her hairline and neck, even though she'd vacuumed yesterday afternoon and the morning before that. She ran the machine over every square foot three, even four times, because there will be NO DIRT IN THIS HOUSE, closing her eyes and sighing because the *whir* was good, calm, her eyeballs rolling back into her head. And when she was done, gasping for breath, she knelt down on her shaky knees and pushed the foot switch with her hand, killing the machine. Gilbert had gone silent. Sue put the vacuum back and retied her robe, unpeeled her hair from her face and tied it in a ponytail, refilled her coffee, and sat down in time for the weather, which is when the phone rang.

—You're five, Mervin said, —start acting like it.

Twice a day: one hundred shots before he could eat breakfast and one hundred shots before he could eat dinner.

It was nothing, according to Mervin. The pros put up one thousand a day at least. Pro baseball players took five hundred swings a day. Pro golfers hit seven hundred balls a day, blindfolded, with their caddies jingling keys in their ears to distract them.

So Mervin said.

—I bet there are kids your age right now shooting *five* hundred. You gotta keep up, Animal, or you'll be left behind.

So Mervin said.

And Mervin put his son on a diet of goat's milk and seaweed, the refrigerator stacked with little Tupperwares containing the day's portions.

Gilbert would gag as it went down, the goat's milk stinky and yellow.

In the cupboards there weren't candy or cookies, only unsalted saltines and dehydrated tofu and zucchinis and tomatoes grown out in the garden Sue tended mostly but Mervin helped out with on weekends in the off-season.

—This is what champions eat, Mervin'd say. —The worse it tastes the better it is. You see, Animal, the body's energy can be maximized by eating easily digestible, contributive foods.

And Gilbert would look at his father blankly, his tongue tingling for candy.

—One day you'll understand.

At school Gilbert would watch the other kids eating their delicious lunches and he'd fight back the tears and force down his can of water sprouts and thermos of the mysterious gray health shake Sue mixed every night, the contents of which remained incomprehensible to him. He guessed bug butts and snake heads.

—These American kids' colons, Mervin said, —are clogged to motherfucking hell with all this processed shit they eat. It's not food. It's fake food. No wonder they're all so fat. And they'll all be lazy and depressed and unproductive because their bodies are being *stran-*

gled. Where did anyone get the idea that food was supposed to taste *good*? You think that's bad you should see what we ate in basic. By the way, how many times did you move your bowels today, Gilbert? Be honest.

Sue spoke calmly into the phone, —No, Mervin's not available right now, honey. I'm sorry. Mervin's on his way to the Boston Center. Don't call me and ask for Mervin and hang up when you know he's got practice and a game today. Go to the Boston Center if you're looking for Mervin. Stand outside with your lipstick and tits with all the others. I'm sure he'll get to you eventually if he hasn't already. Now if you'll excuse me, my son, *our* son, mine and Mervin's, because we have a *family*—our son is playing basketball in the house again and scuffing up my kitchen floor. He's just come in from the snow and so he is in a very excitable state of mood right now and has forgotten I guess that the floor is new and should not be treated like that. I've told him I don't know how many times but you know how kids are. Actually you probably don't, do you? I'd assume you don't have any children. I'd assume your eggs are dried up and shriveled and your pussy is diseased and oozing puss from the clap. You have disrespected my family and so I am allowed to speak like this to you. Your uterus is scraped raw from too many abortions. Well I do have children and I am a mother and I work hard to keep my house clean and my child fed and safe. Go sit at that bar where your kind hang out outside Boston Center. Have a drink and smoke your cigarettes and wait for my husband. He'll be along soon enough. Lord knows he's never here, so he has to be somewhere. But I'm sure you know that's how men are. He'll get done with you whatever it is he gets done with you girls. I don't know how you people live with yourselves. But I have to go now, honey. I have to get Gilbert into some warm clothes before he catches cold. I'll tell Mervin you called. Thank you, dear. Die. Good-bye.

And when the screaming stopped and the shivering stopped and the head banging stopped is when the gate opened and in stepped Mervin, basketball under his arm.

—D-d-d-d-did you w-w-w-w-win, Daddy? Gilbert asked, teeth chattering.

—I won, Animal.

—Did you score forty points?

—Fifty-two.

—Did you dunk?

—I dunked, Animal.

—Are you the best, Daddy?

—No, you're the best, Animal.

2

MERVIN MARCUS TWISTED HIS knee up in basic training coming down from the monkey bars and heading toward the mud pit with the rope that you grab and swing over it to the other side. Mervin Marcus could hardly hear out of his left ear due to his buddy Jason Duval pulling a very funny practical joke on Mervin involving getting drunk and firing an M-16 close enough to Mervin's ear for Mervin to feel the barrel buzzing his earlobe like electric barber clippers. Mervin was recruited heavily out of high school but didn't want to disappoint his mother—who was abandoned by Mervin's father before Mervin was born—by not turning out like a man, as she called it. And so instead of college he enlisted in the army to prove to his mother that he was a man and not like his father. He liked to wonder about what things would have been like if he hadn't twisted his knee in basic . . . if Jason Duval hadn't played his very funny practical joke . . .

The word on Mervin Marcus around The Association and bars where the writers congregated was that he could've been great. But the problem was he seemed to refuse to pay attention to the finer details of the game. If he'd stuck to the fundamentals of the forward position more, like rebounding and staying in position on defense rather than trying to be a superhero all the time, he could've been a very special player, was the general consensus.

The Colonials' front office sat in The Owner's beautiful corner office working out the trade that sent Mervin Marcus (and Gilbert Marcus and Sue Marcus) to San Antonio in exchange for a pair of late-round draft picks. Jerome Alvin, general manager, swore up and down that Mervin would never be more than a loudmouthed third-rate Julius Erving, plus that Larry Bird would throw an absolute fit if Mervin were allowed onto the court at all during official game time except for maybe running out with the giant mop during time-outs. Assistant GM Kevin Harrick—thirty, Yale Law School—tried not to make a big deal of waving the smoke from Jerome's cigar out of his face and said that it was his opinion, with all due respect to his immediate superior, Mr. Alvin, who he went out of his way to assure that he greatly admired and would wipe Mr. Alvin's butt after he pooped if Mr. Alvin so desired it (Mr. Alvin did *not* so desire that, Mr. Alvin declared), but that he didn't think that Mervin Marcus had yet reached his potential and that giving up on him would be a horrible mistake they would all regret for the rest of their professional lives, to which Jerome Alvin said with all due respect Harrick you're a fucking asshole. The coach chewed his pen, not really saying anything because he knew by now that whatever he said would be overruled anyway. In the end, it was The Owner's team, and The Owner didn't like showoffs. But what The Owner did like was lunch and The Owner wanted lunch. So the decision was made that Mervin Marcus and his family would be shipped to San Antonio, Texas, in exchange for a fourth- and sixth-round pick and a case of Miller High Life (an inside joke between Jerome Alvin and the front office of the San Antonio Ramblers) and that they would have Mexican for lunch. And Boston fans forgot Mervin Marcus ever played for the Colonials and the house in Hingham was sold and a new family moved in and the winds took it all away.

Mervin tried to call Jerome Alvin personally to tell him that his hearing was coming back lately if that's the reason but Kevin Harrick smoothly blew him off.

The next season Larry Bird and the Colonials won the title and Jerome Alvin was named Executive of the Year.

Mervin told Sue the night Boston traded him, —Wanna know who *I*
feel sorry for? The people answering phones over there. They're going
to get tired of all the season-ticket holders asking how could they fuck
up this bad with Mervin Marcus.

Gilbert sat on the stairs listening. He was so quiet.

And then Daddy was gone again.

He flew down on a plane and met with The Owner—another
Owner—in a restaurant in downtown San Antonio called Brasil. It
was the kind of place with no prices on the menu and where they
serve you a big chunk of lettuce as an appetizer. There were purple-
illuminated rocks on the walls with little waterfalls trickling down
them. They drank a red wine that Mervin thought The Owner said
was called Filet Mignon. The Owner was a vegetarian car dealer who
was divorcing his third wife, a twenty-three-year-old former Russian
gymnast who wanted nothing in the divorce except for every wall
hanging in the house. Mervin did his best to look impressed when the
waiter showed him the label on the bottle of Filet Mignon. He held the
glass by the stem like must be the proper way, drank the little bit of
Filet Mignon the waiter poured, and went, —Mmmmm. Yeah. That's
good right there.

Mervin's hair was no longer an Afro but now a little tight carpet
that spread down his face into a beard. He got the haircut the day before his flight. He also bought a new suit and new socks. He spent
nearly three thousand dollars. The Owner wore a string tie and spoke
with a flat midwestern accent from beneath his enormous cowboy hat,
weepy green eyes, and skinny pale hands. Mervin had just been trans-
acted into this man's possession. Each time before he took a sip of Filet
Mignon, The Owner stuck his nose into the glass and sniffed very
deeply, then held the glass up to the light and examined the contents
of it. The Owner said that the Filet Mignon went good with a kind of
low-acidic cigar. Mervin nodded and furrowed his brow and said, —Oh
yeah. Absolutely.

And the two men nodded in silence, agreeing that Filet Mignon
went well with a kind of low-acidic cigar.

White people shoveled food into their mouths that cost more than your clothes. The waiters were embalmed, homosexual teenagers, death forced to live. They bent down and murmured to you in gentle voices like you'd wet yourself if they didn't. They ignored The Owner's private booth unless The Owner himself raised his finger and beckoned. One time The Owner called a waiter over to demand the heat be turned off or he would die, and the waiter grimaced and said, —Right away, of course . . . and scurried off to extinguish all sources of heat.

Even though, Mervin thought, the heat wasn't on. It was summer.

—Well, Marvin, The Owner said, —what kind of music do you like?

—Oh all kinds.

—I love how you folks are always playing your music, Martin. Every time I go down there in the locker room to say hello, you know, to make myself available, that sort of thing. I like to do that now and again. Show my face. I'm quite progressive. Anyway whenever I venture down there I feel myself enveloped in your marvelous music. You people love your music, don't you. It must have something to do with your natural sense of rhythm. I think it's great. I'm progressive-minded, as I say, so I love it.

—Absolutely.

—What is the name for it? Urban music I believe? An urban person's style of music?

—No, right, yeah. Definitely. I definitely like that kind of music. Sir. Yeah. The . . . *urban* style of music.

—I love music. Did I mention I was a music major in college? I had my training in the French horn.

—Oh really?

—Yes. I was very good. But the life of the musician is a very limiting one, unfortunately. But enough about me. Marvin, I must tell you. I can't wait to see you play. I understand you're very exciting to watch. Slam-dunking it all over the place. Kind of like this Julius Erving kid back there in, uh, where is it, Philadelphia. Or this Earvin Johnson.

—Magic Johnson, yeah. He's going to be real good.

—You two have the same name. Earvin.

—Ha ha. Yeah.

—So, Earvin, you're from the ghetto they tell me?

—Well to be honest.

—Please. Honesty is very important.

—They used to tell me back in Boston to tone my game—er, my

style of play—down a bit. I think that's what had to do most with my, uh, limited role. But honestly I don't see it. Honestly I just try to put the ball in the basket. I mean. Or, get it to a teammate who can. And I mean, uh, if they want to call what I do flashy, I don't know I can't control that. I just want to win games.

—Winning is good.

—Absolutely. If my team doesn't win a championship, that's a failure, in my opinion. But I uh I don't believe I can help my team do that unless I'm allowed to be myself. On the court.

—I don't think you'll find that a problem here, Irving. I'm very progressive-minded. Did I mention I'm a vegetarian?

—No, you didn't.

—I am. I don't eat meat. Not a lick of meat. Not even baked beans. Because the broth has meat in it. Did you know that?

—No.

—It does. Anyway, I always say that if it's good for the team, it's good for me. I say that.

—Good to hear it, sir. Because, yeah, I just want to win.

—Don't we all, Jonathan. Don't we all. That's why we've brought you in. We think you can be a real breakout player here. Matty, my general manager, tells me he remembers you from Boston University.

—Yeah.

—Says he can't believe no one in this league's figured out how to use your talent yet.

—Yeah. It's been frustrating, to be honest, sir. I mean, just a little bit.

—Well I think you'll find what you've been looking for here with the Ramblers, Bartholomew. I think the angels have blessed the San Antonio Ramblers. I think you've been sent from somewhere special. We're prepared to make you the centerpiece of our team.

Mervin laughed. He couldn't help himself. —You have no idea how good it is to hear that, sir.

In San Antonio there were no tumbleweeds, but in their place an expanse of metropolistic vomit stacked high with glisten and the hair-fiber hold-tight grip of the inescapable odor of meat. There weren't any cowboys giddyupping horses in the dusty streets and quick-drawing their six-shooters at each other at sundown in front of the saloon, no corrals or morally dubious women in great flamboyant poofy dresses and floppy hats smirking from porches and cigarettes, no men spitting and making mud. The streets turned out to be paved and the men didn't carry firearms, at least not visibly. To Gilbert, it didn't look all that different from Boston to be honest except much, much hotter.

It was the early 1980s. The sweat of the people lingered in the air in a fine mist as Mervin eased through downtown San Antonio in his new silver Jaguar the day before his first training camp with the Ramblers. Mervin was happy. He was. All necessary changes had been made. When things get bad you change things. And here he was, having changed things. Boston seemed like a nightmare. How had he survived? It was going to be a good year.

Gilbert sat in the passenger seat with his feet swinging, seat belt behind his shoulder in the way Sue made him wear it because the other way would cut his head off like she'd seen on the evening news.

—This is it, Animal, Mervin said. —Take a look around.

Gilbert took a look around. There was something of death in it all.

—Yes, sir, Mervin said, —see what happens if you never give up, Animal? If you never stop getting better? The world wants to fit you into places you don't want to go. That's the natural order of things. Nature's default position is unhappiness. If you don't fight back you're going to be stuck in a place you're too good for. You're never as good as you think you are, is what I'm saying. Remember that, Animal. Keep on improving, never stop learning the game, always remember that you are not bigger than the game. Your chance will eventually come like mine did and you have to be ready when you get the call. You paying attention, son?

—*Yes.*

—What did I just say?

—You have to be *ready*. When you get the *call*.

The smell of cooked animal sifted through the open windows. The metal groans of the city buses drowned out the music on Mervin's radio, The Young Pop Singer, who Gilbert watched on TV, wearing his glove and dancing, and who, years later, would be on trial charged with fondling little kids with cancer. Every eye that turned to notice this emblem of wealth and stylish cool bore into him. He was six and a half. His eyes peered out over the window frame. The adults, this city's people sitting at tables outside restaurants or standing at crosswalks looking at nothing. They were anonymous. The watchers. They existed to be spectators. Gilbert never wanted to be one of them.

—These people, Mervin said, —are *ours*, Animal. They don't know it yet. The Marcus Gang is in *town*! Yes, sir! None of them can touch us. You, me, your mother. The Three Musketeers!

—Dad, how come there aren't any cowboys?

—The Three Musketeers, Animal!

—How come there aren't any *cowboys* though?

—Say what now?

—I thought there were *cowboys* in Texas.

—Cowboys? Cowboys are Dallas. That's football. I play basketball.

—I *know.*

—This is San Antonio. See, son, Texas is a big state. San Antonio's not very close to Dallas. San Antonio has the Ramblers, Animal. San Antone is what they call it here I think. I'll call it that anyway. San Antone.

—Oh.

—And now San Antone has the Marcuses too! Yes, sir!

And Gilbert watched his father stick his head out the window as he drove to scream at the people milling past one another on the sidewalks, in suits, pretty women, graying men, —Take cover, San Antone! The Marcuses are in town! TAKE COVER, SAN ANTONE!

Somebody yelled back, —Hey, Mervin Marcus! Hey!

And Mervin's eyes lit up and he slammed the brakes. He got out of the car and stood there with traffic honking behind him, his arms out, shouting, —Mervin Marcus has arrived!

Gilbert watched his father yell to the spectators that he never wanted to be like, —Anybody want an autograph? Hey! Who said my name back there?

They mostly regarded him like you regard a singing crazy man on the sidewalk. A skinny Mexican kid about Gilbert's age came up and stared up at Mervin, who said, —Hey there, young fella! Want an autograph? The boy shrugged and Mervin took out the pen and pad of paper he carried around with him for this purpose and scribbled on the pad and gave it back to the boy going, —Stay in school now, you hear?

The Mexican boy took the autograph and didn't look at it and stared up at Mervin. Mervin waved good-bye to everyone but no one waved back. —So hungry, someone said. He climbed back into the car yelling to them, —Viva los Ramblers!

As he put the car into gear he was laughing to himself. —That's what it's all about, Mervin said to Gilbert. —The *people*. The *community*.

They were late. Sue had dinner ready by now. It was never a good idea in the Marcus household to come home after Sue had dinner ready. So Mervin took a shortcut he thought he knew but he didn't. They entered a filthy, old-looking part of town—chain-link fences, peeling store fronts, bars on windows, burned-out shells of buildings, toothless white-haired black men drinking out of brown bags, shirtless young black men standing around on stoops, radios blasting. Mervin turned his radio down and slouched in his seat. Boys Gilbert's age but tough and cool and more manly than he threw rocks at a dog in an alley. Old furniture sat torn and bursting in front yards. These people were frayed like it took all they had to show themselves. They stopped what they were doing to see a Jaguar shimmering down the street. They stared at Gilbert and he stared back and wondered, Are these people ours too? A bare-chested boy his age ran alongside the car and he and Gilbert met eyes and the boy threw a rock at them but missed and Mervin said you little fuck and slammed on the brakes but quickly thought better of it. Gilbert stared through the rear window at the boy who was searching the ground for another rock.

The whole way home Gilbert kept an eye out for cowboys, because he didn't care what anyone said.

Everywhere Gilbert went there were children. Children his age. Children in the city. Unloved children. Black children. Poor children. Rejected children with cold hearts. Children flung around like bags of leaves in a subway tunnel. Black children clinging to chain-link fences. Black children buried by the dust of demolished buildings. Children eating Purina canned dog food. Poor and angry ten-year-old black boys with facial hair in New York playing basketball in a windstorm with a stolen ball and a tied-up milk crate. Black children faint with hunger in Los Angeles playing basketball in order to stay out of jail. Black kids in Seattle playing so they won't get into drugs. Kids in Chicago playing so they won't have to go home to their mother and whatever man she has in there with his balls in her. Black kids playing ball in prison for ten, twenty years. Black kids playing ball with their paralyzed brothers with bullets still lodged between vertebrae watching from the side of the court. Playing because it's the only way they'll make money. Playing for the kids they'll have when they are fifteen. All across America, discarded like old meals, their souls raked raw, black kids playing in order to stay alive. And why?

—Mom, can I have a snake?

She woke Gilbert early and made him put on this sweater that was white and itchy. He didn't understand why having company meant he had to wear an itchy sweater. Why did the reporter want to see him in a sweater he never wore? He'd worn this sweater just once before, to church four months ago. The Marcuses hardly ever went to church, even on Christmas, because Mervin usually had a game. The reason they went to church that time was because it was punishment. Gilbert didn't eat all his gluten burger one night, sending Mervin into a rage. He was yelling, —*Death begins in the colon!* As part of Mervin's rage, he made new rules for the family. Whenever Mervin got really mad he made a new rule. The rule Mervin made because Gilbert wouldn't fin-ish his gluten burger was that from now on, every Sunday, they would go to church. They would wake up early (inevitably a part of every new rule) and attend first service of the day every Sunday at First Baptist in San Antonio. That Sunday, they woke up early and Gilbert put on the itchy sweater and they went to church. Gilbert liked the music and the chance to be good for God and adults. But he didn't like staring at all the old men's ears. Church was full of old men's ears. It's all there was in church. They all had things growing out of them. Gilbert couldn't believe how your ears, when you get old, start growing things in them. He also didn't like having to sit still. But the following Sunday Mervin was in Sacramento and so Gilbert didn't have to wear the itchy sweater and look at all the old men's ears with things growing in them and sit still. When Mervin came home from Sacramento he seemed to have forgotten all about the new rule.

—Mom? Can I have a snake? Can I? Can I, Mom? Mom?

But she ignored him. She was in welcome mode. A reporter from the San Antonio ABC affiliate was on the way to the house on Grey Squirrel Drive this morning, the day before the first game of the sea-son, to do a story on Mervin Marcus, newest member of the San An-tonio Ramblers. She'd be here any minute. The same reporter who'd alerted Sue to the dangers of seat-belt decapitation. And there was still so much work to do!

Sue was wearing a yellow dress he'd never seen before. Gilbert liked how it made her so soft and shapely and beautiful. He wanted to crawl up against her and cling to her, smelling the dress. She rushed about the house while Gilbert followed her saying, —Mom, can I have a snake? I want a snake.

—What? No. Ask your father.

Gilbert found his father in the master bathroom which was hot and smelled. Mervin wore a beige suit tailor-made in Italy he said that had to be kept in a plastic bag when not worn and which Gilbert wasn't allowed to wear. Gilbert stood there watching Mervin stand before the mirror looking at himself in his tinted glasses and long silk scarf also made in Italy. Mervin showed himself his teeth. He showed himself his nostrils. He buckled a big gold watch around his wrist. Gilbert knew the smell. It was the smell his father made when he took a shower. Gilbert hated the smell of the bathroom after his father had taken a shower. He stood in the doorway afraid to enter and said, —Dad?

—Yeah, what is it.

—Can I have a snake?

—A *snake*? Mervin turned and blew by him tying his tie and ran down the stairs where he took off the scarf, put on the scarf, took off the scarf. Sue propped up freshly framed photos of Mervin in his army uniform before the American flag on the coffee table. Neither saw that Gilbert had taken off his shoes and sweater. Mervin noticed and growled, —*Sue.*

Sue looked up and hissed through her teeth, —*Gilbert.*

She stomped over and grabbed the shoes and put them back on his feet.

—But they *hurt*, Gilbert said.

Mervin said, —Think Jesus ever complained about his shoes? Just be happy you *get* shoes.

—But can I get a snake though?

—Oh, shut up about the snake. Goddamn, Mervin said.

Sue went, —Mervin.

—Put that sweater on him already, will you? Mervin said.

Gilbert said, —I don't want to. It *hurts.*

—How does a motherfucking sweater *hurt*?

—It *does.*

—I'll give you something that hurts if you don't knock it off.

Sue said nothing and put the sweater on Gilbert.

There was the sound of a car scraping into the driveway outside. They froze and looked at each other and Mervin whispered, peeking out the window, —They're here. Okay. Kemmon kemmon kemmon kemmon KEMMON!

Hustled them over to the door where he forced Gilbert in front between the two of them, one hand on the boy's shoulder and the other arm around Sue, saying through his teeth, —I want you to smile. I want you to laugh. I want you to speak clearly. *Do . . . not . . . blow this.*

The doorbell rang and Mervin exhaled rapidly a few times and opened it and the Marcuses chimed together, smiling like cherubs, nailing a sharp harmony, —*Welcome!*

Mervin liked white girls best, the pretty rich-looking ones, college age and without a purpose in the world except staying pretty. Nothing better than watching a gorgeous young white girl walk naked into the bathroom after getting fucked by a big black man with a big black dick, was Mervin's humble opinion.

Mervin led the news crew through the house, with a fake adobe exterior to resemble a Mexican, open-type design, to allow for air and the breeze to get in and cool things down, he told the reporter. The cars—the Jaguar and Sue's station wagon—were fresh from the car wash, out in the driveway, hopefully drawing attention from the neighbors' cars out in the street, last year's models, or worse. The neighbors had refused to pull them into the garage at Mervin's request. He was embarrassed at some of the lawns the reporter must have seen coming up the way: balding, brown, somehow still overdue for a mow.

Sue remained quiet but pleasant as her husband led them around, her smile warm and reassuring. She was the calm wife. She played the part excellently. She had had so much practice. The reporter asked her how she found the schools here. Sue raved about how good the schools here were and how much they loved their church too. Their church was such a real close-knit community they were very happy to be a part of, Sue said.

The reporter pointed the camera by grabbing hold of the lens on the cameraman's shoulder and guiding. She wanted to capture the tro-

phies, the big-screen Magnavox, the VCR and the new Betamax which
Mervin told them to get a shot of . . . the San Antonio Ramblers ban-
ner hanging over the kitchen table—hung up by Mervin an hour earlier—Mervin's guitar collection, polished and arranged tastefully
around the amplifier last night by Sue. Mervin attempted to play one
and broke a string.

—That string was very old, said Mervin, laughed as he put the
guitar back on its stand.

Gilbert hid behind his mother. From there the reporter led things
outside. They got footage of Gilbert shooting baskets out in the driveway while Mervin explained to the reporter that those kinds of bushes
are a very rare kind of bush, the name of which escapes him at the
moment. Mervin explained that they were planted here by the previous owners who were champion botanists from France. Gilbert
stopped and said, —Really, Dad?

—Yup, said Mervin.

—I have a pet snake, Gilbert said to the reporter.

The reporter said, —We should get some footage of it, it'd be
adorable.

—Yeah, it's actually his cousin's, Mervin said, —they share it. It
stays at his cousin's, is where it is. His cousin has, uh. See the reason it
stays at his cousin's, who lives in Boston, is that his cousin unfortunately has leukemia and so, uh. See, pets, reptiles especially, are proven
by science to help with the disease. On some unknown level that science can't explain. But.

The reporter stared at Mervin and Gilbert said, —I didn't know
that, Dad.

Mervin said, —Why not show us your layup, Animal. His layup's
really coming along.

—How did you come up with the name? Animal.

—Well it's actually. I mean. Well he was named after my buddy
from the service. The army. I was in the army. Jason Duval. That was
my buddy. We called Jason *Animal* because, well, that's not important,
but sadly he, uh, lost his life shortly before Gilbert here was born.
Don't worry, it wasn't combat-related, but. It's a tribute. I came up
with the idea, I think, didn't I, Sue, Susan? And she can correct me if
I'm wrong about this, but I believe I came up with the idea to name
our firstborn in honor of the memory of my dear friend Jason Duval,
rest in peace God rest his soul.

—We liked the way it sounded, said Sue.

✳   ✳   ✳

Back inside, the reporter supervised as the cameraman set up a makeshift studio in the white room with the piano which no one ever played, the leather couch no one had ever sat in before. This was a room no one, in Gilbert's memory, ever went in before, certainly not him. There were a couple of lights and foil reflectors and wireless mikes. The reporter snapped at the cameraman, bossed him around, asked him if he forgot his morning coffee today or what. It got uncomfortable. Then the reporter was satisfied and interviewed Sue and Mervin.

—Listen, Ellen, Mervin said in the white room surrounded by fake floral arrangements, a view behind them of their perfectly mowed and shaded front yard, oil paintings on the wall of what looked like either women or fish, —my family comes first. Okay? *Always.* Basketball comes second. No, I take that back. What I meant to say was that *God* comes second, and basketball is *third.* So it goes family, God, basketball. God might even come first, ahead of family. But saying that doesn't feel right, putting family second to something. I'm sure God is okay with being second to family, which, as Jesus teaches, is a way of honoring God. So, in a way, God still is first. What I mean to say is that it's just a job, basketball is. It's a good job, to be sure, but it's just how I make my living and support my family. It happens to be what I'm good at and what I enjoy. So to be able to make my living at what I'm good at and enjoy, I'm lucky. Blessed. But it doesn't matter too much in the whole scheme of things. I mean, for example, you enjoy bringing people the news, so you're a newscaster is how you make your living. So you're blessed too. But what I'm saying is this: In this world, we got war. Okay? Famine. Communism. Racism. Homelessness. Friends come and go. Basketball games come and go. But family is forever. Family is all you really got. I could blow out my knee tomorrow, Ellen, and never play again, is how I look at it. And it wouldn't matter to me. As long as I have my family and Jesus Christ, it wouldn't matter to me.

He smiled and kissed Sue. The reporter, legs crossed and leaning forward in her chair with papers in her hand (her ankles fat, Sue noticed), smiled and asked Sue, —How do you like San Antonio so far?

—Good ol *San Antone,* Mervin said, laughing.

—Oh gosh, Sue said, —we just *love* it here. San Antonio is just *such* a great place to raise a family. Everyone's just been *so* nice. Our pastor, at our church, is just *great,* and there are just a wide variety of

youth programs for Gilbert to take part in, as well as lots of other children for him to play with.

—How has he adjusted to the move? Ellen said.

—Fine, just fine, said Sue, —he likes San Antonio a lot. Gilbert
has lots of friends.

Gilbert stood off to the side trying to take off the sweater but Sue
kept giving him the evil eye. He watched the camera guy, sweaty and
dirty and every now and again scratching his ass. Probably waiting for
everyone to turn their backs so he could steal Gilbert, throw him into
the van, drive him to a secret crawlspace under his house filled with
the bodies of other little boys.

He jumped when Sue said, —Gilbert. Mervin was signaling with
his hand. They wanted him to come over. They wanted him to show
himself.

He went over without shoes and sat on his dad's lap, keeping an
eye on the cameraman. The reporter said, —What do you want to be
when you grow up, Gilbert?

He said softly, —A pro basketball player.

Mervin laughed loud and deep and said, —Just like his old man!
Ha ha.

Ellen sighed at the end of her laugh and looked at Gilbert and said,
—Who's your favorite player?

Gilbert looked at his dad and said, —Magic Johnson, and they
laughed again.

Sue said over the laughter, staring into the reporter's eyes, the
conviction in her voice surprising even her, —Gilbert is very happy
here in San Antonio and has *lots of friends.*

Sue dropped Gilbert off outside the school in the Kiss and Ride. All the
boys were dressed identically in light-blue short-sleeved shirts, cream-
and-maroon-striped clip-on ties, dark-blue pants, brown or black
shoes. Gilbert slung his San Francisco 49ers backpack over one shoulder in the way that the big kids did it and walked toward the front
door of Casper Hill Day School (K-6, private, the educating institution
of children of congressmen, lawyers, heart surgeons, etc.).

A group of second-graders bumped into him in the hall and called
him chink and nigger and said he had a stupid name and was he a nigger or a chink?

But Gilbert looked down at the floor at his slightly scuffed shoes not saying anything until they got bored with him and wandered off. He was relieved he wasn't punched and that they didn't take any of his pens which he loved. He got off good this time.

That day during snack time he waited for his peanut butter crackers and chocolate milk at the table where it was only him and Stacia Jacobs who always smelled like pee and so no one sat with her. He loved snack time because he could have a tiny carton of chocolate milk and Mervin would never know. But the chocolate milks ran out before it was his turn to go up and pick. He had to have a tiny carton of plain milk. He tried his best not to cry. He bit his lip, fought the hot flood from behind his eyes. But he cried and the other kids laughed at him for it. These kids could have had chocolate milk at home. These kids didn't hate plain milk. Matthew, whose face was always red and who puked once, like all over himself, like in front of everyone during show-and-tell, said to Gilbert as Gilbert cried, —You like chocolate milk because you're black and it looks like you.

—He's not black, Stacia Jacobs who smelled like pee said. —He's yellow and black. He's a chigger. Do you know what a chigger is? It's a chink and a nigger.

During handwriting he finished his assignment early as usual and fell asleep on his desk and he dreamed that he was in his house only it wasn't his house and he went downstairs to find no one home so he got scared and ran toward his neighbors like his mom told him to do but the driveway and the streets were all melted into a stagnant river of sticky tar hundreds of feet deep, trapping him. He woke up startled but thank God not screaming because then Mrs. Greer would notice and he would get in trouble for sleeping during school which would mean the white kids would see him get in trouble and look at one another with looks that said, —The chigger got in trouble.

Mrs. Greer told the chigger during art that he drew well and that he should be an artist, to which he said, —But I'm a basketball player.

—You can be a basketball player and an artist too, you know. It's really hard to be a basketball player anyways. I'm not sure if you are the right type for it.

And outside after school waiting for their parents to come in vans and station wagons, the white kids removed their ties and whipped one another with them, then turned on the chigger and whipped the chigger in the ass, his tie still on, saying to him, —You're gay and your name is stupid.

—Why are you black?

—Did you get dropped in paint?

—No, he's black because his mom hates him because he's gay and has a stupid name so she put him in the oven when he was a baby and burned him.

—Yeah, and then she took a knife and cut his eyes and that's why his eyes look like that.

—Then she fed him rice and taught him karate.

—Chop suey!

—Chong-chong-a-dong-dong!

And Sue pulled up and the white kids stopped and watched him get in and he stared back at them as Sue drove off.

The interview aired that evening and consisted of Mervin trying to play his guitar then saying basketball wasn't that important before cutting back to the reporter after forty-five seconds or so who ended the segment by sending it back to the anchors in the studio who sent it to commercial. —Waitwaitwait, Mervin said. —That's it? That's *it*? The season started and Mervin played 13 minutes a game and averaged 1.2 points, .4 rebounds, and .3 assists before blowing his knee out. The San Antonio coaches murmured about him over coffee after practice, rubbing their balding skulls and droopy eyes, saying while sighing deeply, —It's like he doesn't *want* to recover. I don't get it. What's stopping him?

—He could be great. I don't get what's keeping him from being great.

After the season, Mervin knew his agent would be calling with the news. When he'd read it in the paper, his gut knotted and he got ill in the bathroom. They were going to cut him. They're going to exercise the injury clause, he thought. They can cut me. It's in my contract. I remember Jimmy saying something about it. And they will because my knee's shot. You never know what's going to happen, he thought. You have no control over anything. Whatever is going to happen is what's going to happen. He waited by the phone. He never left the house. Jimmy, his agent, was a young cheerful type of guy who had a talent for banal conversation. Finally he called.

Mervin said, —Give me some good news, Jimmy.

—I have your good news. I have your good news and I have your great news. You're going to love me. How's Sue?

—She's fine. What do you have?

—Listen. Does she watch TV? Only reason I ask is because my wife, all she does is watch TV. All day she sits there watching TV. It's fascinating. I mean, what is it with women and TV?

—I don't know.

—It's a talent is what it is.

—What's the word, Jimmy.

—Okay. Here's the word. They want to give you an extension.

—*What?*

—They're going to offer you six, eight. Something like that. We're still scratching it out a bit.

—Six or eight what?

—*Years*, Mervin. They want you for life. Or close to it at least.

—Wow. Oh wow. But . . . well, I thought you were going to say they cut me.

—Cut you? Why would they cut you? You're the show, Mervin. You're the franchise. You fill the seats. Listen, how's the new—what was it you got? New oven or something?

—Uh, no.

—Oh, I thought you did.

—No.

—Oh. Anyway, yeah, so the word now is. Hold on. I'm in a restaurant. Okay. The word now is, what they're saying is they're going to trade to get you a guard. A shooter. A veteran. A team player. They're throwing some names around but nothing definite right now.

—No, that's great, Jimmy. That's exactly what we need. That's exactly what I've been telling them. A shooter. A scorer, you know?

—Yeah, and they're most likely going to take this kid Hawkins in the draft. From, uh, UCLA.

—Persuval Hawkins. Percy's good. I watched him in the tournament. He's got some bad habits but he's going to be real good. Real good. Real team player. This is great. To be honest I was a little nervous.

—About what?

—I don't know. It's stupid. I heard some things. You know, my knee and everything. I don't know. It's stupid. It's dumb. You get paranoid.

—People get hurt. That's the nature of the sport, Merv. The fact is the Ramblers are committed to you. They're building the team around you, Mervy. You're their guy. They're talking about five hundred thousand per year. Give or take. Like I said, we're still squabbling a bit. But that's ballpark. And barring any last-minute snags, as they say, I'd say you're sitting pretty, Mervy-poo.

—Man, Jimmy. You said good news but. Damn.

—You earned it, Mervster. Merverooski. This is your time, baby. You know what? This is your time. Because it's like I was telling them. Mervis Marcun . . . Er, excuse me, *Mervin Marcus*. Ha ha, I do that all the time. But listen, it's like I was telling them. Mervin Marcus is a tank. A fucking *tank*. You know? And they're fighting guys with rifles. Their army has a tank and they're in a war with guys who have these little one-shot Civil War rifles that shoot musket balls. But they don't use the tank. They keep the tank back at headquarters in the garage. All loaded up with missiles and ready to go. And these guys with the musket balls are *massacring* them. And they're asking themselves, Why can't we win this war? With their fucking tank sitting in the garage they're asking themselves, How come we lose every battle?

—Yeah. *Yeah.*

—You're their *tank*.

—I'm their *tank*.

—No one can touch you. And they know that. Haven't I always told you that? Listen. What'd I tell you when you signed on with me?

—You said you'd get me the Magic Johnson contract.

—What did I *tell* you when you signed with me, Merveroni?

—You said you'd get me the Magic Johnson contract, Jimmy. Ha ha.

—And what did I get you?

—The Magic Johnson motherfucking contract.

—I don't go back on my word. Listen. I'm in a restaurant right now. Some jerk needs the phone. Some *dick* . . . Yeah, you heard me, you dick. Listen, Mervy, I'm, uh, I'm in a restaurant. I have to get back to the office and get on the horn again with these scoundrels. Fucking jackals. I'll keep you updated.

—You've done good, Jimmy.

—Please. I'm just doing my job. *You've* done good. *We* have done good, Merv. The Dynamic Duo.

A week passed with no word from Jimmy. Mervin called his office in New York daily but he was always out. He left messages with Jimmy's secretary that were never returned. He went nowhere, he did nothing.

I don't go back on my word.

Sue watched him on the couch as he picked his lip and stared at the wall. Old thoughts swarmed her. A boy she knew in high school. A smart boy who went to Amherst, remembering one time standing on her stoop with him in the silver sigh of dusk, laughing. At what? Nothing. And wouldn't that be great? A school night, which made it magical. She'd been happy then. Not like now. No, that's not true. She rinsed off the dishes, dumping Mervin's plate over the trash after dinner because he barely ate nowadays. From the kitchen she watched him on the couch in the living room. Flipping through the channels, a hand down the front of his shorts, which he'd been sleeping in till noon. He'd always woken up before sunrise. Ever since she'd known him. She thought, No, I'm happy. A house, a husband, a child. I should be happy. And I *am.* I'm *happy.*

After a month of this, Mervin finally got off the couch. He took a shower. He could see in Sue's eyes that he was losing her. She was getting resentful. He could hear it in her voice. Short, terse words. Her mind was wandering. And maybe her heart. He knew it. She was beginning to stop seeing him as a man. She was starting to see him as weak. Women have no use for the weak. Maybe she was done having her fun pissing off her parents, he thought. Maybe she was thinking it's time to move on. Get on the ball, he told himself. Take responsibility. He remembered the army, he started jogging. He woke up before sunrise. He ate. He changed, he bathed. He made calls. He dialed everybody he could think of. He got on a first-name basis with the ladies at 411 (they sounded kinda sexy, some of them). He called people he knew in the CBA, the ABA. These were lower-level pro leagues that existed as a kind of minor league to The Association. But there was nothing, not even with the Harlem Globetrotters, who said, whoever he spoke to, that they'd never heard of him. He called L_____, his coach at Boston College, looking for an assistant coaching job. Even though he didn't want to coach, he wanted to play. L_____ wasn't at B.C. anymore. He hadn't been for years. He was playing golf in Scotland mostly, enjoying his retirement. And having left on bad terms, he didn't have any connection to the current program at B.C. Nor did he have any connections anywhere else.

One morning after another day of unreturned calls, while he shaved, Mervin thought about maybe driving off into the desert and parking his Jaguar and killing himself. He would use one of his rifles. He'd shoot himself in the chest. He would use a pencil to push the trigger if he couldn't reach. He saw himself dead. He saw the blood on his shirt. He saw the EMTs standing around his body, smoking and making small talk as they waited for the detective.

Maybe he could coach kids. He liked kids. Children are the future. Teaching them the sport of basketball would be really fulfilling emotionally and athletically. Maybe Gilbert would be on his team. Sculpt the boy into the best player out there. And then he could coach him in high school too. Then college. Then who knows what could happen. Train him in another sport too, like golf, which is easy on the body and won't get in the way of basketball. Or boxing, which is good for conditioning.

Came across the number of the Benny Glenn League back in Hingham. A secretary answered and he told her what he wanted and she patched him over to an old-sounding guy with a throaty high-pitched voice like a gangster who turned out to be Benny Glenn himself.

—You know what you should do? There's this school. They're looking for a coach.

—Yeah? What school.

—It's this military school. Great school. It's in Utah. Let me get Stephanie to find the number.

—School? What kind of school? High school?

—It's a good school. A kid I grew up with runs it. We grew up in Medford together then he went off and became a Mormon. I don't know why. Real good school though. They need a basketball coach. I

remember you, Mervin. I remember you from the Colonials. I remember you at B.C. even. I was there that night at the conference
championship I think it was against North Carolina.

—Yeah. Ha. Yeah.

—When you nailed that fifteen-footer then stole the inbound and
dunked it backward? I was there. I'd never seen anything like it. I've
never seen anyone move like that. Whatever happened to you anyway?

—I don't know, Mervin said, looking for a pen.

3

TET HUT! FORWARD . . . *march!*
March, Mormons. That's it. March, I say.
Forward march, soldiers. Even though the
grass is wet and yes there is some mud. It
won't kill you. Tough it out. That's what Mormons do—they tough it
out. Even when they are nine years old. Hut two, three, four. Hut
two, three, four. Count it off. Hut two, three—Company, *halt*. Hold
it, hold it, company. Halt. Hold it. *Stop.* You there, Marcus. You're
holding your rifle upside down again. See how everyone has their's?
With the butt in their hand and the barrel toward the sky, against
their shoulder? You have it the other way around. I understand
you're still a bit new to all this, Marcus, and that the rifle is a phony
rifle made out of a solid single block of wood that was made right
here at Smith School for Boys in wood-shop class. It's not even
brown, is it, like standard rifles, or black even like you see some of
the newer models these days. It's green. Army green, but still green.
Who here has seen a green rifle? Show of hands. No one? Good, no
liars here. Nonetheless, Mr. Gilbert Marcus, we treat our phony

green rifles like an actual firearm, mmkay? It doesn't matter if your father is gym teacher and sixth grade boys' basketball coach leading our Fightin' Jackrabbits so far to an undefeated record and average margin of victory of thirty-three points per game. Good thing for you though, Gilbert, because if that was a real firearm there in your hands you would have shot yourself through the hand, much like your drill sergeant yours truly did once when he was a plebe at the Naval Academy and thus became ejected from the Academy as a fair consequence. Don't worry, son, don't get too upset about it. No one will eject you from the esteemed Smith School for Boys. We are here to correct mistakes. You'll learn to hold your rifle right side up and how to be a reasonable and good man who respects the proper way of doing things. That's the Smith School for Boys motto according to yours truly, drill sergeant Mr. Henderson, aka fourth-grade teacher, general education. Uh-oh, you have thrown your firearm into the mud. You better drop the attitude, Marcus. We can march down to your father's office if need be and I can tell him about you having quite the attitude. Pick up your firearm, Gilbert. I said pick it up. I don't care if it's muddy, you can wash up later. Do soldiers care about being muddy? No. I know you're a young boy but you're making yourself look like a perfect idiot here in front of not only me, whose respect you should strive for, but in front of your company too which is also your classmates. They already have their doubts about you, based on your race and that you are not from a Church of Latter-Day Saints background, which is fine of course, since we are much more accepting than the secular world would have you believe. We don't all bike around harassing old ladies on their doorsteps to join our church. We don't take multiple brides and hole up in compounds with heavy artillery. At least not anymore. Though I do own an AK-47. The typical stereotype regarding the reasonably priced, conveniently located Smith School for Boys is that our students, no matter what the age, must have done something to deserve being in a military school. Setting a fire or shooting the neighbor's tabby cat to death with a BB gun are popular ones, especially for kids this young, like yourself, who are so small and so must be quote-unquote loco . . . No, in fact it is a gift to be here, where a young man can learn discipline and self-respect and how to be a man, something you just can't get on the quote-unquote outside, in today's society. We do appreciate your father's financial gift toward the new gymnasium, which I sure do keep in mind in moments like now. Normally throwing your rifle onto the ground during drills is cause for very stern discipline. But the fact is this: everybody, raise your hands who has been sent here due to your breaking a law or murdering an animal or an otherwise disturbing and illegal act of transgression. Show of hands. See, Gilbert? None. Not a one. I'm not sure by the way where that phrase comes from—*not a one*. It's redundant. And I don't like redundancy. We have no time for it. You will never use the phrase *not a one* on the campus of Smith School for Boys ever again. Is that clear? For all those for whom it is clear, let's get a show of hands, please. Okay, yes, very good. And now we are going to do this right, gentlemen, are we not? If we do it right we can break for supper and thus ensure that the fourth grade won't be last again to evening prayer and embarrass your poor Mr. Henderson like we embarrass him every night. Now then, company, everybody fall in and stand up straight. Think about our forefathers please when you wish to slouch. And ask yourself if Joseph Smith—our school's namesake—slouched when he led the wagons out West to settle this great state. And everybody fall in and TEN HUT! Forward . . . *MARCH!*

We heard that his family could trace its roots to African royalty. We stayed up late and talked about the new chigger, the foreign invader. He was the only student who didn't have to live in the dorms. We heard that his father was an exiled chief of a cannibal tribe and they had to leave Guinea and come out here to our school because there was a hit out on the whole family. We heard his father fought in wars all over the world for money, like a hired mercenary. Only six kids had the balls to sign up for his basketball team. Andy Anderson said he saw the family the first day they came to Provo and that they didn't wear shoes and rode in on motorcycles, Gilbert on his own full-sized adult one and drinking what looked like blood, which we decided must have been where he got all his strength from. Andy also told us at the rec center one day when Gilbert wasn't there that the Marcuses had a live cheetah in a cage in the basement and they fed it rabbits they caught in the backyard and kidnapped little kids sometimes for like holidays and stuff. When Thomas Richards lost the hamster he smuggled into the dorms, you can imagine who we first suspected. The reason for the cheetah was obviously so Gilbert could take it out into the desert and race it, and that's how he got so fast. Little Robert Morgan, whose fam-

ily did janitorial work (and whose mom we heard sucked the headmas-
ter's weenie) in exchange for tuition, saw Gilbert and Miss Behan the
math teacher having sex after school one afternoon, right on her desk,
and his dick was bigger than a baseball bat. And of course we believed
it, just like we believed that the Marcuses cooked dogs over a fire in
their living room and ate them. We gathered around the window in
Chris Gatling and Justin Gutterson's room and watched their little
house at the bottom of the hill through Anthony Watkins's binoculars,
smoke pouring out in the winter, yellow lights behind the window
shade at night, the shadows of the invaders moving behind them. The
reason that Gilbert never spoke was because he had no tongue because
it was torn out by one of his dad's enemies in a battle back in Africa and
eaten in a satanic tribal ceremony conducted to gain the powers of the
enemy. Imagine how exciting a bunch of Mormon kids felt in the midst
of such people. His mother was Oriental. And Mr. Marcus was *black*.
Even though we were young and hardly knew what sex was—but we'd
heard the older kids talk, and we'd heard our parents when they
thought we were asleep, some of us had walked in on the fresh warm
stench of it—we still knew that Gilbert was having it and that he was
having it with our teacher Miss Behan. And we hated him!

Gilbert spent most of fourth grade in Utah at the Smith School for
Boys staring at his desk in the back of the classroom. He watched the
other kids to know when it was time to take out his math book, how to
march during drills, how to say "Sir yes sir" (just like in the movies).
These same kids stayed far away and whispered into their hands about
him. He did his best to not disappoint Miss Behan. Miss Behan had
humongous tits. When a woman had humongous tits, he realized, you
didn't want to disappoint her. The boys in Gilbert's class were always
talking about how humongous Miss Beehan's tits were. Gilbert imagined what her tits looked like. What tits felt like. He imagined taking
her by the back of the neck and bending her back like in the movies
and kissing her mouth with lipstick all over it.

Nick Friend saw him once smoking a cigarette on the baseball field
after chow. We all believed it without a smidgen of doubt when he told

us Gilbert Marcus could, and did, jump over a ten-foot-high fence not only without a running start but without even flexing his knees. Nick Friend saw him do it once so he has proof. He was from another planet. We didn't know what to make of him. He seemed so much older than us. So quiet and unworldly. Nick Friend's dad managed the Chi-Chi's in Provo and could attest that Gilbert was a regular at the bar. He had to sit on phone books in order to reach. He drank whiskey and flirted with married women. He was an okay tipper. Nick Friend was the one who kicked Gilbert in the balls, in the bathroom, and got suspended for it.

The rec center was a long one-story building that was once the caretaker's quarters, situated in a parklike setting with trees and a picnic area, a ten-minute bike ride from Gilbert's house. Leo, who ran the rec center, still had the crater-scarred face of a pimply adolescent even though he was Mervin's age at least. He could relate to the frowning scrawny chigger. He had been an outsider too. He had once been a frowning and scrawny boy with no friends too. But of course he had been white. He couldn't imagine bringing race into it.

—I know what it's like, Leo said to Gilbert over a game of Boggle. It was after hours. The rec center was officially closed and all the other boys had to be home. But he made an exception for Gilbert. —To be, you know, *mystified* by the world. By other kids your age who seem to not get mystified by anything. Yet when you catch a glimpse of yourself in a mirror, you're mystified by your own face. I know what that's like. I know how you can feel like, Then how am I supposed to understand anything?

The rec center had a little court that was an unmarked chunk of asphalt and a rusted bent hoop. Leo spent hours out there with Gilbert. It was artful to watch how the ball danced between Gilbert's hands like on a string, and how he pulled up and tossed the ball from his shoulder without aiming and made it almost every time or at least came a lot closer than Leo, who dribbled like his hands were numb, heaving the thing up from his chest off the backboard and off and away and Gilbert was off to chase it down the street. Leo watched the boy run, arms pumping and new Nike Airs that cost $150 kicking. Things came alive in Leo as his eyes lost focus on the boy, seeing nothing because it was impossible to see everything.

* * *

From the first days of playing organized basketball in this small local private-school league, made up mostly of other Mormon schools in greater Provo, Gilbert discovered that he was really really good at this. None of the other kids had stood barefoot out in the Boston snow for this. None of the other kids had had to practice before they could eat. The other kids, they fit in other ways—some were funny, some were personable, etc., so none of them NEEDED this. And he played like it too. He was scrawny, but his stomach was ridged and flat and his thighs slender and gazellelike. He was *fast*. He had no shame in taking off his shirt when his team was skins because his chest, as opposed to the concave chests other kids had, was a man's chest. He'd whip off his shirt and the other boys would look down at their toes. Nick Friend, pudgy and rolly with little pert boy-boobs, crossed his arms over himself and felt every eye upon his ugly flesh. You could almost hear all the parents in attendance groan when there was a loose ball followed by a mad scramble and Nick Friend somehow ended up with it, invariably throwing it away or dribbling it off his foot. They wanted the chigger to have the ball. They wanted the black boy. It made them feel good to cheer for the black boy. Gilbert had nothing to fear anymore. When it comes to youth athletics, the best become cool, and the mediocre stay close to the cool hoping to be liked, while the rest sit on the bench or play with bugs and panic.

When he wasn't coaching basketball and teaching gym class at the Smith School for Boys in Provo, Utah, Mervin occupied himself with the Western Independent Basketball League, a spring and summer semi-pro West Coast league. He played for the Salt Lake City Sand Gnats. A league of guys like him for the most part, who due to either a deficiency of physical skills, too many failed drug tests, or a lack of sufficient mental abilities fell just short of The Association. These were guys you watch in the NCAA tournament each year and root for, memorize their faces and quirks at the foul line, the chunks of deodorant in their pit hair, the flare of the nostrils. And then you never hear about them again and wonder what happened to them. This is where they go.

Even with the knee and the vertigo caused by now pretty serious deafness in his left ear, Mervin still cleaned up. Easily.

This was temporary, something to talk about in interviews after

he'd made it back to The Association. A nice angle for newspaper articles that would one day be written.

There were women here too, some barely women at all. He'd meet
them in bars after the game, when his team would venture out while
on road trips to Fresno or Bend, Oregon, etc., deciding they deserved a
little fun after what fate had done to them by putting them here in
this sorry-ass league, give themselves a bit of a break, enjoy their lives
a little, the small-town girls approaching the group of tall black men,
all smiles and glinting eyes and touching them, smelling good, asking
if they're basketball players or something.

—Yeah, baby. I'm Julius Erving. Ever hear of me?

And washing off in the shower alone postcoitus, enjoying the
calm and the silence of a different city, happy, a man, above the earth.
What I have to do to survive. He'd go to sleep a king and catch the
flight back to Provo (coach class, invariably), wrap his arms around
Sue, ask her if Gilbert was keeping up with his training regimen and
how many hours Gilbert had slept and checking the log Gilbert was
required to keep (daily documentation of technique used in drills, how
his muscles felt afterward, what he'd eaten, etc.) for proof.

Gilbert told Sue he was going to Timmy's to watch the World Cup but
instead went to Leo's, that crazy-ass, Wop-ass Guido, as Mervin called
him. Leo lived in a little house a mile from the front end of the endless
driveway between the brick posts that said SMITH SCHOOL FOR
BOYS. Leo had little trees cut into perfect spirals out front and beautiful
tall flowers that were pink and yellow and red. It was a mini-arboretum.
And a brick-and-gravel type of walkway thing leading up to the front
door. The lawn an even three-quarters of an inch all around. Waist-high
fence. Like Grandmother's house in *Little Red Riding Hood.* Gilbert
hopped off his bike and dropped it in the grass and Leo answered the
door with his face covered in shaving cream and said,—Come in. I was
just shaving. Hope you don't mind. Have a seat. Here's the remote. The
game's almost on. Uh, help yourself to some juice in the refrigerator. I
hope you like fruit punch. You do, don't you! Ha ha. Oh I also have
champagne soda too. So. Don't worry, I won't tell on you. Oh never
mind, you're not Mormon, are you. Well neither am I. I'm a little
drunk. Please, just make yourself at home. I'm real glad you're here. The
game's almost on. Uh, I'll be right out. I just have to finish shaving.

After ten minutes Leo came out and was wearing only little boys' tighty-whities, with G.I. Joe on them. Timmy did not really exist. There was no one named Timmy. Gilbert had made Timmy up. The tighty-whities made Leo look like an overgrown boy. There's nothing as disgusting as a grown man in little boys' tighty-whities with G.I. Joe on them. All that male body exposed. Curling dark hairs and pale flesh rising over the waistband. The Death Valley of the male upper thigh. The sad little bulge in the crotch, curled over itself. Leo held a box which he placed on the coffee table and in a voice like a young girl asked Gilbert to please open it. Gilbert opened the box. Inside the box were tons of pictures of Leo, wrestling with naked little boys. Pictures of little boys with no clothes on crawling all over one another or standing there naked looking at the camera with their little dinks. Gilbert recognized the room they were taken in as this one. The couch they crawled over one another on was this couch. The pictures reminded Gilbert of the zoo. He remembered going to the zoo in San Diego once. The walruses spread out on the rocks. Gilbert laughed and said, —They look like walruses.

—They make me horny, Leo said. —Do you know what horny is?

—No, Gilbert lied.

—This is horny, Leo said, pointing down at himself. It had become huge and weird.

Gilbert was embarrassed and didn't look at Leo's horny.

—Do these pictures make you horny? Leo said. —It's okay if they do. They make me horny.

—I don't know, Gilbert said. —I guess.

—Do you have any idea how good you are at basketball, Gilbert? Leo said, standing beside him now, touching his hair. His horny was poking out of one of the leg holes of the tighty-whities. Gilbert pretended it wasn't.

Leo whispered, rubbing Gilbert's shoulders, —Do you have any idea how special you are?

—Gilbert got in a fight.

—What? With who?

—Someone in his class. They were calling him gay or something.

—They?

—This little boy and some other little boys.

—Hmph. You don't think . . . ?

—Mervin.

—What? I don't know.

Gilbert sat on the stairs listening. He was so quiet.

—Kicked him in the crotch, said Sue.

—Who? Mervin said.

—Gilbert.

—No. Who got kicked?

—Gilbert.

—Gilbert got kicked in the sack?!

—The doctor checked him out. Said he's fine.

—He could have crippled him. Did you know you can get crippled from that? You can.

—The doctor said he's fine.

—Well we're pulling him out. We're taking him out of that fucking place. Those kids are going to be nothing but crazed militiamen. That school breeds them. Whose idea was it to teach budding radical polygamists how to shoot guns?

—He needs school, Mervin. And they're not polygamists. That's illegal. Not all of them are polygamists.

—He's too good for school. Especially *this* fucking school. They don't see his potential. They just lump him in with the other little shits and let God take care of it. I know, Sue, I work there. Did you know they think black people are by nature like lesser in God's eyes? That's, like, their *doctrine,* Sue.

—The boy got suspended who kicked him.

—Fuck him. Good.

—I was screaming at Harvey. I don't know what I said. I was livid.

—You tell Harvey I don't care if he is the principal, he can suck my dick. I mean it. He can *suck . . . my . . . motherfucking . . . dick.* I would've gut-punched the fucker. On sight. The kid I mean. I would've punched the kid on *sight.*

—I know you would've.

—We're pulling him out. That's all there is to it.

— . . .

—He needs to be homeschooled, Sue. He can be done with school by fifteen if we do it ourselves. He can be playing college ball by fifteen. Be pro by eighteen. He'll have years on everyone else.

—He has to develop social skills, Mervin. Make friends. Learn how to deal with people.

—Who needs friends? Fuck friends.

—Who's going to homeschool him? Me? Think I want to be responsible for his education? On top of everything else? You do it if you want to homeschool.

—Listen, he can still run and everything, right? Jump? All that?

—Yeah he seems fine now.

—Shoot? Dribble? Right?

—Bouncing off the walls this morning.

—Okay. We'll talk about this later. I got to crash. Thanks for taking care of it baby.

—Mm-hmm.

—I'll go down and talk to this kid's dad. Kick *him* in the nuts. Do they realize they're fucking with a very lucrative and extraordinary career?

— . . .

—Okay. I have to go to sleep. I'm jetlagged as a motherfucker. Thanks for taking care of it baby.

—Don't thank me, she said. —That's what I'm here for isn't it?

—Huh?

—To clean up after everyone? Solve everyone's problems?

—Baby.

—You fly around and play basketball. I stay home and yell at principals. Put ice on crotches. Drive to emergency rooms. Educate people. That's what I do. That's the deal.

—Sue.

—This isn't how my life was supposed to go, Mervin. I want a job. I'm *bored.*

—You're bored? Paint the fucking shutters.

—Why am I in *Utah,* Mervin?

—Sue this is not a good time. Please.

—Yeah, yeah, yeah. I know. It's not a good time, Sue. Shut up, Sue. You have a good life, Sue. You have a family, Sue. You get to travel the world, Sue. You don't have to worry about money, Sue. But listen, I didn't go to college and work my ass off to clip coupons and sacrifice my life for some little boy. I want a *job.* I want a *life.* I want to feel *useful.* And *sexy.* I want somewhere to *be.* It's the eighties. Women have jobs. Women balance family *and* career. Even if I have to scrub toilets, I want to get out of this house and *work.* I want to be productive and sweat and earn money. I want to *struggle.* I want to make friends with my coworkers. Take coffee breaks. Roll my eyes at my stupid boss.

—You have a friend. Marla's your friend.

—I'm just tired of this house, Mervin.

—You're *tired* of this *house*? Boo fucking hoo! Some people would kill for this house.

—Not me.

—Boo fucking hoo. You think it's so easy, don't you? Supporting a family. Working for a living. Boo hoo hoo. You forget, Susan, that if it wasn't for me you'd still be in Jamaica Plain pouring coffee and substituting bacon for sausage and having bars installed on the windows of your one-bedroom basement apartment so you don't get fucking *raped*. Understand what I'm saying? You don't appreciate anything I do for you, is what your problem is. I've given you all this money. A kid. Brought you around to all these different places. This is a *nice fucking house*. And in Hingham the house was a *nice fucking house*. In San Antonio the house was a *nice fucking house*. You. No. I'm *sick* of this shit. *Fuck* this. You women think you're entitled to it all. Just because you were born with a pussy. Work until you get tired of working and feel like having a baby. Raise your baby until you get tired of raising a baby and feel like having a job again. Then when that stops being cute you can quit and go back to sitting on your ass. Why? Because you have a pussy. Think a man can quit when he's tired of going to work? Soon as he does he's worthless because a man who doesn't work isn't a man. You already got a job. You're raising a child. That's your job. You should thank motherfucking Jesus for the opportunity to be raising that boy. He's fucking *special,* Sue. You better recognize that.

—I knew this is how this conversation would go. I knew exactly how this conversation would go.

—You women. You women and your pussies. Where did you get this idea that you can have it all? Who told you you were entitled to whatever you want? Can someone please explain this to me?

—You smell like perfume, Mervin.

—No I don't.

—Why are you so tired? Up all night?

—Watch it, Sue.

— . . .

—As a matter of fact, yes. Okay? Yes I was up all night. Know why? Because it's hard to sleep when you're not appreciated by your own family. That's why. So fuck you.

—Fuck me? she said.

—Fuck you.

—No fuck *you*.

While Mervin went to Fresno for his weekly game Sue packed a suit-case and told Gilbert to do the same as she scribbled the note, and they took the taxi to Marla's and Marla smelled like life, a smoker and drinker, a godless woman alive and content whose husband was old and elusive and did something having to do with international finance and lived in Utah because he liked to ski, but Marla wasn't old, and neither was Sue—they were young and at the edge of the world.

Mervin lay in bed in the Holiday Inn in Fresno, his semen running down the inside of a black-haired Greek girl's thigh beside him. She drank from a plastic thermos and he'd just given her herpes. He watched her, his chest still heaving, wang shriveling, and asked her, —The fuck is that?

—It is, how you say, lemonade.

—Lemonade? Shit.

—It is made from fresh-squeezed lemons I grow myself. And syrup I get from the market. We have been drinking it for years, my family. It cleanses the intestines. It cleanses the body of parasites and, how you say, trash.

—Death does begin in the colon, Mervin agreed.

—For fifty years my great-grandfather is eating nothing but lemonade. He is being ninety-eight years old and still a fisherman in Greece. He is never getting sick. Not even a cough.

—Yeah?

—Hmm-hmm. The strongest man my town is ever knowing. The greatest fisherman.

—Huh.

She took a sip and licked her lips and handed the thermos to him. —Would you like? Drink.

* * *

Gilbert woke up on one of Marla's couches, coffee gurgling, the darkness of early morning. He sat up and rubbed his eyes. Sue and Marla were at the kitchen table, smoking and smiling at him.

—Up and at 'em, stud, Marla said, blowing smoke out of her nose.

—Want some eggs? his mom said.

And Marla was already up and scraping some off the frying pan for him, saying, —We've decided we're going to see to it that you turn out right, Gilby. With our expertise, we'll raise you into the perfect man.

The thrill of being on the run. Being lavished in feminine cooing. It made Gilbert so giddy that he pretended to surf on the wicker rocking chair, going —Whoa! Whoa! Sue and Marla watched him, Sue saying in the warning tone of mothers, —Careful, Gilbert . . . Gilbert went, —Whoa! even though there was no chance of falling. They all laughed, Gilbert's grin opening his entire face, staring at his two mothers gasping, waiting for more praise.

A strange light on Sue's face now when she smiled. A glint in her eyes that made her beautiful because it was sinful. Marla stood behind her rubbing her shoulders. He'd never seen his mom smoke. She stamped out her cigarette and gulped the last of her coffee and went, —Let's get you to school, handsome.

Gilbert liked his mom calling him handsome.

Marla wrapped her arms around Sue and kissed Sue on the head and then brought Gilbert's backpack over, stroked his head and kissed him too and said, —Such a handsome sweet man. He's got such pretty eyes, Sue. He's going to break some hearts for sure.

He was glad he had two mothers now. He was glad that Mervin was gone because Mervin never called him perfect. He hoped Mervin was dead. If Mervin was dead Gilbert could wake up to his mother and Marla smoking at the kitchen table calling him handsome every morning.

They got into Marla's BMW and backed out of the driveway. Gilbert wore his wooly gray uniform and hat and turned to his mom and said, —Mom, do I really have pretty eyes?

—Yes, Gilbert. She was distracted, glancing out the window. Marla driving, scanning the stations with her free hand, swigging from a flask with her driving hand, her eyes dark and pretty in the rearview.

—How come I have pretty eyes?

—I don't know, Gilbert. Your father's mother has nice eyes.

—Did I get them from her?

— . . .

—Mom? Did I get my pretty eyes from Grandma?

— . . .

—*Mom!*

—Yes, Gilbert. Yes.

—How come they're pretty?

—They just are.

—Is it the color?

—Yes.

They're brown. Is brown pretty?

—It can be.

—Yours are brown. Are yours pretty?

—I don't know.

—I think my eyes are prettier than yours.

On the way out of the house and into the car and backing out of the driveway, Marla announced to them that Gilbert would not be attending school today, because he was sick, and that the phone call had already been made by Sue while Sue was in the shower, and this made Sue laugh and sort of shake her head and look out the window, and Marla floored it toward downtown.

Marla never slept with Mervin but Mervin often thought of her on the rare occasion he and Sue did it, which happened on average once every two months.

—You want a job too, Gilbert? Marla said. —We should all get one. We can be a roving band of gypsies, working our way across the world. What do you want to be, Gilbert?

—I don't know.

—You can be anything, Marla said. —Anything you want. Whatever you can think of you can be. Today's the first day of our lives. We're going to seek our destinies. Maybe even find them.

—Basketball player, Gilbert said.

Marla and Sue sort of glanced at each other in the rearview and Marla said, —Sure you don't want to be a fireman or a pilot or anything?

—No.

—Okay. Sue? How does one get the job of basketball player?

—You have to be a dirtbag, first of all, Sue said, not laughing. Gilbert looked at his mother, who didn't look back.

—What about you, Sue? Marla said. —What's your destiny?

—Oh, I don't know. I figured I'd do something like answer phones in a dentist's office. Or work at a clothing boutique or something.

—That's it? That's your destiny? Your purpose for being alive on planet Earth is to fold clothes maybe or answer phones?

—It's been so long since I've had a job, I don't think there's much else I could get. I just want a job right now. I'll worry about the rest after that.

—It's your choice, Sue. But me, I'm settling for no less than my destiny today.

—Yeah? What's that?

—To run for president. To be a poet. No, a singer! No, to fuck somebody who rents!

—That's not exactly a job, Marla.

—No, but it'd be a nice secret to have.

—Okay. Long hair or short?

—Long. A long-haired Irish man. A bricklayer. Tanned and muscley from slaving away in the hot sun.

—Sounds nice, Sue said.

—Then when I'm done with him I'll make him make me a gin and tonic and kick him out. That, my dear, is destiny.

The women laughed and Gilbert looked at his mother who hid her eyes from him and he said to her, —Mom, what's *fuck*?

After following Marla into four restaurants, two arts-and-crafts stores, one circus, three photographer's studios, six dentist/doctor/orthopedist/optometrist's offices, all of which Marla stood in the doorway upon entering and proclaimed, arms wide, —We come for work! Sue's desire for a job morphed into the desire for her husband's arms and a warm couch with a blanket to curl up under and the *blip-blip* of grocery-store purchasing.

—Work is for peasants anyway, Marla said, going into a bar.

Sue hesitated outside and Gilbert looked up at his mother whose eyes glazed with tears and reddened with strain on this empty street corner. Where was she and what was she doing in this small town in this small country? Could she catch a glimpse of her flesh in the reflecting foil bordering the door, and if she could, what did she see, and did she know what she saw? His mother stared out over the buildings and Sue and Gilbert did not belong to time and did not flow with their surroundings, which made them time travelers, dazed and left out, son who was a product of mother but mother a product of what and so son not a product of his own time either but an entity existing adjacent to it all. Because they were unaffected and rich and strange and inherently other and the white people on the streets with pudgy bellies and windbreakers and beards shoved by them, and if excuse me is what is said then Sue could not remember what to say. Or what is right or what is to be done when everything is yours for the doing. Sue trembled with the fear that she would not know what was now or where they were or if now was now and where they were was here. Or what red was or if inside out was outside in or if now was time to panic because the ground sinks beneath your feet and God slices your strings and I can't promise that's me and my lips in my reflection.

Marla was born in a little house in Roanoke, Virginia, to a father who was almost sixty years old and a mother with two other kids by another guy who was in jail. She almost didn't graduate high school, slept with four boys before she was eighteen. She was the prettiest girl in her graduating class and got married to someone in the marines. She got a job when she was twenty-three at a Belk putting makeup on old women. Five years later she was still there and still married and met Herb, a rich man on business as he said, a decade older than she was. She ran off with him to Europe without ever divorcing her marine, and married Herb under a made-up name. —For my MS, she told Sue the first time Sue saw her shoot something into her arm, in Marla's bedroom one sleepy Thursday afternoon as Sue applied an eye shadow shade called Confidence.

—MS?

—Multiple sclerosis. If I don't do it, my hands buckle up like a goddamn cripple's. It's okay. I have a prescription for it.

—Does Herb know?

—Know? More like encourages. It's the price you have to pay if he wants to keep enjoying Marla's World Famous Hand Jobs.

* * *

Marla walked out of the bathroom on her own, avoiding eye contact, scratching her face, and sat back down across from Sue and
Gilbert and put her head on the table. —You alive? Sue said, to no
response. Gilbert spit pieces of napkin out of his straw between sips
of Coke.

Sue lit another one of Marla's long skinny cigarettes that Marla
had to go out of state to buy but she stamped it out without taking a
drag, staring at Marla. Marla lifted her head off the sticky table to yell
at no one, —Hey! Beer! The bartender was an older guy with a toothpick in his mouth that made him look wise, but he didn't look up from
his conversation with two large balding men with dark eyes. Sue said
to her, —You going to be okay to drive?

—Yeah. Yeah. Uh, of course, yeah, Marla said. —Don't worry, Sue.
We'll get jobs tomorrow.

And Sue said, —I want to go home.

—No, no. Stay. Tomorrow we'll get great jobs, Sue. I promise. Tomorrow.

—Marla, I'm going home.

*Inside the doorway, the whole house dark, Mervin in sweatpants and
his face grown shaggy from neglect and eyes bloodshot, Gilbert
standing to the side as his mom and dad fell into each other with soft
whimpers.*

The taxi dropped Sue and Gilbert off at the end of the driveway.
They paid the driver and lugged their bags up to the front door, which
had changed in that it was just as it was, like Sue had never left, and
maybe it was Sue who'd changed. Gilbert watched his mother's shaky
hands as she turned the knob and stepped inside. The windows were
all covered with black trash bags. It was silent except for the sound of
game tapes in the living room, where Mervin emerged from. He stood
there. Man and wife stood staring there at each other. Gilbert looked
back and forth between them. Was this forgiveness? Love? Resigna-
tion?

—Hey baby, Mervin said.

—Hey, Sue said.

He stepped forward and took her hands and she wrapped herself
up in her husband, and they whimpered like puppies. They had
mauled each other, drawn each other's blood, and now it was time to

hug. Gilbert stood there watching, wishing they hadn't come back here. He wished his mom hadn't hugged his dad. Mervin took her bag in one hand and her hand in the other hand and said to Gilbert, — Grab your bag. He led them upstairs, tearing the black trash bags off the windows along the way.

4

THIRTEEN, AND THE RAIN WAS DEATH. Thirteen and the rain was the end of time. The rain was eternal when thirteen. It came only when it was cold, falling fast from the belly of the sky, an army of caped billions, with barbed teeth protruding like a school of prehistoric fish. Each drop in its descent incinerating into gas then freezing into solid then melting back into liquid. A life cycle that was born and changed and ended fast. Gathering all toxic air from man's machines, wetting the last gasps of the recently departed, and splattering onto manhole covers, rain. And washing the grease from the streets and forming little rivers in gutters, rain. And it was raining, and it was raining, and it was raining. The rain turned dirt into mud. The mud squished into the waffle grids of your shoes. Massachusetts rain. The rain scoured the fair skin of Boston men, drove the last-chance depressives to clear-eyed suicide, destroyed the hair of Boston women. The ugly weather of the greater Boston area. He was back in Hingham, like he had never left.

At St. Francis of Assisi Junior High School back here in Hingham they taught Gilbert to honor thy father and mother. And so when Mervin decided that from now on every Saturday morning Gilbert would empty the hampers and lug the family's laundry two miles into town, even though they had their own washer and dryer, Gilbert didn't ask why or whine, but humbly uttered, —Yes, sir. In school they taught you to offer up all your sufferings, especially the everyday kind like being hungry or having too much homework, for the forgiveness of sins. Father Ryan, his religion teacher at St. Francis of Assisi Junior High School, had all sorts of insider tips on avoiding eternal damnation—like how receiving Communion puts you in a state of grace, meaning you're without sin, and if you die right after, you go straight to the front of the line into heaven.

That strange small building twenty miles from Gilbert's new house in Hingham, in Stoughton. Seventh grade through high school but still only three hundred students, in a small building that looked a hundred years old and had dark hallways and low ceilings and third-hand desks carved with generations of bored doodlings. It was not uncommon for students to withdraw from the school because they were severely allergic to the mold in the wood. Girls were not allowed to wear makeup and boys' hair was measured at random against a ruler to make sure no part was longer than four inches. Boys couldn't roll up the sleeves of their uniform shirts, and girls had to wear a turtleneck under theirs at all times. Entire school days were canceled when the staff decided to lug the student body to the local abortion clinic to protest. You could get out of class whenever you wanted to go to Confession. Gilbert thought this sounded nice so he raised his hand and asked if he could go to Confession, and he was let out of class. He walked down to the chapel and stood in the line of sinful boys and girls outside the door, wondering what it was they each had done. But once he was in the little room he didn't know what to do, not being Catholic, so he asked the person on the other side of the screen, but the person on the other side of the screen was Father Ryan, who recognized his voice and said, —Nice try, Mr. Marcus. Get back to class.

Once a week it was Gilbert's turn to stay after school and clean Father Ryan's classroom, which entailed a full sweeping and mopping. His partner was a small fat blond boy named B.J. who smelled like old cheese.

—Goddamnit, B.J. said, —I'm supposed to play street hockey today. This is bullshit.

—Shouldn't curse, Gilbert said.

—Whatever, B.J. said. His face was red. His face was always red.

—Think of it as honoring your father and mother. Second commandment.

—Father Ryan isn't my goddamn dad, you asshole. My dad says Father Ryan's a kid toucher.

—Shouldn't curse.

—My dad says you people are taking all our jobs.

—Why would I want your job?

—Take my job I'll kill you.

Gilbert stood on the corner with the laundry in downtown Hingham, waiting for the light to change. The grays and greens and botanic smells made the world feel like outgrowing shoes. Headlights lit up the drops. The rain was knives that opened up the chests of the citizens of Hingham, leaving them vulnerable. He'd been home a year. Was this his home? It was where he was from. Recently his soul had been stirring. He didn't know how to explain it. It felt like his hands would pass through the lampposts like holograms. Maybe it had something to do with being thirteen and suburban at the onset of puberty. He felt alone. A monster clinging to his ribs and into his brains where words were creating themselves, twisting like snakes into little verses of poetry as he ducked into the laundromat.

> *One day the rain fell from the sky*
> *It fell onto the people's heads*
> *And made all the children cry.*

Wow, yeah, that was good. He'd make a hell of a saint. Gilbert had decided after listening to ancient Father Ryan talk in his Irish accent about Saint Francis of Assisi and Padre Pio that he would be a saint. For some reason he assumed all saints had to write poetry too.

The machines shook his family's clothes into new and he pulled out his notebook, worn and half-filled, and sat in a chair in the corner of the laundromat, watching the fat chatty Brazilian women and the old man who came in and tossed his soaked shirt into a dryer and stood there in his wrinkled old man skin watching it tumble. He wrote words that would one day be engraved in stone beneath a sculpture of his head, revered by the people of the future. *The man washed his shirt and grew old / The boy wrote poems, tales never told.*

He looked around, hoping someone would notice him and come over and ask what he was writing. He'd modestly hand over the notebook and they would read it and they would know that he was a saint.

Hairs were beginning to spiral out of his armpits. His horny could ooze a dollop of colorless gel if he rubbed it long enough. His balls hurt and his leg muscles ached. His feet hurt all the time. It was becoming too clear that he would never fit in. Like Saint Francis of Assisi. Forever alone and weird. *Which is my destiny too,* Gilbert thought. The holy hermit, the blessed mystic untouched and untainted and aloof, thus great.

> *I shall never speak again*
> *An artist, a saint, an idol of men*
> *O! Lord, strike me blind*
> *So I might love Thee*
> *And cherish mankind.*

B.J. said, —Everyone thinks you're an illegal, you know. Do you have a green card? I'll call immigration. Deport your ass. You act gay too by the way. I dare you to try and fuck me. I'll fuck you up.

And for a while he skipped meals, gave his lunch to whoever envied his cookies, even B.J., who envied them the most; bit his tongue when his classmates called him fag, walked away and sat in the corner of the courtyard and got out his journal. And for a while the sun on the grass became poetry, and the desexualized mothers picking up their kids after school became poetry too. He watched them all as if from behind a Plexiglas wall.

There was a girl he was in love with. This girl was his soul mate. They were destined to be bonded in matrimony forever. It was fate that she would be beautiful and he would have her on his arm and she would be smiling, everyone saying how beautiful Gilbert's wife was. B.J. and Nick Friend would see pictures of him with his beautiful wife and be envious. Her name was Colleen and she was twelve, in the seventh grade. Every Monday morning the student body of St. Francis of Assisi Junior High School met in the gym for Mass, and Gilbert stared up Jesus Christ on the cross, hanging over the altar, beaten and humiliated and killed, suffering the death of deaths for Gilbert, who couldn't even stop thinking about Colleen for an hour. He'd look over at her on the girls' side (boys and girls divided at Mass at St. Francis, like families at a wedding), her dark eyes and pink mouth and long dark hair down to the middle of her back, her tall slender body and long dark legs. The mystery that lurked beneath her blue skirt.

Gorgeous hot sexy Colleen, whose gaze his breath stopped for, who laughed at how he talked funny the first week of school when he bravely approached her and her group of girls in the courtyard, wanting to make friends. He'd never said another word to her again. He'd never looked into her big brown eyes lined with mascara again. But she loved him too, he knew it. Why wouldn't she? It only made sense that she would. He was Gilbert Marcus. And every poem he wrote was for her, every shot he made, every steal, every victory he'd look around to see if she was in the gym, standing by the door in her green jacket still in her uniform with her skirt barely below the knee (as per the rules), white socks pulled up high, with her friends, all of them staring in awe, Colleen humbled and impressed and weak with desire. But she was never there.

Gilbert burst through the door with the clean laundry, smelling like wet afternoon. Mervin sat reading the paper from behind his beard, fat and faithful in retirement. He didn't have to work anymore after licensing his name and image to the producers of *Mervin Marcus's Freak of Basketball*, what turned out to be a successful series of mail-order instructional videos for children. He appeared in advertisements for local car dealerships. He did motivational speaking appearances at corporate pep rallies around the region. A college game played on the outdated big-screen Magnavox that no one was watching. With his free time he'd begun reading the paper. He'd become dismayed at the world. He'd begun following politics, taking sides, memorizing the names and voting records of congressmen who had become his enemies.

He collected royalties from a ghostwritten tell-all autobiography about his experiences with racism and narcotics during his years in The Association.

He read the papers with a red pen, a whole coffee cup full of them on the end table. Old yellowing newspapers stacked up in great structures in the corner. Legal pads filled with notes taken from the game tapes piled up on the coffee table. Circling articles that particularly reinforced his idea that the world was a sinking ship and writing ANIMAL or SUE on them for them to read. A smiley face in the margin meant the passage or quote was something he agreed with.

—The world is full of crackwhores and devils, he'd say aloud if Sue were in the room, and she'd nod slightly and offer a small moan of agreement.

He reported half of his income to the IRS.

The days a pregnant woman was murdered or a senator introduced legislation that would let teenagers abort without parental consent, Gilbert would find himself out on the backyard court well past midnight staring into Mervin's drooping face. Mervin played superdefense, knocking the ball from the boy's hand, swiping shots out into the street, sweat dripping from his beard as he crouched before Gilbert muttering, —Crackwhores and devils, Animal. Come on, devil. Come on.

And Mervin'd lay the paper, folded to the article, on the kitchen table where Gilbert and Sue would see it, and he'd stand beside them as they read.

Gilbert never actually read them. He tried, but you can't read when someone's staring at you.

And my voice when I speak to him sounds weak and high-pitched, and his hearing is bad the way grown men's is, so I have to repeat myself over and over, whatever I say. It makes me hate to speak.

This was retirement.

Mervin had an article ready for Gilbert today when he came in. This article was about how some politicians wanted to spend more money on sexual education in public schools and some politicians wanted to spend less money on sexual education in public schools.

—These people think condoms will save them, Mervin said. —But condoms won't save them. Nothing will save them. Condoms are only seventy-five percent effective when used properly. Did you know that, Animal?

—Unh-uh.

—Nothing will save them. Look, what I'm trying to say, Animal, is that there is more to life than basketball.

Gilbert didn't say anything.

Mervin took him by the shoulders and looked him in the eyes. — No, Animal. Listen to me. *There is more than basketball.* Understand?

—Yeah.

Mervin's eyes were huge and crazy. And Gilbert could see the holes where the beard grew out of his face. He remembered Leo. The smell of shaving cream. What else? He couldn't remember anything else.

—No. Listen. There's a whole world out there, Animal. Fuck basketball. Be a doctor. *Help* people. Make a *difference.*

He'd never heard Mervin say fuck before. Not directly to him.

—Promise me you will never touch a basketball again.

—Okay.

—Promise.

—I promise.

Sue sat on the toilet in the master bathroom, tearing lines in her flesh with her cosmetic scissors. The sores were back. They were all over her mouth. From the inside of her lips to the middle of her cheeks. Oozing and painful. She couldn't show herself in public. She hated them. But she deserved them! Didn't she? For coming back? Why had she come back? But that was so long ago. Nearly four years. The last four years had been nothing. The sores were coming more and more often in the last year. And more of them each time. How could she stop them? Suddenly it dawned on her why Mervin wore a beard. Each sore had a name. The names were in her head. They screamed themselves at her: *Jennifer from Cleveland. Theresa from Seattle. Sofia from Bend. Aria from Fresno* . . . Names and faces and teeth and bodies and clothes and her husband's hands searching their orifices. Hundreds of them, never dying, and the only way to be able to go downstairs and make dinner was to sit here and scrape at her wrist, scrape out the names, get to the blood, the blood was where the names were, the blood was where the poison was, the blood the blood the blood.

* * *

Then one day he woke up and he was fucking enormous. He grew a foot in one month. He grew so fast he thought he'd die. He could no longer hide. He looked sixteen at least, and people expected him to be mature and responsible like a sixteen-year-old. He was no longer allowed to be a boy but an illusion, kicked out into public. And he felt ashamed, ducking under doorways and bumping papers off his teachers' desks, girls tapping him on the shoulder in class to tell him to duck because they can't see, and he felt so ashamed always being in people's way, not knowing what to say because all his classmates who had ignored him now had no choice but to see him, talk to him. His eyes darting away. His humiliating puberty. It's humiliating making graying men with children and wives appear like blunted midgets in your presence. It makes you feel intrusive. He was the leading scorer, rebounder, passer, and shot blocker on the St. Francis of Assisi Squires' undefeated eighth-grade team—indomitable champions of the Metro-West Catholic Athletic League Eighth-Grade Division—whom his teammates gave the ball to every time and the opposing coach ordered all his kids to guard, give up your guy just everyone get on 32 I don't care. He made adults uncomfortable he was so big, which made *him* uncomfortable. Girls wanted him to talk to them, but he never knew what they wanted to hear. The only girl he wanted to talk to was Colleen. Colleen never wanted to talk to him.

He stole Mervin's cologne and Sue gave him a crash course in dancing on the way out to the driveway before she drove him through the darkness to the school. The fall dance. The only dance of the year. The students could even *choose the music.* As long as Father Ryan approved of the lyrics. He had all the words planned out. *Hey Colleen, what's up, wanna dance?* She would say yes. She would become his girlfriend. Then he would be able to put his horny into her whenever he wanted.

But only for the purposes of children . . .

He was so nervous dancing with her. His tie was too short, and his feet were too big. His hands were sweaty and it was gross but he couldn't make them stop. She was beautiful. His gorilla hands on her little hips. He could smell her hair. They swayed, stiff, uptight. She looked around. She smelled like cigarettes. She looked everywhere but at Gilbert. She muttered, —I wonder where Chrissy is . . . He loomed over her in the middle of the sparse dance floor. He stepped on her toes and she screamed, —*Ow!*

—Oh, I'm sorry, he said.

—You fucking *stepped* on my *toe! Ow!*

—I'm so sorry.

—Get *away* from me. *Ow.*

Her girlfriends came over, separating him from her. She had taken off her shoe and they all bent down examining Colleen's little wounded toe.

—I . . . I didn't mean to.

The rest of the kids were coming over to see what was going on. A couple of high school boys said to Gilbert, —That's not how you treat your girl, man.

—She's not my . . . She's not my . . . girl.

—You don't step on your girl's toes, the high school boys said.

—I *know*, Gilbert said. —I didn't *mean* to.

Colleen was crying. She draped her arms over her friends' shoulders who gave Gilbert nasty looks as they helped her out of the gym.

—I can't move it, Colleen whined. —Oh my God, he *broke* it. I think he *broke* my *toe!*

He spent the rest of the night standing against the wall. He called his mom from the pay phone outside. —It's boring, he said. —Some kids are drinking beer. I think you should come pick me up.

Every day after school Mervin was there waiting for him in the drive-way with the basketball. Gilbert would drop his bag and take off his tie and they would play and Mervin would beat him in ten minutes. Mervin blocked his shots—smart, are ya?—dunked it over him—think you got it all figured out, eh?—used his size and weight to push Gilbert out to the street and grab rebounds. Giving him bruises on his arms and back, tearing the skin on Gilbert's wrists and hands, swatting his shots into the neighbor's yard, boxing him out for rebounds and throwing his elbows into Gilbert's throat, and utilizing fall-aways and ball-fakes and all kinds of tricks.

—This is the way the game is played at the professional level, Animal, he said afterward, wiping the sweat off the back of his neck as he watched his thirteen-year-old son shed tears of defeat. —Get used to it or don't play.

Since he'd lost, Gilbert then had to shoot 250 free throws before he was allowed inside the house. Before he was allowed to sleep he had to do seventy-five push-ups. Every morning at four thirty he was woken by Mervin blowing a whistle and banging on a metal trash can with a wooden spoon from the kitchen. He had to run four miles, Mervin driving behind him in the car, screaming at him and throwing pennies and nickels at him from the change in the ashtray. He had good aim, he usually hit him. His favorite place to hit Gilbert with the loose change was in the back of the head, at the base of the skull. Loose change can really smart if thrown at the back of the skull at a strong velocity. Other times Gilbert held on to a handle Mervin had welded onto the back of Sue's station wagon and ran like hell to keep up as Mervin drove through the neighborhood. Then it was off to school. This was weekday mornings. On Saturday and Sunday mornings, Gilbert ran stairs at the local high school first thing, then when the sun came up he jogged over to Gold's Gym for strength work (squats, lunges, bench, curls) with his personal trainer, Rupert, a former Mr. Universe. That was followed by the rest of the morning on the court with Mervin, working on his shooting, footwork, dribbling, and fundamental technique. On Saturday afternoons, after a quick gray health shake Sue made for him for lunch loaded with weight-gain powder and more than a dozen different nutritional supplements, he met with Peter, the tennis instructor Mervin hired from the Phillips Exeter Academy varsity tennis team, for a brutal match on the courts in the Marcuses neighborhood. On Sundays, instead of tennis it was crew: he met with the Belmont Hill Academy crew captain, Michael (not Mike, Michael made clear the first day), also hired by Mervin, at the boathouse near Harvard Square (for which Gilbert needed Sue to give him a ride) and spent an hour or two strenuously rowing a boat on the Charles River. There was also the laundry of course, usually on Saturday. After a two-mile run to cool down, Gilbert had to get his ass handed to him by Mervin on the hoop in their driveway again, invariably resulting in 250 more free throws, then a dinner of brown rice and organic produce, a half hour on the exercise bike in the basement, a shower, and bed.

He began losing small amounts of hair. He'd wake up and there'd be hairs on his pillow. The shower would clog and he'd bend down and pull a large clump of hair off the drain and the water would empty.

Gilbert ached so badly and so often from Mervin's training regimen that it caused a high-pitched squeal in the inner part of his ear. He heard this squeal all the time. It got so he stopped noticing it. He suffered a constant soreness in his quadriceps and gluteus maximus. He complained of a sore throat and mysterious raised mounds at the very back of his mouth that burned and leaked a bitter discharge.

—Gonna beat that motherfucker . . .

On the day that Mervin was away in Washington, D.C., to protest abortion at the annual March for Life rally, Sue was making brownies in the kitchen at 2:25, anticipating the sound of the front door opening and Gilbert's changing voice cracking, —Mom, I'm home! He'd be hungry after a day of school, she'd feed him, he'd scurry off to work out.

But all she heard as she stirred the bowl with a spoon was the thud of rubber on pavement outside. And Gilbert talking to somebody.

The grandfather clock played she thought Mozart or Beethoven. She looked out the window and saw Gilbert's backpack lying at the mouth of the driveway and Gilbert running across the driveway and shooting, mumbling to himself. She moved across finished hardwood floors and passed the living room with spindly furniture that was expensive and she opened the storm door with the golden curvy handle and stood on the porch in the late spring heat with the chocolaty spoon in her hand and said, —Gilbert, who are you talking to?

Gilbert didn't acknowledge her. He kept mumbling to himself. She walked over pieces of sticks on the ground looking down at her chipped deep red nail polish and legs unshaved for three days, making sure nothing pricked her bare feet, and said, —Gilbert?

Didn't answer. Maybe he was singing a song. Not that he ever showed much interest in music. Sue bought him a karaoke machine for Christmas the previous year in the hopes that he would discover he had an incredible voice and abandon basketball in favor of music, but the karaoke machine, a Hitachi, lay now with broken battery compartment under a plastic Christmas tree in the basement.

—Gilbert.

Something cut into the bottom of her foot and she went, —Shit!

She limped over to the garage door to lean on it while she pulled out a chunk of glass. A maroon bubble swelled until it broke and road-mapped into the cracks of her skin. She held the bloody glass and looked up at her son, holding it between her fingers. He was now throwing the ball with one hand at the hoop, clanging it off the back board, ducking as it ricocheted back at him, and chasing after it, oblivious to Sue.

—I'm bleeding, Gilbert.

She could only now hear what it was he had been saying to himself: —Gonna beat that motherfucker. Gonna *beat that motherfucker . . .*

She gasped. —*What* did you say, Gilbert?

—Fucking motherfucker. Gonna beat that motherfucker . . .

Jaw open, she limped over and took him by the elbow. He had a feral look in his eyes and was huffing and puffing. —We do *not* use that kind of language, Sue said. He was taller than she was by nearly a foot, but she still took him inside, slapped a bar of soap on his tongue, put a Band-Aid on her foot, the basketball halfway down the street against the curb.

You can't stop, change, it's no good for you, makes you feel worthless, inferior, a waste of skin, you can't live your whole life this way you know, spinning your wheels in the mud. You see the other kids your age who don't have squealing ears. They bounce around with no pressure greater than getting their homework in on time. They are shiny-eyed and glorious and you want to join them, become NORMAL, the pain of being weird too much to take anymore. You dream of spending your afternoons with these kids playing video games and poisoning your colon. FITTING IN. Invisible and liked . . .

In the fall of eighth grade, the months before the season, and despite Mervin's protests (but in those days he was distracted by the news to care too much), Gilbert gave up on basketball. He'd never play again. He spent his hours after school on the sewer grate behind St. Francis, with Brendan and Jimmy, who smoked cigarettes and drank their dads' beers and liked to set things on fire. And for a while it was fun, seeing how plastic straws burn, the danger of getting caught and arrested and put in jail. He took a drag off Jimmy's cigarette once, which Jimmy and Brendan called a *butt*. B.J. followed them there, once cool B.J. but now loser B.J. with dumb clothes and no friends. When B.J. saw that the cool kids were smoking cigarettes and lighting straws on fire he said he'd tell his dad who was a fireman but Jimmy punched him in the stomach so he didn't. Gilbert fished around his house for more matches to bring Brendan and Jimmy so they could light their cigarettes and set things on fire. His English teacher, Mrs. Englewood (Mrs. Dangle Wood, Brendan and Jimmy called her), requested a parent-teacher conference because Gilbert was distracted in class. His grades were slipping. He'd stopped doing his homework. Sue went to the conference alone because Mervin was attending a (sparsely attended) Republican Party fund-raiser in Boston.

Just put your head on your pillow and let your hair fall out of your scalp, stare up at the ceiling all night, closing your eyes but seeing only darkness, turning over but it meets you on the other side. Its face is a skeleton's, eyeless and opening its mouth but cool rank air coming out. Chills your bones, never letting you be. Everything in its place, all in agreement with the earth, this feeling, you realize, is the way it shall forever be.

Gilbert realized one day watching Jimmy cut the head off a praying mantis with a pocketknife that he had no choice in the matter of who he was. Being away from basketball was like something being torn from his soul.

Gonna *beat* that motherfucker.

When the season started every game became for his father. The parents were there to support their own kids, but their attention was drawn to the black boy in the T-shirt jersey with cheap shiny 32 on the back (because it was Darren Dickinson's number) scoring thirty, forty points against the other runts. It was like he wasn't having fun. This serious look on his face. Like it mattered more than it did. And it *didn't* matter. It was a kids' game, for Christ's sake. They all found it a little disturbing. Plus they were more than a little concerned for their sons' safety out there with him, he played with such intensity. Throwing his elbows around, getting very physical and rough. He was so much bigger than everybody else. Fathers of kids on opposing teams yelled at the refs, —Do something with this kid before I do.

Three different times the refs threw Gilbert out.

Two different times a father was waiting for Gilbert in the parking lot. But they never did anything. Not with Mervin there. The former professional basketball player who had played with Larry Bird. After all, they weren't *dumb.*

Gilbert hated that. *I don't need his help. I can fight my own fights. I'm a man.*

Gonna beat that motherfucker.

His shadow on the driveway in front of his house was his father, and he juked it and spun around it and pulled up over it, and no other opponent mattered.

Gonna *beat* that motherfucker.

All the victories and congratulations from the astonished opposing coaches were hollow. They meant nothing because he failed to beat Mervin. He had even failed to ever score against Mervin. He never spoke to his teammates in the parking lot upon arrival, or during warm-ups when the kids would goof around and shoot it from half-court and run around crazy.

He didn't need St. Francis of Assisi or Father Ryan. He didn't need their saints. He had his own saint. His saint still walked the earth. You could see him in real life if you wanted to, touch his clothes and be blessed. This saint was Darren Dickinson. Darren Dickinson was the greatest basketball player of all time. He was the first one you thought of when someone said *basketball player.* He played basketball so well it was like he'd sold his soul to be able to play basketball so well. He was raised in the mosquito graveyards of Jacksonville, Florida, by his father who was a chronic alcoholic and his mother who never left her bedroom. He had to quit his high school basketball team his senior year because his mother had a stroke and his father was too drunk to take care of her and all the college scouts lost interest in him. But he didn't quit. He used the rage that he had inside of him for his father being drunk and his mother never leaving her bedroom making him quit the basketball team during recruiting season to develop an unrelenting work ethic, long lonely hours spent on the dirt court developing his art and walking onto the team at the University of Central Florida and leading UCF to an NCAA championship and being named NCAA Player of the Year. Then after just one year of college making the leap to The Association and from there leading a charmed career of championships and MVP trophies and scoring titles, breaking records for season scoring average, playoff scoring average. He dunked like nobody before him, adding an electric element to the game that had not been there before, inspiring a generation of kids like Gilbert Marcus. He seemed to fly. His excellence came from a strict regimen of work and study. He was said to be clinically obsessive. He often stayed up all night shooting free throws alone, it was said. His game had no weakness. Nobody had seen anything like this. He was better than Dr. J, won more championships than Larry Bird, and was more famous than Magic Johnson (though not by much). He achieved everything one could achieve in professional basketball. He was recognized in Phuket. He spoke in the clear voice of a white man and smiled, had no edge, nothing to fear, kept his hair neat and stayed out of trouble. Wore a suit, like a businessman. He turned himself into a brand, endorsing sports drinks and athletic wear. He made moves on the court that were gravitationally irresponsible. The analytical instincts of a coach, the body of a wide receiver. He gave a name to his team forever—the Detroit Autos. There was no question and no one could argue.

Every now and then, in the old Jaguar with a weird sound in the engine, crawling inch by inch over the city along the Mass Pike on his way home from Boston College, where he was now part-time assistant coaching adviser, listening to talk radio, the sunny glare of impending dusk bursting off the Financial District towers, Mervin remembered when he was great. How many years ago was that? What'd happened? When he was in high school and then eating shit in the service and then at B.C. he was on top of the world. Back before the world caught up with him and swallowed him up.

Mervin decided the day he woke his son up before daylight and had him stand out in the snow in his pj's, barefoot, that there would be no illusions.

His duty as a father was to raise his son to be a successful citizen of *this world*. It was a grim duty for a grim world. It required him to reveal all its ugliness for his son but also to reveal the sport as it truly was as well. It was an ugly, ruthless sport. Let those other fathers pretend athletics are about teamwork and self-esteem, Mervin thought. Sports aren't like that. The world's not like that. Those kids and their self-esteem will be shocked white when they realize in a thunderous moment of revelation the truth of men and life.

—Sports, Mervin told Sue when she showed him all the hairs she found on Gilbert's pillow, demanding explanation, are one man's brutality pitted against another man's brutality. It's savagery, Sue. It's lions on the plains. The only thing that matters in sports, no matter what Little League coaches or anyone says, Sue, is *winning*. That's what sports are for, Sue. To *win*. Animal's got to learn that. Ain't no glory. Winning and losing. *That's it.*

One day when he was about five years old and living on Oak Hill Drive in Hingham, Gilbert said to Mervin, —I want to be a basketball player.

It was dinnertime, brown rice and vegetables, the TV on but on mute, a compromise between Mervin, who liked to watch while he ate, and Sue, who wanted a nice family TV-less meal, and Mervin was talking about how Coach was a son of a bitch whose very existence was proof that any asshole could be a coach in this league, goddamnit, and how he should have gone to Hollywood to become an actor, and Gilbert went, —I want to be a basketball player.

Mervin dropped his fork mid-chew and stared at him from across the table like Gilbert'd just farted. Sue lowered the chopstick-load of brown rice she was poised to deposit into her mouth and discreetly did the *ixnay* sign at Gilbert. Mervin looked at Sue who stopped and looked down at her lap. Mervin said to Gilbert, —Come again now?

—I said I want to be a basketball player.

—Speak up now.

—I want to be a basketball player.

—Do you now?

—Uh-huh.

—That's yes sir.

—Yes sir.

—Okay. I'll teach you.

—When?

—Mervin, Sue said.

—I'll teach him, Sue.

—When do you plan on teaching me? little Gilbert said.

—Oh I don't know. How about tomorrow? How's your schedule look for tomorrow?

And Sue said, —No, he has that thing.

—It won't take long. We'll do it tomorrow. He wants to be a basketball player.

And the next morning Mervin woke Gilbert up when even Sue's father—your stereotypical Japanese workaholic—was still in bed. It was the middle of a blizzard that no meteorologist had predicted. School was canceled and most everybody was staying home from work. But Mervin still had practice and then a game at night. He said to Gilbert, —Get up. Go outside. Put your hands on the siding and don't move.

When Mervin let Gilbert come back inside he said, —How's it feel to be a basketball player?

That night Gilbert fell asleep and dreamed nothing.

It was the summer after freshman year of high school (new school—Brenton Prep!). A Friday evening in mid-June, the heavy wet Massachusetts summer, mosquitoes terrorizing your flesh, lightning bugs sweet in the distance. It happened in the haze of dusk, in the driveway, an orange sky silvery over twisty Lake Shore Road, the gated community on the golf course where the Marcuses made their home in Hingham, Massachusetts, about half a mile east of Oak Hill Drive: He beat that motherfucker. *He beat that motherfucker.* And when he beat that motherfucker, he didn't jump up and down and Mervin did not congratulate him or call bullshit one way or the other. Rather, each Marcus stood where they'd been when Gilbert pulled up over Mervin and sunk an eight-footer off the board. Mervin watched it go in and turned to Gilbert, his hands on his hips. Silence sprinkled over them. For the first time in his life Gilbert saw the trees with their leaves green and flittering against the sky. His destiny came to him then written in stone. As it shall be, forever more. He was fifteen years old. Mervin wiped the sweat off his forehead with the tail of his white V-neck T-shirt. The shirt was so soaked Gilbert could see his father's nipples. The smell of charcoal wafted over them from the neighbors barbecuing next door.

They looked at each other for a while and Mervin said, —Makes you feel good, doesn't it. Beating up on an old man.

Gilbert shrugged.

—Guess you think you're some sort of hot shit now?

Gilbert said nothing and Mervin didn't tell his son his ankle got twisted so bad on the first point that he limped for two weeks after and his ankle swelled to the size of his shin. He didn't tell Gilbert that his blood pressure had gotten so high that it felt like his face was about to pop and there were tingles in his extremities, pinpricks up his spine. Mervin headed into the garage and said over his shoulder, —Wasn't even a pretty shot. You didn't even call bank.

He cursed and kicked over a trash can and went inside. Gilbert watched him go. He picked up the basketball and put it in the garage and followed after his father, thinking about dinner.

5

THAT SUMMER HE WAS HARDLY home. He stepped onto planes and off planes, hopping up and down the East Coast, even as far out west as Indiana, to exclusive basketball clinics to work with the best coaches Mervin's money could buy. He went to Australia with Mervin to meet with a holistic medical practitioner for a week of body purification. He lived with a Pilates instructor named Tali (fifty, tanned crispy) for a week in Miami, Florida, and she made little effort to conceal her attraction toward him, even going so far as to once during a mat-work session—as he was on his back and she was bent over him using her own body weight to try to push his leg back behind his head—sliding her crispy hand down the inside of his thigh and cupping his balls and giving him a wink. This created such a confounding mixture of arousal and repulsion in young Gilbert that he freaked out and kicked her off of him. Literally kicked her off of him. First pushing her off with the leg she was trying to push behind his head and then—since she maintained a grip on that leg—using the other leg to clip her in the underside of her ribs, knocking the wind out of her. Gilbert spent the rest of the day following Tali around apologizing his ass off for kicking her in the ribs, Tali holding an ice pack to her ribs and saying to just let it go, okay, because it wasn't her fault that Gilbert wasn't mature enough to handle the physical proximity necessary for Pilates.

On the Fourth of July Mervin and Sue dragged him to a picnic in Ipswich. There was barbecue and fireworks and men in light cotton shirts with hands in their khaki pockets and little kids running around and mothers in sundresses standing around talking about the little kids running around. She was Sue's old college roommate's daughter. She wore a sundress and had big eyes and her face glowed and she was fifteen like him. She led him off and asked him, —Why are you so quiet?

And he said what everybody else says to that, which is, —Nothing to say.

You don't have to say anything.

He looked down because to look up would be to notice boobies. Her sundress made it hard to not look at her boobies. Her dress made it hard to not look at her thighs, and her thighs were smooth and exposed almost completely. Her name was Sandy. She was fifteen, like him. She touched his face and went, —You're cute.

—I am?

—Uh-huh.

—Oh.

—What's the matter?

—Nothing.

—Do you want to go to McDonald's sometime? With me?

—Yeah. Wait. No. I'm not allowed.

—Not allowed to go to McDonald's?

—Yeah. That stuff is nasty. Did you know the burgers are made out of leftover scraps on the floor of the meat factory place?

—Gross.

—Yeah and there are all these worms in there that feed off your body and grow to like fifty feet long.

—It's good though. I like it.

—I guess.

—So what do you eat?

—You know. Like organic vegetable broth and oat crackers. Stuff that's good for the bowel.

—Ew!

—What.

—That's gross.

—How's it gross?

—Oat crackers? It sounds gross.

—I have to be careful about what I eat. I'm gonna be the best basketball player ever.

And at the camps all the white kids wanted to be the chigger's friend.

They hadn't seen him play but still threw the ball to him when they were trapped.

Give it to the black kid, he'll know what to do with it.

There were other black kids but they weren't like the chigger because they were pure black. They looked at Gilbert and called him mix breed, Oreo, even though that was for white-black. The pure white kids begged for Gilbert's affection. —Hey Gilbert, sit with us . . . Gilbert, we're sneaking out tonight to go to the girls' soccer camp, wanna come? . . . Gilbert, check out these shoes. Do you like them? If you don't I was gonna throw them away . . .

It made him wonder if it was some kind of joke, the way things had changed.

He went to the pure black kids' dorms and pretended to know the rap music they played in their rooms, nodding his head and not asking who it was. He caught a glimpse of the CD cover, memorized it, made a note to go shopping when he got home. The pure black kids wore baggy jeans and Darren Dickinson T-shirts down to their knees. He felt like a clown in his tight jeans and polo shirts, loafers.

The black kids called him Carlton Banks. They asked him if he was going to the library.

But Sandy didn't say anything about his clothes or haircut or about how he talked like a white guy. She leaned forward on the log by the river on the Fourth of July and put her lips on his and The Light exploded and the sky blasted the cap off the world.

When school started again—sophomore year—he had changed. He was no longer Carlton Banks.

ⱽ ⱽ ⱽ

These skinny loners moping through the hallways of Brenton Prep between third and fourth period, clutching their little journals and hating the world. Ugly antisocial freaks with a fear of the opposite sex and poor parents and zero athletic ability, colons ridden with parasites. I bet they think *saltwater enema* is the name of a grunge band, he thought, sneering. He had his arm around Bethany. He whispered into her ear, —Coming to the game tonight? Bethany had a doughy middle, he'd noticed. He watched a scowling art fag shuffling in cheap dark clothes with greasy hair and zits on his neck. Gilbert's eyes narrowed as he imagined this kid writing poetry. His teeth grinded as he saw the kid in a coffee shop smoking cigarettes with fucking Nirvana playing or something. Sweat broke out on his forehead as he said into Bethany's ear, —I'd love for you to come. His voice shaking and hands clammy, but all that mattered was that the art fag had half his head shaved and safety pins in his pants and that his . . . hair . . . was . . . *purple!* These facts made Gilbert light-headed and he took his arm off Bethany and didn't say bye as he blew by the art fag with purple hair, shoving him into the rows of lockers and not looking back. The kid rubbed his shoulder and said, —*Fuck* Gilbert. The other hallway stragglers turned to look at Gilbert, who didn't notice, walking briskly toward room 210.

He decided he was no longer the chigger. He was black. He liked being black in Hingham. He liked the look on the face of the guy at the White Hen, keeping an eye on Gilbert as he made his way to the Gatorades and whole grain breads, waiting for Gilbert to pull out a gun and demand the money in the register.

He liked driving Mervin's Lexus and parking Mervin's Lexus in the mall parking lot and bleeping the alarm as he walked away, heads turning.

The kids at Brenton Prep felt it was their duty to be friendly to him, to make him like them. To let him know they did not hate him and weren't racist. He liked this. They felt inferior to him. He could sense it. He'd been places they hadn't, was better than them because black was style, character.

He was fifteen, almost sixteen, and six feet six inches, Darren

Dickinson's height. He was a skinny kid with a little pea head. He slipped through the door of room 210 as the teacher explained *The Canterbury Tales* to her catatonic students. She stopped and looked at him and everybody looked at him, but she kept her mouth shut as he plopped down at a desk in back. She went back to explaining *The Canterbury Tales*. If it were anybody but Gilbert Marcus she would've demanded a note and strongly considered deducting points from his grade.

Brenton Prep was a private high school, attended by the sons of Cambridge attorneys and daughters of Red Sox. The desks were new and shiny and the teachers baggy-faced and cranky from deteriorated idealism regarding children and the future of our species. Everybody wore what they wanted. There was no uniform. The idea was that it was progressive as far as private academies went. Gilbert Marcus nudged the white kid next to him who wasn't an athlete and said, —Hey. Got the homework? He was already a starter on the varsity basketball team, used to seeing his name in the *Globe*, the savior of a team that hadn't won a game in two years but was now contending for the playoffs. The number of applications for admission had increased by 30 percent from the previous year. Kids were coming to Brenton Prep to play basketball who never would have come to Brenton Prep to play basketball. Division I college recruiters had been coming to his games since freshman year. Tickets to Brenton Prep varsity basketball games were hard to come by. Their price had more than doubled. Scalpers had begun setting up shop in the parking lot outside Brenton Prep's $12 million athletic facility, funded in part by a semisenile Pfizer executive donor who did not prefer to remain anonymous.

Of course Bethany would be at the game. Every sweet-scented girl, every high ass and perky tits and sparkly cat eyes would be at the game, watching Gilbert and wanting Gilbert. The whole town would be there, every human in Hingham and even Boston and as far north as Vermont, adjusting their schedules around Gilbert Marcus's basketball games. If Colleen could see him now. Colleen was never pretty. Not really. He had been wrong about her. She was disgustingly ugly. All the girls in this place loved Gilbert more than Colleen did. She didn't love him at all. She didn't see how special he was.

He whispered into their ears and saw their mouths open into

smiles as he breathed into the wispy hairs that strayed on their ponytail necks, lips brushing their jewelry, their boyfriends standing to the
side and scowling but helpless.

The taste of power, of pull, like meat in your mouth. Full of secrets.

Reporters were already asking what his secret was. Balding middle-
aged men in khakis from the *Herald* with flushed skin and booze on
their breath waiting for him outside the $12 million gym after games
and offering their hands. They wanted him to like them. He saw it in
their eyes. They needed his validation. He didn't like them. But he
needed them. He knew he needed them. They tried to make small talk
about cars and shoes and rap, things they assumed a black boy would
like. —Seen the new Nike Flight series?
—Yeah.
—Pretty cool, huh.
—Yeah.

But he'd never tell them his best secret.

He'd take the commuter rail into South Station and take the T into
Dudley Square, walk into Roxbury, and down to Blue Hill Avenue. He'd
walk past the Gourmet Subs shop and the small grocery stores that
looked like they were from a Third World country. Kids with gold
chains and guns in their waists standing on the corners keeping look-
out. Hip-hop coming from somewhere unseen. The sky blue against
former crack houses taken over by the state and boarded up.

He wouldn't tell the reporters (or anybody) about leaving his
brand new $190 Nike Airs in his bedroom and wearing an old pair of
crappy no-name brand shoes he'd found in the locker room at Brenton
Prep and stealing one of Mervin's empty organic wine bottles and
wrapping a brown bag around it and pretending to sip from it on the
way down Dudley Street through the housing projects with twelve-
year-old pregnant girls in tight jeans looking him up and down.

Of this, no one would know. Of him, no one would know.

He had secrets stashed everywhere he went like knives in jail.

He played pickup games with ex-cons and killers. If anybody on
the lumpy blacktop court with broken-chain baskets and chain-link
fences with poorly trained pit bulls tied to them asked him where he
came from, he told them he was from *the jungle. The jungle* sounded

good and rugged, because it meant the projects, the ghetto. He heard this in a movie. During the pickup games Gilbert spoke seldom but loudly. He talked shit when he could remember the lines from the movies. His face scowling and brows furrowed and his wealthy suburban softness dripping down his forehead as he checked it in to big motherfuckers with jail tats and warrants and illegitimate kids. Gilbert felt his softness exposed when these men's elbows would clip his jaw under the basket or someone would stick out a foot and Gilbert would trip over it and skid face-first to the pavement. But he couldn't call foul. He had to play like he expected it. They'd talk more shit as he walked off toward the T, twelve hours after getting off it, but he would not respond—to speak would be to challenge them, and they were stronger than he was. They had suffered. But he could run if he had to. He ran every day. He ran through his neighborhood holding on to the back of his mom's station wagon, sprinting for as long as three-quarters of a mile sometimes. He ran across town and along the shoulder of Route 3 until he tasted vomit and saw colors and then kept running, running. He could run all the way back to Hingham if he had to.

Gilbert skipped his nightly anal laxative to hang out with Sandy on a Friday night. They sat side by side on the couch in the Marcuses' living room. The team was hanging out at Dave's but Gilbert was hanging out at his house with Sandy. Mervin was in his office, heavy beard now trimmed to a goatee and though he'd lost a bit of weight he was still porky. He was now a full-time assistant coach at Boston College and even taught a class. He taught Basketball Theory 101, a real course only members of the basketball team took.

—See this? Gilbert said, rewinding via remote control. Darren Dickinson zipped backward through the air and back in front of a Rambler. —Watch this crossover, he said, hitting play again. —See? See that, Sandy? Look.

Sandy watched, quiet, arms crossed to hide her chest because it was cold and her headlights were showing. She was very aware of her elbow brushing Gilbert's shirt. Though he could feel the parasites consuming the walls of his small intestine, he was trying not to resent her. The living room was clean and the furniture sparse and matching. Sandy was afraid to ask for a drink. Gilbert leaned forward on the couch and went, —Damn. Look at that. He sort of mimicked Darren Dickinson's hands then hit rewind again, then play again. Sandy wondered what Jenn was doing and wanted to go to the movies to see the new Adam Sandler and technically wasn't a virgin, not since eighth grade, but never told anybody. She said, —Yeah. Wow. Gilbert rewound again, played it, rewound, played, and after like the ninetieth time Sandy who wanted to be a lawyer and marry R. Kelly put her hand on Gilbert's arm and turned to him and leaned in to kiss him, and he turned his head away so she put her head on his shoulder but he got up without warning and her head dropped. He went to the entertainment center which was loaded with copies of *Mervin Marcus's Freak of Basketball* and with seemingly hundreds of blank tapes labeled with the date and teams playing and arranged both chronologically and alphabetically. She watched him eject the tape and pop in another and thought about last weekend when she got drunk with Jenn when her parents went out of town, how she wanted a little girl someday, and she said, —Want to go to Store 24? Or the mall or something? But Gilbert grunted something noncommittal and sat back down with the remote and hit play and Sandy decided to never tell him about getting drunk and to never tell him about any of the things she had done because Gilbert was a man of strong moral character, which is what she liked about him, she decided here, and so this time she kept her elbows to herself and watched the screen and said nothing and while she was thinking all this Gilbert was thinking about how he wanted to have sex with Bethany.

Sandy walked him to his locker after third period, since their second period classes were in the same hallway, the top of her head peaking at his elbow, today talking to him about a dance her church was having that she wanted to go to. —It's gonna be fun. But he didn't want to go. He hated dancing. Dancing meant he'd step on her toes and break them and the high school boys would tell him that's no way to treat your girl. But he didn't tell her this. And they kissed and she said, —See you after class? —Yeah, he said. As Sandy left, she passed Bethany walking in the opposite direction. Gilbert watched Sandy's ass as she walked away then watched Bethany's tits as she walked toward him. Felt something savage stirring in him down below as he wondered if that story about Bethany and Chris Cook, a senior center, was true. Gilbert imagined Bethany naked and on all fours for him. Gasping his name as he pulled her hair, their skin smacking together. He stopped her, put his arm around her, and said, —Coming to the game tonight?

It was the last day of another lemonade fast, which Mervin put him on as a way of resting the colon while cleansing the bowels and digestive system. Mervin said, —This lemonade is great for your colon, Animal. You drink this stuff all your impurities will be washed out. I know this Greek fisherman who was still fishing at ninety-eight. He drank this stuff all the time. Never got sick. Not even a cough.

According to Mervin, the colon stored up to eight meals' worth of waste at a time, in order to reabsorb the water in it back into the blood. But when things got backed up, which they inevitably would considering the crap modern culture calls food according to Mervin, the toxins and impurities your body was trying to get rid of started getting reabsorbed too, tainting your blood, making you tired, unfocused, gassy, sick, slow. —All those other guys are running around with poison in their bodies, while you're running on the pure supreme unleaded. Why do you think you still have energy for your acting classes? Speaking of which I'm thinking of having you try out for the play this fall. You're going to need the experience for when it's time to cross over into movies. I'll speak to your acting coach.

It had been two weeks since Gilbert had consumed anything other than lemonade. He was light-headed and cranky. After English class he went to lunch. He flung his food at the art fag with purple hair in the Brenton Prep cafeteria so his teammates wouldn't notice that he wasn't eating. He couldn't tell them about the lemonade. He couldn't tell them about anything. He'd go through the line with them and take one of the trays and joke with them, pretend to get Phil Orkin (of the exterminator Orkins) in a headlock, aware of all the eyes on him as he told the lunch lady spaghetti, maybe get a pretzel too, and then a Coke from the machines, to be seen with.

6

J N THE FLEETING EMBERS OF EVER-
lasting but flaking youth.
  In its trembling cracks.
  —Do you still love me though?
—I don't know, cookie. I don't know if I ever really did.

After practice Gilbert and his varsity teammates made a couple JV
kids they found in the locker room strip naked and stand there naked
while Omar, a guard, shot them with a stun gun (who knows where
he got the stun gun). Gilbert had to physically stop Chris Cook from
performing an act on the incapacitated boys that was so strange it
would have essentially been considered sodomy. Then they went out
for pizza.

Gilbert bumped his head on the top of the door frame as he entered the pizza parlor. And the families of tiny people sat at tables
and glanced up at him as he strutted by, followed by a single file of

seven other boy-men, laughing and talking shit with little consideration for the other patrons of the place as the host led them to their table.

—Dude, I'd bend that girl over there over that table and just fucking *fuck* that shit.

These rooms, these crowded restaurants where your legs don't fit under the table, your hands always knocking something over, they suffocate you, and you long for the vast open space of a hardwood gymnasium, where the ceilings never end and you can holler to the other side and not be heard, and you can run and stand upright without fear of hitting your head on ceiling fans and you can wave your arms and feel small. Thank God for mountains, for miles, and bottomless lakes, for galaxies of stars stretching forever . . .

They ordered pizzas and Gilbert ate the pizza and footed everyone's bill in cash then went home and puked it all up, wishing he had never spent the time and energy going out with his teammates after practice. It was bull what Coach Lalli said, that he as a leader of the team needed to develop a bond with the other players. They were animals, talking about bitches and screwing and other uncivilized blah-blah, video games, this rap group they wanted to start, never a word about basketball, all the while consuming cooked poison in the form of cholesterol and gooey grease. On the ride home he could feel the worms wiggling to life in the walls of his intestine, and he shoved his finger down his throat in his private bathroom adjacent to his bedroom. Then he took his pants off and lay on the cold tile with his legs in the air and inserted a coffee enema.

In a better mood after the coffee enema, he called Sandy over and they sat on the couch watching *Entertainment Tonight*. Sandy sat back with her thin wrists crossed delicately over her tummy. Gilbert sat forward with his elbows on his knees and irritated because she was sitting so damn close to him. Why did she have to be so damn *close* to him all the time? His chin was in one hand, the other hand wielding the remote with the instinct of a samurai. And Sandy thought, I love him so much. Neither spoke because when Sandy would speak Gilbert would either shush her or not answer, so focused was he on studying Will Smith's turns of speech and Michael Jackson's waves to adoring masses.

Sandy decided that this would be the year she got a boyfriend and fell in love with him. It warmed her heart being beside him and supportive, obediently quiet and respectful of her boyfriend's need to concentrate. It made her feel like a wife. No, that was stupid. She wasn't a wife. Just his girlfriend. But they weren't like any of the other couples in school! Their relationship was more serious than those. More mature. This is what being married will be like. This good talented boy! He'll wrap his arms around her and hide her away from the world.

She watched as Gilbert got up and turned off *Entertainment Tonight* and put in a game tape and came back to the couch.

I'll marry him one day, she thought. But it will be after college, because we'll need our space then to study and get good jobs that let us travel together a lot, and after graduation we'll buy a house and go to our jobs and eat out at nice restaurants and if you don't believe that what me and Gilbert got is true and everlasting then I don't care what you think because I owe you nothing.

Jenn was having a party tonight but Gilbert didn't want to go. That was okay with Sandy. Sandy thought of the rest of her life. It would be like this. And that would be great.

Gilbert had to fart so he sat up on the couch and leaned over on the edge of it, clenching to keep the fart in. Fucking pizza. He knew he shouldn't have eaten it. He must've missed some with the enema. Fucking Sandy. He wished she'd fuck off so he could fart in peace. Why did spending time with her always require the sacrifice of his good health? He tried to focus on the film but all he could manage was to appear like he was focusing on the film. He wasn't interested in studying the game tonight. He fast-forwarded through it, all the way to the end, to Darren Dickinson standing over the sideline reporter, towel over his shoulders and sweat dripping from his nose, watching how he leaned down to hear the question then answered with his eyes looking out at things in the distance behind the camera and wiping his face with the towel.

Sandy's silence gnawed at him and made him wonder if he was a good boyfriend. Probably. But was he the *best* though? Can she see my potential? he thought. Does it show in the glint of my eyes, their squinted focus, in my detachment and inversion, that I am blessed and above the masses and smart, good-looking, a total and indomitable package of body and mind? Do I remind her of Tom Hanks?

I don't love her, he thought. She's cute and lets me kiss her and touch her boobs and she has a pussy that she lets me touch sometimes too if I try hard enough and the way her ass sways when she walks, how her hair smells, how her voice gets small when she's tired. But I don't love her.

The way she sort of hits me when I tease her. I like it. But I don't love it.

Should I dump her? Should I break up with her right now?

He thought of the other guys lined up waiting to get a piece of her—he'd seen them ogle her. Soon as he'd break up with her they'd be there, trying to get a piece of Gilbert Marcus's ex-girlfriend. She'd fuck all of them. Or a few of them at least. He got ill as he imagined them sticking their dicks in her.

He thought, No, I don't want them to stick their dicks in her. I won't break up with her. Not tonight.

Gilbert stood by the wall in the Brenton Prep hallway and waited for Sandy and Pete to see him. Sandy waved and smiled and Pete tensed and said bye to her and scattered. Gilbert watched him go, glaring, and took Sandy's soft meaty arm, squeezing until he felt bone, and dragged her, nearly tripping on her own shoes, over to his locker, snarling into her ear, —What are you doing to me?

—Gilbert, stop. Ow.

—Do you want to have sexual intercourse with him?

—*Ow*! Who?

—Pete. You want to have sexual intercourse with him, don't you.

—His name's not Pete.

—I don't give a shit what his name is. What's his name?

Often he'd find himself in Chinatown walking among other Asians who looked tired and overworked, feet dragging and moving along the sidewalk like slugs, tiny people up to Gilbert's waist, like animals, expressionless heaps of flesh grinding their invisible lives to death.

—Answer me.

—*What.*

—I'm onto you, he said. —Okay? Just know that I'm onto you.

—Onto me? What am I? Some sort of criminal?

—Yes. That's exactly what you are.

—They're my *friends,* Gilbert. I have friends who are guys. So what?

—I want to break up with you.

—*What?*

— . . .

—*Why?*

—I don't know. I think we should break up.

—Why though?

—I just, I think it would be best to break up now so that we can remain on positive terms.

—Just because I was walking with Charlie you want to break up with me?

—Don't be ridiculous.

—What did I do?

—It's not like there was something you did. It wasn't *one* thing that you did.

—Then *why,* Gilbert.

— . . .

—When did you make this decision?

—It's something I've been thinking about for quite some time.

—Tell me why. You have to tell me why, Gilbert.

—Sandy. Don't.

—Tell me *why. Talk to me.* You never *talk to me.*

—Don't be absurd. I talk to you.

—No you don't. Tell me why you want to break up with me.

—You really want to know?

—Yes.

—It's going to hurt.

—It already hurts. Tell me.

—You sure you really want to know?

—It's only fair to tell someone why you want to break up with them out of the blue.

—Okay. Fine.

—Tell me.

—You want to know? Fine. You're just not pretty enough for me. Okay? You happy now?

There was silence.

—I can't believe you'd say something like that to me, Gilbert.

—Hey, you said you wanted to know.

Tears were streaming down her face.

—It's how I feel, he said.

He watched her standing there crying because she was not pretty enough for him.

—Look, I take it back, he said. She covered her face. —Sandy? Stop. I didn't mean it, okay? Stop covering your face. I just said it. I don't know why. I was mad.

—I don't *feel* like that though, she said from behind her hands. —I don't *feel* how you said I feel! I don't *want* to do it with anybody! I want *you*! I love *you*!

—I really didn't mean it. Seriously. It's just that I'm tired and—

—We were meant for each other, she said. —I wish you could see that.

—I do, Sandy. I *do* see that. But *Jesus*, you know? What am I supposed to think?

—We'll get married someday, she said. She stopped covering her face and started wiping her face with her fingers.

—Someday? he said. —Yeah. It's very possible. I could certainly foresee something like that down the road.

—We're in love.

—We are. I agree. We are in love.

—So you love me? she said, sniffling.

—Yeah.

—Say it then. You have to say it.

—I love you. I didn't mean what I said. I'm sorry. I take it back.

Sandy threw her arms around his waist and buried her face in his stomach, and he flexed instinctively. She whimpered that she loved him too, into his Darren Dickinson T-shirt that came down to his thighs, and he looked around to see if anyone was watching, which they were.

Sandy never liked possessive boys. She was born the daughter of a lawyer named Earl who specialized in lease agreements—both writing them and getting tenants out of them—and who once slept with four different girls in three weeks in law school. And to a mother named Vivica who was a substitute teacher at the same elementary school she'd gone to. They were the only black family in Medfield, Massachusetts. The only ones in both their families to graduate college. Victoria met Earl when Earl was at BU Law School and Vivica was an undergrad there with an ex-boyfriend who she had to get a restraining order against. And now the family claimed as close friends two DAs, a nobel laureate, Ted Kennedy, Jim Rice, Doug Flutie, a former keyboard player from Parliament-Funkadelic, Diane Chambers, and a one-time Boston Colonial named Mervin Marcus, whose own family, including his wife, Sue, and their little boy who happened to be Sandy's age, was not only enviably close-knit to the point of it being cultlike but also graced Sandy's family's annual Fourth of July picnic at their summer home in Ipswich until they moved off to San Antonio and then Utah. No one heard from them. There were rumors the Marcuses had become Mormons. Soon the Marcuses weren't mentioned in conversation anymore. It was like the Marcuses had died in a tragic accident too gruesome to bring up in polite conversation. And then the Marcuses came back to life. How the boy had grown! He had become a polite and clean-headed young black man with his father's good looks and his mother's grace. He was soft-spoken with the still gaze of deep waters. Tall, handsome. Sleek features and soft brown eyes Asian eyes that made him look like an Eskimo, as Vivica said.

—Watch out, Sue, hon, Vivica said to Sue Marcus, —you're gonna have lots of broken hearts showing up at your door.

And Sandy had grown too into a miniature of her mother, with the same magnetic ability to make people smile (and the same ass too, Mervin observed approvingly), so studious that she was known to cry if she got lower than a B+.

—You'll have quite a few yourself, Sue said.

And then it was summer and both kids had finished their first year of high school. Sandy helped set out the paper plates at the Fourth of July picnic and played with some of the little kids running around as Gilbert stood off by himself, watching the fuzzy baby ducks in the soft ripples of the late afternoon water and sneaking glimpses at Sandy. She looked over and waved, and Gilbert looked away.

Then she was coming over!

Earl opened a Diet Coke and looked on as the two kids took a liking to each other. He watched them walk off toward the water, thinking, Kid better keep it in his pants.

Sandy and Gilbert played together as little kids but then you turn fifteen and go to the same prep school and in forced company you stare at the ground, not knowing what to say to each other, wondering if the other remembers splashing in puddles, catching inchworms and making homes for them in shoeboxes, giving them water and grass. It would be stupid to bring it up though.

Gilbert had a very lonely year in ninth grade, eating lunch on the stairs every day, had no friends, met Sandy.

When Sandy turned twelve it happened that she lost connection with the world. The hormones bubbled and burned inside her brain. Her father stopped loving her and she couldn't talk to her mother. She started throwing up after she ate. She starting hanging out with this boy Robbie who sold drugs and got into fights behind the elementary school. It was said that Robbie had doused a neighbor's cat in gasoline, set it on fire, and threw it off a roof. Robbie ordered pizzas (this was true) to abandoned apartments and robbed the pizza guy when he came. He saw Sandy the first week of seventh grade, in her Keds and pigtails. He sat behind her in social studies and teased her about being smart, asked if he could copy her homework, and she let him, asked her to come to his house after school, and she did.

With Robbie she was safe. His stubbly cheek scratching hers. Even when he jammed his fingers in too hard the first time, she was safe. (He examined her face as he did this, contorting in pain, the tears welling in the corners of her eyes, fascinated at the science of what he was doing to this rich girl.) She was safe even though he made her lick his fingers off afterward and told his friends about it so everyone knew that he had fingered Sandy and that she'd licked his fingers afterward. He technically took her virginity but she panicked and made him stop. He taught her how to smoke weed. She brought him food from her pantry, Cool Ranch Doritos, his favorite. Robbie liked to get this rich girl fucked up, to be seen with this rich pretty girl, liked to see her panic when she realized it was time to go home and she was still high. Because he was forbidden, a monster, and ugly.

She snuck through her front door apocalyptically stoned and she averted her eyes from Mother and Father looking up at her from their dinner plates saying she wasn't hungry even though that was a goddamn *lie.* She went up to her room and tried to kill herself with half a bottle of Tylenol before climbing out her window and disappearing.

Long days and never-ending nights followed, and Vivica didn't sleep through any of them. The Medfield police came and sat around the family room, sipping watery coffee as Earl and Vivica paced vigorously.

—Why is she doing this? Vivica said. —What did you say to her?

—Vivica, said Earl.

—You treat her like an employee, Earl. Now you've driven our baby away.

—That's good. That's just good. See, officers? See what Sandy has to deal with? A control-freak mother? Anyone can see except us that our family is fucked. *Fucked*. No respect. No goddamn *discipline*.

—Like you know *anything* about discipline.

—I *do*. And there isn't any.

—Why aren't you people out there? Vivica said, turning to the cops. The officers looked at one another and shrugged. —Why don't you have dogs? Do you have dogs?

The officers looked at one another and one of them said, —Do we have dogs?

The others shrugged.

Vivica said, —*Get dogs*. Where are the helicopters? The searchlights? The news reports? Why are you *here*? What the hell are you doing drinking my goddamn coffee?

A cop wearing sunglasses, heavy Boston accent, said, —To be honest, miss, it needs sugah.

It was up to a security guard at the mall to finally apprehend the perp, as he referred to Sandy in the report he was required to fill out when he detained her for stealing lipstick at Macy's. Vivica was secretly proud when she arrived with Earl and the guard displayed the evidence—Sandy had chosen a *very* flattering shade of lipstick to steal. By then all anger and confusion was washed out by the sight of their little girl, skinny and dirty and alone in the security office. Earl and Vivica smothered the sad-eyed twelve-year-old with kisses and hugs and led her out, Earl thanking the guard over his shoulder for not calling the police, and the guard, face scarred with the traces of teenage acne, the kind of guy who gets a hunting license, said after them, —If I see her in here again I will.

Back in her frilly room in the enormous house, teen-idol posters, teddy bears, and pictures of Prince torn from teenage magazines, Sandy didn't feel a part of it and looked out her window at the plastic foundation, the pink bed sheets a lie, the house built from molds and

lawns carved from Astroturf, a prison of lawnmowers and homeown-
ers' associations and churchgoing sinners, robots, traffic zombies, and
she called Robbie but he didn't answer and she hugged her teddy bear
and prayed that Luke Perry would appear in her bedroom window and
jet her away on his motorcycle.

—Hey I got acid, Robbie said, appearing behind her as she walked into
school. Three of his minions were with him. Sandy took the product
from Robbie. It was a tiny square of tinfoil. She unwrapped it to reveal
a tinier square of blue construction paper. She put this into her mouth.
—It works best if you keep it on your tongue and let the juices trickle
down your throat, Robbie said. —I know you like to swallow, but don't
swallow this.

His minions snickered accordingly from behind him and Sandy
glared at them and put it on her tongue and was careful not to swallow.

As she sat in algebra, the class one by one and at random turned
to face her and slowly raised their middle finger and mouthed, —
Fuck you . . . then turned back around. The teacher joined in from the
front of the class, holding up all of her fingers and then using her
other hand to mime a gun shooting each finger until only her middle
finger remained, and she pointed this middle finger at Sandy and
mouthed, —*Fuck you*. This kept happening for what seemed like
hours. Sandy was confused, indignant. But she knew it would be catastrophic if she were to speak. Then she got very thirsty. She had to
fight the urge to get up and jog. And then she was out of her desk and
clawing the floor and screaming, —*Very funny! Very funny!* And the
teacher didn't know what to do so she called the principal who called
the police who called an ambulance who took her to a hospital. They
tried to give her heavy doses of multiple bipolar and antipsychotic
and sleep medications that would have turned her into Gumby but
she managed to mutter in just the nick of time, —I . . . I'm not psychotic —I . . . I'm on acid.

When she came down she was tired and defeated and hooked up to
a feeding tube because she was eleven pounds underweight and finally
told Earl and Vivica who gave the acid to her. She said he made her eat
it or he'd chop her hands off with a machete. Earl called the police and
pressed assault charges on Robbie and Robbie got sent to a detention
home.

In the hospital room Sandy and her parents cried and hugged each other, Sandy kept going, —I'm sorry, I'm sorry.

I want love, a boy, a boyfriend who sweats and makes me laugh and loves me, a man to call a husband, to look over at a man and think to myself, That's my husband, the sweet fragrance of a boy who picks me up at home and talks to my dad about sports and helps my parents with the dishes, who says my name as he drives with both hands on the wheel, a quiet boy with good teeth who is well-dressed and not possessive and never thinks about any other girl but me, and we study together in my room late at night to make sure we get into a good college and we act grown up and look good waiting to be seated and he wears a tie and we walk arm in arm to the car, and the sick dark girl I was dies from neglect because I never visit or give her air to breathe. She is forgotten and I live and we fall in love and marry and the *future*! and I choose *love*!

Sandy's mom and dad on the Fourth of July in Ipswich after Sandy's freshman year in high school watching her go off with the Marcus boy who had grown up so handsome, the pedigree of Sue and Mervin, a strong family who knew the importance of leaning on one another, and Vivica cried at the sight, sobbing through her hands, —Our baby's back.

Sandy went to Gilbert's games with Mervin and Sue (and the rest of the state, she thought) and felt a buzz in her knees as she sat beside them, the crowd increasing with every game, lines snaking down the street for tickets. Her in-laws. She enjoyed being the wife. She cheered louder than anyone, and hoped the people around her noticed her devotion. She hoped they envied her for being the one Gilbert Marcus loved. As she fellated the boy she loved afterward in his bedroom Sandy's heart pounded as she again felt the thick jab in the back of her mouth and choked, but Gilbert didn't hear her gag and she pushed the memories away, washing the wet goo from her tongue, of being stoned and naked and, no, fighting it, holding her breath and closing her eyes and praying, I love *him* . . .

The chastity of her, the smallness of her girl-shoulders and girl-waist and her big doe girl-eyes and the way she could raise one eyebrow and how she would bite her lip when she was thinking, an untouched being that he handled like a china doll with his hand on the small of her back heading into the movie theater, and he liked that about her, that she might break, and that it was she who was drawn to him, she saw something in him that no one else saw and she couldn't quite place it, but, he thinks, she couldn't resist it. I made her into a woman, he thinks, and she's smart enough to be grateful for it, though she whispers no when I try to stick it in, which is good because that means she's not a whore and belongs to me. Even though she probably won't get into Harvard and she wouldn't fit in at a country club, and although her belly rolls a little when she's naked and her left tit sags a little lower than her right and her legs could be longer and sometimes when she speaks it drives me nuts and I find myself wondering why she's with me at all because I'm so cold and she's so warm.

In the backyard where it was hot and where bugs whose buzz was bigger than their bodies hovered over blades of grass, she stood ankle-deep in an inflatable kiddie pool, one hand holding her skirt up around her waist and the other holding a Coke. Her tiny feet bloated and discolored by the water. —You're gonna see my panties, she said as she squatted into the water with bits of grass and dirt floating on top. Her panties were pink with purple polka dots. She squealed even though Gilbert dumped a couple pots of boiling water in to warm it up. He watched the neighbor's head scan back and forth along the top of the fence as he mowed his lawn, Bethany's neighbor, because this was Bethany's backyard, and this was Bethany, on a Sunday, when her parents were out of town. Gilbert stared as Bethany knelt down into the water letting the water take her skirt and spread it big, big, big, like she was melting, and when the water touched her pink polka-dot panties her eyes popped and her mouth dropped open and her nipples became erect beneath her tank top she wore without a bra. —You're gonna see my panties, she said again, before she sat down and pinched her nose and leaned slowly back until she was submerged like she'd been buried at sea and Gilbert said, —I'll see them anyway.

7

BETHANY EYED SANDY, WHO SHE
knew she was prettier than, as she led her
father—John McNeal, head coach of the
Boston Colonials—into the Brenton Prep
gym, saying to him, —You *have* to see him play, Daddy. He's *so*
good. He's *amazing*.

Mervin Marcus's kid. He vaguely remembered Mervin Marcus.
Made videos now or something, he'd heard. Mervin Marcus's kid was
probably putting it to his daughter for all John McNeal knew. Of
course she thought he was the greatest thing ever. Brenton Prep had
never had much of a basketball program (was that one reason he in-
sisted Bethany enroll here—to keep her away from the type of man
he knew so well?). So how good could this kid—a fucking
sophomore—really be? There were never any good ones all the way
out here. A school like Brenton Prep was too rich. These kids were all
too soft and spoiled to really be hungry and suffer for it. They half-
assed it on defense, thought they were Darren Dickinson, cried when
they didn't get calls, panicked when their shots were off, played video

games, and chased pussy (like my daughter's, John McNeal conceded) instead of practicing. In their opinion, they already had one foot in the Hall of Fame and didn't need to get better. He had no use for any of them. He was a professional. He was interested in professionals.

But, shit, it was about time he spent some QT with Bethany. He was always on the road or in the office or doing interviews. Doing his weekly radio show. Flying off to look at draft prospects—twenty-four-hour-a-day job, coaching is, seven days a week. Three-quarters of that spent on airplanes. No weekends or really time for much else in your life. Slip up just a bit, you're out the door. And who knows how this has affected Bethany, he thought. What choices she's made because of him never being around. Doing who know what with who knew who, in search of her lost daddy. Her mother didn't exactly keep her in line, that was for sure.

John McNeal thought, I wonder exactly how many guys she's— no, good God, knock it off.

—That's him right there, his baby girl Bethany exclaimed as the teams came out for warm-ups. —That one, with the . . .

—Yeah, I know, buttercup, John McNeal said. Such a sweet little girl. Nothing like her mother. And John McNeal stared at Mervin Marcus's kid and instantly remembered Mervin Marcus and said again, —I know which one it is.

Was there any doubt? The way the kid became the only one, even in warm-ups. He turned the other kids into scenery. He watched him shoot a couple jumpers and stood up and said, —Okay. Come on. Let's go.

—But you didn't see him play yet.

—Don't need to, my little tulip. I've seen enough.

—But.

—Tell him next time you see him that I want to meet him. Maybe we'll have him work out with the team this summer. What'd you say his name was?

—Gilbert, Bethany said.

—Gilbert Marcus. Tell Gilbert Marcus to give me a call. Come on, let's go get some ice cream or something.

The picture, the wall. Gilbert found the picture of Darren Dickinson in *Sports Illustrated* and lovingly sliced it out, careful not to tear it. Darren Dickinson in a gray Italian suit amid a crowd, which he didn't seem to be aware of, sunglasses on his forehead, quiet wife looking on, serene, beside him. Dickinson, the god, with his championships and MVPs and merchandising empire. *The Basketball Player. The Athlete.* The master of psychology. Cool no matter how many millions were watching or what was on the line. A Buddhist wizard, blessed with clarity and short memory. He framed it and hung it on the wall, knelt before it. Basketball, Darren Dickinson's picture said to him, is as much a battle of respect as a battle of physical ability. Talent means nothing without respect.

What lurked beneath the suit? What happened when he put the shades in the locker and slipped out of the cotton shirt, exposing muscles twitching with anticipation?

Gilbert went into his walk-in closet and came out with the costume he wore to Blue Hill Avenue. He told his father he was going to Sandy's and drove Sue's station wagon into the city, parked in a parking garage at Kenmore Square, lucky that there wasn't a Sox game.

The quiet high school sophomore got off the T at Haymarket and walked into the Adelphia Center, where the Colonials were holding summer workouts. The doors to the gym were locked by a two-inch chain and five-pound lock wrapping the outside handles, and the key was in the enormous pocket of a massive piece of meat dubbed Baby. Baby let Gilbert in after talking to somebody on his walkie-talkie.

As Gilbert entered the doors slammed shut and he heard the lock clink behind him. He entered a world of sweat and torture, like a CIA training compound, the echoing thud of basketballs and shrieks of exerted men, dark bodies greased up and shoes squeaking, every inch of the court occupied. The men were all but naked, shorts low and baggy, toned muscles bursting beneath wet flesh, the air damp and hot and smelly, lights set to a bare dim to sustain undercover. Big, big, *big* fucking guys. He saw Thadeus Marshall, the rookie from Kansas, who they said would be the next Darren Dickinson, pulling up over Clarence West. Thadeus Marshall even looked sort of like Dickinson, and Gilbert looked kind of like Thadeus Marshall, they looked sort of like each other—the wristband, the bald head. That you look like somebody else, who is where you want to be. Thadeus was oblivious to Gilbert, as were the other members of the squad, spread out on every basket and focused on their three-on-three games, dumping water on their heads, panting with hands on knees, stretching, getting taped up, barfing into trash cans. Men whose job it was to rub players' knees rubbed players' knees.

John McNeal, in the middle of it all, a dark hemisphere of sweat staining his white tucked-in polo shirt, glanced up, sensing the foreign invasion into his practice. He used his finger to draw Gilbert over to him.

Gilbert jogged through the tangle to half-court, held out his hand to the coach, saying, —Hello, sir, I'm Gilbert Mar . . .

—I'm thirsty, John McNeal said, handing him a squashed paper cup. —Get me some water.

Gilbert's breath was short as he made his way back across the court to the water fountain, which was located by the door he came in through, exploding black eating away at the corners of his vision, the degradation, the contempt. Who does he think he is? Hasn't won shit in his life. Telling *me*, Gilbert Marcus, who starts on varsity as a sophomore, to fetch water? Pot-bellied old man. What were they last year anyway? Like 2–80? Lucky if he still has the job when the season rolls around.

No, no. Got to keep it together. Get perspective.

Gilbert Marcus versus Thadeus Marshall. One-on-one.

John McNeal watched with his whistle in his mouth and athletic shorts hiked up to his belly button, sweat rivers down his wrinkled forehead, as Gilbert checked the ball in, crouched with it in attack mode, Thadeus Marshall bent and swatting and balanced, ready to react, crossed through his legs once, started hard right but Thadeus met him there and cut off the lane, so he slowed and worked his way backward against him, steadily back toward the hole, keeping his body between the ball and the defender, in rhythm, like music, gave a shot fake that got Thadeus in the air and Gilbert laid in an easy hook. McNeal watched the kid drive hard then pull up and fall away. He watched him knock the ball from Thadeus's hands. Watched him spin, throw it up recklessly without looking, but it always found a way in. Thadeus Marshall worked him back toward the hole, sticking his butt into Gilbert's crotch, perfectly acceptable for some reason in the context of defense. He dribbled in slow rhythm trying to lull Gilbert asleep. But Gilbert held his position, a forearm hovering over the lower back, the other hand sort of floating motionless relaxed but ready, not fouling. Then in the fastest movement Gilbert had ever seen, Thadeus swung his elbows and the right one caught Gilbert's skull so suddenly that his knees went weak and his teeth went cold and sounds snapped off. His vision somersaulted. Thadeus scored. No foul called. The next play, Thadeus lost his footing allowing Gilbert to slip by undefended, and he dunked it as hard as he could, his mouth open and screaming as he hung from the rim, raising his knees, which he'd learned on Blue Hill Avenue.

—Game, right? Gilbert said as he landed with a thud, in the silence. Thadeus climbed to his feet and said, —Bullshit.

The team stood along the sidelines watching Gilbert look bewildered after Marshall stormed off to the showers, nobody answering when Gilbert said, —Right?

—Real game you'd get the snot knocked out of you going into the lane like that, Coach McNeal said.

—Yeah. I—

—Thanks for coming in.

—That's it?

—What's it.

—I thought. I don't know. That I'd play some more? Run with the team a little? Maybe some five-on-five?

—I got a practice to run, son. McNeal turned and blew his whistle and the players stirred and split off to resume where they left off, and Gilbert closed his eyes and almost fell over, touched his lips for blood, wasn't any, slowly trudged to the door and knocked weakly, gasping for air, listened to the chains being worked, and left. Coach watched the boy go. Turned to his assistant and raised his eyebrows as if to say, How 'bout that?

—Best high school player I've seen in my life, he said.

—He's soft, the assistant said, —watches too much TV. Thinks he's Darren Dickinson.

—He's *fifteen years old*, Del, John McNeal said.

—Doesn't mean he knows the game just because he can dunk and act like a highlight reel.

—Well. That kid's something. He's Mervin Marcus's kid, you know.

—Who?

—You remember Mervin Marcus.

The red-haired assistant shook his head. He didn't remember Mervin Marcus.

John McNeal said, —Well, I want that kid in here every week.

* * *

Gilbert didn't remember that conversation. He didn't remember the elbow, and he didn't remember blowing by Marshall to tomahawk-slam, winning, or gathering his things and leaving. All he could tell you was that Baby was still outside the gym and that he was singing to himself but stopped and muttered to Gilbert, holding his head, —Trainer's down the hall. On your right.

Gilbert looked at him and walked out in a coat of gel, a mask of ooze, the windy North End with its narrow roads and bird-stained statues of saints, Italian women in scarves and pastry shops, his shirt stretched and hanging loose off his skinny frame, thoughts bottle-necked in the clamped neurons of his brain and so intense and chaotic, stood there on the sidewalk watching them tear their way along through the Big Dig and the pigeons, flying rats and so much to look at, and, light-headed and bones melted in his skin into radium to turn against him and lungs filled with excrement and impurities, he stag-gered for refuge toward the shaded alley among crushed aluminum cans and fast-food containers with gobs of ketchup and mustard at-tracting flies, and thought as he collapsed against the brick wall and closed his eyes to steady the world, The alley is the indicator of soci-ety. Slid down the brick surface tearing his back a bit until his wet butt was on solid concrete, and he was grateful for it. He put his forehead against his knees and spit blood between his feet, throat scorched and eyes leaping against his lids from their sockets, puke rising, and tried to catch his breath, but it was too late, and he slipped into uncon-sciousness.

Passersby glanced down and saw a poorly dressed unconscious man in an alley.

He came to with dusk settling in, made his way to the T, and rode to Kenmore Square facing his reflection in the windows.

Because why bother if not to be the best?

He liked to ride in to Roxbury wearing his costume, brown-wrapped bottle dangling from his hand, but empty, his disguise—certainly not the clothes of a boy who drives his father's Lexus—to the playground where they pushed, shoved, ignored fouls, but Gilbert learned quickly that psychology existed as a war tactic, and soon he was grabbing ball sacks too on defense, but mind the fine line, and beating his chest and screaming. Threw their elbows like clubs down there, knocking his teeth loose, blood drying on his lips. Beasts. They'd gang up and chase you out if you didn't get back up. You've got to get up and play. Dunk it on them, make them pay, it's a ball game, throw elbows of your own, if you foul hard, put them on their face, make them earn the point. He liked to remember Mervin swinging his fat elbows and fouling the snot out of him and knocking twelve-year-old, thirteen-year-old Gilbert on his ass. And so when Thadeus Marshall's college-educated midwestern elbow caught him in the gooey sweet spot of his skull, Gilbert's body kept playing, gritted into the man's ear, —You're in Boston now. This ain't college no more . . .

He didn't let the pain have life until he had won. He allowed it life only when there was no more basketball to play and there was no one around to see him bleed.

8

HIS TENDER FEET RUBBED AGAINST each other as he slept, sheet wrapping his almost naked frame, calf muscles cramping around the bone, his battered body strangling itself in protest.

The things that happened in there.

The dank thud of sweaty socks hitting fungusy floors. Enormous feet imprinted with sock ribs stretching in exposure. Fuzzy things between the toes. The chuckles, the cackles, the wide teeth and red tongues and mischievous eyes, the jingle of expensive watches buckling on swollen wrists . . . Loud black voices whose timbres shook the back of your throat and laughs that made you wonder if they were laughing at you. Gilbert laughed too, especially at the story about the girl in the pink-striped skirt and the bar of soap in Atlanta. He could see her as Brian Morris, a white guy, a Mennonite who had to defer his drafting a year while he did mandatory work around the farm, told the story. Gilbert saw the thighs, the light hair on the bronze shoulders, the freckles on the cheeks, the green eyes, pink lipstick. Hoping they noticed him laughing with them because that would have meant he understood them and then he would have been liked.

Gilbert ran five-on-five in the Adelphia Center, playing guard in summer workouts with the Boston Colonials, holding his own. Afterward he showered with his bathing suit on. He didn't want them to see his horny. He dressed quickly in a bathroom stall, hearing them talk about him:

—Didn't know we traded for Dickinson's little brother.

—Hey, take it easy.

—We can all take the season off if we play with this kid. Won't need us.

—He can win it all by himself apparently.

Afterward he tried sitting with them around the locker room, laughing with them, to show he wasn't so bad. Respect is important, he thought.

—Ain't you got school? Maybe when you grow pubes you won't have to wear those trunks.

—Ain't you got homework?

—You still a virgin, junior? You ever fuck before? We'll take you out and get you some pussy sometime.

—Yeah, his voice will drop two octaves, ha ha.

Then he knew showering with a bathing suit on and changing in the stall wouldn't cut it, but he remembered what happened when he tried changing out in the open with everyone else, the shame. Never again would he let anyone close enough.

They came from the cities and the suburbs, large houses and castles, wives with pretty hair founding charity organizations. They were young men, but old in their world.

Wise Coach McNeal appeared in the doorway of the locker room one day, a toothpick hanging from the corner of his mouth, as they toweled off and sat bare-assed on the benches rubbing deodorant and cologne onto their skin and ice packs strapped to their limbs, the scent of Icy Hot, patting baby powder into their crevices, eating double porterhouse steaks and black spaghetti prepared by the team chef, the trainers shooting painkillers into them. All talk ceased. The hip-hop cut off as Coach John McNeal strolled to the middle of the room and shouted, —Basketball is a game of humiliation!

They eyed the mixed-race boy showering under one of the spouts, in his bathing suit, pretending not to hear. Alone but listening, they knew, like the rest of them. You had to hear McNeal. He was one of those men whose talent is their gift of not being ignored. He was not impressed with you; he was fine-tuned in the art of an unreadable face. Which was the problem with the boy because he had the same sort of thing, only he was one of them and so they resented him having an unreadable face. The problem was in how they all felt their uniqueness sucked up by the boy's, leaving them to wonder just what purpose they served at all.

—Missed shots, McNeal said, —stupid passes. Brain farts. Tripping over your own feet. Falling on your butt after slipping on sweat. Losing your cool in front of millions. Your face all twisted up like you're crying. And everyone sees you. No helmets or hats or shades or dugouts. Just you out there, under the lights. And when you screw up everyone knows it. And they know how much money you make and how much they paid for their ticket. There's no way around it. So who's the best? The one who humiliates himself and gets back up the fastest. He who suffers humiliation without getting humiliated.

What he was doing wasn't playing basketball but losing himself completely, a raw attack on the hoop. This was street shit. That was the big complaint. He didn't play the game the right way. He didn't play his opponents. His teammates might as well not be there. It was unsettling the way the game fizzled in his hands. He had the power to upend all their hard work, to devalue their lives. And even in the bathroom stall it was known but unspoken, his being in there, listening to them with his air of superiority, never offering a word of small talk during downtime. Rashawn Adams tried. Rashawn Adams asked him about colleges, who was recruiting, how his golf game was, knowing he had a hell of a drive that was nearly as accurate as his jumper, but the kid just looked through him with his unreadable face.

It's like when he's not playing he just shuts down.

—So, uh, what are you, by the way? Like Hawaiian or Mexican or some shit?

—I don't know. I'm black. Like you.

—How'd a black dude convince a Chinese girl to fuck him? GHB?

—No.

—Because I know a black girl would never in her right mind fuck a Chinese dude. No way. She wouldn't feel shit after getting fucked by something like this all her life.

— . . .

—Thing about GHB is make sure you flip them over on their belly with their face hanging over the edge of the bed. Otherwise they might choke on their own barf.

—Yeah.

—All's I'm saying is it's unusual. That's all. I'm just curious is all. It's unusual. You have to admit it's unusual.

—I don't know. Yeah.

—Seriously though. Was she a whore or something? Your mom? Not to be offensive, but was she a stripper or something?

He felt so guilty after scoring twenty-three points in a full-speed scrimmage the next day that he showered without his bathing suit and let everyone see his horny.

He changed, smiling at Thadeus Marshall describing what a particular semifamous actress's vagina smelled like. He was glad he'd gotten over his fear of being naked around them. But then Derrick Bannon, a center with a face like a chewed-up chunk of meat and an odd bald spot on the side of his thick hair looked up in the middle of his story of what he did to the rectums of two T.G.I. Friday's hostesses who weren't much older than Gilbert last month in Las Vegas with his mammoth hands to shout to Gilbert who was across the room pulling up his boxer-briefs, —Cold in here, huh, Wong?

They all laughed as their dignity returned. They had demolished the kid with the unreadable face. They had given the kid who had scored twenty-three points in a scrimmage what he deserved. Gilbert glanced down at his horny poking out sadly and from then on was sure to pack his bathing suit into his Nike gym bag on the way to Adelphia Center.

Sue got a call from a young man from New York who said David Letterman himself was personally in the next room asking—nay, *demanding*—that her son Gilbert come on the show sometime soon and talk about what it's like to be a basketball prodigy.

—A prodigy? she said.

—Sure. Well, the deal is, the young man said, —we had a savant on last week. A real actual savant. A seven-year-old kid, with acne, great big glasses. His thing was he could do math. Any kind of crazy mathematic equation you could come up with and ask him, he could do it in his head and give you the answer in about ten seconds at the most. Just like *Rain Man*. I can't tell you how many hours of entertainment we got out of him after the show. Dave loves that kind of stuff. This kid was seven. Seven years old. What were you doing when you were seven?

Sue said, —I'll have to talk to my husband. But Gilbert's not a freak.

—No no no.

—He's just a young man who knows what he wants to do and happens to be extraordinary at it. Due to hard work.

Gilbert got elbowed in the skull and never told anyone about it. And he told no one about Derrick Bannon grabbing his scrotum down low when he was fighting for position for a rebound. A quick squeeze and twist that made his vision double. The bloody underwear in the locker room afterward, his testicle the size of a golf ball.

He didn't tell anyone about the finger that scooped his eye as he drove in for a layup.

As much as they resented him, Gilbert resented them back: he thought they were mediocre and comfortable in their mediocrity. They talked about anything besides basketball in the locker room. They didn't carry themselves with dignity like Darren Dickinson did. They lacked composure and focus. They were born with talent but had stopped making that talent grow. They'd given up. They did not want to be the best. They'd been told there already was a best and they couldn't chase it. And they believed it. Which disgusted Gilbert. Gilbert woke up at four AM before going to the Adelphia Center every day that summer to dribble a tennis ball for a mile through the neighborhood while running. After Thadeus Marshall's elbow somersaulted his vision, he drove home and ran five miles. Gilbert couldn't imagine eating double porterhouse steaks and black spaghetti. He couldn't imagine not being the greatest. *I wouldn't be able to live with myself.*

What he did like was listening to them talk about the girls. He learned so much. The kinds of things you could do with girls. How the bodyguard stood outside all the hotel rooms stopping the girls the players brought back to check their IDs and to tell them that this was a one-time thing, just sex, nothing more will result from it. He won't date you, you won't be his girlfriend, he'll probably forget your name by the morning. You won't see a dime. Go in if you understand. If not, go home.

The money they paid girls to forget.

Greasing the remote control up with free lotion from the little bottle in the bathroom and getting her up on all fours on the tight-sheeted bed and shoving the remote control in until it disappeared and then changing the channel on the TV. (Rashawn Adams)

Fucking three different ones in the same night. (Thadeus Marshall—at Kentucky)

The pretty girl with fake tits looking up with a streak of throat yogurt going from ear to mouth and laughing, —Someone should take a picture! (Jason Thomas)

What *throat yogurt* is. (Brad Reyes)

Snorting coke off pierced belly buttons and shooting human growth hormone into their thighs. (Thadeus Marshall, Derrick Bannon)

A white girl who you should have seen her face when she pulled it out of my pants. (Brad Reyes)

Then afterward how if it was necessary they would call the body-guard in with the code word *salsa* and the bodyguard would lead her out naked and make her dress in the hallway where anybody could see and call her a cab and the bodyguard repeating what he told her before or giving her a check sometimes if she seemed like the type that would need a check.

The next morning going to do a spot for United Way, an interview with the Saturday morning kids' show, a meet and greet with sponsors at the stadium, a telephone conference with their financial advisers and portfolio managers, phone calls with business partners regarding the juice-bar franchise they're opening in West Virginia, making an appearance at the children's hospital to give hats to crippled kids, then catching a plane to Las Vegas with a couple other Colonials to drop a couple hundred grand on a fight and to gangbang a stripper in the limo-bus, leaving the used condoms on the floor of the limo-bus and tipping the driver three hundred dollars.

The boy sat alone, at the end of the row of lockers, alone, all showered up, alone, though the grime of the unsanitized bathing facilities leaves you with the inescapable sense of a layer of filth between you and the water, alone, a hand on a knee, alone, not sure when the proper time to get up and make an exit was.

He sat alone, alone, listening to all this, his eyes huge, alone.

How do you leave a room? How do you say good-bye to them without feeling like you've wronged them somehow?

Alone, laughing when they laugh, hoping to be noticed and accepted but no one ever seemed to notice or accept him. He laughed harder than them, and Brad Reyes and Jason Thomas glanced at him with funny smirks.

I'm young but old for my age, he thought. Can't you see it in the way I listen? How I only laugh at the funny things? I don't ask stupid questions, or any questions at all even, like, What's that mean? *Who* was that? *What* are you talking about? Except for the one about *throat yogurt.* But how could anyone be expected to know what *that* means?

I'm one of you. I see little bursts of light in your faces. But none of you know it. I'm not a little kid. I'm not soft. I know pain. I want to be one of you. I can be one of you.

Let me be one of you.

Mervin never told him about *this.* Well, that sort of thing licks your wick when you're fifteen, sixteen—discovering how naïve you are and that it could *happen* that two beautiful girls you have never met before (who weren't Sandy, who weren't Coach John McNeal's daughter) would be interested in having sexual intercourse with you and would perhaps be enthusiastic about you putting your *throat yogurt* onto their faces.

And these guys weren't even Gilbert Marcus.

Imagine that.

He did. He imagined it every night that summer, sometimes two or three times a night, lying in bed with his horny in his hand, imagining vigorously and loyally, vague naked female bodies, faceless tits and ass, legs, hair, smoothly tanned bodies crawling over one another for him, in the midst of girl pretzels, envisioning the guys' stories as he imagined and imagined and imagined . . .

He imagined into a tissue held in his free hand.

He folded the tissue twice, wrapped it in another one, then stuffed the little package into a ziploc bag which he pressed to get all the air out and zipped shut, slipped out the front door without a sound with a gardening shovel from the garage and squatted down in the darkness behind a small shrub and buried the bag in the mulch of the landscaping Sue and Mervin spent weekends carving out, went inside and scrubbed his hands and groin and thighs with Dawn antibacterial on a fresh puff of steel wool, two times to be sure, pat-dried, ate a B_{13} and a new multivitamin he thought he'd try, downed with a peanut-based protein shake, did fifty sit-ups and fifty push-ups, went to sleep, and woke up four hours later.

It dawned on him with the rush of religious conversion that the reason he couldn't connect with the Colonials, a fairly lukewarm team the previous season in what they called rebuilding mode, though no one involved with the franchise wanted to admit it—a faulty product you're paying for and everyone knows it, but still you hold out hope—the reason he had such a difficult time getting along with the Colonials was because he was simply on a different level, or at least would be with time. I'm not ready to rest on my laurels and accept my place as a cog in the machine, he thought. If they won't accept me then that means something. Gilbert had no obligations to anyone. He was free. They weren't free. They didn't accept him because he didn't belong. But being accepted is being bogged down. Belonging is giving up on your destiny. Categorized and shelved and forgotten, your potential curbed, your soul compromised. Any of these guys could have been one of the greats. Not like Dickinson was made of anything they weren't. Magic wasn't from another planet. Bird sneezed and coughed and had moments of doubt too. Anyone could have had it. They just couldn't handle being so alone.

9

OMAR RAN UP TO GILBERT IN THE Brenton Prep locker room, both naked, Omar's eyes ablaze with decision. It was the look of someone who never follows through on an idea. Omar was a six-foot-tall 170-pound waif who couldn't execute a 3-1 fast-break opportunity if his manhood was on the line. He ran up to Gilbert as Gilbert applied a green stick of deodorant to his underarms after a particularly grueling practice and said, loud enough for everyone to hear, —Yo, Gilbert-san! Rehearsal today, yo. Be there. Know what I'm saying?

—Rehearsal?

—You know, for our rap group? Know what I'm saying? Remember we were talking about forming a rap group?

—Gilbert-san?

—Yeah. That's your name. Know what I'm saying? I thought of it when I was sleeping in geography. Know what I'm saying? It's your *persona*. Know what I'm saying? You're like a kung fu wizard of the East. You play mind tricks. Know what I'm saying?

—Persona?

—You *got* to have a *persona*. And knock it off.

—Why can't I be Gilbert Marcus?

—Who wants to buy an album by someone named Gilbert Marcus? Who wants to crank the new *Gilbert Marcus* joint in their six-four? That's why. Know what I'm saying?

—I assume you know that you're in dire need of a haircut, Omar?

—Yeah, Omar said, —I'm growing it out. Know what I'm saying? I decided I'm going to be the crazy one. The color guy. Know what I'm saying? Like Flavor Flav.

—Who?

—I need crazy hair. See, the dynamic I figure is you'll be the laid-back Snoop Dogg type and I'll be the fucked-up zany type. Know what I'm saying?

—Whatever, Omar.

—See? That's perfect. And get this: *you'll rap in Chinese!* No one raps in Chinese. That'll be your thing! Know what I'm saying? The guy who raps in Chinese.

—I thought my thing would be basketball. And I'm not Chinese.

—It'll totally fuck everyone up! Know what I'm saying?

They had talked vaguely about forming a rap group six months ago, and since then Omar had been going around telling people about his and Gilbert's rap group and making points to discuss the rap group whenever possible, like at lunch, especially when girls were sitting nearby.

—What are you guys talking about? the girls would go.

—Oh, Omar would say, —just our rap group.

—Uh-huh.

The idea took kindly to Gilbert-san. He saw the concept floating before him, the pro basketball player/famous rapper . . . No, no, the GREAT basketball player who is also the BEST rapper, getting props from Run DMC and Dr. Dre et al., invited to be on their albums and in their videos. He'd rap on the court. That'd be what differentiated him. His court-rapping. Like Dickinson had the tongue, Gilbert would have the rhymes. All the kids would copy him. A great marketing angle too by the way—he'd *rap* in his *commercials*! He had a vision. He saw himself in The Association. After every game a microphone would lower from the rafters and the lights would dim as the defeated opponents trudged off the courts, a stage rising at center court, thumpity-thump music coming up, and the crowd rushing the court as Gilbert mounts the stage and grabs the mike and they scream as he begins to rap . . .

The Booyashaka Clan was something that popped into Omar's head one day as he dozed in math. The group consisted of Gilbert, Omar, and someone Omar knew named Willy P. Willy P. went to public school. Gilbert and Omar were members of what would be the best basketball team in the state of Massachusetts at the high school level. Gilbert was widely regarded as one of the best high school basketball players in the nation and was being recruited heavily by Duke and Kansas and pretty much everyone else—slipped clothes and cash and CDs by boosters and scouts. Omar was widely regarded as the best hip-hop producer at Brenton Prep Academy. Willy P. was widely regarded as the best Mario Kart player in Newton.

The first Booyashaka Clan rehearsal took place that day in Omar's parents' finished basement in Newton that had a new rug, a matching set of black leather couches and love seats and easy chairs set up in front of an entertainment center and a tremendous TV, a fully stocked bar, a popcorn machine that they didn't use—the utility size like in movie theaters—and a pool table.

Omar answered the door wearing a San Jose Sharks Starter hat flipped inside out and turned sideways, a tremendous Mercedes medallion around his neck, an XXXL Atlanta Falcons jersey, and a pair of brand-new jeans hanging off his ass. He raised one hand for Gilbert to slap, standing on the other side of the finished oak door on the porch among potted plants and a wind chime.

—Gilbert-san in the house! Booyashaka Clan represent! Omar said. —What up, son?

—Chilling, Gilbert said awkwardly.

—Yo, I got my mom's camera. We can take some pictures of Booyashaka Clan. You know, for promotion. Soon as my boy Willy P. gets here, we'll get started. Know what I'm saying? Have you met Willy P.? He's a musical *genius*, yo. He's a *lyricist*, yo. Know what I'm saying?

Gilbert lay on the black leather couch legs crossed trying to find a name for the color of the ceiling which was not quite white, but can white ever be totally white?, MTV on, Willy P. and Omar playing pool, Willy P. saying, —I know a guy in Philly who has a record label.

Willy P. might or might not have been stoned, Gilbert observed with disapproval. Omar said, —Philly? *Fuck* Philly. Know what I'm saying? We're from *Boston*. The 617. Or the 781, depending on what part of Boston. The point is, *fuck* Philly.

Earlier Omar's mom came downstairs, a heavily Jewish woman with the new confidence of recent weight loss who always seemed sort of drunk because she liked to tease Omar's friends about girls and talk a lot and dressed like the girls their age, dyed blond hair. Gilbert thought about fucking her as she shot some pictures with a disposable camera of the great Booyashaka Clan standing together before the pool table. Omar stood up front, in the middle, with eyes wide and hands held out with fingers twisted in a weird shape.

—It's a gang symbol, he explained.

Gilbert thought, These guys are holding me back. I'm the real artist, I'm the one with vision, these guys owe all their success to me. I'm the poet, notebooks filled with it, born with it, I come from an artistic background.

—You need to work on your name, Willy, Omar was saying. — Know what I'm saying? Something more kung fu–sounding.

—Fuck that. I'm Willy P. It's a good name.

—It's not *kung fu*–sounding though. We're Booyashaka Clan. Know what I'm saying? How does Willy P. fit into the aesthetic of Booyashaka Clan, goddamnit?

—I'll kung fu your ass. Gilbert will karate-kick your ass. Won't you karate-kick his ass, Gilbert?

—The point, you *asshole,* is that we have a theme here, Willy. Know what I'm saying? The theme, the dynamic we agreed on, is *kung fu*. Lyrical assassins. Ninjas of the decks. Know what I'm saying? Kung fu.

—You're name's not kung fu. *Omar.*

—Don't call me that. Don't you ever call me that. It's Chow-Chow. I told you that. Call me Chow-Chow during rehearsal.

—That's a gay-ass name. And we ain't rehearsing shit. This shit's corny.

Bone, Gilbert thought. Sedona beige. Ivory.

—Corny? Omar said. —Why don't you quit then if it's so corny?

—No.

—And Chow-Chow isn't a gay-ass name, by the way. Do you even know what a chow is? It's like the most ferocious dog in the *world*. It's *Chinese.* Okay? A *Chinese fighting dog.* Okay? Emperors use them for fucking up prisoners.

—Okay, Willy P. said, —then I'll be Cream of Some Young Guy.

—Nuh uh. No jokes. Take this seriously or get out. This is for real. This ain't no game.

—Whatever, Willy P. said, —we don't have beats. We don't have lyrics. This is bullshit.

—Okay, then guess what? You're kicked out. You're out of the group.

—What?

—Leave. You're out of Booyashaka Clan.

—Fuck you. *You* leave.

—It's *my* house.

Whatever.

Willy P. threw his pool cue down and went outside through the sliding glass door and Omar watched him. —Gilbert-san, what do you think about all this?

Gilbert uncrossed his legs and put his hands behind his head and went, —I'm a little nervous about all this inner-band turmoil. It's really getting in the way of my music. Which is what it's all about, right? I mean, I can't create in this environment. I'm sitting here trying to think of a good idea for a flow and all I hear is arguing. This isn't good for my creativity. It hinders my creative process.

Senior year was the Year of the Big Decision. The year ended the way most senior years of high school end—with a national press conference in the school gym. Brenton Prep dismissed classes early for the occasion and made attendance mandatory. They gathered to learn what he had decided.

Would it be Duke? Or North Carolina? Or would he be staying local and following his father to B.C.?

Or, as it was rumored, would he skip college altogether to make the leap to The Association?

He paced his bedroom. It would start in an hour. He could hear them gathering already, spears raised, storming the premises with burning torches and white hoods, calling for his blood. He'd already been to school this morning to take a precalc final on which he would score an 89, a blow to his 3.8 GPA. Then he had jogged back home, with the principal's blessing, horns honking at him and men leaning out to yell, —You better pick Duke, Gilbert!

—UNC, Gilbert, UNC!

—Boston College if you know what's good for ya!

—You suck balls, Gilbert Marcus!

He got home and did push-ups until he lost vision in his left eye. He took off all his clothes and lay in his underwear over the sheets of his bed, groaning, sweating. I won't leave this room, he thought. Eventually they'll lose interest and go home. I'll run off and live in a hut and change my name.

He threw himself down before the great Darren Dickinson. He would hate Gilbert. Wouldn't he? Sneer at him for being so fucking scared.

—Tell me what to do, Gilbert cried to Darren Dickinson, —because I want to be you. They will all say The Second Coming of Dickinson, and I'll earn your respect when you see my work ethic. Six hundred shots a day, four hours in the gym. No one works as hard as Marcus, they'll say. The hardworking kid from Boston. And we'll face off in the finals, classic head-to-head battles in which the rest of the court fades to dark and there is only us, faking, sweating, slapping, cursing, panting, grinding our teeth, and feeling the blood in our ears. King Dickinson and The Prince. That's what I want. Our wives proud before the cameras. Looking on warmly as we sign autographs for kids. But only a couple of autographs now, because there isn't time for everyone. I can see myself in slow motion, spinning. In your highlight clips but with me instead of you. And I can see my house, a white castle, with armored gates, and no one can touch me. The dark stars of the world will only exist in movies, because nothing will exist but me.

Then what? Peace.

Gilbert slipped into his suit, nearly identical to Dickinson's but not custom-made from Italy, and not gray—greenish—and placed a pair of sunglasses on the top of his skull, kissed Dickinson's picture, and said, —Coming to get you, motherfucker.

School security guards blocked the exits and Coach Lalli, The High School Basketball Coach, sat behind an ESPN camera whose fat operator was oblivious to him. Both were attributes he was noticing was common among camera operators. In attendance were columnists from *The New York Times, Washington Post, Sports Illustrated*, etc. Steven Tyler from Aerosmith stood by the back wall with Dick Vitale and Bob Ryan. John McNeal was there. An aspiring sportswriter named Bill Simmons had snuck in and was eating a hotdog he'd bought at the concession stand, inadvertently overhearing Michael Wilbon and Charles Barkley's conversation about the Arizona housing market. And once everyone was seated and appropriately anxious and bored, HE strolled in, a new greenish suit, sunglasses resting on top of his head, skull shaved, grinning at the applause he deserved as he shook hands with somebody who might have been Jay Leno, hugged Sue and Mervin who sat in the front row near the stage, stepped up to the podium, stood there for a second, taking it all in.

Sandy sat with Sue and Mervin to his right, but he didn't look at her, just leaned over the microphone and went, —Hi, thank you for coming. My name is Gilbert Marcus and I am pleased to announce what I have chosen to make of my future. It has been a tough decision but I believe I've made the right one. Thanks to my mother and father for their support.

They loved him. Sandy picked at a piece of skin around her thumbnail and imagined traveling the country with Gilbert for games, petting his head as she nursed him with ice after grueling practices. Her star, her man.

—Well, Gilbert said, —so I'd like to, uh, announce here and now that I have decided to enter The Association draft and . . .

He was drowned out as the crowd went wild, mad applause, on cue, for him. He didn't know what it was, but it was electric. He thought he saw Connie Chung leaving the gym. The student body horded him, shoving their yearbooks at him (the only thing they had on them) for him to autograph. And *The New York Times* et al. wanted his answers to their questions, and this was awesome! Power! He owned them! I deserve this, he thought, as he said into the microphone, as they scribbled his words into their notebooks, —It's a rare opportunity. In life you have to take chances, the sky's the limit. My father told me that. And if I fail, then so be it. But I don't want to say I didn't try. I want all the kids at home watching to look at me and remember one thing. And that is: You don't get anything if you don't risk anything. Keep playing, keep practicing, keep learning. Never stop improving. You gotta be ready when you get the call. And stay in school.

And he winked and the crowd around him laughed.

* * *

Though Coach Gerry Lalli had leaned over so far he was nearly parallel with the floor, he was still unable to see around the hefty camera operator who, Gerry realized, could have been *either gender.* He didn't see Gilbert announce that he was going pro, but he could hear him. *Fat fuck. Thanks a lot.* Gerry had countless times found himself shaking his head in wonder at the blessing that'd been bestowed upon him in the form of Gilbert Marcus. Four years ago he had a career high school basketball win total of one. And that came only when the opponent, Phillips Exeter, had to forfeit when the team bus's gas tank was rudely violated by a frustrated and confused young black bear who'd wandered down from the state park.

He was forty-one years old and had received a full scholarship to play for UMass out of high school, but after redshirting his freshman year his coach came up with a brilliant strategy that consisted of playing only retardedly inept nonathletes. The idea was that this would be a sneak attack on the institutionalization of the sport—the trained and prepared opponent would never expect a bunch of five-feet-eight-inch guys who could hardly dribble and who had no set plays beyond tossing the ball over their heads in the general direction of the basket—but of course the Beginner's Luck strategy didn't succeed longer than one and a half quarters, and the college had to save face by having the coach committed and cleaning house, starting its program all over again from scratch. Which meant that Coach Lalli almost immediately found himself in Middlesex Community College getting his gym teacher's degree and losing his hair.

He got the varsity head-coaching job at Brenton Prep, his alma mater, not by his own merits or résumé but by way of nobody else wanting it. He quickly discovered why when only seven kids showed up for tryouts and five of them—the starting five, it would turn out—were asthmatic. They pulled on their inhalers as Gerry Lalli explained that he expected every one of them to give 110 percent. As for the other two, there were only two and three-quarters legs (as in *natural* legs) between them.

Gerry Lalli spent his nights alone that year, in his boxers, watching late-night talk shows and staring at the phone, praying for either a call or death—quick or painful, he wouldn't be picky. He didn't have much in his apartment. He had given his wife, Maureen, half his possessions in the divorce even though she made three times his salary as a private masseuse (nonsexual, and he believed her). She even took the end tables. His bank statements now laughed mercilessly when opened. He sent his black joke of a résumé to UMass to be an assistant or anything they had available, hoping a UMass rep would call back with an offer to hand out cups of water to the players on the bench. He never got a callback from UMass, which was no surprise, though he did get a call the next day from an athletic supply company based (appropriately) in Littleton, Colorado (this was pre-Columbine) to tell him that his order of seven size extra-small jockstraps had arrived in the warehouse to be shipped.

He never got a callback from UMass-Boston either, nor from Clark, nor from Automotive Tech College in Lowell, nor Middlesex Community College, which turned out to be okay because he still owed them $10,765.34.

The phone finally rang early the next morning, waking him where he'd passed out on the lawn chair in the living room, TV still on, hands still down pants, during a dream in which a degenerative bone disease crept out from behind a forgotten gene and rendered him invalid, allowing him to never have to pull into the Brenton Prep parking lot again.

It was his ex-wife's lawyer who said his client decided she wanted the fish tank and the fish and someone would be over later to take it, and Gerry looked over at Bilbo, his prized twelve-year-old barracuda that he'd bought himself as a congratulations for graduating college, floating before a tropical backdrop and staring back at him, and Coach said, —There really isn't anything I can say except *okay*, is there?

—Nope, the lawyer said.

—But *she* cheated on *me*.

—Divorces are clearance sales for women.

—With *forty-seven people*.

—Yeah, well, look at it this way: at least it wasn't forty-eight.

Threw on some clothes, wandered into school slightly hopeful that there would be a school shooting for him to get in the way of, trudged past the open gym door on the way to a nap in his office, saw this skinny black kid who looked liked an Eskimo sorta and taller than he was twirling like a ballerina through the air and dunking it.

The kid's name, it turned out, was Gilbert Marcus. He didn't seem to have any friends or come from any particular place or even speak the vernacular of the high school species: absent from his vocabulary were words like *cool* and *man*, never uttering *and stuff* or *or whatever*, replaced instead with words like *particularly* and *certainly* and *actually quite to the contrary, sir.*

No one had any answers: he eats lunch by himself on the stairs, he never talks to us, he might be a drug dealer, he destroyed Dwayne the starting point guard in one-on-one in front of everybody after school once. He's a snob. He's pretentious. He doesn't speak English. He's a fag, Coach, I ain't playing with him.

The kid, in his junior and senior years of high school, won Gerry Lalli back-to-back Massachusetts State Championships.

After Gilbert graduated Gerry Lalli became one of the winningest high school coaches in state history (in *any* sport), was hired by Villanova as an assistant, used his university salary to hire a pit bull of a lawyer to get Bilbo back, was hired as head coach at an NCAA Division II school in Ohio, married a twenty-eight-year-old former lingerie model who was a philosophy professor at the school, died a rich happy old man with an impossible legacy of victory. At his funeral his oldest daughter stood weeping before the congregation and read a note Gerry wrote with a quivering failing hand, as his last living act, lying in bed listening to the birds sing on this the final, beautiful morning of his life:

To Gilbert Marcus, who proves angels do exist.

Jay DeCourcy sat cross-legged beside a player development executive from the Boston Colonials, wearing contact lenses and a vertical-striped button-down shirt with a *Sports Illustrated* press pass clipped to it, pudgy stomach, pens in the breast pocket. The words coming to him like they were spray-painted on the wall: *The suit, man. Way too cool for college.*

Nice one, and DeCourcy licked his teeth and jotted it down and looked around with his eyes narrowed making sure none of the other writers was looking over his shoulder trying to steal it. But this was too good to keep to himself. He had to tell somebody. He leaned over to the development executive, whose name was Tim Anderson, wearing nearly identical attire, and, shielding his mouth with his hand, muttered into his ear, —The suit, man. Way to cool for college. Eh? *Eh?*

Anderson didn't like DeCourcy much. He always made him feel uncomfortable and irritated. The way he grinned and chummied up to him in hallways, pestering him for inside info on trades or philosophy rifts between coaches and players. Ass lickers, Anderson thought. All of them.

DeCourcy was nudging Anderson in the ribs, winking, that creepy grin, and going, —Eh? Eh?

And so now Anderson just grunted and hoped DeCourcy would fuck off. But of course he didn't.

—The *suit*, man, DeCourcy uttered again, leaning closer to Anderson's ear, his breath smelling of coffee. —Way too cool for—

—Yeah, DeCourcy, I fucking heard you. Christ.

That afternoon and in the weeks that followed, radio shows and newspaper columns exploded shrapnel shit from their rectums, quivering drooling old men smirked and licked their toothless gums and jabbed with disposable ballpoint pens injecting into their columns words of ire, smearing their column space with their own failures and bloody chunks of stool spelling out words.

He thinks he's too cool for college. The way he wore his shades. No respect for the principles of the game. He's just a kid, he's not ready for this life.

Which, Gilbert thought, came as a surprise to no one considering that these guys might as well be paid by The Association. They're a club, a fraternity—they all think the same thought.

But I won't let them talk me down, he thought.

But Mervin defended his son. Mervin contacted his contacts in the months before the press conference, determined that not only was it a slam dunk that Animal would be drafted into The Association but that he would most likely be taken in the top fifteen. The Association wanted his youth. They wanted his race. They got boners over the prospect of his marketability. The Association had cash they wanted to give him, so he would have something to give them when they fined him for wearing the wrong color socks. And Reebok had a shoe they wanted to pay him money to wear, Mervin discovered. And besides, Mervin told the scouts and the general managers who were calling, Gilbert grew up around The Association. He was its surrogate son. He knew the unwritten rules of the life—how to make sure the girl is eighteen, how to deliver short precise sound bites in TV interviews to make it easy to replay on twenty-four-hour cable news, etc. Mervin had the experience to guide him. Gilbert was already aged well beyond his years. He was wise enough to avoid the trouble most kids of The Association run into on the road—drugs, gold-digging whores, etc. Because what Gilbert had under his belt of Life Experience was something no one else had yet pugilated with: being alone.

—Listen, Mervin said when he called in to WEEI from his car after hearing the hosts calling for his and Sue's blood, —all these guys will be out at clubs after the game and Gilbert will be back at his room playing Nintendo, studying film. This isn't a normal eighteen-year-old kid. Have any of you guys who say this is the wrong thing to do, have you seen this young man play? Have you? He's very mature. Very.

What they didn't know, or refused to admit, to themselves or to the public, was that he'd had money slipped into his pockets by boosters from every college you can think of, and agents had been taking him out to dinner and giving him clothes and CDs so that he'd sign with them after graduation. They'd offered him drinks, girls, cars, all of which he passed on because none of that had anything to do with basketball. And he could have gone to Duke and played for the great Coach K and won the Final Four and become Grant Hill and be the number-one pick or he could have gone to Boston College and resurrected a once-proud institution, played four years and gotten a degree in something or another, but whatever it was it would have been a waste. Because the more you gamble with the more you get, he thought. Security gets you nothing.

Who was to say that Darren Dickinson would still be around for him to beat and topple when he was done being used by some university to generate millions for their pockets while he ate ramen and peanut butter and jelly and hoped he didn't blow out a knee and see his career end in some thin-walled stuffy off-campus apartment with four other slobs and cockroaches?

Go to college, you play like a college kid, he thought; go to the pros, you play like a pro.

Because college ball isn't about stars or greatness but about studying the technical know-hows, treating the game like a science, playing however Coach wants you to, just a cog in his system, curbing personality and improvisational nuances that make you great. But the game's not a science. College makes you play just like the next guy—just ask my dad, he thought. Dickinson knew it, could only take two years at the University of Central Florida; Dad knew it, went pro after two years too; college makes you soft. It makes you mediocre. You play afraid because if you don't do what you're told you'll get benched in favor of some other robot with an accurate jumper. He knew that. He wanted more than a degree he'd never touch. It was either play basketball or die. Put it all on the line or don't bother. A legend or an embarrassment, a disaster. All or nothing. He'd always known there was something different about himself, like he'd become either a murderer or a saint, a genius or a bum, a monk or a rapist.

Never average. Because what was average?

Mervin Marcus.

Prom was the week after the press conference (such a busy time, the end of high school) and he took a local model/actress named Kelly Levy, a blond beautiful girl who was training for Miss Teen Massachusetts and was a sixteen-year-old homeschooled senior who had appeared in a series of regional furniture commercials that got her recognized once at the Natick Mall and had been accepted into Harvard but was deferring her acceptance to go out to L.A. to start auditioning for major acting roles since she had an agent who was already scheduling auditions for her.

Gilbert smiled as he walked through the door of the hotel with the blond beautiful girl on his arm, her wholesome cheeks and suburban sex appeal, to the explosion of flashbulbs and newspeople awaiting in ambush. The blond beautiful girl's dress showed tit but not too much tit. The blond beautiful girl wore hair extensions and professionally done makeup. *The perfect china doll for Gilbert Marcus.* The rest of the boys were dapper in black-and-white tuxes and the girls classily showed tit and they stopped their dancing and chatting to turn at the commotion, whispering to one another, —*Here they are, look, they're here!*

Gilbert exuded pride and confidence and he showed his teeth for the photographers amassed outside and he twirled the blond beautiful girl around for them, just as virginal as she came across in her commercials lying on mattresses talking about back support.

The Light between her and Gilbert cracking the zoom lenses and melting pens, the unofficial King and Queen of prom, dazzling and sudden celebrity.

He met the blond beautiful girl at a charity basketball game in which he was playing and at which she was singing the national anthem, local news cameras following her around for a piece.

And the power couple stayed at prom only half an hour because paparazzi kept sneaking in and everyone wouldn't stop staring so it was impossible to have fun so the high school basketball star and the blond beautiful girl snuck themselves up the elevator to a private suite an agent courting Gilbert had paid for, in the tux the agent paid the rental fee on.

—Uh-oh, he laughed when they entered the room. —Only one bed.

But Kelly Levy didn't laugh or say anything and he sat next to her on the bed. She smoothed out her dress and fanned her face with her hand and said, —It's so *hot* in here. Isn't it *hot* in here? Gilbert turned the air-conditioning up and got a couple beers out of the minifridge and struggled with the caps, laughing coolly as Kelly watched, expressionless, sighing audibly, arms wrapped around herself.

—You need a bottle opener, she said. Now she shivered, rubbed her arms.

—No, no, I got it. It doesn't want to come off, heh heh. *Aaaah, nooo, don't drink me, noooo!* Heh heh.

—Here. Kelly took a beer from him and slammed it against the corner of the end table with a Bible in its drawer and the cap popped off, foamy head dribbling onto the rug.

—How the . . . ? Heh heh, Gilbert said. She handed the bottle to him and he said, —No, go ahead.

—I don't want it. I don't drink. I'm not old enough.

Turned on the TV, sat next to her, but not too close. She was prettier than Sandy by far. They watched a sitcom he'd never seen before He laughed whenever she laughed even though he didn't get it.

—Ha ha, this show is pretty hilarious, he said. —What is it?

She looked at him with disgust. —It's *Seinfeld*. You've never seen *Seinfeld* before?

—Oh. Yeah. Duh. Of course I have. I don't know what I was thinking.

He put his arm around her, leaning in to the side of her face, and he tried to kiss her. Kelly sort of froze and waited for him to stop. —Gilbert, she said.

—Did you know Reebok wants to give me ten million dollars to wear their shoe? he said, nearly in tears. —Did you know that?

—Let's just watch TV.

—Please, he said.

—Are you okay? You're sweating.

I need a girl. Don't you understand that? I need a wife.

His eyes were wild, sweaty lip quivering, mouth sticky.

—Magic has one, he said. —Dickinson has one. You *need* . . . to have . . . a . . . *wife*.

—You're scaring me.

—Why do you have to act so goddamn *sweet*?

—Gilbert, I don't know what's wrong with you.

—Fine. Go.

—Gilbert.

You hate me so much, then go.

—I don't hate you. I hardly know you. I have to tan in the morning or I'll lose my base. Plus I have voice-over class in the afternoon. I need my rest.

—Let's fuck. Please? Please let's just fuck. It's not a big deal.

—Gilbert. Jesus.

He crossed his arms and looked away, and she closed the door and Gilbert stood there for a while, getting his breath back, feeling the room coming back together, and before he went to sleep he jerked off, thinking of (in order): Kelly, an advertisement he saw for And 1, Marv Albert, Sandy, a patch of sand somewhere in the middle of the Pacific with one palm tree and maybe a rusted toilet seat ten feet up its trunk where no one knew it even existed, healthy populations of lactobacteria in the intestinal tract, Kelly again.

In the morning, he woke up in his tuxedo, alone.

10

THE LINE OF SHIMMERING BLACK robes voided personal traits such as faces and identities, succeeding in creating a uniform snake that beheaded itself one segment at a time then inched forward to regenerate. The crowd—parents, younger sisters, grandparents, disinterested cousins, under-age girlfriends—could not tell who it was they came to see, where they were sitting, why they were here. An assistant principal, a be-spectacled man with thinning gray hair and flesh-colored thin lips, read into a microphone off to the side of the stage, —Gilbert . . . Marcus. There was a small burst of hoots and applause of recognition, vi-olating the principal's beseechment to hold applause. Flashbulbs went off all over the place. The ones in the seats belonged to curious par-ents. The ones at the foot of the stage belonged to media. They cheered for themselves, for knowing the name.

Congratulations. Happy Graduation. You clenched your stomach muscles hoping the outline of your perfect physique showed through your robe. You smiled warmly, your teeth immaculate and untarnished by processed foods and added sugars. You were a man now. As you moved across the stage you were aware that your features were chiseled and your jawline was angular and clean, that your eyes sparkled in the bombardment of flashbulbs. You exuded perfect confidence. Though it was not you whose image they captured but rather the thick cake of flesh that had grown over your bones, and inside this cake you were hiding. A warm fleshlike debris, its lips rubber, a creation. And as the large strong hand clenched the cold soft one of the principal's the other waved to the crowd, and the eyes glanced up to the seats and scanned their faces.

The Light was with you, crouched down somewhere deep, curled up like a fetus, your hands bound and eyes stitched, tranquilized and buried in goop. These people had to be pleased and teased. They had to get their money's worth.

The crowd applauded the recognition of it but its ears did not hear.

Though they were proud to be in the presence of it, they did not realize that what they clapped for was nothing, that Gilbert Marcus was not graduating today, Gilbert Marcus was graduating never, Gilbert Marcus was not there, Gilbert Marcus . . . was . . . *gone.*

In his place, a secret twin: The Athlete.

He waited for his parents afterward in the lobby outside the Brenton Prep auditorium, zoning out on all the shoes and hands. Mervin touched him on the back of the shoulder holding a copy of *USA Today*. Gilbert took it from him, glanced at the article and his picture, "GILBERT" written in red pen at the top: *USA Today*'s High School Player of the Year.

—You know what this means, don't you? Mervin said.

—Yeah. Pretty cool.

—Pretty cool. Right. State champion. Player of the year. Every time there's a column sniveling about how Gilbert Marcus skipping college to get paid is the first sign of the apocalypse, that's more zeros in your contract. One more spot in the draft you move up. Irreverence is a high commodity, Animal. Even today with everyone who's worth a damn skipping college. That article you're holding is worth *millions*. How do you feel about a rap album? Or your own record label? Def Jam is talking about giving you an imprint.

—Hmm. I don't see what the big deal is though.

—They just like to jerk themselves off is what.

—I mean. Kevin Garnett did it. Why's everyone acting like it's such a big deal?

—It's their job to act like it's such a big deal. It's like WWF. People listen to get outraged. Their business is making people outraged. Hey, how do you feel about Alpo dog food?

—I just want to play basketball. I mean. I wish I could just play basketball and not have to deal with all this stuff. Never talk to anybody. Just play.

—Comes with the territory, Animal. That's lesson one. Can't just play.

—I don't know. Whatever.

—Of course basketball is number one, Animal. Of course. But as much as basketball's a sport, it's also a business. It's show business. It's real estate. It's everything balled into one. Sooner you learn that the better. You have a product to push and that product is *you.*

—Me? No.

—Your youth. A prodigy. That's something they can grab on to. All-American and nonthreatening. Polite black boy who won't rob you. You're a Cosby kid. You speak good clear English. People are sick of Ebonics and gangsta shit. Big black athletes fucking white bitches and beating up their baby mommas and pulling guns on people and all that *shit.* People are sick of people who play sports. They like seeing people like you. You look like them. You act like them. Listen. To be not just a ballplayer but THE ballplayer, okay, you can't be yourself. You have to hide it. Give them something they can name what it is. That they've seen on television. Tell them how to see you and they'll see you that way. That's how people are. You've made it this far on talent, you need something else now.

— . . .

—And whatever you do, don't challenge. I mean challenge, but challenge in a way so it's clear to them you're being challenging. Challenge scares people, turns them off. Confuses them. Alienates them. Makes them indecisive. You want to be someone everyone can like. Take Dickinson. Ghetto thugs love him, twelve-year-old white kids love him. Their parents love him. Everyone. And what do all those people have in common? Eyeballs and TVs. You getting this?

—Um.

—You have to know what you want to be, Animal. What do you want to be?

—I want to be idolized. I want to be a man. I want to be Darren Dickinson or Magic Johnson.

—Magic? Don't give me Magic. Magic's a minstrel show. Magic's blackface. Smiling and dumb as a rock with his big black AIDS dick swinging down his pant legs. Ever wonder why he's not living in a cage somewhere ever since he got AIDS?

—I don't know.

—Not only kept around but given his own goddamn late-night talk show on network television? With *AIDS*?

—Nuh-uh.

—Because the people knew what it was when it happened. Of course they said it was a shock. But who was shocked? No one. Of course he got AIDS. What else would he be doing when he's not playing sports? Fucking. That's what. They were *shocked? Really?* Please. He's black, of course he fucks everything. Of course he doesn't use a rubber. He needs to fuck so bad there's no time to put on a rubber— you paying attention?

—Yeah. Yeah.

—What'd I just say?

—He needs to fuck so bad there's no time to put on a rubber.

—That's how they see it. He runs around for the people's entertainment, smiles for *massah*, shits out in the yard, then mates and goes to sleep. Without the self-control to know a woman of questionable merit. And they say they were shocked. Ain't nobody shocked, Animal. Relieved is more like it. They were relieved that they were right when they think all black people do is fuck and kill each other and play sports.

— . . .

—Nobody was challenged, everybody wins. He fed themselves to themselves and he gets to *stay alive* because of it. You're entering a very stinky world here, son. This world isn't just getting paid to play basketball. You're becoming something else entirely. As far as reporters like this know, it's a dream come true! It's such a blessing to get a chance to live my dream and I just want to help my team win, *suh*. Thanks for the money, *massah*. Listen, it's going to change you. Being a chunk of pumped-up meat on a leash, dressed up in their goofy uniforms, paraded around on TV, rubbing against each other. And if you're hurt they don't care. They'll pump you full of painkillers and send you out there and if you hurt yourself for good, too bad. You're public property from here on out, meat.

They went outside and Sue was there standing alone in makeup, antsy and cranky, and Mervin stopped Gilbert and said, —You understand what I'm saying though, Animal? But Gilbert was pulled away by the elbow to stand with someone for a picture, and Mervin grabbed him back, ruining the shot, and said through his teeth, —You understand my point though, Gilbert?

—Yeah, yeah. I hear you.

He thought, Crazy old man. Nobody knows but me.

They were walking toward the car. Mervin shook his head and looked at his son, grinning, and Gilbert noticed the yellow on his teeth and looked away, and Mervin went, —Look at that face, Sue. Fresh *meat*.

The conversation occurred away from home, in another sector of the multiunit, square-lined happening that is Metropolitan Outskirts, USA, the lingering knots of jurisdictions and tax-bracket settlements, landscaping companies fighting to the death over territories, new houses springing up like zits, the interstate expanding until deer give birth under overpasses, and all the while the people looking at one another and at their glasses of water, flat cola, wondering where, if anywhere, they are.

Time was almost up. Suddenly before you knew it it was time to say good-bye. To what exactly he was supposed to be so sad about leaving he wasn't sure. High school was little more than useless facts and sleep deprivation. Aside from the posters on the walls, the carpets of the hallway, the smells of books and shampoo, it ended up meaning nothing . . .

But one day you'll look up and you won't be sure her voice was like how you remember it or if her kisses were really as sugary as you remember them or if the warmth bubbling in your gut was imagined or not.

For Gilbert Marcus it was So long, shit town. Crying over the memories of the people he'd been forced to spend the last four years with was last on his priority list.

They'd all be nothing. They would stay in the place they were from forever. But not Gilbert.

They never meant all that much to him in the first place.

Gilbert thought, That is what separates me from them. I have the grit and the balls to do what I want to do. I chase the life I imagine. I gamble. I take risks. I have a mission. They take what's given them. The standard issue life. It's easier than chasing. It's safer than gambling. They prefer anonymity. They want nothing but to go to fun parties and to have cable television after work to quell their minds from the banal horror of their existence. How do people do that? Gilbert couldn't understand. How could human beings let themselves become unremarkable and inconsequential? Boring baby-machines, buying-machines? How could they do so little with their lives? Wouldn't it make them want to die? If it were Gilbert, he would want to die. Because what would be the point?

Sue was on Prozac and an antiviral for the cold sores and had just witnessed her baby graduate high school. She sat with Mervin during the ceremony wearing a purple dress, distantly aware of the parents of nonfuture professional basketball players staring at them. She slipped out afterward leaving Mervin to find Gilbert. She stood in the afternoon sun alone outside the school. She opened the orange-tinted bottle with Xanax in it that she begged off her family practitioner, Dr. Pramoke (to offset the anxiety caused by the Prozac), and tilted a few into her mouth. They were bitter and sticky without water.

The night before, Mervin woke her up by rubbing himself against her thigh, and when she opened her eyes he climbed on top of her, hot breath, nose, and she was still half-asleep and didn't realize until he'd ejaculated inside her and withdrew and rolled off her and fell back to sleep that she wasn't dreaming.

His face had changed recently. She didn't like this. It wasn't good when men's faces changed. But it was after he came home late from B.C. one night with a dozen red roses and a bottle of wine, smelling like smoke, out of the blue, and kissed her on the lips and said Hi Momma that she realized where she knew that look from. Mervin went upstairs to change and she sat at the kitchen table staring at wine and flowers. Wine and flowers made her ill. He hadn't brought her wine and flowers in a long time. Years. Not since Utah. When he came back before she left to go to Marla's he'd brought wine and flowers. Wine and flowers. She knew what wine and flowers meant.

What a nightmare, the shadows the memories released inside her. The Xanax quelled the trembling, made her hands steady, eased the feeling that she was jumping out of her skin. What Dr. Pramoke called akathisia.

The Xanax quelled the akathisia. A little bit.

That night Mervin rolled her over in her sleep and jammed himself into her before she was ready, the stinging, tearing. Copulating madly without mind, even though she murmured, —Mervin, wait, *wait . . .* It was like a dog, overcome with the primal need to fuck *now*. She thought of her son as her husband panted in her face, his sweat dripping into her eyes. The son that this same act had once produced.

Soon, she thought, there will be no buffer. No common point. Soon my son will be gone and it will be just me and this person.

Afterward she was tired but couldn't sleep and she got up and went to Gilbert's room and put her hand on the knob and listened.

She went downstairs in the dark and put on her jacket over her nightgown. She stepped into the wide-open summer night and walked up and down the street, drinking the bottle of wine, smoking cigarettes. She waited for something to fall from the sky to tell her why it's true that the curse of mothers is to create life, love it with your entire soul, so it can use your love to grow up strong enough to leave you forever.

To love that which leaves is woman.

The mystery of abandoned summer late night, when the streetlights buzz and the frogs and crickets and a bottle of wine, the reservoir evaporating toward the stars, cars at rest and shining and no one knows your name. The same world Gilbert snuck out his window into when he was thirteen and bursting from his skin too (but not because of any drug), to wander and sit in the abandoned parking lot of the community center and write poetry about the moon in his sports sandals.

Sweating, touching her thin low breasts through the neck hole of her nightgown, cupping them, nipples flat soft between her fingers, letting them drop with a flap. Once the source of food and life. And now? Kneading her belly which had grown wobbly. She stopped walking to pull her gown up over her waist and stare down at the place. The place was glinting and flagrant. She stumbled into the front yard of the Needhams' house, collapsing like a toddler under a tree. She spread her legs to get a better look at the place. She admitted to herself that she was drunk. She marveled that Gilbert had come from the place, what her body had once been able to do. Sue cried as she stuck a finger into the place. Maybe there was another baby hiding in the place and she'd find it right now and then get to start all over again. And what a baby she had been and didn't even know it. But that's how you know if you're a baby: if you don't know that you are. And she still was a baby, wasn't she? She withdrew her finger from the place, having found no baby. Her body had given in to time and gravity. She could tell because her thighs and rear, her breasts, were all deflating and pulling themselves toward the middle of the earth. She stood up, gown falling back down, hiding the place.

Sue snuck back in as the sun rose, before anyone woke up, wondering why she was sneaking back into this house. She put ice on her face. She put ice between her legs. She threw away the empty wine bottle. She buttered a frying pan and cracked open some organic brown eggs. She made breakfast for her son who was leaving and for her husband who bought her flowers and wine. She made breakfast for her family on Graduation Day.

The 4Runner was a gift given to him in his senior year, early in the season. It had a twelve-disk CD changer, power locks and windows, and custom leather upholstery. The keys were slipped into his still-sweaty palm in the midst of a hubbub outside the Brenton Prep gym after Gilbert poured in 34 against Revere in a 25-point margin of victory. A gawking crowd had already formed in the hall as Gilbert jogged out after the final buzzer, into a gauntlet of back-pats and people with no names who wanted to talk to him, and then there were keys in his hands, and he looked up to see a small man with white hair and a red face, in a suit, a calm glaze in his eyes as he held out his hand and said, —Abe Birnbaum.

—What school are you from? Gilbert asked, disinterested, pocketing the keys.

—School? He smiled. —Just don't lose my number.

The man handed Gilbert a tasteful business card (eggshell, with raised Romalian type) and slipped off into the crowd. Gilbert fought his way to the locker room, dressed in his private locker that he'd had Coach Lalli rig up with curtains and all surrounding lockers unoccupied, stared at the keys, holding the secret with a mix of sin and glee, not telling his teammates about it, and he waited until the lot had cleared out and the only car remaining was a 4Runner that shimmered, off by itself taking up two spaces, lonesome and magnificent under the orange streetlights, and the registration in the dash had Sue's and Mervin's names on it with a Post-it that said only "SPECU-LATIVE CREDIT. REGARDS." He touched the bulbously curved fender, liked it, the headlights like the eyes of a giant reptile. The system thumped as he roared down the streets high above the sedans, their roofs rusted and peeling and drivers invisible inside.

He flew out with Mervin to Los Angeles and puked on the plane and pulled up in a taxi in front of the offices of Miller Greenstein Talent Agency, an impossibly imposing building with black windows and white stone. It was a factory of money and destiny.

Abe Birnbaum stood up behind his desk, suit pressed and shoes shined, the faint lingering cigar smoke, as Gilbert and Mervin entered, and gave the boy a hug and Mervin a handshake. He offered both a drink, a bottled water at least, we have limes too you know. Gilbert said, —No, thanks, I'm fine, I brought my own.

Abe Birnbaum invited Gilbert to sit and pointed to a stack of paper, slid a twenty-four-karat-gold fountain pen across the finished mahogany desk, and said, —Sign here and we're on our way.

Gilbert in a gray suit, looking very professional. He and Mervin had already pored over a version of the contract that had been faxed to Hingham, which, Mervin deciphered, was a standard representation agreement and not racist in any discernible way and so was acceptable. The same day Gilbert received a letter from Los Angeles and inside the envelope was a handwritten check for fifty thousand dollars from an account called Lyson and Sons, LLC, and a note scribbled in fountain pen that said, "THE CONTRACT IS PREPARED. JUST WAIT-ING FOR YOUR WORD. REGARDS."

Another page came through the fax of what was a POWERade wrapper removed from a bottle and laid on paper and xeroxed, and it had a picture of Gilbert on it, hanging from a rim. Written was, "THIS COULD BE YOU."

He deposited the check in an overseas account. It took nearly two weeks for it to clear. But when it did he withdrew six thousand of it in hundred-dollar bills and went with Omar and Willy P. to Off Tha Wall, a sports apparel store in the mall, and spent three thousand dollars on jerseys, hats, jewelry, shoes, etc., tipping the cashier one hundred for no reason. He had to bring his new 4Runner around back to load it all in. He drove home in the 4Runner with merchandise hanging out the windows, blowing in the breeze, music thumping, boys laughing, tucked the rest of the cash under his pillow, and woke up in time to catch the plane to L.A. to officially sign with his agent, Abe Birnbaum.

Abe Birnbaum came up representing athletes out of New York in the 1970s but in the 1980s he moved to L.A. and switched to entertainers and was known there for his fetish for vomiting on strippers. He became a partner at Miller Greenstein after getting an actor named George Hedford, the worst actor anyone in Hollywood could remember—plus the ugliest son of a bitch you'll ever see in your life—a supporting role in a Brian De Palma movie, considered a legendary piece of agenting still to this day. In the 1990s, Abe Birnbaum had to admit to himself that the only way to stay interested was to go back to athletes. And the first one was this kid from Boston, Gilbert Something-oranother.

Standing at the window overlooking La Cienega Boulevard, SUVs and Bentleys cruising below, his hotel room with black marble shower and TV speakers in the bathroom, tying the tie to his gray Gucci suit for which he paid four thousand dollars in Boston, plus a two-hundred-dollar tip for the tailor, the HOLLYWOOD sign barely visible through the afternoon smog in the distance, sunshine and palm trees and tits and ass forever: LOS ANGELES.

He put his sunglasses on his forehead and met Mervin in the hallway, told the cabbie to go to Miller Greenstein, signed a representation agreement with Abe Birnbaum, ate dinner that night at a Tex-Mex place on Sunset, caught the red-eye the next morning back to Logan, and slept with three thousand dollars under his pillow with no hairs on it.

11

A SUNNY AFTERNOON IN HINGHAM after getting back from acting class, at the cusp of his gritty descent from youth to famous adult, and the scene he remembers vividly in perfect snapshot, the seamless features of her nude female body, the marvelous curves and drops, and the green ring on the second finger of her little right hand as she gripped him and slowly worked away, the surprising pleasure of seeing himself handled by another, like it created a whole other realm of existence— another dimension, clinging to him tight like a little girl, he felt the warmth against his thigh, the particular bristle-wet, as she panted and looked up at him, lying on his back, grinding against him and moaning, whimpering and starving, hair sticking to her face, saying to him breathless and urgent, —Gilbert.

All of a sudden Sandy was disgusting, her neediness repulsed him. She was naked and needy and disgusting.

He went limp in her hand.

—What's the matter? she said. But the way she said it irritated him. It was such a desperate thing to say. How she said it was irritating. Why was it irritating? He didn't know, just was. She was a talking dog in heat. She was pathetic. It was pathetic, a girl wanting it so bad. Needing it so much. *Too* much. Girls shouldn't want it. Not any girl of his. Where was his quiet virgin? The respectable prude girl who didn't like to kiss in public? Had she been acting this whole time? Was she really some nymphomaniac slut? And if so, were all girls? Can you trust any of them? Were they good for anything other than fucking three in one night? He broke into a sweat and shoved her off. She nearly tumbled from the bed, yelping.

—God, you're such a whore, he said.

It was a week after prom. She didn't attend even though Martin Barnsbury asked her. Martin Barnsbury had followed her around like a puppy since eighth grade. But Sandy watched the local news at home alone and saw the footage of her boyfriend arm in arm with the blond beautiful girl. She'd curled up on the couch in her pj's and cried for the rest of the night. A week went by and they didn't say a word to each other. She avoided him. She didn't call. It was torment, but it was what he wanted. Then she saw him talking to Bethany McNeal in the parking lot outside Blockbuster, and later that day she showed up on Gilbert's doorstep, ashamed but still ringing the bell. And he looked down on her silently and she knew she had to say something and finally she said, —Can I come in? He let her in and they went to his room, made out, got naked, the box of Trojans in her purse that she bought at CVS on the way over, and all of sudden Gilbert went soft and he shoved her off and she fell off the bed and he called her a whore and jogged into the bathroom, slammed the door, saying as he did so, —I'm thinking about taking art history classes and investing in some modern pieces.

Sandy stayed there on the floor for a moment before jumping up and gathering her clothes, yelling at the door, —What's the matter? You said you wanted to fuck! You always wanted to fuck me, well here you go! Fuck me! Come on out and fuck me!

But he didn't come out and he didn't fuck her. After letting her scream for a while, listening to her trash his bedroom and smash something heavy it sounded like, catching his nude reflection in the mirror and pleased with his physique, he heard her leave then snuck out of the bathroom and put on his clothes, his parents at work, chased after her, catching up with her in the driveway where she was digging through her purse outside her car, brushing her hair back, stomping her foot and saying, —I can't find my goddamn keys!

He stood there watching her as she dumped the purse all over the sidewalk and squatted down, her dress wrinkled, the one she'd put on especially to go to Gilbert's house and just talk, because they could at least be friends, right? It made no sense that they couldn't at least be friends. It didn't seem right that they couldn't talk.

And she was crying, and he said, —I can fuck. By the way.

—No, you can't.

—Yeah, I can.

—No, you can't because you're better than everyone so you can't fuck anyone.

She found her keys and was stuffing handfuls of lip gloss and tampons and tweezers back in, the box of Trojans.

Gilbert said, —What are you talking about?

Sandy ignored him and opened the door, which was squeaky, and climbed in, tears under her eyes, lip trembling, skirt caught on her thigh, but she didn't care, nothing mattered anymore, not Gilbert, not that he was saying, —What does that mean?

Not that her hair was sticking to her face or that she was starting the car. Not that she hadn't told her parents that Gilbert Marcus had dumped her.

Gilbert tried the handle but she'd already locked it. He knocked on the glass and said, —Are you being, like, facetious?

Which is when the phone rang. The phone was in his hand though he didn't remember grabbing it. He said to Sandy through the glass, —Don't go. Wait just a second.

He pushed TALK and said into the phone, —Hello?

The voice on the other end was raspy and direct and was Abe Birnbaum's. —Milwaukee wants to work you out to see if they want to draft you or not. Your flight's in the morning.

Standing in the driveway in sandals atop the oven-baked slow burn of a summer afternoon, listening to Abe Birnbaum and watching Sandy drive away in her father's Camry with the squeaky door: The last time he ever saw her.

And then he was on a plane, in the aisle seat in first class, watching the stewardess's ass, who he was pretty sure wanted him to put his throat yogurt onto her face, a gym bag stuffed between his feet. He had expected Mervin or Sue to go with him, but Mervin said from his cell phone with bad reception, —You have to get used to traveling without us, Animal. You'll be doing a lot of it. Your mom and me won't be there to wipe your butt all the time.

Landed in Milwaukee, the professional athlete in town on business. (Or, at least, the soon-to-be professional athlete.) They'd be in awe of him. Maybe they'd want to put him up against one of their guys, their Thadeus Marshall (who was now out of the league due to multiple failed drug tests and facing jail time for domestic abuse). They'd call Stephen Buchannon, a third-year guard out of Syracuse who they were saying could be the next Darren Dickinson. They'd order him to come in and play Gilbert one-on-one and Gilbert would beat Stephen Buchannon easily and Stephen Buchannon would be doubled over in exhaustion and Stephen Buchannon would be shaking his head and looking at Gilbert in disbelief, and Stephen Buchannon would ask the executives, —This kid is *how* old now?

He looked around as he got into a taxi at bland forgotten Milwaukee screaming desolation and shadows. He looked out the window of the taxi on the way to his hotel on a dreary balmy day—Wisconsin was a boneless extraneous digit on the hand of American democracy.

It was a hell of a thing, being eighteen and on your own in a strange hotel room, not knowing anyone or how to do the card-key thing, dropping your bag on the bed and standing there before the quarter-tucked comforter and personally autographed card that says a maid was here earlier and that she sterilized your room of all hairs, excretions, fluids, and exfoliated skin cells. He stood there not wanting to touch anything. He turned on the TV but turned it off because the channels were different and it made him uneasy. He masturbated in the bathroom, using the free hand lotion, thinking about the maid.

The little Latina maid who under the beige one-piece suit no doubt hides a sculpted and taut body, cleaning his room, bending over to vacuum under the desk, little dumb Latina whose tits flap and knees wobble and thighs soak slippery as he does it to her, quickly, gasping in hypnotized ecstasy, then he sends her out to continue her maidly duties, fucked by Gilbert Marcus.

Gilbert watched himself in the mirror over the sink as he did it, admiring the defined ridges of his abs and the swell of his biceps. The good thing about being black he thought was the definition brought on by the dark skin. He touched his pecs pretending they were the hands of a Latina maid touching his pecs. He held his hand still and thrust away, pretending it was a Latina maid's vagina. He came into a handful of the onion-skin toilet paper and flushed it immediately then showered, folded his towel after showering, scrubbed the bottom of the tub with toilet paper, threw away the little bar of soap from the ridge of the shower wall, ate the three-dollar bag of peanuts, and sat on the edge of the bed staring at his reflection in the TV screen for two hours until the car came to take him to the Harrison Center.

They'd heard the hype, the tall tales, the legend of the Prodigy from suburban Massachusetts, but, as the other Associated franchises would find, there existed little actual game tape of him to study, as high schools taping their games was a rare thing, more rare than colleges at least. The fire of the mystery was fueled, as, Gilbert learned, people claw more ferociously for what they cannot have.

—They want to test-drive you before they throw bags of cash at you. Into you. You're an investment now, son, Abe had said.

—What kind of tests?

—Oh, usually just parade you up and down the court a bit. See if you can jump and run and all that.

—Okay.

—Talk to you to make sure you're not retarded or psychotic.

—Yeah.

—Make sure you're mature enough that you won't flop on them. Or flip out and get into drugs. Or kill anyone. If they do draft you.

—Okay.

—Don't be nervous, Gilbert. You'll be fine.

—Nervous? About what?

Taste the thrill of money pumping through your well-toned arms, revving your clean-tubed heart like eight-cylinder diesel, and there ain't nothing anyone can do to stop it—the power he holds is nuclear, the wealth of attention and approval of the money holders, Association franchise execs flying him in and footing the bill to put him up just for an opportunity to watch him shoot and speak words to him . . .

* * *

Walked through the ramp onto the floor of the Harrison Center and immediately noticed that Stephen Buchannon was not there. Waiting for him were front-office executives in suits, conversing in a cluster at half-court. They stopped talking and turned to face him, hands in pockets, expensive shiny shoes squeaking, eyebrows raised, intrigued but not all that entirely impressed at this darty-eyed minor who showed up already in his workout clothes and looked like, oh, fourteen years old.

This is him? Sure he's a basketball prodigy and not, like, a violin prodigy?

Not wearing the rags or the old white no-name brand shoes which he'd stuffed without ceremony into the trash can at the curb of the safe and big Marcus house in Hingham, but baggy shiny mesh shorts and T-shirt that still smelled like the store with name brand stamped large and cartoonish on the back, sleeves cut and hemmed, the new Dickinsons which retailed for $215, new Adidas socks, all bought at City Sports on Commonwealth Avenue in Allston for $20 altogether because the manager recognized him. Not the scowl like he had practiced but a wide goofy grin. He shook their hands with the same hand that a couple of hours before was the little Latina maid's vagina and smiled warmly like he belonged.

They tossed him a ball and moved without breaking the cluster to the sideline. They watched him play basketball.

It was quiet as he dribbled onto the court and to the basket and took a shot, fielded his own rebound.

Was this what they wanted? *This?* Where was Stephen Buchannon? Maybe they would like some dunks. Perhaps he should rap for them.

He glanced over as he took another shot and there they were with a finger on their bottom lip, all of them, each, elbows atop a fist, blinking, eyebrows low as if trying to comprehend an impossibly obtuse piece of art. Did I piss them off somehow? Was I not friendly enough?

Beauty in his motion. They were all aware of it. They were drawn to it like flies to sweat because human eyes pinwheel at true beauty. Sweeping those limbs like melted ice cream. Sudden and true. His first step, which was fluid and instinctually swift like some sort of explosive gas. The ball teasing to dance from his hands but never giving in. Lovely ballet, good art. The best kind of art because everybody feels it in their gut.

We didn't know what to do. We just stood there and watched. None of us knew what to think.

And the general manager and his colleagues of the Milwaukee Lobos watched the kid glide around and hit jumpers soft in the net, trying to comprehend what was happening. The way it made them feel. Like life and death, he played the game upside down and backward, the angles he discovered were unheard of but ravishing, how he wrapped himself up in them and obliterated them from the inside.

The general manager played with his bottom lip and tried to be unformed and unswayed. This was the kind of man who speaks in clichés without irony and doesn't listen to music. His face was expressionless and his soul hidden. It was the only escape from the beautiful things occurring inside him . . .

His suit was gray but grayer than his hair which with his baby face made him look like an unfortunate twenty-one-year-old. He'd looked younger than he was since he could remember. He got carded thoroughly and skeptically at bars until he was thirty-four. He knew his colleagues were glancing at him trying to gauge what he was thinking, but they knew how good he was at not reacting, Ian Martin, general manager of the lowly Milwaukee Lobos, perennial losers, doers of bumbling personnel choices . . .

He liked it, coming across as old and jaded. When he was younger he had been intimidated easily. He had been aware that he looked meek, the pitch of his voice going up a few notches in the presence of taller older men. His wife was an attorney (partner) and was pretty in the richer-middle-aged-woman sort of way. Dark shortish hair and pumps and stockings. Theirs was an open union that allowed both to philander gleefully with their careers, to indulge in long intimate hours with their office furniture—but on the rare nights when they could forget the responsibility and money, they drooped into each other's arms on the big leather couch before the remote-control fireplace and emptied a bottle of white Merlot, making out like teenagers and laughing at silly TV, screwing, asses and feet high in the hair, messy and grunting, relieved for the chance to unstitch their rawhide and let their ridiculous underbellies out for air. For now at least they could be human, children, and no one would ever know.

Ian Martin was now, for a moment, as he watched Gilbert Marcus work out, deeply embarrassed remembering last night when he humped his wife like he was in heat right there on their antique coffee table imported from Namibia and then rubbed her feet while cooing *I feel so close to you when I'm inside you, Baby Girl*—oh boy, he could feel his face getting red—and now he stood with finger on lip, in suit and tie, neat to the point of odd. Serious, cold. A professional. Darting his eyes, he saw that his underlings were now standing just like he was, the morons, playing with their lips too, furrowing, no wonder they were mere assistants, the sheep. And now he closed his eyes and fought the redness from his face, which made him look unimpressed and even irritated and went, —All right, Gilbert. Bring it in, son.

Gilbert smelled like armpits and hot feet on a courtside seat, back sloped and hands hanging between his knees. These seats would cost you around five hundred dollars each. And Gilbert was between two men—one of them the general manager, whose name he had already forgotten—who smelled like nothing.

They asked their questions slowly, deliberately, like bad actors forcing it: Where do you see yourself in five years? What do you want from your career? How do you feel about coming off the bench? And they raised their eyebrows and their eyes glassed over as he responded. It made him think maybe he was saying the wrong things. He shifted in his seat. He wiped sweat on his shirt, cracked his neck, noticed he had this habit of sort of stretching when he spoke, sat forward, cracked his neck again, plowed forward to just get through this.

The interview.

He wanted to express his ambition. He wanted to open his mouth and beckon forth his Light and let them see! And then they'd know why words came so hard to him, because words couldn't illustrate his future. His words were not true, but his Light was, and how could he show them this, how could he tell them that he knew, and wasn't it enough?

The general manager was the one immediately to Gilbert's right, with graying hair and a young face and tight pale lips. Gilbert imagined the man slept in his leather chair somewhere in an office overlooking the arena. Gilbert saw this man driving home late at night through deserted interstates to stand in his bare suburban kitchen in his enormous house, with his reflection in the sliding glass doors, drinking a glass of water. He was unmarried and alone, Gilbert thought. He didn't know what love was. It pleased Gilbert that the general manager wore an expensive gold watch. It gave him joy picturing the general manager ordering Chinese or consolidating his credit on the telephone.

He—the general manager—said, —I'll be honest here, Gilbert. I believe in honesty. I'm a straight shooter. That's how I run my organization. But your maturity is a concern to me. You're young. You're no doubt talented, but playing against teenagers is a lot different from playing against professionals.

—Oh, no. My dad's told me all about that. And I've been practicing with the Colonials every summer since I was a sophomore and.

—It's all so very tricky. Morally speaking. The money. I've seen kids just as talented as you come into the league. They get some money. Some fame. They listen to the wrong people. They get into some bad situations. Uh, it's not pretty.

—That's the thing though. I mean. You guys think I'm like just another player. I'm not. I know in my heart that like I'm special. I can be special. I'm different from all these other rookies.

—Sure. Without a doubt. But Gilbert, anywhere you go in this league right now they will tell you the same thing I'm telling you now. We're looking at years of development before you're going to see any real playing time. You're not getting any kind of head start on anybody.

—I don't know. I just want to win. I'm not a coach. Or a GM. I don't know what to tell you people when you ask me all these questions. I can't guarantee anything. It's like you need everything like proven beforehand. All I have is that I'm ready to work. I'm ready to play and I'm ready to win. I'll come off the bench if I have to. I'm going to make an impact in this league. If not immediately then eventually.

—Okay, son.

—I don't think anyone has any real idea what I can do. You think you do. I mean. Just because I didn't go to college. So? Maybe I don't need to? Ever think about that?

—Gilbert, I—

—I mean, like, I just want to win. You know? I want to give it my all and be the best. If I get drafted, man. I'd totally like take total advantage of the chance. Like. Not giving it my all in the Association? Man. Nuh-uh. I couldn't live with myself.

—Okay, son.

—I *can* play. I *can* win. I *can* be the best. Maybe, like. I don't know. Like maturity will come with time? You know?

—Sure.

—But ask anybody. I'm not my age. I don't act my age. I've always been very mature. Ask anyone. I'm more than an age. I'm very mature.

Ian Martin was quiet and biting his upper lip, arms crossed, staring at the door that Gilbert had disappeared through.

—I like him, a red-haired assistant said.

—Not me, said another.

—He's arrogant, the coach, whose name was George Manfredo, said, the one in the polo shirt stretched over a vast gut and man-breasts and khakis, a balding large head, the tallest of the ten and with the constitution of men who consume too much space. —I'm not putting up with that kind of shit. Ego the size of Miami. The kid thinks he's Darren Dickinson. Doesn't even bother to learn the game. Send him to college. Let them deal with his shit. I'm not babysitting him, Ian. I'm not.

—All right, George.

—If you're thinking about drafting him I'll walk. I swear to God. I won't babysit him.

—Shut the fuck up, George.

The Milwaukee Lobos hadn't had a big-name draw for years, since Lance Bolton in the seventies. And the team felt it in the revenue. There hadn't been a sold-out game once in all of Ian Martin's time with the club. But Ian saw Gilbert and saw merchandise, filled seats, and people in those seats screaming until their throats were sore, advertisers and national TV broadcasts, the taste of success. He had been a general manager in this league long enough to know that success in the Association wasn't measured simply by winning. It wasn't just championships the fans wanted. Victory wasn't what they wanted. Not really. Not entirely. He put his cell phone up to his head and turned his back on George Manfredo who was still huffing and puffing and now telling the red-haired assistant that he was not going to babysit the kid. Ian said into the phone, —Abe. It's Ian Martin, how are ya. I'll tell you what. That was the best workout I've ever seen. Spectacular. Yeah, absolutely. Mind you we're at number

four in the draft but if he's still there—without a doubt we're taking him. He'll be an All-Star one day. Without a doubt. Yeah. Listen,
I'll have my secretary fax you over some things and the whole nine
yards. Great. Everybody's very excited about him. Great. Yup. Okay.
Thanks, Abe.

Ian shut the phone and George was standing there holding his
long arms out with his mouth open like when he argued with the refs,
his sideline stance, and Ian closed his eyes and said slowly, —Shut . . .
the fuck . . . up . . . *George*.

Gilbert didn't like it that these men who meant nothing to him would
determine his career and thus his life. But, he thought, so it is, and I
have to accept that and work through it. He was proud of himself as he
boarded the plane back to Boston for having such a logical and mature
mind-set. It was the thinking of a pro athlete. For that's what makes
one great, one's thinking! A lesser mind would be hotheaded and focus
on the injustice of the system rather than his playing. A lesser mind
would whine to his agent, throw tantrums until maybe even quitting
altogether—death. Can't let them kill you. Gilbert wanted to play and
wouldn't let a handful of air-conditioned businessmen get in the way
of that. I accept it, he thought. I accept everything. Nothing shakes me,
work through everything. The professional.

To exist above. To conquer the flaws of man with his ability and
drive. Untouchable and bulletproof.

After landing at Logan and walking through the terminal, all eyes
on him though no one knew why, he got a call from Abe Birnbaum,
his friend and agent. —I talked to Ian Martin. I don't know what you
did up there, Gilbert, but they're salivating. I can hear it in his voice.
You really knocked them on their butt. Good job. Every team in the
league has heard about it by now I bet. But sit tight, son. You're not
going to Milwaukee. Not if I have anything to do with it. Who the
fuck decided to put an Association franchise in fucking Milwaukee,
Wisconsin, is what I want to know. Let's just say I have my problems
with the limitations of that particular market. Sit tight. We're just
heating up here.

Gilbert had to ask Abe to repeat himself because a guy walked up
to him in the middle of what Abe was saying and went, —You a basketball player or something?

Gilbert went, —Uh, yeah. I'm on the phone.

—Who?

What?

—Who you play for?

—Um. No one. The Lobos, maybe.

—The fucking Lobos? Heh. More like the Lo*blows*.

But the word was out. Abe's phone rang nonstop in the ensuing days, and Gilbert found his hand turning into the vaginas of Latina maids in Detroit, Toronto, San Antonio, Minnesota, Atlanta, New Jersey, New York, Seattle . . .

He left Sandy as a ghost in their decaying hometown which would never be worth anything and shot off around the country, a traveling salesman, always the stranger, sneaking into cities under the cover of night and fleeing before the sun set again, feeling his skin shed off as the ground dropped from the belly of another metal flying object, the roads mapping themselves and trees turning to toys and imposing buildings going going gone, existing in the air now, an angel, weightless and carried by the whims of the wind, ears popping beneath his headphones, death the earth and home an ashen skeleton filled with dirt, darkness the past, the future the only life, as the draft prospect ascended toward mach speeds.

Escape . . .

As Abe told him on the phone on his way to board the plane for Dallas, —The city's huge. Big market. And now is the perfect time. They're rebuilding. They're looking for a star. A foundation. Someone to give an identity to their franchise like, I hate to say it, but like what Dickinson did in Detroit. So that's you. The future. Only problem is their pick in the draft is so late you might not be around by then. Don't worry. We'll see what we can do. Tell Jeffrey I say hello.

And Gilbert went there, met Jeffrey, the Dallas general manager. He was a nice if quiet little man. He was a legend. He actually also designed the Association's trademarked logo on a bus ride to Chicago back in the early days when he played for St. Louis (now New Orleans).

Dallas!

The city pumped with sex and death and cash and fame and oil. He aced the interview, pleasing Jeffrey he could tell, who came from Boston like Gilbert, only Jeffrey came from gritty Irish South Boston. They understood each other. They spoke the vernacular of champions. Jeffrey picked him up personally in a black Lincoln Town Car outside the airport as Gilbert waited at the curb among the taxis, bag in hand. And as they drove through the city slowly, all that life on the streets, a world that never existed till now, Gilbert knew every beautiful oil-fed female body here was for him. The bodies grew up on pedestals in their small towns in the plains, the prettiest and most popular bodies, and the bodies left their boyfriends to come here for success in the Big City. But in the chaos of the city the bodies only found themselves tossed atop the heap of other beautiful bodies and they'd offer the bodies to him, the famous basketball star.

—What do you think of Dallas? Jeffrey said in the car, loud, saying *Dallas* in a Texas twang.

—Man, Gilbert said, looking out the window with a semierection, blue sky endless, a breeze calming everything. —I'm staying. I'm not going home. I'm staying.

And he and Jeffrey laughed, the future and the past.

How could he ever have said he loved her? They were so young. They hadn't lived yet. This was living, right here.

As soon as he noticed one body, another would come along and he'd forget all about the first body, and this went on over and over, without end. It wasn't the desire to actually have sex with all these bodies scampering to and fro that consumed him. The need was to make THE BODIES want GILBERT MARCUS, to be attracted to GILBERT MARCUS, to crawl into the bodies' darling little heads and settle inside the bodies' distracted little brains and exist there, indelibly. He hoped that he caught the bodies' eyes but that they didn't let on, because bodies like this couldn't afford to, and that the bodies hoped he would approach them but when he didn't it made the bodies want him even more because the body must not be beautiful enough for him (maybe her stomach was not flat enough, or her ass was too flat). Which made the body want him. The bodies would notice him more because he ignored the bodies. He wanted to be the center of the bodies' pink perfumey world. He wanted the bodies writhing for him. He wanted to turn invisible and go up with the bodies into the cute matching bedrooms with lace curtains and teddy bears and the tiny outfits hanging in the closet and who knows what other kinds of wonder.

He walked past the Dallas Convention Center with Jeffrey and some of the other Lonestars front-office guys after his workout and headed toward a restaurant with a purple-illuminated waterfall on the wall where they serve you a chunk of lettuce as an appetizer for the interview. The waitress was dark and cut through the room like a cat. The body was thin and the tits were huge. Gilbert knew he would be caught staring at the huge tits and so kept his eyes on his plate when the body neared. He ordered so quietly and quickly that the body with the huge tits had to lean over close to him and the hair brushed his hand and he repeated himself, stuttering. The tone the body with the huge tits spoke with changed, suddenly the body was above him now, as the body asked, —Excuse me? And he humbly repeated himself. But what now? How do we escape from this? The alienation of untouchable beauty, unrequited desire, the humiliation of being a man? Exposed and your nature sinful and insulting, wrong and criminal though beckoned and manipulated, your attention undesired, repulsive, threatening, though called upon and asked for. Gilbert curdled under the shame, and as the body with the huge tits walked away he prayed he wouldn't end up here in Dallas. It would tie him in a knot. He longed for Sandy. The comfort of her. He was sorry he had said to her, —God, you're such a whore. He wanted to be back in his bedroom in Hingham where he could wake up early and jog through the golf course, away from all the bodies. Unfailing and safe from the unmerciful torment that all women were bent on inflicting upon him.

Afterward Abe called him and said, —Jeffrey said it was the best workout he's ever seen in his life. Gilbert, this is it. I've been around long enough to know when it's it. And this is it. Listen to me. He said we've got to find a way to get you to Dallas. And I agree.

Good ol' Abe, trustworthy and loyal, blond hair barely hanging on to his spotted dried-out scalp, nose hairs curling from his nostrils, an aardvark, is what he reminded Gilbert of.

How could Gilbert tell him that he would rather die?

* * *

The Meadowlands was a sudden enormous structure bursting from the flat expanse of concrete that was New Jersey. Backstage at a round table with a card in the center with his name on it, in the greenish Italian suit, blue and black silk tie, so dashing and handsome, Gilbert sat between Sue and Mervin, both dressed for church as well. Abe Birnbaum sat alone across from them, always alone, and with a phone up to his head, unafraid of tumors.

He watched the Milwaukee Lobos—who picked fourth—pass him over more than an hour before, and his hometown Boston Colonials, who, even though Coach John McNeal had been fired the year before, could have chosen him eleventh but didn't.

He knew then he could never go home again.

He began to wonder if he had made a mistake and should have gone to college.

It was Washington's pick. Then Dallas had the next one. He hadn't worked out for Washington. Though he'd been there on vacation with his family when he was eleven.

He would go to Dallas with the bodies and the body with the huge tits would ask him to repeat what he wanted to eat because he'd stuttered.

His gut sank.

But then the ESPN camera crews that until now had been circling the room like sharks began shuffling over to his table, and over the public address The Commissioner of the Association announced, —With the nineteenth pick overall, the Washington Grays select . . . from Brenton Prep Academy . . . Gilbert Marcus.

Then he was onstage, blinded by the lights, wearing the hat of the Washington Grays, whose colors matched his tie, like he'd planned this, like this meant something, though no one had, and destiny.

But this was not Gilbert. Onstage now was his twin, from graduation. It was The Athlete. Gilbert watched and admired The Athlete from the side of the stage. The Athlete looked just like him. Only The Athlete looked better than Gilbert Marcus. And The Athlete acted better than Gilbert Marcus. And a sensation bristled Gilbert's skin as he watched The Athlete shake the little Commissioner's slimy claw and bare his healthy white teeth for the cameras, the little Commissioner (a Jew, Mervin pointed out) licking his slobbery lips with dried spittle in the cracks and his bug eyes watery and dull behind the retinas, like a frog. Gilbert was alone and transfixed by his twin, The Athlete, who was so poised and noble amid the flashbulbs turning him into an object and preserving him forever. Sue cried, confusing The Athlete with her son, Gilbert. Mervin stood with his hands in his pockets winking at The Athlete from the wings, also confused. He had them all fooled. Grinning like a minstrel. Gilbert was proud of his trick. The half-empty arena smattered with applause. Gilbert could see Abe with a finger in his big old man ear with things growing out of it barking something into his phone and throwing his hands around.

So proud. So *proud*.

Gilbert Marcus, the Washington Gray. *Gilbert Marcus's Washington Grays.*

Not *Gilbert Marcus's Dallas Lonestars.*

It sounded like it was fated from the origins of time.

He'd been right all of his life. It had all come together. The stars had been for him after all. There really had been a Light. All was right in this wonderful world. How could anyone ever be unhappy, he thought, in this perfect world? Where good things happen to good people?

He was with The Athlete as The Athlete proudly walked offstage, happily, but cool, and said into the spongy red microphone held by Dan Patrick, a short man also in a suit, smiling up at the mighty tall Athlete, charismatic and positive as he responded, into the camera, —I couldn't be happier to be a Washington Gray. It's a dream come true and I look forward to getting my hands dirty and helping my new team win a championship. Or a couple.

Thank God for Washington, D.C., magnificent little square district, warm and rife with charm and culture. Museums to walk the halls of. All those historic monuments and things to learn about. He would become cultured. He would become an expert on American politics and law by surrounding himself with senators and maybe even the president. He would talk to them about policy. He would remember what he learned from them for his own political career on which he would embark after basketball.

Washington, D.C., splendidly ugly D.C., without bodies with big tits who made him repeat his order because he stuttered. Washington, D.C., had gross, wretched bodies with magnificently pale skin and the heavenly fat rolls and the blessedly small uneven tits! God bless small uneven tits! He would call Sandy, he would apologize for saying *God, you're such a whore.* She would forgive him and they would get married, live in D.C., she would be his First Lady. And he could say when he was expected to fuck a body with big tits in order to keep the guys' respect for him as a man, —Not hot enough for me. Nose is too big. Don't like the hair. Just not good enough for Gilbert Marcus.

Washington, D.C. The name was salvation, like music on his tongue as he stood with his parents, the hat on his head that was the same color as his tie. Has there ever been a prettier name? Washington, D.C. He could sing it all day. Washington, Washington, Washington. Thank God for good ol' Washington, D.C.

Because basketball players are not soft . . . Because basketball players are not quiet and never stutter . . . Because they are never unsure . . . Because they have no insecurities . . . Because they beat their chests and holler hanging from rims, balls swinging between their legs . . . Because they're never alone . . .

. . . Because their skin is thick and feels none of the shards of being alive.

But his is thin to the point of transparency and feels everything.

Because the point is to swallow it all down deep, so your face is object, eyes animal's.

Shut off your insides, because.

And they have to approve of you and respect you and you can't stand out.

Put a target on your back and use it against you in the court of competition. Because you must glare steel.

Because you must become of the pride.

Because you must be a man.

Time to try to do some work.

Abe, smiling, politely pulling The Athlete away from Dan Patrick and from the throngs of congratulators, and saying, —Take that stupid hat off.

—Why?

—You're bait. That's why.

—What? Bait?

—You're not going to D.C. You're not a Gray. They got you for trade bait. That's it. They don't really want you.

—No, sure they do. They drafted me.

—Okay. Then why are they telling anyone who will listen that you're a malcontent. Exact words. That you'll never fit in there?

—No way. They wouldn't do that. They drafted me.

—Son. I hate to burst your bubble here. But just be aware that a trade is in the works. Okay? Washington wants a center. A veteran. They don't want a project and plus they view you as cocky and cold. They got you to dangle you for a center who is a veteran. That's what they do in this business.

—Meat.

—Don't take it personally. It's the business. Get used to it. But listen to me. Keep smiling. Those cameras over there. Listen. Forget D.C. because the Dallas Lonestars want you more than they want to breathe. Jeffrey's exact words to me. The *Lonestars*, son. Much huger market than Washington and closer to L.A. too so you can take some of those movie offers you've been getting. And you can do more endorsement spots from Dallas. Just hop on over to L.A. and hop on back. Live in L.A. if you want to even. Just buy a condo in Dallas for the season. *Dallas.* It's what we *wanted*, son.

—Oh. Great. Great, Abe.

—Think about that though, Gilbert. How does that feel? Soon you'll have the money to buy not one but two very high-end pieces of real estate. I'm expecting a deal any minute now. Dallas has a guy D.C. wants. Ford. I won't tell them he's a bum.

—Yeah. Cool. Very . . . cool.

—You're gonna be a Lonestar, Gilbert. They're building the franchise around you. You're the sleek new superstar that'll bring in the fans and T-shirt sales. They're already calling you the next Darren Dickinson. Do you know how much power you'll have around there if you, excuse me, when you start winning championships? Hoo boy. Forget about it.

—Wait. You're sure?

—I'd bet my ass on it. My *ass*, Gilbert.

—Well. Okay. Hey Abe?

—What is it, Gilbert.

—Um, I was just thinking. Is there any way that . . . I don't know.

Can you like call Jeffrey and ask them not to do that? Can you call Washington and say that they should keep me? Tell them, I don't know, maybe that I really am mature. That I'll do my best to act grown up and do some work and help win ball games?

—Are you out of your goddamn mind, son? What the hell's the matter with you? No. No way in hell.

—Okay. Forget it.

And though they both smiled, clasping hands, Abe's eyes still looked at him like a new person, an unexpected sinner. It was disappointment, suspicion. And the relief draining from Gilbert like on the autopsy table.

To put the guilt to rest, of failed responsibility. To do what is expected of a man. To do what he is required to fit in, become one of the team. Since he has never fit in before. Not one day in his life.

PART TWO
The Athlete

The Man Who Has It All

THE WORLD IS FULL OF PEOPLE. Inhabited by ones who have paired off in order to love each other and mate. The earth contains a bajillion people. Here come two of them. Here comes your Athlete and his regal model wife, who is in *Sports Illustrated*'s swimsuit issue, out of the limo and down the red carpet at the Hollywood movie premiere. A certain percentage of people stand out in order to be observed by the rest who don't, and it is directly important what they do and how they look. How the wife looks is good, on The Athlete's arm, both in sunglasses and she in a pink tight top that shows the public how big her body's tits are. Her hair blond, eyes green, lips red, skin cared for, good tan. A gorgeous firm young couple, bodies fit and primed for reproducing strong dominant-gened offspring. And she quiet and eager to let her husband shine in the spotlight in loose-fitting clothes like one of the actors in attendance here. Breezy and relaxed garments of light colors. Here they go down the gauntlet of photographers who shout their names so they may put their image onto glossy pages of gossip weeklies for sale in the checkout line for purchase by the ones who are not gorgeous and do not stand out.

The Man Who Has It All: good looks, a great job he loves, unheralded success in his field, victory, recognition, wealth, a wife any man would cut off his big toe for a night with her TV body. The people's choice!

Here for the movie premiere, the latest film starring his good-looking young actor friend, the bad boy wunderkind with the reputation for fashion-model tomfoolery, The Athlete here to show his support for his movie which will sink like a dead body in theaters and gather dust on rental shelves, its DVD sales boosting in a decade when it has become ironic and funny among college-aged boys.

She clings to his arm. He doesn't find himself enthusiastic about screwing her body anymore as he stands with her smiling for photographers yelling their names so they can put their picture into grocery stores.

12

A MAN EXITS A PLANE. A TWENTY-seven-year-old man on business was up over the clouds thirty-one minutes ago and now he is on the ground in Las Vegas, stepping off a plane. He wears sunglasses that are classy brown and round, the delicate understated sunglasses of an older gentleman, suggesting he is precocious or that he wants others to think so. He wears a tucked-in red polo shirt that is wrinkled in the back from sitting against vinyl in the same position for an extended period of time, and pleated khaki pants, the seat of which is wrinkled the same way the red polo shirt is, the cuffs tailor-hemmed and gathering perfectly over wingtips of a darker brown. A baseball cap with prefolded brim and "TITALIS" printed on it, an inexpressive mouth, thick lips, two lobeless ears, smooth, hairless baby face. The white wires of a pair of iPod earbuds dangle down his neck and he has a thin mustache and the white wires of the earbuds go into the neck hole of his shirt where they merge into one near his abdominals, which are well-defined and flat, coming out again at the tail of his red polo shirt where they plug into a white iPod toting along deep in a spacious but otherwise empty right pocket, putting a solemn violin concerto into his ears.

Of rectangular proportions is a black zippered bag with a flap of material covering its zipper, a functionless piece of faux leather hanging from the key of the zipper, at the center of the front of the bag, which follows at the man's heels by way of a retractable plastic handle extending from its top and gripped by a freakishly large hand, dwarfed, the bag is, by the size of its owner, made mobile by two small plastic wheels on the bottom so that when tilted the wheels go into motion and glide the bag—which is more of a soft box—and its contents—athletic shorts, a couple pairs of clean undies, four T-shirts, shaving kit, toothbrush, deodorant, vitamins, portable enema kit, lemons—pretty much without sound except for a muffled windy noise made by the suitcase's wheels on the carpet which is thin and blue-gray and covers the also angular and square accordionistic tube connecting the exit of the plane to the entrance of the airport terminal. The man himself, considering his abundance in height, is an orbit of attention. He is a well-built grand spectacle of a man. This is not helped by his being flanked by three men an inch or two shorter but way, way fatter—two in front, one in back—each pulling along his own suitcase on wheels. There is a set of four quick clicketeys-clicketeys as each pair of wheels bumps over the metal strip that bids farewell to the accordion connector tube and greets anew the gauntlet of the terminal.

Beneath the khakis the man's average-sized penis is folded into itself and his testicles are cupped snugly—smelling of Gold Bond medicated powder—inside a pair of gray cotton boxer-briefs with the manufacturer's name repeatedly expressed in white stitch-print along the elastic waistband, never before worn. On the left ankle, a flesh-colored—though the flesh of a white man, whereas his flesh is not white—a flesh-colored brace holds secure the pieces of splintering bone and strained ligaments of his ankle together, giving his walk a bit of a limp that is noticeable only to athletic trainers or doctors and doesn't hinder his step. Mere static emits from the earbuds wedged in the outer hole of his ears like paper crumpling.

The plane was small with no commercial logo on it. The flight attendant on the plane was polite with big tits but forty. His bodyguards have been hired through a company called Terrence and Sons and they are all wearing sunglasses too though theirs are black and more sporty-looking, curvy and wraparoundish. Two black and one white, speechless, serious, and without humor. They are the only passengers deboarding the plane that eat ten people and had personal satellite TV portals, a bathroom with a bidet, wood toilet seat, two built-in speakers pumping in TV audio, potpourri, an array of long skinny tubes of lotions on the sink, and where the man, famous all over the world, the spokesman for a major soft-drink company, majority owner of a major West Coast hip-hop label, winner of four Association Championships, owner of the record of the youngest player ever to appear in an Association game, the youngest All-Star ever, the youngest Rookie of the Year and youngest league MVP, multi-multi-multimillionaire, youngest All-Star Game MVP, youngest to score 50 points in a game, who once scored 50 or more points in 8 straight games and 87 points in a single game, where the man before the plane landed dropped his khakis and the snug boxer-briefs and dangled his bare ass over the toilet with bidet without coming into contact with the wood toilet seat, grimacing because of his ankle, and, carefully, laboriously, and to the soundtrack of a popular sitcom, took a neat and admirably formed dump.

It is nighttime and there's a wrinkle in his sock. He did not pay for the sock but received it free from the athletic shoe and clothing company (same thing for the boxer-briefs) that pays him millions of dollars a year to wear their products and that also owns 4 percent of General Electric and 12 percent of Viacom. The wrinkle in his sock made it difficult to sleep on the plane, and he did not remove the shoe and straighten it out because he has a thing about taking his shoes off in public (he considers even a chartered airplane public). Stragglers in the terminal are weary-eyed and tired of motion and wish for home but cannot deny the presence of the four men, which is actually felt intuitively—almost *heard*—before it is seen, the man in the middle with his head down aware of the exposure strolling briskly by. People read articles written by Harvard alums in political and (waningly) literary magazines and they glance up from these glossy magazines they sorta regret buying at the newsstand so they'd have something to read on their flight because in all honesty they don't really understand what they're reading and when they glance up they see the man who has exited the plane. Their eyeballs move in their sockets and their feet stop twitching atop their knees, and they nudge their companions and raise their eyebrows like, Is that somebody? A foreign man with a brushlike mustache and big eyes behind the register of a newsstand does not notice. He stares through all the people at some far-off point. One of those oversized golf carts with orange flashing lights and chirpy beep driven by a whistling black man swerves around the men without slowing down, nearly running over a sixty-something woman, who, judging from her face, was already bewildered by everything before nearly being run over by the oversized golf cart with orange flashing lights and chirpy beep. The air-conditioning is on too high, even for summer. Nipples protrude from tank tops and T-shirts. Sullen teenage girls who hate their little brothers walk with their arms folded in front of them while in the crotches of men's jeans and shorts penises shrivel and scrotums tighten, the man who exited the plane's included, though you wouldn't know it from the way he walks, which is detached, aware. The terminal is heavily inhabited and slot machines whir and clink. People carry around open containers of alcohol happily. There are napkins and ticket stubs and discarded food containers on the rug. People wait fifteen, twenty deep in silent impatience with carry-ons over their shoulders, lined up and waiting to board. Unintelligible cackled intercom speech comes and goes but to the travelers it means nothing, they stare off into space, watch the digital screen that repeats in red scrolling light-text the number of their flight and when their flight departs and the name of their airline. People look out the window, they look at their shoes, they look at the head of the guy in front of them. He passes a group of five strangers standing shoulder to shoulder with heads tilted and mouths slightly agape in front of an eight-bunch of TVs with flight information in multicolored rows of text. One at a time they look away, check their watches, wander off. A heavy woman runs by, shrieking. For this season, which ended four days ago, he earned $23 million in base salary, plus his many endorsement deals, plus an All-Star Game bonus and a bonus for playing in 75 percent of the games and a bonus for averaging over 28 points per game and a bonus for not getting injured during the regular season and an installment of his signing bonus which is spread out over four years. He makes on average around $81,500 a day. He'll get more next year, as he will for each year he stays with the team, which, unless they for some reason they decide to trade him—and they wouldn't—he will.

Sheldon Washington, the human moon waddling to the man's right in a black size XXXL T-shirt cascading down the multiple rolls of flesh that make up what he calls his torso, breathing so heavily and audibly through his open mouth that one feels for his heart, stuffs a hand into a pocket and comes out with a cell phone that is playing 50 Cent and opens it and mumbles something along the lines of, —Hello? At which point The Athlete reaches into his own pocket as if inspired or reminded by Sheldon, looks at the LCD monitor of the tiny portable white music-playing device, uses the thumb of the same hand to push a silver slim button, then stares, still walking in his cocky gait, pushes the button again, looks up, slides the device back into his pocket.

They pass the security stations, where people remove their shoes and allow strangers who are earning a bit more than minimum wage to poke around their crotches and butts because they have a wand and wear a uniform. The people whose crotches and butts are poked around in make no fuss about it because they recall recent Tragic Events and are vaguely grateful for the charade of intensive security and are eager to remove their shoes and have their crotches and butts poked so as to display that they are alive. He passes the entrance of the inner-airport Hilton (which, as passing a Hilton hotel always does, makes him think first of Paris Hilton, then of Paris Hilton's sex tape, *One Night in Paris*, which he owns and has watched dozens and dozens of times; in fact, it might just be his favorite porno of all time) where on the other side of the window wall, like a display, businessmen in suits and polished wingtips examine newspapers and drink coffee, remarking to one another about the facts they find in the newspaper. They are cross-legged and composed, hair parted carefully and faces scrubbed into inhuman masks of eternal youth. A middle-aged woman on a cell phone sitting alone in an outfit that might have been designed with females fifteen to twenty years younger in mind ignores an older Spanish-looking waiter who approaches her table and lays down a fruit salad, nods, leaves. She switches ears and pokes through the food with a fork as she talks, impaling a fork-load of fruit salad but only to hold it chest-level like she has forgotten it's there. Then the smoke room and then gray men, ignoring the girls with Southern accents and rooty hair lighting menthols and waving them around excitedly as they talk to one another about being a dental assistant, legs crossed in the girl way, sandals hanging off a big toe with a silver ring on it and chipping polish, twitching. Europeans with enormous backpacks chatter in their native tongues passing a group of preteen girls standing with their arms crossed in their pajama bottoms habitually catching their lips on their braces and popping their eyes wide at one another as they talk, mouths awkward and pouty in repose, in matching white T-shirts that tell you in blue lettering that they are a soccer team. Their coach, a man in his early thirties who seven-eighths of the girls will marry when they are twenty-one and have graduated from college and are dolphin trainers argues at the ticket counter with a heavy black woman who is telling him that the effort to gain what he wants is futile, she has the power, she's in charge and the situation will not be solved. The man, who is The Athlete, has no hair on his chest beneath his wrinkled red polo shirt save for around each nipple where thin shallow-rooted hairs impersonate a child's drawing of the sun. His face can grow maybe six or seven hairs, tops. A trail of hair begins two inches above his belly button and gradually thickens on its way to his crotch. His skin is an ashy hue as it always has been. There is baby-blue lint in his navel. Three members of the twelve-year-old-girl soccer team stare at him as he passes with his mini-entourage. They suck on their braces. They know him. They don't know why they know him. Posters with his image hang on two-thirds of their bedrooms. They will marry him if they don't marry their coach. They don't know this. And the rest of the girls see them staring and so they stare too, but none of them knows that he is who he is, the concept not occurring to them. The confidence with which he carries himself—almost tangible, the practiced filtering out of attention so exponential he must ignore it. The walk of an important man with affairs to attend to. How he has chosen to deprive himself of the sense of hearing by choosing deafness-by-music shows he cannot be bothered to experience any of this right now, as it doesn't matter to him because this transient point will disappear when he exits the terminal and reaches the destination at hand. He is the opposite of those staggering around the terminal with a blank gaze and nowhere to be. All of this is designed so that he blends into airport terminals. His lack of eye contact eliminates the chance to be remembered. Despite his physical impressiveness, he is another traveler sick of traveling, hurrying through. He walks with hurried step past the bar where one white man in a baseball cap and khaki shorts sits with his back to the action. The man at the bar bounces his knees and rests his sandaled feet on the crossbars of the stool, hand on a half-full mug of beer with a napkin beneath it onto which he has poured a small amount of salt in order to keep it from sticking to the mug, talking into a cell phone, and watching *SportsCenter* muted on the TV over the bartender's head and he needs a shave and says into the phone, —Nuh-uh . . . as The Athlete is for a moment both on *SportsCenter* and passing behind him.

Three weeks ago the Dallas Lonestars missed the playoffs for the first time in The Athlete's career. It was the fifth year in a row they failed to win the championship, after previously winning three in a row (a fourth would have solidified their place in the upper echelon of historic teams). When they lost the must-win final game of the season that would have put them in the playoffs, the live TV cameras captured The Athlete lying facedown at center court, not moving, jersey over his head, as his opponents blurred past him, and he stayed like that for so long that eventually the team trainer went over to stick his finger under his nose to make sure he was still breathing. The trainer nearly knelt in a puddle of urine The Athlete lay in. The Athlete, it became clearer, was pissing himself. The commentators made a stammering half-assed effort at explaining away the substance pooling around The Athlete's body before giving up, calling him disgusting, apologizing to the viewers, demanding that The Athlete be punished to the full extent of league sanctions against peeing yourself on the court, reminding everybody that there were children watching, apologizing some more, and eventually cutting away to commercial. The footage nonetheless was replayed ad nauseum on *SportsCenter* and *Pardon the Interruption,* and *The Best Damned Sports Show Period* and ESPN News and CNN and Fox, etc. Bill O'Reilly denounced Gilbert peeing himself on the court on his blog. Keith Olbermann applauded it, simply because O'Reilly denounced it. *SportsCenter* is still—three weeks after the fact—devoting, on average, seven minutes a show to the topic, bringing in experts, covering new developments in the story (though there have been none), putting together a montage of memorable instances of athletes urinating on the field of play (many more than you'd think). Gilbert Marcus peeing himself after losing that game is already widely considered the most shocking outrageous moment in the history of televised sports since Ron Harrington smashed an ESPN camera all over the court during a game in Milwaukee, nearly starting a riot.

The man who exits the plane and walks through the terminal of the Las Vegas airport has a heavy Grande Complication watch on his wrist that cost four hundred thousand dollars. His undies and red polo shirt and everything else he wears were delivered to his doorstep two months ago in a package and last night he finally got around to sitting down on his enormous brown leather sofa which stuck to his skin to cut the box open with scissors and he pulled out the garments, individually wrapped in plastic, manufactured and sent by the athletic shoe and apparel company with which he has an endorsement deal. He put the clothes on when he woke the next day with the limo already waiting idle for him in the driveway to take him to the airport so that he could fly to Las Vegas and invest in a new casino. He looks like he is dressed in someone else's clothes. The fold lines are still prevalent and the chemically new-clothes smell is still rich.

Larry, the white bodyguard, front right, walks with his arms down but away from his body in the way of men with bloated muscle mass and high blood pressure, his bone-colored denim shorts past his knees and revealing surprisingly skinny legs. He points up at a sign that says TAXIS with an arrow pointing left, and so the four men take that left and follow Larry who now has assumed charge since he pointed at the sign and steps onto a downward escalator beneath another TAXIS, this one with an arrow pointing down, their wheeled suitcases beside them, each standing there descending on his own step, until Larry grumbles something and grabs his bag handle in his stunted fist like a baby's and thumps down the steps, and the other men say nothing and follow suit.

When The Athlete lay there pissing himself on the shiny hardwood court, before tens of thousands of people, and millions more on TV, some of which are in this airport, he was sweaty and dirty, the cameras sending up to the sky to satellites then dispersed throughout the country and beyond images of the champion in his moment of failing. This man's darkest moment displayed before the entire world. The team that eliminated them from playoff contention was unglamorous and undeserving, but they were a team, and The Athlete finished sixth place in the MVP voting—a *shock*—and—midway through the season—was not selected to be a starter in the All-Star Game for the first time in his career. The Athlete was filthy then but now is clean and here he comes, the past behind him—how impressively athletes can forget failure and move on—through the grayer and less accommodating lower level of the airport, past the baggage claim covered up by its metallic skin, the abandoned car-rental stations, ignoring the sleeping bodies, parents pulling their sleepy children by the arms, out through the automatic sliding doors and into a concrete world of nighttime outside an airport, his wife at home with the baby, her dreams of being an actress dashed and her country album forever in progress, taxis lined up a quarter mile long, a shuttle bus zooming over the crosswalk, a man in a suit smoking, a police officer leaning against his patrol car eyeing the four men, bored but attentive and picking his teeth with a toothpick as his radio squawks ignored. A heavy buzz of distrust generates from the veins of the sidewalk, echoing in every human and automobile standing along the curb in the sort-of-terrorized weird new millennium.

The Athlete stops when his bodyguards stop, and Will, the other black one, is saying something to him, so he takes out an earbud and raises his eyebrows, like, *You've disturbed me.*

—Limo ain't here.

—Fuck, says The Athlete. —Why? Where is it?

—I don't know. Said they'd be out here.

Sheldon Washington says, —Yeah, but security won't let them just fucking sit out here.

The Athlete goes, —Fuck.

Larry (the white one) says, —Let's get a cab, man.

Will goes, —Let's get something to eat is more like it.

Larry (the white one), —Why don't we just get a cab? Fuck it.

The Athlete says, —No. Call them. Fucking call someone. Do they know who it's for? Tell them who it's for. Tell them it's for me. Tell them it's for fucking Gilbert Marcus.

On the flight to Las Vegas he has a headache, but when the flight attendant who has big tits but is forty asks him how he's doing today he still mutters, —Fine.

The headache is a secret grip of pain that he almost likes. It was creeping up his spinal column as he sat in the bucket seats in the private VIP terminal back at LAX, L.A. being his home in the off-season, awaiting departure, his foot twitching and staring at an electrical socket wishing he'd thought to buy a magazine. And now it, the headache, has fully ruptured atop the radius of his skull like an egg cracked over his head, and if he'd remembered a magazine then it would make it better maybe.

Onboard, he tries covering his mouth with his fist formed into a makeshift chin rest, reads the warning again on the fold-down tray that says to keep it upright on landing and takeoff in order to take his mind off the headache. He listens to his iPod but the headache has turned his earbuds into applicators of invisible shards of glass, feeding violence into his brain. The music forces him to imagine the process of making music—which exhausts him and makes him feel ill. Midair the headache is now so severe that it is doubling his vision. It pushes from the back of his eyeballs. Thank God he sits alone. You have to take what you can get.

Struggling to maintain this goodness when the flight attendant's body comes along with its big tits, the makeup accentuating the age wrinkles around the mouth of the face, the stockings on the calves, blue skirt wrapped around the ass, telling perhaps by mistake that she has the droopy ass of a forty-year-old hotel-room adulteress, which sways into bathrooms and steps gracefully into showers, reaching the hand out with raised veins on the back of it to adjust the water, making room for the married man she's with. She likes rich older men and chicken salad and expensive benefit dinners. The Athlete puts all his waning energy into a dig-deep surge of positivity, everything now depending on what the flight attendant's body thinks of him.

It started that night three weeks ago when the buzzer rang which meant there was no time left in the game and the opponents had more points than the Dallas Lonestars and jubilation ensued around him. The Athlete stared up at the giant cubic scoreboard hanging from the rafters, blinking, trying to comprehend the meaning of the scoreboard, and slowly understanding. Nobody seemed willing to *do anything about it*! And as the reality revealed itself, his body began to shut down, and he couldn't remember feeling like such a child, so helpless, alone, the overwhelming emotion as the frustration of the world crept in, realizing that he had been alone his whole life. He calmly knelt and pulled his jersey over his head and lay down at center court, and felt himself pissing. It was hot. He was aware of but numb to the cameras at center court filming The Athlete, who disgusted him. He used to admire him. Not anymore. He strove so hard to become him. Why had he wanted this? He couldn't remember. He was reminded of a little boy in Utah, scolded in the bathroom for not knowing he needed a pass, the yellow teeth of the male teacher whose name he can't recall inches from his face, barking in a language he didn't understand, while the other boys went in and out whistling, ignoring his predicament, going about their lives in joy because they knew the rules—the death of it all was where it came from, like a tube stabbed into the base of his skull to drain the blood.

The buzzer. The buzzer was what did it. Instantaneously after that

buzzer the headache crept in. First the headache, then the loss of blad-
der control. It was the buzzer's fault. What if there had been no buzzer?
Then what?

To the reporters who asked the now dry-eyed and somehow
showered Gilbert Marcus clutching his temples and massaging them
uselessly, the Dallas Lonestars locker room eerily quiet, he said, —I
feel terrible. I've never felt worse in my life. I never want to feel this
way again.

Winning is life and not winning is death, but either way there is a wife
(speaking of headaches). His wife is Austrian but she was born and
raised here and she has fake tits but you can barely tell. She's a model
and is pretty famous but hasn't modeled since they got married, especially with the baby. Her body is beautiful, white, and in shape and
brings him much respect and envy. Her voice is relatively pleasant.

For the next three weeks after that loss he floated around his comi-
cally large house in gym shorts and a T-shirt, teeth unbrushed, body
covered with an increasing layer of grease, mysterious lint in his un-
washed hair, going outside only to feed the tiger and fly his pigeons.

He eyed his wife who actually seemed to be happier now that he
was down—doing her makeup while he suffered, singing along with
dumb TV commercials while he suffered, making goo-goo faces at the
baby and squealing with delight while he suffered. He spent hours on
the couch, glaring at her, grumbling to himself.

All she had to say after the Disaster was, —I'm sorry baby . . .

The baby cried when he picked it up and it stared at him like he
was a stranger. His own child.

He watched TV, hand down his shorts, eyes closed, volume off, a
warm wet rag on his forehead that he had to locate, wet, and apply
himself because the wife was always either shopping with the baby
with his money or talking on the phone with her hot but insufferable
sisters and laughing, while he suffered.

Is she not my wife? Is she not supposed to take care of me?

How could she love him when he was a failure? Shouldn't a model
who is in the *Sports Illustrated* swimsuit issue rather be with a win-

ner, someone happy and successful? Didn't she deserve someone who was more *perfect*?

He would come across himself on TV, by chance. He would be on the news, or on *SportsCenter*. He liked watching himself on TV. Sometimes he'd be watching TV and would see a clip of an Association basketball game and see a guy who looks familiar, until it would hit him that it was *him*! The Athlete!

This was one of the only things that put him in a slightly better mood.

Brianne, his wife, found him once staring at a news segment about himself on CNN, remote held midair and jaw open like he'd paused in the middle of breathing. She asked him what was wrong, intrigued by his eyes which were wide and skitterish but blank. It was as if she'd walked in on something secret, but she wanted to help her husband, who seemingly nothing could reach when he got like this.

He said in a monotone, so quiet she could hardly hear, —I'm trying to imagine what it's like. Watching from a stranger's point of view. I have this feeling. Watching it. Sort of a feeling of dread. Danger. Like I shouldn't be doing this.

—You probably shouldn't be.

—I know. But if you think about it, maybe it's pornography. Maybe this is porn. A type of porn. I'm taking pleasure in myself. Only it's not that kind of pleasure. A different kind. Because watching him makes me feel uneasy.

—Him?

—Like I'm dizzy. Or wobbling around. Like I could collapse.

And poor Brianne, the blond beautiful girl, holding the baby, patting the pudgy stinky baby on the back, looking from her husband to the TV, without a clue.

On the plane to Vegas, from the depths of pain brought on by the headache, suddenly he finds himself thinking of his father, Mervin, and his mother, Sue, and that perhaps he and his parents are no longer family but are merely strangers now. Like everybody else. He doesn't need them. He doesn't need anybody. The Association has people to help him with his finances, his personal assistants wake him up on time, his personal chef cooks his meals, his maids do his laundry and clean, Abe Birnbaum gives him career advice, he has his financial adviser to put together business deals like this one for him. His parents, it is clear, are unnecessary.

When he told them he had given an $620,000 ring to a seventeen year-old blonde white swimsuit model they moved out of his house and across the country back to Hingham.

The shock is considerable. The comparison between now and then. Past versus present. Once he was a member of a family that was so tight as to clutch to one another as they moved through the world. But no more. The suddenness of the amputation makes him wonder if it wasn't a dream, and if it was real then if it really mattered since it could be gone. His family was grown out of and tossed out like old shoes. Were they betrayed that he wanted to start a family of his own? Or had they wanted to pick his wife for him? Did they feel it was their business to arrange his marriage and select the best candidate to vehicle the next line of Marcus DNA carriers? They would interview families, do credit checks, call references. They would set up the special wedding-night bed in the living room and sit beside it in chairs drinking tea, cheer them on, congratulate them when they were finished, rush her off to the bathroom to check her uterus for signs of life.

They threw themselves down in front of his Mercedes as he pulled out to go propose to the seventeen-year-old white girl and he called the police to have them moved out of the way. When he came back he was engaged and they were gone and so was all their stuff, which wasn't a lot since most everything in the house he paid for, so fuck them, he was Gilbert Marcus.

His new fiancée was with him. He walked inside first, she behind him, and she went, —Where'd your parents go? He didn't answer and made himself a bowl of triple chocolate ice cream with gummy worms in it, asked her if she wanted some, she said no thanks, and he asked her if she wanted to watch *The Wizard of Oz*, his favorite, but she said maybe later. His fiancée watched him eat the ice cream, then when he was done he left the bowl where it was and she followed him downstairs to the basement, where he turned on the TV and flipped through the channels, and after laughing at an episode of *Seinfeld* and asking if she wanted to have a water balloon fight (she didn't), he turned to her, undressed her, had sex with her on the couch. During it he was thinking of his father and his mother. He slammed away into her, grunting and sweating, feeling nothing, choking for air and telling himself how many men all over the world had masturbated to her picture in French *Vogue*. But it didn't work. He kept looking over his shoulder for the presence he felt in the doorway, and she went, —What's the matter?

—Nothing. Just tired I guess.

—It's okay if you want to stop. Really. I don't mind.

—No.

—It's okay. If you can't, it's okay.

—Can't? Can't what?

—You know. We can try again later.

—Can't? No way.

But he finally rolled off her and lay there beside her catching his breath, sweat cooling his face. —Mommy, he said.

—What'd you say?

But he didn't answer. He rolled over so she wouldn't know that her husband—her *soon-to-be-husband*, the famous athlete—was nearly crying, desperate, pretending to sleep so she wouldn't try to talk and hear the tremor in his voice. He lay in silence listening to her breathe for hours.

The first time with Brianne Marcus, before she was Brianne Marcus (aka The Wife), when she was just Brianne Kuld. When she was seventeen years old.

Also the first day he met her.

He met her in the second half of his rookie season (the Lonestars in the thick of the playoff race) on the set of a photo shoot for a print campaign for a new line of candy bar he was endorsing. She was in bra and panties, on a toilet, while he stood in front of a sink brushing his teeth with one of the candy bars.

Gilbert approached the girl during lunch at the catering table as she stood in a thick fluffy robe picking over the fruits and whole grain crackers that Gilbert's contract stipulated had to be there. He knew right away, by looking at the eyes.

And he knew, as they sat through the movie he took her to afterward, that he could cling to the body because the world was so full he couldn't keep them all straight, sometimes he felt like he was the only one and the others were just sent to poison him.

Drove her back to his house after the movie where he snuck her in through the back door, disarming the security system, Mervin and Sue asleep, and fell into the perfumed neck. She smelled like girl, the soft

bare thighs wrapped around him, guiding him along as if by instinct—
she was made for this. He sucked on her tits and pulled off the condom
as he felt the orgasm approaching and collapsed beside her with his
knee up to conceal his withering horny as she giggled and reached for
tissues. And how she STARED at him. He could feel the big green eyes
burning into the side of his face, not dimming even when he stroked
the head and kissed the cheek, like she had just been defiled and now
she watched him to make sure it'd been worth it for him.

*Are you pleased? Now that you have taken from me what you
wanted?*

The perfect teeth, exfoliated skin, like cream. Crusted white spots
all over the sheets. He dropped the condom and flushed, leaving a
sticky chemical slobber on his horny, and on her face lay the residue of
the damned, smeared like fingerpaint and drying.

There was instantly guilt, mixed with the pleasure of conquest.

When he came back from driving her back to the house she was
renting in Huntington Beach with her parents he balled the sheets up
around the wads of tissue she'd used, which he fished from the trash,
and stuffed it all into an old gym bag and in the morning threw it into
a bin behind the private athletic facility where he worked out when he
was in L.A. A janitor saw him but The Athlete glared at him, daring
him to comment so he could have him fired. And the next time he was
in L.A. her parents wouldn't let her out of the house so he stayed home
and masturbated to her memory. That she said she was a virgin shocked
him. No way in hell. But it made him want to marry her—she'd fended
off the hornies of every male in the fashion and modeling industry
since she was twelve, resisted the gorgeous male models' charms and
tricks, the skeezy producers' lies, the dirtball musicians' drugs and bullshit. She'd outrun the wolves somehow even in her jet-set coke-and-
heroin phase with lesbian actresses twice her age coming on to her at
raves, attractive young actors bringing her to orgies. But the ass had
been put on earth for The Athlete and no other. The body had budded
breathtakingly immaculate for his hands only. She did her countless sit-
ups for him, starved herself for him, the tight skin, the blond hair, for
him for him and for him.

Picked her up from the beach a week later where she was on location
for a shoot for a new GlaxoSmithKline erectile dysfunction medica-

tion. He waited for her in the parking lot in his Range Rover and saw her walking out beside a black dude who whatever he was saying made her laugh, and the guy's hands were almost brushing hers. So the decision was made and the next day when she walked with the black dude whose hands were almost touching hers and climbed into Gilbert's Range Rover with her backpack and kissed him hello, Gilbert reached into the glove compartment and pulled out a ring and put the ring on the finger, and said, as the eyes blinked into comprehension, — This cost six hundred and twenty-eight *thousand dollars.* The next day when he went to pick her up from the beach she did not walk with the black dude almost touching her hand whose name, Gilbert had found out by hiring a private investigator, was Aaron and was the photographer's assistant and had been telling Brianne that he was in serious negotiations with a totally big-time producer to direct his own feature film.

It was his reason to live.

His reason to live was composed of his wife's eyes and his own nose and eyebrows. His reason to live cried the first time he ever held it. And the big clear infant eyes roving accusatorily around the room, seeing everything in the wonderful new world—walls, doors, carpet—except its father, the human being half-responsible for his chance to be here, to ignore him. When he was born he held him close, wrapped warm and clean in the blankie, whispering to his reason to live, —We'll always be this close. You'll have a happy life.

He promised to the traffic lights on the way home from the hospital that he would be the good father, remembering his own father who was a coach. He wouldn't be a coach. He would be a father. But the baby didn't return his affections, cried whenever The Athlete came near, and so, hurt, he shut himself off from his reason for living, the rejection too painful. Knowing he was away too much and the coldness between them was his fault. His own father would disappear and be forgotten for days then plop back into his life to rearrange the rules Sue'd set, vetoing requests for expensive new shoes, throwing out candy and cookies from the pantry in exchange for bananas and wheat grass, dragging him out into the Boston winter dawn and making him play until sunset, a magnificently dire shadow in the doorway with an enema bag saying, *Get up, get dressed, go stand outside in the snow . . .* A stranger who his mother bowed to. A ruination of a person grasping for control. *I am losing control.*

Last night he tried to feed his reason for living but it wouldn't open its mouth and The Athlete was saying, —Come on, what the hell?

He wanted a beautiful family—a wife on one side, child on the other, for the charming photographs. Not this. Practically stabbing his reason for living with the mush-covered spoon shaped into an alligator when Brianne pranced in and gasped in horror and yanked the utensil from his hand and went, —*What are you doing to him?*

Brianne picked up The Athlete's reason for living and stroked the back of its bald little head until the crying ceased, glaring at him like he was a rapist, a loser, which fueled his resentment, blood in his ears, either cry or yell, and so he yelled, —You're keeping him from me!

—I am not.

—You hog him!

—Do not.

—Yuh-huh!

—He's a baby, Gilbert. What's the matter with you?

But he'd already smashed the jar of baby food onto the floor, and his reason for living was crying again, so he kicked over the chair he was sitting on, stormed out, went up to the bedroom, packed for his trip to Las Vegas, not speaking to either one of them between then and when he left.

Losing, everywhere he turned. Once he was a winner, now he was a loser. Do we not screw enough? Do I not screw her enough? Can I screw her more and bring us closer, and then if I'm closer to her she'll let me be closer to the baby. If I don't screw her right, someone else will. He thinks maybe he should buy her some lingerie. Some sexy red panties.

But he's stopped trying to touch her awake in the mornings, nor does he come from behind her when she's dressing and cup her huge tits and kiss her neck, because he knows the future, and the future is her sort of laughing and waiting with waning impatience for him to stop. The future is her groaning, —Gilbert . . .

Somewhere along the way he fell into a trap he had promised himself he would avoid—how can traps be avoided if you don't know you've fallen in until you're clawing at the walls?

* * *

When the man exits the plane these are the things he is grateful for: the earth that the retractable wheels rest upon; the concrete that has dried hard and keeps us all from sinking; the comfort of blackened acres plowed clear for expedient air travel. That's it. When the man walks through the terminal he is glad that he is a man and alive thanks to a woman, and he notices that for the first time since who knows when that he is not thinking about basketball; how this feels is like kicking off your shoes after an eighteen-hour practice and falling into your $35,000 sofa to watch TV in your empty penthouse in downtown Dallas. Thanks to woman. Puts in his earbuds and exhales and follows his bodyguards past the security station, impatient to get to his hotel and check in, take it easy for just one night in his life. He's earned it.

He found solace in his rookie year in the Association by drowning himself with the sedatives of labor. He channeled everything into his work. He came off the bench as a reserve but that was okay, good even, because that meant there was much more work to be done. The world outside the court was a baffling thing where no matter what he did he never felt a part of it. How did he fit into the baffling world? Only one way: as a worker. He stayed so busy all day every day: sprinting and working on his pull-up and crossover, studying film, talking to the press and showing them The Athlete's smile which they loved. It worked. All desire for the bodies—so close yet unreachable, not the first clue of how to go about attaining them, since he was not yet a star—were quelled. His life consisted of a holy simplicity. Silence. He was a monk. His life was stripped down to what mattered and was rid of what didn't. He stirred before daybreak and drove to practice and worked on living up to his hype. There was always work to be done to live up to his hype. And he was proud of himself for having the desire to improve. Coming home to eat the meals Sue cooked for him and playing video games in his room alone then jerking off so he wouldn't have to think about the bodies and how he had failed to sleep with the bodies that day. And in this way only was the world tolerable.

* * *

That first year, it was like Hingham had been picked up and dropped in Texas. He had Mervin and Sue living with him. They slept in their bedroom while he slept in his. Sue made his health shakes in the morning. He ran through his neighborhood while Mervin drove Sue's station wagon (a new station wagon—a Mercedes station wagon) and threw loose change at his head. He had basketball. Texas was a better state than Massachusetts by far—more sun, less snow, less stress. But it made no difference. It could have been any state. What difference did it make where The Athlete lived? He could have lived anywhere. Because he was playing basketball. It was what he was living for. He was rid of the mess of having friends in his life. He was cold to his teammates to keep them from being his friends.

But then, like a breaking of hot light from a chasm in the earth, lava seeping out to the city: BRIANNE.

He was starting by the time she came into his life. It was his second year. He was becoming a top dog, a leader bossing his teammates around, an All-Star. They were calling him one of the front runners to be the next Darren Dickinson. And he felt Darren Dickinson within reach. He could be him. He knew it. And so Brianne Kuld knew who he was when he introduced himself. He was a champion (well, not yet—but soon!), a winner. Her eyes cleared and her face relaxed. She smiled and held out her hand in return.

In L.A. where he had bought a house to live in during off-seasons to do endorsements, etc., he ran into Jay-Z and invited Jay-Z to his photo shoot the next day for a new candy bar that was supposed to give you energy, in order to be seen by people with Jay-Z. He'd never heard of the model whose name was Brianne Kuld but she was blond and beautiful and The Athlete hoped Jay-Z was impressed by the way The Athlete handled himself around Brianne Kuld. When Jay-Z let him know after a half hour (the majority of which, The Athlete noted grimly, Jay-Z spent on his phone) that he was taking off but to come down to this club tonight, he felt an acute disappointment that Jay-Z didn't say anything about being impressed with the way The Athlete handled himself around the blond beautiful model.

Brianne was created from the ashes of everybody he had turned from out of panic on the streets of Dallas then thought about when he got home later into a wadded-up tissue in his bedroom. What he had here was a one-time shot at rectifying every sinful failure to obtain the bodies, and this creature then had to be conquered or the guilt would eat at him forever.

He offered his hand and she smiled and took it.

Screwed her, didn't feel exactly right about it, but couldn't figure out why. And one day while taking her shopping on Rodeo Drive (letting her get whatever she wanted), he caught their reflection in the black one-way windows as they entered Chanel Boutique, and it looked right—The Athlete and The Model.

She was proof that he spun the planet on his finger.

She was the final piece of It All.

And he remembered the picture of Dickinson on his wall back in Massachusetts, and he thought, She'll do.

Held the door for her as she went in, waited uncomfortably as she left him by himself to try on clothes. He stood there not knowing what to do with his hands, staring at racks of women's clothes, ignoring the leers of the salesgirl who may have been a salesboy.

He married her, his parents objected, she gave birth to a baby.

The strangers are a challenge to his peace. The strangers all look the same. The strangers might as well not have names. Graying mustaches and ball caps, goatees and shorts and tennis shoes without socks, toting along their children as a decoy—upbeat men with midlevel managerial positions who think they know sports and want to offer him their hand to touch and give him their name as if it costs him nothing to hear it, unaware that being forced—by common decency, no doubt— into conversation with a person he doesn't know anything about, who could be insane and decide The Athlete must be stabbed to death right here in this airport—a stranger whom he doesn't know anything about but who knows everything about him. The Athlete isn't as excited about himself as the strangers are and so the conversation forced upon The Athlete by the fan who approaches him in a public space— such as this airport terminal—will die off in a lull because the fan is now self-conscious but not sure why—he knows only that he does not like The Athlete anymore, and will from here on out mutter and sneer from his easy chair during Dallas Lonestar televised games and heroically boycott the stadium.

It is a weird feeling, knowing that people out there you will never meet specifically hold something close to hatred for you.

He's tried hello, thanks, thank you very much, I appreciate it. He's tried everything, but nothing is enough. It is a stressful way to live.

You can never be alone. Some of the other Lonestars like it though for some reason—they smile and shrug if approached at a restaurant, like Elden, for example, the guard/forward, who goes out to crowded shopping malls and amusement parks with the specific intention of being recognized—walking around making eye contact with everyone, his eyebrows raised, as if to ask, —Know who I am?

But for The Athlete it grinds him down so much the upper part of his back near his neck hurts.

The fan will always jump out in front of him with his hand out, asking him something from the get-go to reveal that he already knows who he is, like, —Nice game the other night. But where'd those refs go to school, eh? Ref School for the Blind?

Wanting to touch him, for him to like them.

The Athlete can't help but consider the situation a bit homo-erotic—their gaze, their nervous chatter aimed at pleasing him. Which makes things even less comfortable.

This is why he will default to his confident man-smile and deep voice, looking at something over the fan's shoulder and go,   I don't know, the refs are okay. They try their best.

Why he'll stay distant, give them little. He'll scribble a half-assed autograph if there's a kid, which there usually is. Without a kid the fan is a pathetic man. But with a kid the fan is an honorable father.

—Hey, thanks a lot, sorry about this, but my kid really is a big fan and you know how kids are, eh? By the way, nice game last night, but where'd those refs go to school? Ref School for The Blind?

And if he walks away without giving them all they want, he knows what they will think: I pay lots of money to go see you guys, I pay your ridiculous salaries you spoiled pricks all of you, I spend a lot of time and energy supporting you, so I think I deserve at least a friendly hello—needling into The Athlete's back without relent. You owe me.

And that will make the headache come back and is why he wears a hat and wears shades and avoids eye contact and doesn't have to tell his bodyguards anymore, who spent the ride playing poker, as they enter the terminal, —Walk fast.

Thank God Brianne's never had the nerve to ask him, in postcoital secret-telling when the endorphins are swimming and the pillows fresh and sheets smelling of sweat and spring and they are safe in each other, how many girls he's been with before her.

If anything, she jokes. Never serious though. Never *really* wanting an answer. Naked and clinging to him, sometimes staring into the side of his face, with him oozing down her cheeks onto the clean sheets, requiring him to dig his nails into his palm in order not to get a towel to put under her or something, she jokes, never serious, —Hope that made you forget all those other girls before me.

Thank God because he is twenty-seven years old and has slept with only nineteen women counting The Wife, a disgusting and loathsome number for a man of his financial, physical, and professional pedigree, he thinks.

Thank God because the truth would lower him in her eyes. She *wants* there to have been a small national population's worth of girls each used for physical pleasure for one night then discarded.

The more there were, he knew, being smart, the more she would feel she had beaten out.

Where men like purity, girls detest it. They want their men experienced and desired, with quietly filthy pasts.

He blames partly his decision to skip college and partly for being half-Asian. Asian men, in his opinion, can't get laid to save their lives.

What kind of man am I? he thinks. Think Dickinson had slept with only nineteen girls when he was twenty-seven?

I owe more to my wife. She deserves a better man.

Will steps out of the airplane's bathroom and as he walks down the aisle back to his seat Gilbert reaches up and grabs his arm and says, —Will. Hey. I was wondering. You don't have to tell me if you don't want to. But I don't know. Like. I was thinking. I don't know much about you.

—Uh-huh.

—We spend all this time together. You've been my bodyguard for how long now?

—I don't know. A year.

—Yeah. See? And we never talk.

—You never talk to us.

—And I feel like I don't even know you. I think it's time to get to know my security. I've been busy and now I have some free time to relax and—

—I'm playing poker. What do you want to know?

—Okay. Um. Well, for starters. How many girls have you . . . you know. Don't laugh. Come on, Will. I've never seen you pull any pussy. You like girls, don't you?

—Fuck you, Will laughs.

—You gay, Will? You like dudes? Larry's pretty cute. I don't know if I can have a gay bodyguard. I mean what if you get lonely one night when I'm sleeping? I mean you see me coming out of the shower all the time. And I know I'm pretty and all but—

—Listen. Maybe if you gave me a day off. Why don't you throw me some of that Association pussy once in a while? Share the wealth.

The two men talking pussy on a plane laugh and Will rejoins his poker game.

That wasn't good, The Athlete thinks. That didn't go okay. Real men don't talk about it—only people who are hard up talk about it so no one thinks they're hard up, so Will, since he doesn't talk about it, probably isn't hard up, choosing self-deprecating modesty, which I've used before on Brianne but for opposite effect, telling her *No, there weren't that many . . .* in order to make her think the same thing I now think about Will. Or maybe Will is using the same technique I just used now, which is a sort of reverse psychology, as a defense.

But The Athlete's whole life is becoming a defense he realizes now, a shameful secret to protect, just another chump who has fucked only nineteen fucking girls.

His parents, the bed, movie night.

The house in Pacific Palisades, the night before a meeting with Juicy Fruit that he was dreading because there was no way he could ever endorse Juicy Fruit in good conscience.

In Mervin and Sue's bedroom, after the summer league season, before his rookie year, in the house he bought and which they all lived in, just back from Dallas and the four-week practice-season, the star of the Lonestars' summer league team who sold out even visiting arenas with his YOUTHFUL ENTHUSIASM and BOYISH CHARISMA.

It was like he just loved to play. You could feel the love of the game wafting off him like heat. How hard he played in these meaningless exhibition matches. He hit the court hard like it was the last game on earth. He dominated. He stole the show from all the other rookies who were each heralded in his own hometown and each of The Light and his jealous opponents/teammates then had no question about the hype and understood why all they ever heard about in their first interviews was:

How about this high school kid?

What do you think of this Gilbert Marcus?

Pacific Palisades was where the waves beyond Sue and Mervin's bedroom balcony crashed. The realtor had listed off the celebrities who lived in these parts like award nominations: Tom Hanks, Goldie Hawn, Eddie Murphy, Pamela Anderson.

The Marcuses tonight were watching Jack Nicholson in *A Few Good Men* on the enormous TV that Gilbert bought for Mervin and Sue's room.

Jack Nicholson lived two houses down.

Sometimes Gilbert saw Jack Nicholson in Jack Nicholson's front yard bending over with a plastic bag over Jack Nicholson's hand to pick up Jack Nicholson's dog's poop.

Sue entered, smiling, as she lightly shook a bowl of unsalted and unbuttered popcorn, popping a kernel into her mouth and wiping her hand on her thigh as she slid onto the bed with Mervin and Gilbert and went, —Did it start yet?

—No, the son said, —we were waiting for you. *Again.*

—I was making *popcorn.*

—All right, guys, Mervin said affably, pointing the VCR remote and hitting play. Mervin made grabby fingers as he reached into Sue's lap for a pinch of popcorn to hold in his hands and pick from. And the family on the bed watched a movie, the son whispering to the mother every now and then who that was and what was going on, because the mother was the type who couldn't follow movies for the life of her without getting confused and asking who that was or what was going on.

The ocean was an animal but the walls would bear the force. The waves would well up into tidal monsters forty feet high and wash away the town like toothpicks, and history would end, but they would remain, dry, because they had shelter.

Or not that night.

Rather, two nights later:

Gilbert went out to eat at La Bohème with Omar, who Gilbert had bought a $750,000 two-bedroom apartment right off Sunset Boulevard in West Hollywood with a simple recording studio in one of the bedrooms to help Omar get started in the music industry. Gilbert pulled out his cell phone and told Mervin that he was at La Bohème getting some food and the valet took care of the Range Rover so don't worry and he would be home later and Mervin thanked him for calling and Gilbert said, —Make sure Mom knows so she doesn't make too much for dinner.

—I'll tell her. I appreciate it, Animal. Have a good time.

And Gilbert called again when he was leaving La Bohème and told Sue that now he was going to stop by Omar's because Omar wanted to show him this new beat he made, so don't worry if he was home late, and Sue responded, —Thank you for calling, Gilbert.

And she hung up and turned over to her husband, Mervin, who was reading beside her in the bed with his new reading glasses on the edge of his nose and she smiled and went, —What did we do to deserve such a blessing?

—We *have* been blessed, Mervin said, closing the book *(The Prudent Investor's Guide to Hedge Funds: Profiting from Uncertainty and Volatility)*, taking off the glasses, and placing both on the nightstand, turning off the light, getting under the blankets and closing his eyes, spooning Sue, and saying, —He's still a good kid.

Those were the best times. Nothing like being eighteen in a strange city, so big that it makes you feel bigger, like you could stomp the buildings and burst through the sky, your future set, the possibilities endless, that first year when the sun was bright upon the west and the streetlights shone purple and pink, a city left out in the sun too long, with life and music and basketball, the ghosts of the city's pioneers sweeping up and down the blocks, walking dogs and stepping out of doorways puffing a pipe, the faded rich stucco colors of Pacific Palisades, in the shade, the cliffs and rocky hillsides with vines and trees growing over them, showing you what lies before your fingertips like a prayer candle, old women collecting cans in downtown L.A. and poor forgotten men wary and drunk working their way toward home in clothing disarrayed and glamorous.

—We still have some contract issues to work out that I can't get into at this juncture. As soon as my people and their people get everything straightened out, I'll be there. It's a business and I understand that. I love basketball and am very happy about having the opportunity to play professionally in the Association. It's always been a dream of mine and I look forward to getting to work on my career.

The coaches were frustrated. So were his teammates. Gilbert Marcus was holding out. He was staying in L.A. Even though the Lonestars ordered him back to Dallas to begin training camp. He'd signed a contract but it wasn't good enough for him. This was Abe Birnbaum's idea. Abe Birnbaum called him one morning and told him that he had decided his contract was shit and that he deserved more money than what he signed for. But the press held their fire, knowing it's a business, and that these people put their physical well-being and the future of their careers on the line every day. The act of getting paid to play basketball is gambling that you will be able to continue playing basketball. Their bodies are their meal ticket.

—I need the best contract I can get, he told the press. —I need something I can believe in so I can go out there and give it my all without any worries. I need to know that if something does happen I'll be okay. Only in that way can I play my best.

The strangers at home read about the holdout and thought, How can he complain about not getting enough money when he has a house in Dallas and one in L.A. and all his commercials I won't be able to get away from and in a month all the soft drinks I will buy will have his picture on them and my kids will be wearing shirts with his name on them and I bust my ass and live in a no-name town with a wife I am not happy with and a life I am disappointed living but don't have the finances or will to change and he says it's not enough?

Abe Birnbaum called with a message from another agent—a film and television agent.

—The model-actress Kelly Levy from your home state of Massachusetts, Abe said, —wishes to invite you to attend the premiere of the film *Terror Train 2*, her big Hollywood debut, to be her escort. Dress accordingly.

He had to think for a second but then he remembered—the blond beautiful girl. From the Brenton Prep prom.

It seemed like years ago. But it had been only three months.

A date was arranged, and they reenacted prom. Her doll-like features smooth as melting ice cream, radiant on The Athlete's arm in her custom dress, breasts noticeably larger, nose smaller, body skinnier, tanner, eyes now blue instead of green, smiling broadly and clutching the arm of the handsome modest young athlete down the red carpet outside Grauman's Chinese.

He laughed when she leaned in to his ear and said through her bleached teeth, —This is fucking torture. This dress makes my tits feel like they're gonna fucking *pop*.

Then afterward, she leaned up against him in the limo, their legs and shoulders touching, and he wasn't so sure where to put his hands, or what was what, remembering the last time they met. He didn't know what to do or what to say. So he put one hand on her back but on fabric so she wouldn't know how cold his hands were and said, —That was really cool. Your movie.

Kelly sort of laughed and said, —Whatever. It's just a start. You have to do shitty movies like that before you get the good roles. At least I won't have to suck any more cock to get an audition anymore I hope.

Gilbert couldn't tell if she was kidding and said, —I thought it was good. For real.

—You don't have to be embarrassed.

—About what.

—Prom. Boston. Don't worry about it.

—I'm not.

—Yeah you are. I was a different person then. Fatter, for one thing. I think we both can admit that.

—You weren't fat. You kidding?

—Please. We both were. Let's just admit it.

The Athlete with a semierection in a limo, not sure what to make of it. Kelly impatient with traffic and smelling like peaches.

—God, she said. —One day after I've made it and have my Oscars and kids and all that, I'm going to just lock myself up in my house. Never leave. Never deal with traffic ever again. I mean it.

Went to an after-party at the house of the director of *Terror Train 2*, whose name was Milo. Gilbert stood drinking grapefruit juice alone behind a tall fake plant while Kelly hugged and air-kissed and laughed uproariously with people who were very enthusiastic about everything. There were guys with graying ponytails in leather jackets, short young-looking girls with almost-white hair and huge tits and big raccoon eyes, tall men with their shirts barely buttoned, a fireplace, plastic cups with limes in them, women who were skeletons raising their chins and exhaling smoke, tanned brunette girls with sparkly tits and raspy laughs. The Athlete did his best to not appear lost. The meaning of this party was to defend yourself. He shrugged and apologized when an Asian guy around his age asked him if he could have a cigarette and Gilbert shrugged and said he didn't have a cigarette. Then Kelly reappeared and took his cup from his hand and said, —Okay, Milo is being creepy, so let's go.

He called his parents from the limo as he and Kelly headed back to her house, his hand on her bare fake tit where she had placed it, and he told his parents that the premiere was great and that they had an awesome time and that he saw lots of celebrities and that he was staying at Wayne Thomas's tonight because he was too tired to drive out to Pacific Palisades and Wayne Thomas lived nearby—Mervin and Sue liked Wayne Thomas, who played for Los Angeles, the shooting guard, the big-brother figure with a clean haircut, who'd been in the Association for a few years now so could help young Gilbert learn the ropes, a good kid from Boston (Roxbury—but still a good kid though), a former first-rounder himself with a smooth solid game who Mervin remembered trying to recruit to BC and watching him take UMass to the Final Four.

They went to her house and she took off her custom-tailored dress in her living room, and as she led him naked up the stairs and into her room she said, —I think you're cute.

He lasted about thirty seconds, rolled off her, and she went to the bathroom, and when she came back he said, —I can do better than that, I promise. And she kind of laughed and her parents lived with her too and were down the hall in their room, asleep, and there were pictures of her in beauty pageants all over the wall, a poster-sized photo of Kelly competing in the Miss Teen Massachusetts pageant, and she kissed him quick and said, —It was good . . . rolled over with her back to him, her ass in his crotch. He got out of bed as she slept and opened the door with a frilly pink curtain over it, stepped out onto a balcony overlooking a pool with leaves in it. He watched the sun wake the sky, adorning everything in fresh citrus shades. He went back in and stood watching the blond beautiful girl who he'd just had sex with. The first girl he'd ever had sex with. The first time he'd had sex. With a girl.

The surface of the pool rippled blue, and birds came to life somewhere unseen, and he felt familiar with this new life, somewhere between dead and alive, teetering on right and wrong, like the world was pulling him by the wrist somewhere nobody would tell him. Inside, Kelly was naked and curled up like a fetus on top of the covers, horizontal on the bed, and he tried to picture her as a little girl and went into her bathroom and stared at himself close in the mirror, expecting he didn't know what, but he remembered the ads, remembered saying, —I don't have a condom, and remembered her going, —Who cares.

He called her the next day because calling is what good men do. He was a good man. He called like a good man and he asked her if maybe she wanted to make plans sometime, this weekend maybe, or later, whenever, if she's busy it's not a big deal. But he knew from the way she sounded caught off-guard when he said it was Gilbert from last night that he had committed a grave sin.

She said, —Hey listen, can I call you back? I'm tired. I was taking a nap.

—Oh. Okay. Well.

—Yeah so. Let me call you later.

—Yeah. Cool.

He hung up, confused, and tried to call her back to explain that the reason he called before was not that he was clingy or anything, just that he was being a good man, so don't go around saying, like, Gilbert Marcus is, like, clingy and psycho or anything, but no one picked up, and he felt clingy and psycho, and he never heard from Kelly Levy again.

He saw this as further proof of the ugliness of the world, of which he wanted no part. Driven by the need for solitude from the ugly world, against Abe's advice not to, he went to Dallas and joined his new teammates in training camp.

Because of his contract dispute, Jeffrey wouldn't let him participate in workouts. He sat and watched his team and learned their habits. He called Abe Birnbaum three times a day to beg him to resolve the contract dispute.

—Gilbert, this contract is a death trap. I know what I'm doing.

Abe was crazy. He was going to ruin his career.

He tried to take advantage of this situation like a clear-headed professional would. He ignored the glares from Ben Jermaine, the enormous dreadlocked center. They called him Papa Bear. It was Papa Bear Ben Jermaine's team. They were already putting Papa Bear Ben Jermaine on the list of hallowed all-time greats. Jeffrey's master plan almost complete—everyone needs a big man, a battery, like Magic/Kareem, Stockton/Malone (though they never did win a championship, did they?), unless you're Darren Dickinson.

But I'm not everyone and no one told me my spotlight would be shared.

Papa Bear said to the reporters about Gilbert Marcus's contract situation: —The trouble is these kids want Big Dog contracts when they're not even Big Dogs yet. Small Dogs have to earn the Big Dog contract.

They eyed each other across the gym that first day, the Big Dog and the Small Dog, The Athlete alone in a folding chair on the sideline, Ben surrounded by younger admirers, dreadlocks like a bundle of snakes down his back, and Ben said to him from across the court, loud enough so everyone could hear, —This is a closed practice, bud. No fans allowed.

And the younger admirers laughed at the Small Dog.

Failure is knowing your father. A headache as a taste of the man who spawned you. The immediate beginning of mystery.

He's found an empathy for his father. He knows him and forgives him. He loves him. He acknowledges the suffering his father has lugged around on his back for the benefit of The Athlete.

A father must suffer. Without the father there would be no Athlete. The migraines the man must have endured, the love for his son too much for his cerebral cortex to handle, and his son ignores him and why?

Because of a *girl*. A *white girl*.

The Athlete, on the plane, clutching his skull, biting his lip, has a sudden revelation that maybe his father isn't wicked after all. He sees his own child, the human who crawled into this world through his wife's vagina to cry when his father picks him up.

He decides now as the flight attendant makes her way down the aisle that when he gets to the hotel he will put down his bags in front of the dresser and he will arrange his bathroom products (toothbrush, toothpaste, razor, cologne, deodorant, tweezers, etc.) in order of impor tance along the sink and he will sit on the edge of the bed and possibly—though he will have to think more about this—cross his legs and he will dial his parents' new house in Hingham and he will say into the phone, —I understand that you thought Brianne and I were jumping into things too quick. Perhaps we were. I understand. You were worried about me. In fact you were right after all maybe. I contacted a divorce attorney. Back in February. I just asked some basic information. Nothing final or anything.

—No no no, his father will say. —Listen, son. Don't do that. You don't want to do that. She's a good girl. She's the mother of your child. Take that into consideration please. Don't do anything just because of your mother and me.

—No no. Yeah. No.

—See, the problem was we felt we were losing you. We were losing our son is how we felt. You hold this family together, Gilbert, is the thing. We worked hard for you.

—I know you did.

—I guess we just thought that I don't know that maybe we were being replaced.

—Dad. No way.

—I know, son. But that's how we felt. Now though? I only feel proud now. Real proud. With everything you've accomplished. Maybe I never told you that enough. You've gotten everything I wanted but never got. You earned it.

—Dad, remember when I'd call and say I was going out with Omar? In L.A. sometimes before my first year?

—Uh-huh.

—Well, I wasn't. I wasn't out with Omar. I wasn't out with anyone. Usually I'd just drive around. By myself.

—That doesn't matter, son. Think that matters? I don't care, Animal. Listen. You have to try to keep your family together. It can be tough. Toughest thing you can do. Basketball isn't that important. But listen. Count on me to be there for you. My dad wasn't there for me. But I'll be there for you. No matter what. You're my son. I love you.

—I love you too, Dad.

13

PAPA BEAR BEN JERMAINE PLAYED like an angry overgrown child. The ball was tiny in his hands. His hands were meaty like a big puppy's paws. To The Athlete the name *Papa Bear Jermaine* meant a seven-foot three-hundred-pound creature from the dankest Mississippi mud raised unsheltered to scrape his knees and break his bones on the unpaved earth of stark simple poverty.

This was a man aware of his size.

The Athlete was nearly ninety pounds lighter than Papa Bear Ben Jermaine. He shrank farther when the man would peer down on him. Papa Bear Ben would barrel into the locker room preceded by his voice, a jumbled boom. He liked to palm the point guards' heads. The man reminded The Athlete, for reasons he could not articulate, of a slug. The Athlete felt unmanly, nonblack, around The Behemoth. The first time he saw The Behemoth in the shower he was shocked by the size of the man's balls. His dick was big enough to knock out rodents with. He kept glancing over at it until he was sure he'd get caught—

my God what a dick! With a dick that big you don't have any troubles.

It's clear from the start with some people who will be your friend and who will be your enemy—the waves you send each other.

It was such with The Athlete and The Behemoth. It was clear that they would never understand one another. It's even worse when you're bound by contracts. Loyalty to victory. Rely on one another to make each a winner. Gilbert tried to make friends—*whatever discomfort you get from this guy is your problem and must be overcome, so that you shall be liked. Not being liked—hated even—is almost as bad as losing.*

He said to Ben as they walked off the court one day after the first day of training camp, —Whew, this'll get you in shape in no time, huh?

Ben didn't answer, kept his eyes straight and made a grunting sound, lifted the corner of his mouth a bit.

—But I liked it, The Athlete said. —Though I'm not used to such extreme practices. Not to say I didn't expect this or am shocked or disillusioned in any way. Of course my body can handle it. I run six miles a day at least. In the morning. Since doctors say that's the best time to exercise, because the air hasn't been polluted by the day's cars and all that. Not to mention it's thinner in the morning and statistically cooler which makes working out easier on the body.

— . . .

—What I mean of course is that I enjoyed it. I was just commenting on its roughness. It will help us win, so I like it.

Ben sort of raised his eyebrows and grunted, not looking at him, and The Athlete became self-conscious and walked ahead so that he was first in the locker room. He put on his headphones and sunglasses and changed in the sanctuary of music and darkness, thinking, He likes me. He does. I'm crazy if I think he hates me. There's no reason for it. He likes me. Don't be crazy . . .

He spent two and a half minutes trying to decide whether to acknowledge his departure with a general good-bye to the room or to just leave. It would have been awkward to say bye and have everyone look at him like he was a moron for saying bye. But then again what if he didn't say bye and it turned out everyone says bye before they leave the locker room? He'd have to ask Mervin about this. But for now he chose silence because not doing something is easier than doing something. He left without saying good-bye to anyone and without a shower (still unable to face being naked with naked men and their balls). He drove home fast, biting his lip at red lights, praying that all the humans on the road would disappear so he could find peace. Showered at home, looked at his horny in the full-length mirror in his room for twenty-seven minutes before going to sleep, exhaling warm and long into the pillow and stretching his toes and spreading his legs beneath the sheets, taking up all the room he wanted.

He thought, They think I'm young but I'm not young—I'm older than anyone else my age. I'm not typical. Name one other eighteen-year-old doing what I'm doing. Maybe if I wasn't half-Asian I'd be more liked. Maybe if my penis was bigger I'd be more liked. I wonder what the average size for a penis is, or at least what is considered small, because I wouldn't mind just being average, though you can't go wrong with big. But what's wrong with eighteen, he thought? Who said eighteen was so young anyway? You can buy cigarettes (not that I would). You can get drafted into the armed services and sent to defend your country. I can be given a gun and be allowed—ORDERED—to commit murder so that Ben can continue to be free to be an asshole. I can sign up to do it. I can volunteer to kill and be gone tomorrow.

He imagined himself in the army. Driving a tank, creeping through the jungle, sweat dripping into his eyes, barking orders at his men, running with his machine gun screaming. Though not a girly scream but a deep brave scream, a war cry. Running through a forest, the last surviving member of his unit, an enemy helicopter behind him shooting missiles exploding inches from his heel. Diving off a waterfall, and swimming for days to sanctuary, keeping an eye out for the enemy but *making it*! Then accepting his Congressional Medal of Honor and shaking hands with the president in his hospital bed. He thought, Maybe I'll do that. Maybe I'll join the army. I'll ship out tomorrow, with no word or explanation, and everyone will wonder why I did it.

I'll refuse to talk to reporters, he thought, and then a war will start and they'll think of me. But I won't think of any of them. Then when I'm a platoon leader and leading my muddy men up a hill during a key strategic battle, I will jump on a land mine to save the mission and all their lives. My body will be sent home, there will be a grand procession through the streets of Boston. A monument will be erected in Washington, D.C., to remember me, and the president will call me a hero and challenge athletes to *be more like Gilbert.* That will become a national slogan: *Be More Like Gilbert.* And one day when Ben is washing dishes or choking a coked-up stripper in a hotel room, he'll stop and wonder if maybe he should've answered my observations regarding the difficulty of that morning's workout with something other than just smirking and grunting. He'll feel guilty. It will be the worst guilt anyone has ever felt. But there will be nothing he can do about it because I'll be dead.

And somewhere out there, as he spent entire games on his ass, in his warm-ups, holding out, no word from Abe Birnbaum about progress, staring off at the crowd, zeroing in on faces, crushed under the complex weight of all these people, cameras in his face until one of the assistants shoos them off (but hiding under a towel would make him be ridiculed in the papers and on ESPN), watching Coach and Ben avoid his eye during times the offense struggled, he could hear someone breathing behind him, lurking, an unignorable presence.

His face on the Jumbotron and kids wearing his jersey in the stands.

Imagined his mother in front of their old home in Hingham which had been sold to a woman who might or not be a lesbian (gone forever— his room, the kitchen, the toilet, the stairs leading down to the basement . . .), his mother saying to the reporters camped out on the lawn, —He says he can't tell you why he joined the army. He just says that he wishes you'll respect his privacy while he's in the army and leave him, and us, his family, alone. That is all we have to say at this time.

Tattoos all over his back and up and down his arms and on his neck. It was like a permanent shirt. He was covered in ink like smatterings of ancient maps that were curved and green and impossibly intertwined. That along with his hair made Papa Bear look like a savage tribesman. He had a thin wife who was sweet as pie who came up to the middle of his stomach.

Thinking of them screwing, The Athlete thought, Damn she must about split in two!

She would come to the games with the kids dressed in turtleneck and jeans and white sneakers smiling serenely. A wealthy black woman secure and protected by her large husband.

There were moments when Gilbert realized she was flirting with him. Gilbert would watch her and imagine what she would look like performing fellatio on him, getting his semen on her chin.

She wasn't here today. It was before a practice after which Gilbert would find that someone had placed a dead pigeon in his locker with a note that said "THIS IS YOU. "The two stars were posing for pictures in the gym. It was a photo shoot for *Sports Illustrated* set up by the Lonestars' PR department. The future was good as gold with these two as the foundation of the franchise, was supposed to be the message.

The Behemoth and The Athlete sitting on opposite ends of a seesaw as suggested by the photographer who was an uncombed graying man in jeans. The Athlete way up high, The Behemoth squatting and shrugging and making a face at the camera like, Oops . . .

The Athlete thought, The point guard and the big man, taking historic photos for the record books. The Dynamic Duo, perhaps they'll call us when we dominate the league for years and years and are spoken of in the future whenever there is a conversation about great teams.

The Athlete grinned wide, giving a thumbs-up to the camera. The photographer laughed at The Athlete giving a thumbs-up to the camera, which was good because The Athlete found it important to make the photographer laugh.

The Athlete called down to The Behemoth, —Hey. The Dynamic Duo.

—Hmph, The Behemoth on the other end of the seesaw grunted, raised a mouth-corner lazily.

—That's what we are, said The Athlete.

— . . .

—Okay. Don't talk to me.

— . . .

—What's your problem? The Athlete said. —You expect to come in here and be the star? Everyone to just move aside for you? Well, too bad. Because this is a team, Ben.

—Talk to you? Why should I talk to you? Why should anyone? You never talk to us unless it's to call for the ball. You think you're hot shit. You have no concept of team. When you get the ball everyone else should just walk off the court until you're done with it. But that's because you're young.

They both smiled and held their poses as the flash flashed.

The Behemoth said, —Ignore us on the court, ignore us off the court. Think you're Dickinson. You're not Dickinson. You're just a kid who grew up watching Dickinson on your big-screen TV just like every other kid. Lucky for you your dad played pro ball so he bought you all this equipment to play on. I know all about it. Everyone does. Let you play all you wanted, encouraged you, made you play all day. Boo fucking hoo. Never told you it was stupid and to not put your hopes into it. Didn't tell you you'd be better off joining the army. Lucky lucky. Otherwise you wouldn't be here.

—No, you're wrong because I didn't have a big-screen TV.

—And think being a good player means flying around making crazy-ass plays. You think you can win by seeing who makes the crowd go *oooo* the most.

—No I don't. I don't. I don't think that. People think I think that but I don't.

They smiled as the photographer took a picture.

—You're too flashy is your problem. You don't know the game. Too flashy. Way you hog the ball. Why do you think you never play? *Too. Motherfucking. Flashy.* You probably think it's because of Coach don't you. It ain't because Coach nothing. Of course he hates you. Everyone does. I can see why too. I don't hate you. I like you. But Coach'll put you out there even if he did hate you if you could help Papa Bear win games. If you got the ball to Papa Bear, you'd play. Know why?

—No. Why?

—Because this team is Papa Bear's team. That's the way it is. Because I said so. Feed Papa Bear the ball. Papa Bear's hungry. Feed Papa Bear.

—Whatever.

—Give Papa Bear the ball or get the fuck out of the way. Feed Papa Bear the ball, we win. Don't, we won't. Don't, then you're better off at school. Do some homework, learn something. Get a degree. Play some college ball, learn how to feed Papa Bear. Come back and show Papa Bear what you learned.

—I'm going to be the best.

—Yeah the best towel boy. You'll win MVF: Most Valuable Flop. Poster boy for stay in school.

The photographer said smile and they smiled. That evening Gilbert left the stadium without saying bye and drove around Dallas, yelling at his steering wheel. The city was hundreds of miles wide, spreading coast to coast, the only city on earth. There was always another turn, another person to look away from, always somewhere to go but never going home.

* * *

The picture of The Athlete and The Behemoth on the seesaw came out the next week in *Sports Illustrated*.

A boy in a baseball cap in suburban St. Louis saw the picture and became a photographer because of it.

A girl with braces in Connecticut who just had her first period saw the picture and became curious about basketball, got her dad to teach her how to play, took to it aggressively, a hideout from the terror of being an overgrown and pimple-ridden adolescent girl, got good, graduated high school with a full ride to an NCAA women's basketball power-house, was raped by one of the men players at a party, never told any-one, quit the team she said because she was not playing enough, lost her scholarship, dropped out of school, gained seventy pounds to make herself undesirable, an artery got clogged, and she died of heart failure in the bed she grew up in.

A young man in college, a virgin, came across the picture while flip-ping through the issue of *Sports Illustrated* after class, his roommate a subscriber, the apartment otherwise vacant, got an erection, admitted to himself he's gay, stopped balding, went on to live a comfortable full-headed life with a handsome balding boyfriend.

A white woman with a preference for black men read the issue in the abortion clinic waiting room and thought that the guy in the picture looked kind of like the guy who knocked her up, her ex-boyfriend who she still slept with, and so maybe the baby would look like him when it was grown, put down the magazine, walked out without a word, had the baby. The baby didn't end up looking much like his father but was about as intelligent, failed out of high school, became a mechanic and addicted to crystal meth, installed someone's new brake pads incor-rectly because he hadn't slept in four days, a minivan belonging to a married mother of three getting the car fixed before taking it on a long trip to Disneyland, and on the interstate somewhere in Arkansas in the dark the brakes gave out on a sharp curve and they crashed into a tree and the mother was decapitated and the husband and the three kids all bled to death on the interstate.

Then Abe Birnbaum called and the holdout was over. Gilbert would now be getting $657 more a year.

The next night: Gilbert Marcus's first appearance in a game! Which was for six minutes, against Minnesota. He took one shot which was blocked by Byron Guitierrez (a Light Baby who skipped college too four years earlier) and had a pass stolen. He had his first record: the youngest player ever to blow it in an Association game.

But then he became the youngest to start a game that January when Rashanti showed up in the locker room before game time with the flu and was puking up modern art.

And The Athlete huddled up around Coach and took the court for tip-off. He played for five minutes before he dribbled off his foot and Coach took him out in favor of Terens, whose idea of building team chemistry was to videotape himself with girls and to show the tapes in the locker room before games.

The game ended and he went into the press room and sat behind the table as usual to answer questions.

He told the reporters, —We won the game. That's what matters.

But that night at home in his penthouse in downtown Dallas Gilbert lay awake and winning didn't matter. What mattered was that he'd hardly played. And as he watched on the TV the game tape of The Athlete's performance that Mervin had taped for him, rewinding at his every dribble, the two shots he made—one off a rebound and the other a ten-foot jumper—the pass down low to Papa Bear Ben who turned and bounced it in off the glass, pausing it when he got the ball to see how he looked with the ball, he thought of all the people who rooted for him in high school when he was a star who had been watching the game on TV back in Boston. Mervin and Sue had told everybody to watch.

He wondered if Sandy was watching somewhere.

And as he realized that he should have gone to college he started to cry facedown into his pillow. He stopped crying and sat up, got out of bed, lay down on the floor, stared at the ceiling, stood up, and leaned on the windowsill in his underwear overlooking the city. On the TV,

The Athlete passed to Papa Bear Ben Jermaine who scored. Gilbert turned from the Texas skyline to watch the camera tighten in on Ben running back to play defense, sweating and huffing, long dreadlocks flopping, looking for the first time like not so much a superior male specimen in a world dependent on physical gifts but like a child. Gilbert watched as Ben pointed at The Athlete to say, *Good one.* And you could see The Athlete point back, *Yup.*

A rush of warm blood gushed through Gilbert's heart—it should always be like that, he thought as he turned off the tape and went back to the window where he watched his breath fog the glass in front of the silver moon, mother of madness and tides.

If we could just play all the time and never stop—a life lived on a court—it would be perfect.

Life would cease to be a trial to endure and something to embrace. There would be no death and no crime. God would have no trouble selling us on faith. All would flow smoothly, pulling and soothed by the moon, a perfect rhythm impossible to break, never pausing enough to say good-bye, pulling and looking back at the mark it made before turning around and diving back in again.

And then what?

Joy.

Saying to Kelly Levy that morning when she woke up and rolled over and saw him there, propped on his elbow, watching her sleep, —Why me? She kind of laughed, not that she was caught off-guard but like she'd heard this before. She shocked him by standing up naked, not draping the sheets around her bare body like he would have expected, and walking daintily across the room toward the bathroom. —I don't know, she said before she closed the door, —I just like basketball players the most I guess.

The chiseled mass of The Behemoth's body. A hairy soldier of Jah. The head a widening of the neck and the sudden appearance of face. Great cords of hardened hair wiring from his scalp and browning at the tips. A thick bush of hair dense as that on Gilbert's head spreading from chin to jaw. Shoes a feat of God's vanity.

Whereas The Athlete's body was pieced together in well-planned parts, a magnificent work testifying to the Lord's artistic perfectionism. There were two kinds of humans smashed together into Gilbert Marcus. Just like how he played. Both were composed of strategized whims, cuts as sharp as his face.

My goal, he thought, is to be a machine. The Behemoth's a messy wobble with no discernible theory. Slow moving and without surprise but unstoppable in terms of sheer power—

The sharpshooter and the tank.

Now that he was starting he wanted to stand out immediately. He had to. He wanted to make a statement. He couldn't make that statement without the ball. So when he got the ball he kept the ball and scored with the ball.

Method, he thought, coming up the court, is for the GOOD. Disposal of method is for the GREAT.

The goal of the game was to score, and he scored. The game must be won by any means necessary. If it wins, it goes. By winning he would be exalted by his teammates, respected, and liked. And years later in special shows on ESPN dedicated to his career these guys would say before a black backdrop, with sweet moving music playing, maybe a tear or two in their eyes, —Sometimes we wondered if . . . Well, I know this sounds crazy but we thought maybe this kid is some sort of modern-day saint. That kind of talent? And focus? It was unworldly. A lot of us guys, you know, liked to have fun in the locker room. We'd bust each other's balls, tease each other about their haircuts, you know. Having fun, bonding. But Gilbert Marcus always had bigger things in mind. We knew that right away.

Every time Papa Bear Ben Jermaine scored the Dallas Lonestars' PA guy played a deep and ferocious *ROAR* to the crowd's delight. When The Athlete scored he simply said, —*Gilbert Marcus!*

Gilbert sent a handwritten note up there during halftime of a game against Utah suggesting maybe the PA guy could say *hi-ya* or something after The Athlete scored, like a ninja. But the PA guy never said *hi-ya* or anything after The Athlete scored.

* * *

He got on the team plane back to Dallas after a road game, put his
headphones on. Tilted the seat back. He liked to get on the plane first
to make sure he got a seat all the way in back by a window where the
whirs of the engines would be loudest. Usually he sat next to the
trainer, an old man with black hair growing out of his nose named
Gary, who wore a navy hat with the gold crests on it and was usually
too busy drawing pictures of battleships to want to communicate with
The Athlete. But Papa Bear Ben bumbled aboard before Gary and
came down the aisle with a funny grin on his face, plopped down in
the seat beside him, put a meaty arm around his shoulder, burying
him in folds of sweaty flesh. His was an armpit whose depths no man
should ever know.

—Hey rookie, Ben said, pulling his face close to The Athlete's,
voice throaty and deep, like the effort required to enunciate wasn't
worth it, —you smell real good. Real clean.

—Leave me alone Ben, Gilbert said.

—You need some stink. I'm going to sit next to you the entire
flight and get some of our stink on you.

His breath smelled like weed or food. He was dangerous. His size a
potential liability should a wire come loose.

—I'm going to talk about fucking bitches and how I like to have
my balls tickled when I fuck bitches doggy-style. How's that sound to
you? You like your balls tickled too, Gilbert Marcus?

—I'm ignoring you, Gilbert said.

—Private-school faggot. Chinese motherfucker. You good at
math? You want to fuck my wife? I see how you look at her. How
many times a day do you shit? You're so quiet nobody knows anything about you. You jerk off? Do you fart? I see the way you look at
her. You dirty dude. You Chinese are into fucked-up shit, aren't you.
I've heard about you Chinese and your fucked-up raunchy shit you're
into.

Ben winced, lifted a leg, and farted. The Athlete tried to push him
away but Ben squeezed him tighter. He had him in a headlock. —Smell
that, Gilbert Marcus? Mmmm! You think you're better than us, don't
you. Way you don't talk to us. Are you a virgin? Mmmm! Smells good,
huh.

The Athlete closed his eyes and covered his face and The Behemoth gave him a noogie and said, —I've decided I'm going to make it

my responsibility to break you down and teach you how to play all over again. How would you like that? I'll teach you how to play with Ben Jermaine and you'll win a championship and get a Big Dog contract.

He farted again and said, —Might have shit my pants on that one.

—Fuck you.

—Oh yeah? Fuck me? I didn't know you curse. The golden boy says *fuck*? Does the golden boy poop too?

—Get your arm off me.

—What else does Gilbert Marcus the Golden Boy do?

—I'm being told how to play by a guy who just stands in the lane the entire game waiting for someone to give him the ball? The Athlete said.

—What now?

—I'm going to play how I play and you're going to get the big contract because of *me*. You stay down there and get my rebounds and stay out of *my* way.

—You're something else, Tiger Woods. If only your game was as big as your attitude.

—I'm trying to—

—I bet you woke up your first practice and thought, I'm going to act like Dickinson.

—I'm trying to—

—Maybe if I act like Dickinson long enough they'll think I'm Dickinson.

—I'm trying to—

—I bet you thought, Even if I don't become totally Dickinson even a piece of him is good.

—I'm trying to—

—You're fake is what you are.

—I'm trying to lead this team. I'm working hard to lead this team and get some wins.

—F-A-K-E.

—I'm trying to help this team win a championship.

—Yeah yeah yeah. Save it for the press conferences. You can't lead anybody, Gilbert Marcus. You're too soft. You're not Dickinson. You'll never be Dickinson. And if you do win a championship it'll be because of me.

—I said get your arm off me.

—No. This is my team. You play how I tell you to play. I earned this. I have a proven track record of success. You haven't proved or earned anything. Clean rich kid from the prep schools. You sure you're even half black? That's not just a tan or anything?

—If you don't get your arm off me I swear to God.

—This is my team, little guy. Little skinny Gilbert Marcus. You're young so you have an ego. It's okay. Everyone your age does. One day you'll grow up. Then you'll help Daddy win a championship.

The next game The Athlete played 42 minutes and scored 46 points, 8 assists, 7 rebounds. Won the game, and the next, then the next, etc. The Athlete and The Behemoth were a dual on-floor assault. Opponents couldn't handle them. You doubled Marcus, and Jermaine ran shop, and vice versa. They played off each other, high-fived each other, bumped chests and screamed at each other during time-outs (this was a good thing; it looked angry but warriors were mean when they were happy). He was voted a Second Team Western All-Star. He went to the Meadowlands in New Jersey for the All-Star Game, where it all began. He watched with a blank face as the Eastern All-Stars, the opponents, were introduced. Through the gauntlet of hands and shorts in warm-ups jogged Darren Dickinson, back from retirement yet again, to a standing ovation.

Behind the eyes of The Legend Gilbert remembers seeing a vague human—a man who could be hurt and often felt guilt and regret—who sinned and failed and had dreams of his kindergarten teacher—but before those eyes was a steel programmed weightlessness as he dribbled up the court toward Gilbert, who had been put in the game during the last foul and assigned to guard The Legend by Coach George Manfredo (who after being fired in Milwaukee then bought out of his contract in San Antonio, took Charlotte to the conference finals, and was now the coach of Philadelphia), who was coaching the Western All-Stars. In a synaptic flash devoid of color Gilbert remembered the videotapes, the picture on his wall, the commercials and fantasies alone in the darkened gym—all relics of a past now meaningless for now he crouched down to meet Darren Dickinson at the top of the key, trying to wash from his mind the marvel of how ordinary human beings can come into your brain and stop being human—they are now a THING that exists over you, threatening to storm, a finger on the trigger. Your life stops being your own and becomes the chase of a stranger's. This becomes clear once nose to nose with the physical reality—ears, jaw grinding gum, eyeballs darting, left ankle fat due to a brace under the sock—staring you down. The world shrinks. Our similarities multiply. What this was like for him, this was like meeting God. The phenom born of the sun whom the suits peered down upon from up in the luxury skyboxes with one hand pocketed and the other on a soft moist lip, tieless in pink shirts, observing their investment with giddy judgment. He became helplessly aware of how small he was and how little he had accomplished in his life. This was a despair that comes only with being younger than you are. He was caught in the glacial crawl of time so crippling that all he could do now was to deny his age and all truth. So he bounced up on the balls of his feet and tugged his shorts which he wore like The Legend wore his shorts. He played defense as well as he had ever played defense. Because the crowd was on their feet. And the reason The Athlete was in at all now was because The Commissioner, knowing whose blood they craved, had an assistant call down to one of the towel boys on the West's bench to tell Coach George Manfredo to put the kid in on Dickinson, saying, —They want the lions, then give them the fucking lions.

Dickinson blew by him, scored, and the crowd went wild. Some people booed. Others screamed that Gilbert Marcus sucked. Others screamed that Gilbert Marcus could do it. Gilbert was shocked to find himself not devastated by self-doubt but coolly relieved: the world was still the world. All was in its place.

He got the inbound and sprinted up the court, past the defense languidly jogging to their places (many hungover), switching hands to avoid them casually swatting at the ball, dribbled it behind his back, making the crowd go *oooo*, threw up a reverse layin as he fell over onto the shoes of a photographer from *Sports Illustrated* who would put the action shot into the next issue with Gilbert Marcus on the cover.

Dickinson shot a three-pointer over him and then Gilbert got the ball on the perimeter and backed Dickinson up all the way to the lane before hitting a turnaround fadeaway from thirteen feet.

Then Gilbert dunked it, hanging from the rim (but not long enough for a technical foul). Then he alley-ooped it to Byron Guitierrez, who had a shaved head. Then he crossovered it, juked it, tomahawked it, 360ed it. He left the game in the fourth quarter to cheers and no one screaming that Gilbert Marcus sucked.

Walked off the court wiping his face with the tail of his jersey to no high fives or butt-slaps from the other Western All-Stars on the bench. He glanced up at the scoreboard and didn't see that his team was losing—what he saw was his point total, listed along the side. He smiled at how high his point total was. He liked that his point total was more than the point total of anyone else on the Western All-Stars, even that of The Behemoth sitting at the end of the bench wearing a giant foam hand and paying a red-faced white fan behind him to sneak him beers in mini Gatorade cups.

He sat in a folding chair and accepted a fresh white towel draped over his shoulder by a Hispanic boy who didn't care. Kids leaned in grinning and screaming at him, as far as they could get over the railing dividing them, either hustled away or watched with passive pleasure by their dads. Though he heard them he pretended not to, because there was so much more work to be done, so far to go. And the kids did not know him. They were so naïve about that which they idolized that it gave him a tinge of disdain. *They don't even know what it is they're cheering for.* He was a man who was not smiling. He was The Athlete not satisfied with his performance. He was being The Athlete who was focused. The Athlete bent on improvement.

The Athlete didn't let on that he heard his fellow Western All-Stars on the bench saying to one another, —Somebody tell him this game doesn't count . . .

—Maybe he thinks all this is for him.

—He's young, got confused.

—Tell him to pass the goddamn ball is what somebody should tell him.

—Easy to score when no one's playing defense.

Dickinson got the MVP because it was his first All-Star Game back from retirement. Gilbert was vaguely hurt because he'd hoped that maybe he had earned it since he had scored the most points. As he made his way off toward the tunnel to the locker room to change (not shower—he'd shower at his hotel room, where Mervin and Sue would be waiting) and tell the press how much fun he had and what a real dream come true this was, a wet arm slapped around his shoulders and a steamy face breathed into his ear, —You having fun yet?

It was Darren Dickinson. When The Athlete glanced at him he

saw a few gray roots in his goatee. He carried his All-Star Game MVP
trophy in his hand like it was his lunch.

—Man, Gilbert said, —all of this is so crazy. I can't even try to explain it.

—The pressure's on. They're watching you. Sizing you up. Seeing
how much it takes to crush you.

—Nah.

—The question is how much will it take? It varies, but not by
much. You're just the newest one. Anfernee Hardaway. Harold Miner.
Where's he? What is Harold Miner? Right? Look at these people.
They're not paying to watch you play. That's not the game they like.
They watch to see what will crush you. That's the game. Balls and
hoops don't have much to do with it. The game is man versus machine. And every year their machine gets stronger and upgraded and
more deceitful. But what their machines don't have is heart. Or desire.
Like you do.

—I do. I do have desire. Yeah.

—Yeah, but everyone has desire. What's the big deal about you is
what you have to ask yourself. What makes *you* so goddamn special?

—Okay. So what do I do then? Give me some advice. How'd you
do it?

—You're smart. You'll figure it out. If not they'll push you aside
and someone new will be along next year. The next savior. I've had this
exact conversation I can't even tell you how many times. Next time,
who knows? Maybe the savior will be eleven years old.

—Ha ha. Yeah.

—That's the thing about it though. There's always someone new.

14

AFTER THE ALL-STAR GAME GIRLS on the road began wanting him to sleep with them. So he slept with them.

To become dirty like Papa Bear Ben Jermaine and his teammates so that they would win a championship, he started smiling back at the bodies in clubs and restaurants who recognized him and wanted to meet him. He began making them laugh with smartly placed one-liners. He was confident of his good looks and kept in mind as he spoke to them that he was The Athlete and was great.

It took practice because he choked for words around them. But then he learned that they didn't care what he had to say.

One day you look up and this has become your life. This is you now, you realize.

* * *

Everything was going along handsomely with a girl in Sacramento when she suddenly made a noise and went, —No. Stop it.

At first he fought her a little bit, thinking that this was a weird kinky thing she was into and that she wanted him to restrain her, but then he thought about Allen and jumped off her holding his hands up like after a foul and said, —Whoa.

Allen was one of the players' assistants who traveled with the team, with no discernible job description beyond saying very little and standing out in hotel hallways all night checking IDs of any girls who happened to come back with the players. The other half of Allen's profession was entering the room if he heard screams and cleaning up whatever mess he found there. Allen carried a checkbook in his back pocket whose checks drew from an account at a Dallas bank under the name Rachel Green funded in part by unclaimed Lonestar cash from food and beverage sales—his mop for Big Messes. One of the first times Gilbert traveled with the team there was a commotion in the hallway in the middle of the night and he stuck his head out to see Allen inside an open door of another room, Ben Jermaine sitting on the bed naked with a pillow over his crotch, smiling and playing with his new lip ring, the TV on full blast and a bubble machine blowing bubbles throughout the room while two naked black girls with bruises on their legs scampered around picking up their clothes and cursing and threatening to call their cousins who *rolled deep* and who would fuck them *all* up because *nobody* does what *dis sick motherfucka* just tried to do to us.

Players who made Big Messes for Allen were fined money that went into the Rachel Green Fund, suspended for a number of games determined by the size of the Big Mess (*injured toe* or sometimes *flu-like symptoms* to the press), placed on restriction on future road trips, etc. The guys would rag on you the next morning or talk about you. Basically dealing with Allen put a spoiler on any night and was best avoided. Gilbert remembered this and got off the body, but she immediately put the hands on his shoulders and pulled him back onto the body, the eyes closed, and after a few more minutes for making out etc., he decided now was the time and so he reached down there and she let him at first and he was happy and he got the head in but she stiffened and went, —No. *No. Stop it.*

And so he pulled back out, frustrated and nearly salivating, but he managed a smile and went, —You okay?

She said nothing but put the arms around him again and pulled him onto the body again between the legs of the body wrapping the thighs around him and she started breathing really hard and whispered in his ear through the teeth, —Fuck me.

So he did, gladly, enjoying it for two maybe three seconds before she said no again and tried to push him off her, but by now he was overcome by an animal-like urge and she didn't matter anymore and he used all his weight and strength to push her legs back and pin her arms down, grinding his teeth and grunting into the neck, pumping away mindlessly at the vagina, unaware that she had quit resisting and then it was over and she left and he never saw her again or knew her name.

He was in Seattle and he had two young-looking bodies in his hotel room and he made them drinks and put way more vodka in theirs than in his and kept refilling their drinks until the two bodies agreed to make out with each other and he watched and masturbated as one of them who was blond took off her top and said, —Oh my God I can't believe I'm doing this . . . and the other one who was blond too but with much bigger tits was quiet as she took off her pants and thong and sat on the other one's face and sipped her drink, a screwdriver that was three-quarters vodka, while the other licked the asshole. The one licking the asshole would take a break now and then to laugh very loud and say, —I *swear* I have *never* done this before. And Gilbert and the big-titted one, implants, stared at each other the whole time and an hour later both the bodies were passed out on the bed without any clothes on and Gilbert ejaculated into one blonde's hair (he wasn't sure which) then called Allen to get rid of them.

After shooting a Sprite commercial in L.A. the guy who held the overhead microphone thing asked Gilbert if he'd like to sleep with his girlfriend who, though she was not very attractive, had smooth thighs and was white and Gilbert said sure. Later that night she came to his hotel room and she wanted him to stick as much of his hand down her throat as far as he could, which he did and enjoyed somewhat though it covered his fingers with a thick saliva that disgusted him. But he

couldn't maintain an erection with the condom she made him wear
and so he called Allen in and she got dressed and left his hotel room
and the eyes were so blue you couldn't look away and she asked for an
autograph on the way out and he signed one of his pictures for her,
making it out to her boyfriend who was actually her husband, she cor-
rected him—his name was Josh and he was home with the kids.

Because the city has a way of executing all others so that only you
matter because you're not allowed to look them in the eye as you pass,
and they don't look at you, all you see are your shoes and your reflection which is a relief when it's there.

The Athlete went out with the guys after a game in Houston and met
a beautiful body dressed in black and the beautiful body dressed in
black smiled at him and something clicked and as he put his arm
around her on the dance floor he cracked a joke that she laughed at
and when he kissed her he could see out of the corner of his eye Ben
standing at the edge of the dance floor holding a drink with Garrett
and Tony watching him.

This was his second season. He was already being asked when he
would deliver a championship to Dallas. It was a time for new beginnings—new coach, new attitude: the complete player, the leader.

He washed up in his hotel room after closely beating Houston and
met the guys in the lobby. They went downtown in dark SUVs chauf-
feured by Allen and other TEAM ASSISTANTS to a private party
thrown by a record producer he'd never heard of but girls spilled out
of the club onto the sidewalk smoking cigarettes and flirting with security. Bodies in high heels and mascara and skirts and eyes and skin
and all the life night exudes. They went in through the back and he
saw a girl when he walked in who was looking at him from behind the
bangs, and he didn't consider talking to her (just one of a seemingly
infinite number of girls there that night) until someone he didn't
know introduced them by saying, —Look, you guys are wearing the
same color!

And The Athlete said to the girl who was behind the bangs, —Yeah.
Black.

She laughed very hard at this so he took her back to the hotel. He didn't know the name. And in the cab she put his hand under the backless shirt so he could feel the nipple become erect in his palm, the tits not huge but a comforting size and fitting the frail but curved frame. And she sucked on his earlobe and asked the driver—the voice drunk and lazy—to turn the radio up and she shifted closer to him and licked him like a cat on the side of his face, and he laughed at this but she grabbed his face and held it still and looked very serious and licked it again. The hand was on his thigh and he was cupping both of the tits now with one hand. They could have been racing at time-warp speeds through neon tubes, the world on fire. But it was important that the mouth was small and warm and she took his hand out of the shirt and put it down the back of the capri pants, the ass cold and magnificent. The body in his hands allowed him to see that he didn't like himself off the court where it was a constant struggle for himself—but here in the back of the taxi with the body was like being on the court, where there was no such thing as evil.

She said to the driver, —Oh my God I *love* this *song*. Can you turn this up please?

The cab driver glared at them in the rearview mirror (my God he KNOWS—but not caring) and the driver didn't turn it up.

—Excuse me, she leaned forward, shouting, —turn this up!

The cab driver turned it up and she sucked on The Athlete's finger and curled into him, whimpering, then another song came on and suddenly she straightened and yelled, —Driver, change the station! I hate this fucking song!

—What's your name, The Athlete asked her.

The driver pulled over and said, —Get out.

—What? she said.

—Get out. Both of you. Get out.

—No!

—Look, The Athlete, level-headed and smart, said to the cab driver, —I'm sorry. She's a little drunk if you can believe it. Heh heh. She'll be good for the rest of the ride. Lord knows you don't deserve this, being a hardworking man driving us crazy people around all night. Heh heh. We'd really appreciate it if you could just take us to our destination, the hotel. It's not too far if I remember correctly.

And how cool the famous Athlete, slyly drawing what he hoped was a one-hundred-dollar bill from his wallet and slipping it over the driver's shoulder.

The driver took it and said nothing and pulled back into traffic. She laughed into his neck, the breath. They got to the hotel, walked through the lobby with his arm around the girl not caring if anyone could see that he had an erection. They made out in the elevator and she said, —Calm down. Allen checked her ID and told her what he told the girls the players brought back to the hotel. They got inside his room and had sex in the dark without a condom. He was in there for only a couple seconds when he was overcome with a panic that did not allow him to fully enjoy the moment as he felt the climax rushing through him with a full head of steam and the purpose of all things became to NOT COME. He cursed and pulled out of her, taking deep rhythmic breaths as he had overheard a well-accomplished male movie star remark how it helps you last longer. She was confused and said, —What's wrong? He said, more terse than he meant to, —Nothing. He put it back in and continued and began to come almost immediately. He said, —Sorry. He pulled out again, moved to the face, held the body's head there even though it tried to squirm away. He said as he came on the face, —I'm sorry . . . And as usual, the first concise thought afterward was of Papa Bear Ben Jermaine.

She seemed like she'd sobered up as she got up and walked to the bathroom. He wanted to tell her when she came back that she was the first girl whose face he had come on, but thought better of it. He was glad to have the body back in the bed, after he lay there alone fearing—unfounded as he knew it was—that it would never return from the bathroom.

His life was so boring. Strictly regimented from rise to repose. This was compounded by the fact that he had his father's genes, with their propensity for military and structure. As a member of the Association he had to follow a strict routine of prepractice workout, practice, postpractice workout, games, meetings, diet, exercise, departure times. He was told how to talk to people. He was allowed to say to the middle-aged white reporters, —I just want to help my team win basketball games.

He could not enjoy the anonymity of going for a walk or getting a hobby in order to meet new people outside work. One thing he would have liked to do, he would have liked to join a gun club if he could have or perhaps open a recording studio. Sometimes he wished he could work in the office of a big corporation as a faceless drone being paid a moderate wage. He dreamed often of eating fast food on his lunch breaks and paying off a mortgage on a modest home in the suburbs in the Midwest. Coming home to an increasingly unattractive stay-at-home wife who had cut her hair off. He wanted to wave hello to his neighbor in the mornings as they each climbed into sedans.

A life where nobody knew he existed. A life where he didn't think of Ben Jermaine when he copulated. He wanted to work in sales and drive with the windows of his Saturn down with the newest U2 album on his twenty-seven-disk changer. That was his fantasy. No contract, no fines for being three minutes late to practice.

It's true that he often looked up into the crowd on his way into the locker room at halftime and could not understand their enthusiasm— well-adjusted adults smiling and waving for his attention. His confusion became disdain.

Haven't they ever seen a fucking basketball game before?

When the girl in Houston left, he took a noisy shit and did some quick yoga stretches before spreading out on the bed in his boxers and watching an episode of that season's *Real World* he'd never seen before, wondering if Ben saw her leave. What if he didn't? He would want proof. If he does want proof, he thought, I'll tell him to ask Allen. But Allen won't say anything. I'll show him my fingers so he can smell them. Unless he would settle for seeing the bed all tangled up. But I could have conceivably messed the sheets up myself. Best to give Ben some details about the body then. Such as the thong was black, the pubic hair was shaved into a thin strip, the second toe was longer than the first toe. Were there tattoos? I can't remember. I'll tell him we had sexual intercourse but I won't tell him about coming so soon, obviously. Nor about coming on the face. Or maybe I should tell him about that. Or maybe I won't tell Ben Jermaine anything. He saw me leave with her at the club. He'll ask, of course, as soon as I go downstairs. I'll speak to him like I speak to the media—in broad noncommittal terms. Leave it up to his imagination, which is always more interesting than the truth anyway.

He imagined saying to Ben and all the guys gathered around him in the hotel lobby, —And so then we got to the hotel room and I took off her clothes then had sex with her.

But then Ben stopping him and going, —Whoa whoa whoa, wait a minute. You mean she didn't suck your dick?

Garrett and Tony and the rest of the guys would then look at him and say, —Yeah, we agree with Ben. She should have sucked your dick.

—If you didn't see to it that she sucked your dick then you will never be one of us.

—We'll never trust you enough to form as a cohesive unit under your leadership if she didn't suck your dick.

Caught off guard, he would then respond with, —Well, yeah, of course she sucked my dick. See, you didn't let me finish. After I fucked her, she sucked my dick. I thought it'd be better that way. That's the way I usually do it.

They'd groan and roll their eyes and walk away and it would've been all for nothing. He thought, There would have been no point in her seeing me standing beside the bed taking my boxers off and Little Gilbert going *ping*! We'll never win, and I'll never be held high in their esteem not to mention the esteem of the other players around the league. I'll end up being—oh my God—just another very good player who never wins anything. Like Dominique Wilkins or Charles Barkley. I'd rather be dead than be Dominique Wilkins or Charles Barkley.

Decided he'd say, if Ben asked him, —We just went back to the hotel for a couple hours.

—Oh yeah? What'd you do once you got there?

—What the fuck do you *think* we did? You nosy pervert.

And the guys would laugh at Ben Jermaine for being a nosy pervert.

The next morning he woke up wired and looked out the window at the boulevard, the muffled hum of the city stirring—trucks huffing and traffic whooshing, voices—people milling about, the sun praying upon the cars and the road gray, a race of children so decadent and tired. A sky so blue it must have been computer-generated and he was scraped empty by fear of STDs, perhaps having a virus spreading death through him at that very moment. But if death be the price of a championship then let him pay with his life. Clean old women staggered through their morning strolls and overworked laborers blistered in the Houston toil. A morning way too warm for February. A valet attendant stood out in the street enthusiastically waving a bus into the hotel's parking lot. He was woozy and wondering if she had been real and how it had happened. Perhaps because his eyes were bloodshot and he could see through concrete it was possible that it didn't happen. There was nothing but him and the morning and the opinion that Houston was beautiful when it wakes up as are all strange cities and the sun like a wise grandfather keeping its big hand on him shushing those below who were loud and admonishing them, —Let him be.

He thought of Sandy. He felt ashamed for thinking of Sandy. The reason he felt ashamed for thinking of Sandy was because he shouldn't have been thinking of his high school girlfriend anymore. Especially considering the fact that he thought nothing in particular about her really—just her face and maybe the general essence of her. What he remembered as Sandy was no doubt warped and twisted by time from thinking about her to thinking about the memory of her to thinking about how he remembered the memory of her and so on . . . until what he was thinking about wasn't her at all but a THING called Sandy. Which made him feel guilty. Because he knew that every time he thought of the THING he called Sandy it was unfair to both of them and not based in reality—which by the way disgusted him further because he saw himself as a man firmly rooted in reality. He wondered what Sandy was doing at that exact moment. He heard from his parents that she went to Northeastern as did half of his high school class. He liked to think that that proved she was not spectacular enough for him. He imagined her at a college party and smiling and laughing with friends and flirting with guys and NOT THINKING OF HIM. This was where he always let the THING called Sandy go. He did the same now. The thought of Sandy softly slipped from the buoyant mind of The Athlete.

Her name was Danielle and she was twenty-six years old and lived in the suburbs outside Houston, with her parents—in their one-level house where she grew up, seven miles from the airport—because they helped her take care of her baby. She was a salesgirl in the women's shoe department of JCPenney in the mall. Every day she drove past her high school remembering when life was little more than friends and drama about who said what about whom, friends being one thing she had little of anymore since most of them had moved away or were still around but not tied down like she was by her baby, a three-year-old daughter. The first year after her daughter was born they would invite her out or stop by, knowing she was lonely, and her mom would babysit as the girls would load into a car and go to the bars and get loaded and dance and try to act like nothing had changed. But everything had changed, and it became painfully clear as she sat at the bar one night, staring into her empty glass, as her friends danced ten feet away, squealing and calling for her, that there was no use in pretending otherwise. Her friends faded away; Danielle got used to spending weekend nights with her parents and baby in the blue glow of the TV. The baby's father wanted nothing to do with it, which Danielle was glad about because they couldn't hand the baby off without ending up in a screaming match that inevitably led to someone getting bitten and someone going to jail. She didn't bother suing when he stopped paying child support and disappeared. She wasn't happy with her life but couldn't see any way to change it, considering she had no qualifications for a more lucrative career besides four fractionalized semesters at community college. She sank deep into a firmly rooted depression that she didn't even realize was enveloping her until it already had. Locked herself in her room and called in sick to JCPenney and refused to open her bedroom door even for the baby. And she was very close to doing something drastic about this when her phone rang one night and, shocked because her phone never rang, she answered it. It was Crystal, her best friend from high school, whom she hadn't seen in almost two years.

Crystal, who was Persian, worked as a secretary in a recording studio in Houston where a producer Danielle had never heard of hung out, but apparently he was famous and was throwing a party at Tequila Sands that some Association basketball players were supposed to be attending. They were renting out the entire club for it and everything. On the Tuesday before the party the producer who was addicted to heroin noticed the secretary sitting at her desk with headphones on because her body had huge tits and a face that had makeup on it. The producer gave Crystal an invitation as he left with his entourage and said, —Here's extra for your friends. Bring some friends.

—Okay.

—*Girl*friends.

She went through all her girlfriends. Lindsey was going to a wedding and Kirsten was running a 10K in the morning and Rachel was obsessed with her new boyfriend and didn't want to leave his side for one night, etc. Crystal didn't want to go to the party alone because she was still scarred from showing up alone to the homecoming dance in eleventh grade after taking her neofeminist mother's advice that she didn't need a male escort to have a good time but ended up being called a lesbian in the bathroom by girls who had dates. So she called Danielle, her best friend from high school, one of the ones who had called Crystal a lesbian in the bathroom at the homecoming dance, who still lived in the area and was still attractive hopefully and would be approved of by the producer who Crystal had a borderline obsessive crush on.

Danielle had been meaning to catch up with Crystal anyway and rekindle the friendship since they'd once been so close and really had no reason for not being in each other's lives anymore besides Crystal's maybe private disdain for Danielle for still living in the same town and in the same house she grew up in and for having had the baby which was, in Crystal's mind, an obvious attempt at giving her otherwise small life some meaning. They met in Crystal's apartment in the city, Crystal's roommate at work (waitress) as usual, put on Top 40 pop music and made mimosas and got dressed in outfits they'd separately bought on clearance at United Colors of Benetton, trading pieces from their makeup bag, took a taxi to the club. As they left the apartment when the cab buzzed up, Danielle grabbed Crystal by the shoulders as she locked the door and said, —I'm so glad we're hanging out tonight. I've missed you *so much.*

—Me too, Crystal said. Danielle's voice hadn't changed.

—No seriously. I don't know why we ever stopped being friends, but let's start again. Starting tonight. No matter what happens tonight let's not leave each other's side.

—Definitely.

—We'll use the night to catch up.

—Totally. Because I've been so busy and should totally have not let us drift apart.

—I've missed you so much Crystal. Seriously. Tonight's about us, okay?

Danielle got drunk in about forty-five minutes upon arrival and they were only there an hour when she left with one of the basketball players who was maybe Filipino and cute but kinda creepy who made no effort to conceal that he was . . . how should she put this . . . *excited* on the dance floor with Danielle. Crystal wished she had a girlfriend beside her to laugh at this with. Crystal watched them leave Tequila Sands, extremely pissed and lonely, feeling used, hating Tequila Sands and all the douche bags licking their lips at her and hating the producer who was sitting on these giant floor pillows in a dark corner with a couple Asian girls who looked twelve and hadn't even said hello to her and hating Danielle who apparently hadn't been inspired by motherhood to stop fucking a different guy each week (Crystal wouldn't even share a glass of water with her) which was so obviously, to Crystal, a symptom of terribly low self-esteem from having accomplished very close to nothing in her life, unless you count a baby as an accomplishment, which Crystal did not.

Crystal went home and never spoke to Danielle again, who after leaving Gilbert Marcus's hotel room took a cab back to Crystal's apartment where her car was, not bothering to go up and see her knowing she was pissed, and went home, singing along to "You Give Love a Bad Name" on the radio with the window down as the morning came to life, feeling the best she'd felt in years, seeing her face in the mirror as she drove out of the city as a pretty girl who could get a celebrity to sleep with her and so could no doubt accomplish some other things too. The next Monday she skipped work again to reenroll in classes at community college and didn't drop out. Two years later she graduated with a degree in business and started an online dating site that was instantly successful, making her very rich. She got her own house in a community on a golf course and married a private contractor who thought she was the greatest thing to ever happen to him and who loved her kid and eight months later she sold out for millions and never had to work again.

Outside it was clouded over, a cloak of melancholy gray that at once evoked adolescence and security, and he felt as he stepped onto the plane to fly back from Houston that he had for the past year or so been wandering in transit—though his house was big and full of furniture it didn't feel like his, nor did his life. It was a good feeling. The Behemoth was wedged into an aisle seat, leaning over the armrest, and he slapped The Athlete's butt as The Athlete passed and pulled a headphone from a disproportionately small ear to say, —That's bullshit.

The Athlete shrugged, and The Behemoth said, —She said she liked me. It was in the bag. She said, So you're the great Papa Bear Ben Jermaine. One minute we're talking. I swore she was going to be naked in my bed later. I was already imagining it. One minute we're talking, making out, I'm feeling on her tits, next minute she's leaving with your dorky ass.

—Don't know what to tell you, he said, smiling and shrugging.

—Yeah, Glen said, chewing gum, in the seat next to The Behemoth, —she was hot. You fuck her?

—Yup. (Deliberately distant, calculatedly dismissive.)

—Doggy-style?

—Psssh.

—Put it in her ass?

—Yeah, of course.

—She suck your dick?

—Yup.

Garrett and The Behemoth were silent, he took his seat, flew back to Dallas where it was sunny and the next month when he was in L.A. doing a commercial he met a model named Brianne Kuld and he fucked her and brought her to practice so Ben could see her and then proposed to her and then his parents moved out and he lived with her alone.

We were there. We watched him. We bear witness. Our emotions were scattered but we were many and were watching. We can tell you about the newly engaged Athlete who was fit and cutting through the lights and hardwood floor, sweat dripping off his face, his famous beautiful fiancée in the stands cheering him on so graceful like a First Lady:

Leading the charge against Miami in the Association Championship.

We can tell you about the Coach pot-bellied on the sideline with eyes of stone stroking his bare chin, only three years removed from a quadruple bypass now having led his team to sixty-nine wins, the best in the league. Papa Bear Ben Jermaine with tattoos and dreadlocks dyed fire-red for the war, cocky and strutting through the first two games, catching alley-oops from The Athlete and driving the crowd into a frenzy. A man against boys. The two were in perfect sync. It was like they'd been there forever. We all felt it. The harmony chilled our spines. It was as though nothing could get in their way. They were empirical. Soviet soldiers void of compassion.

We can describe the emotions we felt as The Athlete argued a bad foul called on The Behemoth and was ejected for it. The shock on his face when the little bald referee blew his whistle and reached back and threw his hand at nothing—leaving The Behemoth like the surviving twin out there as The Athlete was forcibly removed into the tunnel and out of our sight.

We heard they didn't get along off the court. This was to be expected from two superstars. *But we didn't believe it.*

How they put aside their differences in the name of a greater cause gave us hope—but hope was quickly lost.

Not only that but then came word The Athlete had a strained ligament in his ankle and was being examined by the trainers in the locker room.

What would happen without The Athlete? Coach was concerned, we could tell. But he was careful not to let his face show this so as to not worry his team, who relied on him to know how to feel. They looked to him as we looked to them—like children.

Let down and disenchanted by the cruelty of fate, some of us, at the seemingly relentless catastrophe of life, while the rest of us snickered with envious glee, glad to see the strong ones fall. It defined us as people.

As Game 4 began let us tell you please how WE ROARED as OUT HOBBLED THE ATHLETE, slapping hands, tearing off his warm-up pants, hopping in place, a man in search of redemption. He scored 38 points and then The Behemoth fouled out with three seconds left and Dallas down by one and Miami with the ball. Could we believe that The Athlete was racing across the court? Did we trust ourselves when we saw The Athlete steal the inbound and lay it in at the buzzer, winning the game, *winning the game, WINNING THE GAME?*

Nothing comes easy which we knew from being the watchers and so we weren't surprised when Miami and their star, Tracy Combs, who was known for having the composure of a sniper, fought back and seized hold of Game 5, and then Game 6, evening the series at 3-3—

—but The Athlete would be avenged. You could see it in his eyes as he made his way off the court.

He would have to be. Because we had faith. Not just in him. *In ourselves.*

The game was up for grabs as Game 7 was winding down in Dallas, another evenly matched clash of titans, the players' bodies battered and their vision blurred and their minds goo. The liberation in this, letting go. We were children and we cheered. Miami was up by one with 1.7 seconds to go. The men we depended on were smeared into piles of sweat, their limbs tangled and useless. Coach screamed red-faced into deaf ears. For no one could help these men but themselves . . . There was a scrap heap of bodies scrambling for it. We prayed to God to make our team win. There was a foul. The ref made it up. One lone soul emerged atop the scrap heap who was brave enough to find it inside himself to grasp it. We were silent and praying as he took the free throws in the face of fire. Millions of eyes followed each bounce of the ball, each flex of the knees, the suffocating smother of a nation of held breath. And the cool rush of air as they exhaled as he sank both of them, as if he were mindless to us starving for his blood. His skill was a soft blanket we could wrap ourselves up in and be rid of fate.

That a man could declare his own greatness and seize for himself his destiny.

When the buzzer went off and the game was over and the Dallas Lonestars were the Association Champions, we were unable to deny the moment of the team rushing the court, and the fans, confetti falling from the rafters and The Athlete looking for The Behemoth in the melee and finding him and jumping into his arms. They were on top of the earth.

The Athlete reaching for the ceiling and begging for the touch of the impossible constellation of hands reaching back down to him, just one hand, any hand, our hands, these hands, his hands.

—How do you feel, Mr. MVP?

—I can't believe it.

Brianne and Gilbert lay on the floor of their Dallas condominium right inside the door with no clothes on.

Brianne left the Circuit City Center after the game alone because he had more press conferences to do and had to kiss the trophy with champagne dripping down his head for historic photographs, wearing a hat and a T-shirt with the tag still on it that someone had slipped on him. The first thing you learn after becoming a champion is that people now feed off your time. You must explain your victory. You must tell those at home what it's like and what you were thinking. Brianne had never been prouder of anybody than she'd been of him tonight. Her eyes glowed seeing her man choose what he wanted and plow through all the other men to obtain the thing he wanted. The people in the stands around her didn't know The Athlete. But she did. They were going home to their ordinary lives. Throughout the game they kept turning around to check her reaction, aware of who she was, and her heart jumped with VIP glee.

As he stood with the trophy on the bandstand at center court with his team, as the Commissioner named him Association Championship MVP, the white hat skewed on his head, the big white T-shirt, sputtering into a live microphone words that didn't begin to explain how he felt but nonetheless were what people wanted to hear, Brianne was led by security down from the stands and onto the court, following the hulking security guard and shouting into his ear as he parted the mess of people, —I want to go home! Take me home!

Men screamed high-pitched into her ear, vibrating down her shoulders. The sweaty backs of camera guys backed into her. Teenage boys hopped up and down, and a skinny one with zits and shaggy hair landed on her foot, which was protected by nothing but a sandal.

Outside, in Dallas, people were burning cars, destroying windows, being pepper-sprayed.

She found herself clinging to the belt loop of the security guy, in a pale-blue polo shirt and an earpiece, shaved head. He turned around and possibly sneered at her, and someone's elbow caught her under the arm, and she gasped and pushed back meekly. Smiling middle-aged men in suits with shiny faces, black girls screeching at nothing. A vague disgust filled Brianne. These enraptured people reduced to submission. Just when she thought she would pass out or throw up onto the shoes of a drunken teenager who she recognized as a minor television star, she was spit out into a silent concrete corridor, alone, the security guard nowhere in sight.

As she drove home through the city in the brand-new baby-blue Mazda RX-7 that The Athlete had bought her when she moved in she was unable to comprehend how all these people in the streets weren't as utterly fused to success as she . . . how the acts of the man she belonged to had revved these drunken men into a riot. And what's wrong with belonging to him? A man such as he. Yes, she did belong to him, and so what? Every girl in America could only dream she could belong to him.

She said to herself, —They don't get it. It's there for them but they choose not to have it.

She stood in the penthouse condominium's wide-open country-style kitchen fingering the edge of the counter. She turned on the kitchen television (a forty-two-inch Panasonic plasma HDTV) to ABC for the live coverage then scampered up the stairs and took a shower, shaved, put baby powder on her vagina because he didn't like it when her vagina smelled, put on a short skirt that barely covered her ass and high heels and a thong from Frederick's of Hollywood. When her fiancé came home she met him in the doorway and they made love right there, the way he liked to—by pulling her skirt up and pulling down the thong from Frederick's of Hollywood and bending her over a chair, his hands gripping her neck. It was the first time they'd done it since Sue and Mervin moved back to Hingham, which was a month ago, before the playoffs.

Afterward they lay on the hardwood floor which was pristine and polished since the housekeepers buffed it every other day and she studied the side of his face in love and wished that there was some way for him to penetrate her deeper.

To go all the way through. To pierce my heart and come out the other side.

She said, —So how do you feel, Mr. MVP?

He laughed and wiped his forehead and she laughed too and he said as he looked up at the chandelier, —I can't believe it. It's the greatest day of my life. Like, I don't know. It feels like the *last* day of my life. I just mean it doesn't seem to me like any other day is ever going to feel as good as this one. This is what I've lived my whole life for. I mean, nothing, *nothing* will ever compare to this. *Nothing.*

Brianne nodded and put her head on the inside of his shoulder. Though she said nothing, you could feel how her blood thickened in her veins.

But what about the day we get married?
But what about the day we have a child?

As the months of their engagement ticked off, Brianne often felt as if the world were closing in on her. Most of these times were when she was looking at her fiancé—she would be so unbound by love for him that her heart would close in, overcome by the weight of an emotion so fierce that she couldn't tell you what it was—one minute he'd be rubbing her little pedicured feet on the couch after a mindless summer day, off-season, no charity golf tournaments to attend or movie cameos to make, no Association promo spots to film or interviews or charity 10Ks to run in, watching a DVD of the movie *Die Hard*, his favorite, or a highlight reel of himself he had the Lonestars put together for him, on the remote-controlled pull-down projector-sized screen that lowered from a slit in the ceiling, in the wide-open Pacific Palisades, a breeze cooling the green leaves of trees, the sun in shades and squares, their castle, their solitude . . . and the next he'd be gone, closed off and staring through her when she said, —Want a glass of water? I'm getting one . . . Perplexed that she could speak, amused but baffled that she was offering him water. Where was he, and where did he go?

She wanted to tell him about a pair of jeans she was going to buy, but she felt as though she were somehow bothering him, so didn't bother.

He'd wake up in the middle of the night, bolt upright, and she'd wake up and see him staring and gasping at nothing, and she'd ask him what was the matter but he'd grumble and go back to sleep and in the morning he'd say he didn't remember and didn't know what she was talking about.

Their lives would belong to each other, forever, a concept that in dull moments, like telling the housekeeper to remember to use dryer sheets because her socks had been sticking to her lately, hit her in the chest: FOREVER.

Or walking out of a Rodeo Drive perfume store with a small brown bag with rope handle containing a $289 bottle of exfoliating eye-wrinkle cream made from the object material of male babies' circumcisions, for Gilbert, and putting on her sunglasses and looking up and down the street, old rich women coming from all sides, suddenly unsure of which direction to go next: FOREVER.

He was gone for weeks at a time, on business trips to meet with companies that wanted him to endorse them, or meeting with his financial consultant in New York, unsanctioned minicamps with the Lonestars in a high school gym in North Dakota. But when Brianne cried about the neglect one night he bought her a thirty-thousand-dollar platinum necklace and canceled all other trips for the duration of the summer.

15

HIGH AND IN NEW YORK WITH KARL
Babcock at a club called Rifle.

Karl Babcock used to play for Chicago
until he got thrown out of the league
after his fourth failed drug test and had recently returned from two
years spent detoxing in a cave in the Andes. There was a warrant out
for Karl Babcock's arrest (failure to pay child support—he owed more
than $380,000, spread among six women) but the concern was not
great enough to deter him from going out with Gilbert Marcus to
this club that some investment bankers he was friends with had recently spent more than $8 million opening.

Another season, another championship.

They'd won two in a row. Next year would be three in a row.
Three in a row was called a Threepeat. Last person to get a Threepeat
was you know who. Gilbert felt as though he'd earned the right to be
himself and not The Athlete for one night. So tonight, in that regard,
he figured he would sleep with the bartender who had been giving
him eyes from across this VIP room of a multistory club with a strict

dress code and sport utility vehicles parked along the curb and a two-block line of eager young men with collared shirts and polished shoes, cell phones to heads, wads of twenties in palms ready to give to the bouncer and half-naked girls huddling together smoking cigarettes and fighting with their psycho boyfriends on their cell phones.

Though the mouth was three-eighths of an inch too wide and the butt could have benefited from a regular step class the bartender's body had nice tits and she was the best-looking girl in the VIP area which was a shame considering that Karl who was coked to the gills and chain-smoking filterless cigarettes had promised Gilbert that models and dancers would be there but so far it seemed to be only twenty-three-year-old white males with gel in their hair and shirts with the collars up who must have snuck up there somehow and would brag to their friends in the morning about being at a club where Gilbert Marcus and Karl Babcock were. The presence of these males would have normally filled Gilbert with horror but knowing that all of them were attracted to the bartender made him feel a little better and at least Karl was easing his rapidly compounding boredom by telling him again about how he was awake for three days blowing coke at his house in Westchester County with his friend Terry and his friend Terry decided to check his stocks online and discovered that he had made nearly forty thousand dollars on a stock that Karl Babcock had just dumped the week before after losing money on the stock for months (Karl Babcock forgot what the stock was) and Karl Babcock was so fucked up at the time that he got so mad about Terry—who was probably the world's worst investor—making forty thousand dollars on that stock Karl had dumped that he went and got one of his shotguns from the small armory he kept in his house and went out to the barn and shot his three-hundred-thousand-dollar horse—bred from a Preakness runner-up—in the face, and when his friend Terry came out to see what the gunshot was, Karl pointed the shotgun at him and told him to go back inside, Karl was saying to Gilbert, because he wanted to pull this practical joke he had decided to play on Terry and wanted more than anything to carry out, which was cutting off the horse's head (resembling a watermelon crushed by a sledgehammer at this point) and putting it in the driver's seat of Terry's brand-new black Escalade that Karl had bought for him, not realizing until he came to in the morning alone in the barn with the shotgun in his hands and his very well-bred horse dead with its head halfway sawed off just what the fuck he was doing and not only that but also that he had stolen what he had thought was this brilliant idea from *The Godfather*.

Gilbert laughed very loudly and looked around to see if any of the girls noticed how white his teeth were, or the frosted tips of his newly straightened hair, or the results from the new triceps regimen he had recently implemented. And of course two or three were gawking from the corner and making no effort to cover it up but they obviously ate too much meat and didn't tan, nor did they put any effort at all into not looking fat and disgusting, which really started to anger him.

Gilbert Marcus was here in New York, as he had told Brianne, to meet with his financial adviser about investing in some real estate in Alabama and to work with a really top-notch private defensive trainer because his reaction off the dribble was lagging, but the real reason he was here was to work with a private investigator he had hired to find out where Sandy was. The PI was a lot younger than he expected him to be and had a distracting eye twitch and told him that Sandy was living outside the city in a house with her husband who she had married a year and a half earlier and earlier in the day before meeting Karl Babcock Gilbert hired a taxi to take him past the address the PI provided though he had a personal driver and a limo with him and he stared at the front door of the house Sandy lived in with her husband from the car window imagining her bringing groceries into the house. He had the taxi drop him off on the corner and he sat on a bench beside the community pool which looked like no one had ever sat in it before and called another taxi to take him back into the city laughing as he waited because he was Gilbert Marcus sitting on a bench on a Saturday afternoon in the middle of your subdivision. As he waited he called the telephone number the PI gave him for Sandy and a man answered after the first ring and Gilbert hung up.

Here he was now nearly twelve hours later drinking a seventeen-dollar rum and Coke because he didn't know any other drink and didn't want to ask Karl or the bartender what other kinds of drinks there were and though his drive-by of Sandy's house had left him dreading something that seemed just beyond his periphery, he had no choice but to be here.

And here he was on the eastern coast of the United States the number-one country in the world and this was what you did and this was the life you lived when you were the best and were twenty years old and had more money than you could keep track of and would never have to lift your finger the rest of your life if you retired tonight and your name was known by families in places you'd never heard of and your face recognized by people who meant nothing to you.

Karl ran off with someone who was either a New York Jet or a young state senator from Illinois to go to Scores but Gilbert Marcus stayed and finished his rum and Coke even though it was just ice that kept sliding down and hitting him in the teeth. While he did this he tipped the bouncer fifty dollars for no reason and watched a black girl dance on a stage and shook hands with three black guys who asked him if he *had bitches waiting back at the hotel.* Then he put his glass down on a table and smiled and made his way toward the bartender.

He dumped her and moved West to become famous and she got into Columbia. The shock of their breakup never fully dulled and she spent her four years of college in her dorm room alone, uninterested in boys because of how Gilbert Marcus had treated her. To keep them away she smothered her beautiful body with thirty pounds of fat and flab until she was buried beneath her own flesh.

The words they had spoken hovered over her. That last day when she spilled her purse in the driveway.

Sandy had no choice but to turn away and leave the room when the TV in the communal area of her dorm had a Dallas Lonestars game on but then again the red-faced kids with beer cans and baseball caps never were for her, but soon it wasn't enough to leave the room as his face began appearing on the front pages of newspapers and in commercials for sports drinks and clothing companies springing up out of nowhere during her favorite shows to bite her in the neck, MVP this, champion that, until she had no choice but to avoid TV altogether, even the sight of one giving her heart palpitations.

Without the rigorous sitting and watching involved in television consumption, Sandy had fewer opportunities to eat as she used the time instead to study and read books and stare at the ceiling, and then one day she read a book by an author whose name she couldn't remember but it was about this girl who falls in love over and over but only as a way to avoid learning how to love herself, and when Sandy finished the last page she let the book drop on her chest and let out a slow gust of air and let the copper tones of sunset soak into her through the window. She stole her roommate's shoes and crept down the stairs and pushed open the front door, bent down and touched her toes, pulled the right leg back and then the left, and she started in a slow trot, right foot in front of left, one step at a time, down the sidewalk and up over the hills and around the buildings, the world popping huge before her.

Lost thirty pounds and graduated in the top five of her class, met the guy who was number three, married him, became a social worker counseling troubled young girls who since they were rich didn't know where their troubles came from, and she showed them how to love themselves, a career not financially rewarding but since her husband was appointed a professor of psychology at Columbia she had comfort to go with her spiritual satisfaction.

She woke up at 4:30 AM as usual, ran a couple miles before work, saw on CNN.com which she checked by habit every morning that Gilbert Marcus had been arrested in connection with a rape and murder, let her coffee go cold. When reporters began to call she didn't tell them about how she still dreamed about him sometimes and that it made her feel guilty, but not as guilty as sometimes thinking of him when in bed with her husband, but if she told them that she'd have to tell them the same about Robbie. Nor did she tell them about using connections at work a few months earlier to track Gilbert's number down and calling him late one night while her husband was asleep and the sun began to rise and hearing him say hello before hanging up on him. What she did tell reporters was that she and Gilbert Marcus had gone out for a little while in high school, that he was an old family friend, that mostly they just watched old Association games together, a silly teenage romance, puppy love, just like what happens to all of us, but it was nice, he was sweet, she had a hard time remembering to be honest, she told them, it was no big deal really, just something that happened a long time ago.

He'd turned a corner in his game that got the critics off his back and made his teammates like him—passing, defending, closing in on becoming the ultimate all-around player. There was a freedom in getting his teammates in on things. Trusting them to make the shot, setting them up to make plays, dumping it in to Ben who opponents structured their entire game plan around stopping. And when they did stop him—usually by fouling him or getting him to foul out—then Gilbert could take over. Gilbert became a crouching tiger. This was how men played the game. Smart, with subtleties. The way he played the game was a wise jazz needling as opposed to in-your-face hip-hop. His maturity was a weapon. And also—perhaps not coincidentally—he had begun listening to jazz quite a bit on the advice of Brian who was quite the aficionado. His defense improved thanks to tireless personal sessions with Al Kennon, a well-regarded defensive coach who used to be on Detroit's staff in the nineties and now made his living off his sessions with Gilbert, and his passing improved thanks to a man recommended by Karl Babcock who was a middle-aged white guy who otherwise worked as a consultant on basketball scenes in movies. His game held water at all corners. The Athlete and The Behemoth became buds and talked about working on a rap album together. The team was running slick greased with diesel fuel. Morale was sky high. Endorsement deals were pouring in. He had developed such a strong chemistry with Coach that they went for entire practices without the need to speak. They were like father and son. Gilbert thought of Coach as *Dad* sometimes to himself. *Because I never had a father—only a coach.* Gilbert had a much more substantial relationship with Coach than Ben Jermaine had with Coach, Gilbert happily noticed. The two formed dendrites in their brain stems for each other. They could tell you the name of the man by the rhythm of his breath.

The team they played in the championship that year was none other than the Boston Colonials. Boston was a city where the fans never forgot nor forgave. They found a sick joy in their inability to win. The Athlete heard them scream, —Traitor! And a staff member in the Bose Center tunnel in Boston as he headed toward the court before Game 3 muttered in his ear, low enough for only Gilbert to hear, —What's the difference between a chigger's brains and a bucket of shit?

His father's team and his team when he was a boy.

—The bucket, the man said, grinning.

The Colonials were now led by a little solitary black-as-night point guard named Ron Harrington who white people also called a ball hog and hated because he had cornrows and didn't smile for them and looked like he would rob them. He held the record for the biggest single fine and longest single suspension handed out in the history of the Association ($130,000; remainder of season), which he got the season before for snatching a television camera from an ESPN cameraman in the first ten minutes of a game against Milwaukee and smashing the camera all over the court then diving into the stands because a drunk fan called him a cocksucker for breaking the camera, causing a melee between fans and players and between teams that went on for nearly seventeen minutes before the police started shooting tear gas. Ron Harrington earned $113,000 per game and had three illegitimate children and had been arrested for possession of a concealed weapon and for possessing dried urine.

They liked to put Ron Harrington up next to Gilbert Marcus and feel good because Gilbert Marcus was clean and engaged and had no illegitimate children and spoke correct clear English without Ebonics and was from their kind of neighborhood and had neat hair and didn't curse or hang around thugs or have a probation officer. He was a focused athlete without an attitude and with a commitment to excellence—he was someone their kids could look up to in an age when pro athletes were overpaid and spoiled and ungrateful and BLACK. Here at last was a black athlete who was quiet and demure and stayed in line.

A black man who wasn't too black.

The Boston crowd booed him during pregame introductions each of the three games that were played there at the Bose Center. He heard a little girl's voice cut through the chaos, —Fuck you Gilbert! He felt nothing. The ire was not directed at Gilbert Marcus but at The Athlete. The Athlete never belonged to Boston. The Athlete never belonged to anyone. Gilbert Marcus did not belong to them anymore. They did not matter and were not there. There was only The Athlete and the victory to obtain, and they would never understand each other.

He thought, I stopped doing this for you people a long time ago.

Sue and Mervin didn't take the tickets he'd bought and set aside for them, the pain of which he was able to brave by bending in its wind, as Coach would say, like tall grass does until there is no more wind and it's able to stand straight again and continue being grass—a basic Tao principle. Coach was known for his Taoist philosophy. He could quote Taoist principles like that offhand.

If they didn't like The Athlete, they could bury themselves in their endless winters and brood upon their championshipless lives. Because at the end of the day he'd be leaving here first chance he got and would never come back.

He smoked weed with Karl Babcock in the hotel. He would drink a masking agent that he would have his barber order for him which cost forty dollars a gallon so that he would pass the next random drug test, tipped off the week before by Gary the trainer. He couldn't say he enjoyed being stoned. He was acutely aware of every foreign body intruding on his cells; the feelings of adulteration that he could not shake. This was something he vowed when he was twelve that he never would do after seeing three high school kids at St. Francis of Assisi Middle School doing it in the woods with a Coke can behind the gym and how evil they looked sneering at him, how he crippled in their gaze. He had a fear that ingesting a recreational drug of any sort would dull whatever frail edge he had over the rest. The only reason he did it tonight was because Karl Babcock offered it to him in the hotel room and Gilbert was in the mood to do something like smoke weed. He had made up his mind that he would enjoy himself for a minimum of one night. Whatever he had to do to have fun for one night, he would do it. Smoking weed seemed like something people who had fun might do. He wanted to be somebody who had fun and smoked weed.

He was unsure of how to do it and Karl laughed at him and Gilbert became terrified that he would tell other players and they would laugh at him too. Karl Babcock was the same blabbermouth who'd just finished telling Gilbert about how Patrick Dott from the Vancouver Dukes came out with him once and ended up in bed unconscious shitting himself drunk. Karl had coke but didn't offer Gilbert any to Gilbert's relief because he probably would have done it. The thing that they were smoking out of was called a bowl to Gilbert's surprise who thought they were called bongs, but he didn't tell Karl this—Karl was to know nothing.

I've been so stressed. All my life I've been so stressed.

Karl laughed as Gilbert held the lighter to the bowl and said, —You almost burned your eyebrows off.

And Gilbert exhaled and said, —Yeah well I've fucked fifteen girls. Did you know that?

Karl was playing with a butterfly knife he'd taken out of his bag and said, —Yeah?

The room was filled with smoke and Gilbert saw what must have been a smirk on Karl's face, a joke he was enjoying, keeping from Gilbert—my God, is fifteen NOT A LOT? A panic washed over him as he realized that Karl had no doubt slept with more—way more—than fifteen. Maybe fifty, even. No, more than that. Two hundred maybe. It became clear to Gilbert that Karl would tell everybody that Gilbert

Marcus had slept with only fifteen girls and was going around brag-
ging about it. He thought he might vomit. He hated weed, he was realizing. He hated fun. He considered that maybe he should snatch the
knife from Karl and before Karl knew what was happening stab him to
death with it. I could kill somebody if I had to, he thought. He'd jab
him quick in the side of the neck like in the movies and drag him into
the tub so blood wouldn't get everywhere. Then he'd call down to the
front desk and extend his stay for a week. He could say it's turned out
that another business matter has come up, if they asked, which they
probably wouldn't since they respected their customers' privacy. Then
he could wash up and go down and buy some clothes from a thrift
store so that he would look like a bum and put them on in an alley behind the Dumpster in which he'd throw away the clothes he was wearing because they'd have blood on them. Then he would spend a couple
hours staggering around so that any potential witnesses would tell police about the crazed homeless man they saw nearby the night of the
murder. Then he could find a hardware store and buy some lime and
tell the guy casually that he's the groundskeeper at a local park and
they need some lime right away for the baseball field. He could bring
the lime back to the hotel and pour it over Karl's now-dead body and
let it dissolve his flesh so that by the end of the week it would be
bones that he could put into his suitcase and walk out of the hotel
dragging his suitcase on wheels containing Karl Babcock's remains
which he would eventually dump in various Dumpsters across town.
Then he'd fly home, get on with his life.

   He sat on the bed hoping Karl didn't notice how dizzy and nauseous he was—his heavy lids and pale face. He waited until Karl
opened the sliding door to go out on the balcony to holler down at
passersby before sneaking into the bathroom to shovel water from the
faucet into his mouth. He locked the door and stood there staring at
the tiles and rubbing his temples and on the tiles was a single black
curled hair that might have been a pube and he pissed and puked and
flushed and went back out to where Karl was waiting on the other side
of the door. Karl pinned Gilbert against the wall and put the knife to
Gilbert's throat and said, —If a motherfucker wanted to do this to you
there ain't shit you could do about it.

   Gilbert forced a laugh until Karl pulled the knife away and threw
it across the room where it didn't stick in the wall but put a dent in it
and Karl looked disappointed about this.

   Then they went out and a couple years later Karl would kill his gardener by shooting him in the side of the head while playing with a .50 caliber handgun while heavily intoxicated and he would plead guilty to manslaughter and get a couple years' probation.

Somewhere between convincing the bartender to come back to the hotel and taking off the thong, which was pink, a dread consumed him that made him lose interest and he suddenly felt hideous and could see himself behind the bartender slobbering on the neck as the possibilities of the world vanished one by one before his eyes into a confounding simmer. The skin was cold and he could not name himself and he was not here, as memories of the season just ended raced back in a proud stream that made him wonder if it really ever happened until he was forced back into the present compromising moment aware of only the fact that he was a man who was panting heavily with his tongue hanging out into a stranger's open crotch. The name was Michelle and there was no mystery between the thighs anymore. And there were tiny raised bumps where the thighs connected to the pelvis and a stubble on the lips of the vagina. She was catching on that something was amiss and it made her self-conscious but she didn't come here for male dramatics so she sighed and reached down to find him limp as a noodle and started prepping him for entry. He reluctantly poked the vagina with a finger which stung her because she was absolutely dry.

Which was when the noises started.

She assumed they were the sounds of the air-conditioning kicking on but then they got louder and she worked her hand to minimal reaction as she looked around trying to find the noise until it became impossibly clear that it was not the air-conditioning nor was it the full-sized refrigerator in the suite's large kitchen—rather the sounds were coming from the basketball player on top of her who she had heard of but only knew it was him because a busboy pointed him out and what the basketball player on top of her was doing was growling like a dog with his face down and his eyes closed, louder and with quickly increasing urgency until he was roaring and squealing in her face, still incorrigibly limp-dicked. This wasn't the first time she'd had a man growl at her but even if it were she had been finding lately that nothing men did shocked her anymore. She rolled her eyes and said, —Wait. She pushed the basketball player off her and got up and turned around toward the nightstand and bent over with a knee up and she was not surprised to find that he became instantly erect, his snorting quelled as he began to fuck her.

Though Gilbert could hardly stand it he sat in the bed with the sheet over his crotch and watched the bartender wipe the face and neck off with a white towel from the bathroom then gather the clothes, not looking at him.

The flesh, the hair, the inside of the body.

He said, —Um, I should probably explain that, huh?

The way this girl picked up clothes off a hotel room floor was she got the shirt first then the bra then the pants then the thong. She shrugged and didn't look at him as she muttered, —I guess.

—Are you mad at me?

—Ha. No.

—You sure?

—I'm not your girlfriend. Don't be so assumptuous.

—How is that assumptuous?

—Because you're not my boyfriend. So I don't care. So I'm not mad.

—No, I mean listen. I'm depressed is the thing.

—Really? Wow.

She went into the bathroom and closed the door and he listened to her pee and when she came back out he said, —Yeah well. It's not uncommon. Depression I mean. It's a chemical imbalance that comes with being stressed out.

—Honestly though I'm not interested in what kind of life you live.

—Are you mad because I, you know.

—No. I'm not mad because of that or for any reason because I'm not mad. I don't care enough to be mad. I just don't like it. I've had guys do that before. Most of the time they ask first, but . . .

—Yeah but that's my thing though.

She buckled the bra and lit a cigarette, unable to hide that the hand was shaking, and she put on the shirt, which came halfway down the belly, and when she put the hair in a ponytail he saw a dark discoloration at the base of the neck and said, pointing at it, —Is that why you're mad?

She laughed, covering the spot with her hair, and said, —Good night.

He chased after her and caught her before she could go and wrote her a check for five thousand dollars, saying, —Please don't tell anybody.

And the bartender took the check and blew smoke in his face maybe or maybe not on purpose and the bartender had some sort of winged creature tattooed on the back and as the bartender left the bartender looked like she might cry, touching the hair and the neck again. After closing the door after the bartender Gilbert stared into the closet for half an hour, listening to his breath coming out of his nostrils, and the next day on the plane back to Los Angeles he found himself staring out the window at the clouds and the sun lighting them golden and texturized and came to the brink of tears because he didn't know what to say about himself. He bought Brianne a pair of diamond earrings from the duty-free shop at LAX. Brianne liked the earrings so they had sex, and he did not touch her neck which set off alarms in her head and he was wary of her because she was sleeping with him and seemed to enjoy it and so what kind of person was she? Was it the money she liked? He saw little difference between Brianne and the bartender. Both were whores. Most everyone he knew in the Association wrote checks to pretty young women—considering they were unremarkable and lingered somewhere in the middle of the ladder, mediocre, therefore normal, that made them the rule—he could not expend the energy required to think about anything outside of himself and he could not control anyone but himself.

—I think I'm depressed.

—What?

—I think I am. Do you know the symptoms? Of depression? Guilt, unhappiness, sleeplessness. A constant sort of bad feeling.

—Where'd you hear this?

—I don't know. A commercial.

—And you feel this way.

—Sometimes, yeah. But at least I can pinpoint the problem, you know? So I'm going to the doctor in the morning and getting some antidepressants so I can start working on it.

—You're fine though.

—No. It's going to be a long battle but I'm prepared to fight it. I can always find ways to improve. If you think you're perfect and don't need to improve yourself then you're lazy. Never stop learning. Never stop improving. You gotta be ready when you get the call.

—Yeah, but Gilbert, you're not depressed though.

—Brianne, I am. I need to fix it.

—My sister was depressed. I mean like *really* depressed. Being depressed is not being able to get out of bed. It's like trying to slit your wrists all the time. She tried to kill herself, I mean. I saw her. She looked like a cat attacked her. I mean, she was totally fucked up.

—Which sister? Geena? It was Geena I bet wasn't it.

—Yeah but it's not just being unhappy though. Because that's everyone pretty much.

—You're not happy?

—I didn't say that.

—You said everyone though. You're everyone. I don't make you happy?

—Gilbert stop.

—See what I mean? Everything is about me. I cannot stop making everything about me. That's a sign right there. Listen. Did you . . . you know. Come? Just now?

—Oh my God.

—Did you have an orgasm?

—It doesn't matter.

—You didn't.

—That has nothing to do with anything Gilbert. You're not depressed, okay? It's the off-season and you're not playing. Once you start playing again you'll feel better.

—No. It's never been like this any other off-season.

—You're fine. Look at you. You have it all. A beautiful fiancée.

—Yeah yeah yeah.

—I'm kidding.

—I mean I can't even give my so-called beautiful fiancée an orgasm. I'm selfish and totally self-absorbed and—

—No you're not.

—You don't know everything about me, Brianne. I'm sorry but you don't. Not everyone knows everything about me. They think they do. There are things you all don't know. Okay? I'm fucked up for one thing. Okay? There it is. Gilbert Marcus is fucking fucked up. I'm not clean-cut and like awesome like everyone thinks. For whatever reason. I'm twisted and horrible and really quite astoundingly disturbed and I need help.

—You're not horrible.

—No? Yes I am. I'm a rotten depressed person and you don't know anything.

I think about IT when I could be thinking about basketball   I am self-indulgent for thinking about IT so much rather than basketball I am selfish and self-absorbed and undesirable for I still have miles to go and tons of work to do on my game, improvements to make such as my front-court game and my defense is good but not dominant it should be an inescapable force—most of my game is indeed phenomenally good but not the best in some places—and until my game is the best in EVERY PLACE!!!

I hate IT and won't think of IT anymore because IT's a sin choosing the pleasures of the world THIS IS A sick materialism that is a by-product of growing up in a society so focused on objects AND IS a way of trying to weasel out of self-improvement and growth   I am a broken man who cheats on his fiancée   *I AM MY FATHER, MERVIN MARCUS*   I need to get over it so I can marry Brianna I mean Brianne who I have been engaged to for four years now out of fear of getting married

The world does its best to tempt you&works against people who strive for great heights like myself & but it is the job of the individual to possess the strength of will to shut out that which is evil & I am WEAK for letting my brain stray, my heart wander, and I am flawed for losing focus   there IS such a thing as the devil and the devil is that which is not what you are but what you are tempted to be and THAT IS GOOD&EVIL!!   *MERVIN MARCUS*   The Athlete must be on top of the world& NOT AFFECTED BY IT   In times of weakness my darkness shines through & the tainted parts of me that have chewed away   brain corrupted by TV
& advertising& our general culture's declining morals   &luring me into their grasp with IT IT IT I must overcome IT IT must be corralled to the outside worldMERVIN MARCUS   kill IT   I am better than IT   resist "THE DEVIL"   and I am better than the world which has given birth to IT & but I won't let IT touch meMY FA-THERanymore   *the world must DIE so that I will never sin again.*

*   *   *

He knew that George, the Dallas Lonestars' team physician, would hardly listen to him and end up writing him a prescription for a sleep aid or get him some human growth hormone and be done with him, so he shelled out the thousand clams to go to a Beverly Hills doctor recommended by a successful mononymous R&B singer, at this doctor's private practice, a cozy shady building in the same strip of offices as a pet funeral home and a tanning salon, with matching decor and manicured shrubbery in various geometric shapes and swirls, one bush that was in the shape of a dinosaur.

Dr. Bruce Bennet sat cross-legged on a stool with the paternal gaze of a man schooled in bedside manner and Gilbert could see a piece of white nearly hairless leg, and this made him forget the receptionist who was white and beautiful and young and with eyebrows artfully plucked and the receptionist looked up at him with desire in the eyes and he had to look away. The doctor held a thick stack of medical records on his lap, eyes clear ocean blue that made him look psychotic. White hair and orange skin that made Gilbert wonder if he ventured next door to the tanning salon during lunch. The creepy glow of youth in those who are not young.

—We're having a bit of a rough time? said the doctor and Gilbert smiled and went, —Well yeah I guess you could say that. Thing is though I know it's physical.

—It is.

—And so I'm ready to take the steps to get myself back on track and enjoy life to its fullest. I'm ready to get better.

The doctor's stare made Gilbert feel like a pink bundle of nerves whimpering for nurturing. The doctor nodded and said, —You know to be honest we don't get a lot of basketball players in here. Or any athletes at all to be honest. Unless you count bowlers as athletes. Do you count bowlers as athletes? I don't.

—Uh, no, I don't think. No. I don't know.

—I'm a little surprised to have you in here, with all due respect.

—None taken.

—And I do respect you Gilbert. A lot. You have no idea how much I respect you. I'm surprised, I have to tell you, not just because of who you are but rather what you do. See, athletics, physical exercise, has a way of making us happy.

—Yeah, yeah. Endorphins and—

—It causes endorphins to rush to your brain, which is like a natural antidepressant. They call it an endorphin rush because it's like a natural high of sorts. I should know. I happen to play a lot of racquet-ball.

—Yeah I don't know though. I mean I'm just telling you how I feel. This is the way things are for me. This is where I'm coming from and I want to get help. So. Before the season starts I mean. So I can be focused when it does.

—I've had a few of them come in here. Bowlers I mean. Depressing bunch, bowlers. Let me tell you. It's not hard to see why either. Personally I don't qualify as sport something you can do while smoking a cigarette or drinking beer. I feel very strongly about this. Sports take *skill. Acumen.* Physical *exertion. Intense mental training.* A certain purity of body. I could go on.

—I'm not sure though what this has to do with.

—You smoke marijuana?

—No. Nuh-uh.

—It's okay, you can tell me. Who am I gonna tell? Patient-doctor confidentiality. You shoot heroin? Don't laugh, I know how you guys are during off-season. I read ESPN.com daily. Young guys with money, living it up, enjoying yourselves. You guys lead very stressful lives. You train very rigorously, and so when you get a break you enjoy yourself. How much marijuana would you say you smoke? Per week.

—Um, seriously, I—

—Just, you know. Guess. Rough estimate.

—Honestly? Just once.

—Once a week.

—No. Once ever.

The doctor wrote something and looked back at Gilbert, jittering his nonsocked loafered left foot, and said, snapping his lips, —How many alcoholic beverages would you say you consume on average per week? Again, roughly.

—I don't know. Not a lot.

—Yeah but how many?

—You mean since the season ended? Because I've been like you said taking this month to just relax. It's been a weird month is what I'm saying. Or do you mean to average this month into the rest of the year? Because I don't drink anything at all during the season. Nothing. I hardly drink now even. It's not like I'm an alcoholic or anything. Like, I know Vin Baker, okay? I know what he's like. If that's what you're getting at. I'm not like that. That's not my thing.

—No one's saying you're an alcoholic.

—It's just been a strange month. It's been very stressful. I know I said this is supposed to be the one month that isn't stressful. But. Well, that's why I'm here I guess. It's, you know, unique circumstances.

The doctor wrote something and whispered to himself and sort of shook his head while smiling and Gilbert tried to see what he was writing but couldn't. This made him uneasy. He didn't like when somebody was writing something about him and he couldn't see what they were writing. Dr. Bennet had a full head of white Brillo-like hair and a melon polo shirt with the collar flipped up beneath his white doctor coat and no undershirt so Gilbert could see his wiry gray chest hair. There was a blown-up poster-sized picture among his diplomas of a younger version of himself and three other similar-looking white men white-water rafting, paddles angled, helmets tight, mist spraying over the bow of their inflatable yellow vessel, faces wincing in a profound and simple joy. Dr. Bennet clicked his pen and said, —Yes or no. Have you ever felt fatigued now and then for no apparent reason?

—Sure. Now and then. I mean. I'm busy as hell and—

—Just yes or no please.

—Oh. Yeah. Yes.

—Do you ever feel wooden or lifeless?

He was staring directly at Gilbert as he asked these questions, pointing with his pen for emphasis, his brow furrowed and glasses slipping onto the edge of his nose, voice crisp and booming.

—Um . . . yes. I guess.

—Have you ever experienced drug flashbacks?

—No.

—Do you feel less alert than you used to?

—Well yes but it's the off-season and I'm relaxing like I said and. Yes.

—Do you sometimes get a feeling of light-headedness or a feeling of being spaced out?

—Yes. I guess. Why? What is—

—Do you feel irritable without reason or cause?

—Yes. (Right now.)

—Do you have unexplained aches and pains?

—Yes. (The one you're giving me in my neck.) No. What do you mean though by *unexplained*?

—Do you find it difficult to get excited about people and things?

—Sure. Yes. (You. This.)

—Do you find you feel anxious and don't know why?

—Yes. All the time. Constantly.

—Do you have trouble learning new things even when you are interested in them?

—No.

Dr. Bennet nodded and looked down at his lap, muttering, counting something with the tip of his monogrammed gold fountain pen, and Gilbert held out a meek hope that the reason Dr. Bennet could afford to run his practice in Beverly Hills was because he held the key that would unlock the doors to a world unlimited in its potential where men are satisfied with their wives and women fear nothing and where there is no guilt or unbearably attractive women to sleep with and so no one inflicts horror onto one another, rather all that is relevant is written out and told to you at birth so that you might pursue that with your time here and not waste it trying to figure it out yourself—where people live and succeed and are liked and fit and wealthy and want nothing. The ideal world!

Dr. Bennet crossed his legs and said to Gilbert, —You're experiencing a case of severe body pollution. You have a detrimental level of accumulated toxins making you dull and wooden, with lessened ability.

—I'm dull?

—It's affecting your capacity to think clearly.

—Yeah but okay but like what kind of toxins though? How do you know this since you didn't run any tests or anything? Because I flush my digestive system regularly and don't eat anything that's not organic. I eat water-based foods. On an empty stomach. And I don't mix meats with carbohydrates. Nothing I eat contains preservatives or added sugars or even flavoring.

—Are you kidding me? Who knows what those trainers over there are putting into your body. Do you ask them? Do you know? Do they tell you what is in a cortisone shot? Do you have any *idea* what's in a B_{12} injection? Do you grow your own produce?

—No.

—And just being in this city. With all the smog. Cigarette smokers. The drinking water.

—I have a Brita. I don't drink tap. I have a Brita.

—It's no wonder really. Quite a shame you didn't come to me sooner. But everyone is in the dark. I'm not going to get too far into it, but they're brainwashed. Lucky for you there's help. Listen. We're not putting you on antidepressants. Do you know what those things do to you? They're essentially amphetamines. They're tested on rats and are deemed successful if they make the rats aggressive enough to kill each other. It's pretty much brain damage what those things do to you. I could go on. They dim your life. They're toxins.

—Wait a minute. Wait. Okay, I see where this is going. You got me.

—You have to listen to me right now, Gilbert. The Detoxification and Deprogramming Method developed by Mitchel Oliver . . .

—I've already been through my religious phase, so—

— . . . is the solution to handling these problems.

Gilbert stood up and went to the door and said, —Listen, thanks a lot but . . . and he turned the knob but it was locked and Dr. Bennet took a book from a box in the corner and scribbled a phone number on the inside and handed it to Gilbert saying, —This is forty dollars and you can pay Margo for it on your way out. I'll tack it on to the bill but listen. Read this book. Call the number I wrote inside. You have no idea what the Systemism Joy Church can do for you, Gilbert.

He went home and read the first seventeen pages of the book and decided not only that he was polluted with toxins but that these toxins were the cause of the turmoil within himself that he could not shake and that by becoming a member of the Systemism Joy Church he would get the answers he needed to purify himself and find the peace he'd never had. He'd been brainwashed by American society and that's why when a body with huge tits in a skirt would step into his path his entire universe would collapse around the desire for the body. He called the number and paid thirty thousand dollars for enrollment in the introductory course which included reading material, instructional videos starring the movie star John Lui whose action flicks Gilbert had seen all of, went to his first class which talked a little bit about how to handle being famous and giving people what they need from you while maintaining your personal being, hung out in the Star Quarters which was where all the famous Systemism Joy members congregated, met the actor Eddie Fulton who had earlier in the year won his third Oscar, told Brianne about it when he went home that evening, and after seeing how boyishly excited the man she loved was and how it made him happy she signed up. Brianne thought that this might be the thing that would cause them to get married. She was only twenty-one but had still been engaged for four years of her life without a wedding date and it was coming to the point where a decision had to be made one way or the other. Brianne and Gilbert began exclusively eating walnuts (following the diet set forth by Mitchel Oliver) in the on-site cafeteria between classes, and he and John Lui arm-wrestled and made plans to go up in John Lui's plane because John Lui was a pilot as was Eddie Fulton, though John Lui could fly fighter planes while Eddie Fulton had to stick to recreational single engines and heli-copters, and that weekend Gilbert and John Lui flew to the deserts of Utah where they ingested salt tablets and went rock climbing and rode dirt bikes, even though such dangerous activity was forbidden in in-disputable language in The Athlete's contract.

Systemism Joy was a religion of rebellion. Systemism Joy was a religion without deity. The only one you had to answer to was your-self.

Karl Babcock called and left a voice mail (sounding like a wretch) saying he was in town but Gilbert didn't answer because he saw who it was on the caller ID. He told Brianne, in the passenger seat of the Hummer, driving home from the Star Quarters, —The guy just has the wrong idea about everything. He doesn't get it. His thing is, he's too into the negative. Systemism Joy is all about the positive.

Brianne smiled and reached over from her seat and played with the hair on the back of his head and said, —Good. Because for a minute there I thought I was losing you.

—No, you were never losing me, baby. I just got a little crazy be-cause I didn't know how to handle what people expected from me, you know? I didn't put my life first. I got stressed and it was giving me a low self-esteem and I was just kind of flipping out, you know? But all that's over, thank God.

—So you're not going to do antidepressants now?

—Christ no. Those things. Listen. John Lui was telling me like how like fucked up those things are. I can't remember exactly what he said. But. He had some really good points. The guy's really smart. Modern psychiatry he was saying is basically a bunch of crap where they don't actually help you. They just drug you up and make money off you. It's amazing how much crap there is. Like how many lies. You know?

She smiled and pinched his earlobe and he laughed and said quit it, snatched her hand away, kissed it, shook his head and went, —I don't know. I just feel like the world's opening up, you know? I feel so

happy right now. There's so much possibility now. Everything's just
falling into place it feels like. This is the best day of my life. Seriously.
It is.

She leaned over, kissed him, laid her head on his shoulder, sighed.

Soon it was time for Gilbert to fly to Dallas to meet with coaches to
prepare for the season and to consult his dermatological team based in
Kansas City and nutritionist and bowel specialist (both based in Miami)
and so he had to cut back on his class load to make room for private
conditioning programs and acupuncture and time in his sensory deprivation chamber and watch film of himself so he could find what he
needed to improve on. Brianne therefore passed into the Second Phase
before he did and he let her pay the $54,000 with his American Express
Black Card. They had slow, uninhibited sex. He had never felt so close
to somebody before. The way her breath tasted when they kissed. Her
face in his hands. Her rich lips. Their bodies cut from the same bone.
And he thought, She is the most beautiful woman in the world and I
am lucky to have her. They talked about the wedding. It would be in
Nepal or they would lease an entire cruise ship for a month. They
talked about children. They volunteered to host Systemism Joy fund-
raisers at their home to raise money for cancer research and child
paralysis treatment, wearing their Systemism Joy T-shirts and drinking
fruit juice squeezed fresh, attended by producers and studio execs and
Dr. Bennet and John Lui (who wore only black T-shirts and prefaded
jeans and was shorter than you'd expect) and ranking Systemism Joy
officials (though not Mitchel Oliver who was old and didn't venture
out of the Star Quarters much anymore) and a story editor on *Sur-
vivor* and a couple retail CEOs and the successful mononymous R&B
singer and Eddie Fulton and Eddie Fulton's wife who looked like a
walking skeleton with very nice hair and the fund-raisers Gilbert and
Brianne hosted at their home were catered by handsome boyish models
and ice sculptures of swans and nude young actresses in body paint
standing around the yard. Gilbert and Brianne were invited one day to
the Star Quarters to meet Mitchel Oliver in his private wing and
Mitchel Oliver rode up on a Segway scooter which he stayed on the entire time and he had a beard and spoke with a heavy Eastern European
accent that sounded fake and his hair was cut, it appeared, into a
widow's peak and his voice was high and on the webbing of his left
thumb was a horrific open wound that his assistant warned Gilbert and
Brianne beforehand was an insect bite. The meeting consisted of being
introduced to Mitchel Oliver and shaking Mitchel Oliver's hand with

the horrific open wound on it and touching the horrific open wound with your own thumb then being hustled away by the assistant who was in her early fifties and wore a business suit and resembled a high school principal.

He'd say to Brianne twice a day, —This is the greatest day of my life.

And she said she wanted a baby and he agreed, so she stopped taking her birth control pills, took an EPT first once a week then every other day. He came to the brink four times of confessing to her about all the other girls he had slept with since he had been with her (there had been over a dozen in all) in the belief that it was necessary and would shatter whatever remaining glass wall was between them thus allowing them to connect totally.

Systemism Joy was a religion of honesty.

He was completely over all that anyway. Now he could see how he had just been doing what he'd been brainwashed by the American media to do as a young man of color with a lot of money. You're not a man unless you screw a lot of chicks, is what society told you. You're not successful unless you have a lot of sexual intercourse. You're not a man unless you idealize the physicalities of women to the point that they are not people but mere sexual objects to obtain and fertilize, which is why, he realized now, after all this time, that the bodies were always such a big deal for him. Thinking of his old ways disgusted him. Thinking of his old ways gave him the same retching reaction in the gut you get when you think of children being molested. He'd turned the corner and all that ugliness was over. She didn't deserve the pain that would be caused by confessing everything to her. And neither did he. Telling her about it would be allowing it to do more damage than it'd already done. I'm a doer anyway, he thought, not a sayer—always have been, and saying you're changing means nothing. What's done is done and the future shines bright, and I've learned from the mistakes of my youth. I had a tough road because my father was such a poor example for me. It's understandable then that I would make mistakes. But now it's time to grow up.

It was good all the way through summer and into September which snuck up on him because the summer of 2001 had been by far the greatest and richest summer of his life (even though her results were always negative) and there was no doubt that his Lonestars would defend the crown again and achieve something rare (a Three-peat) and be remembered for it.

16

AND IN ANOTHER DREAM SHE WAS confused by him. In another he met her again in the future, and her face was cold and she offered her hand but was indifferent toward him.

—What happened? she said. —One day you just left.

And then the sun, thick knit glove on her hand, and fine hairs on the side of her face, eyes concealed behind thick shades. Her face had aged, roughened.

These he awoke from in the middle of the night with his pillow damp and Brianne curled up beside him. He listened to make sure she was still asleep and lay back down and stared up at the ceiling wide awake like he'd never been asleep at all.

This was the truth of the world, the way things came to be. Before the storm came the calm. Peaceful men looked around themselves busy and desperate to find something wrong only to recoil in horror when something became wrong. As the summer of the year 2001 crept toward Truth time began eating its way to the end, which was a bright blue sky and oddly warm. Men stepped out of taxis and dropped their briefcases and vaguely noticed the beauty of the day, feeling a charge in the sky that could not distract them from their work and schedules. And someone spoke and another one uttered and a horn honked and waitresses at breakfast bistros stuffed cash into their apron pockets as then a third poked his dish asking if this was over easy as a woman with a new hairstyle touched her lips in the reflection of her spoon and a man along a brick wall in a baseball cap stomped out his cigarette and moved aside for an old man coming by with a walker, people slipped ringing cell phones from their pockets and put them to their heads and asked hello as summer interns forked undressed salads and teenagers screwed stoned vowing their unending love and all of this was done walking in circles with the television on because that's the way lives were lived in the summer of the first year of the second millennium—a time that couldn't look itself in the face and turned its back to your eye. They sighed bored and wondered how they looked for this was the country where they were born.

It happened at a quarter to nine in the morning after showers and coffee and during bus rides when the people were fresh and childlike. As the sun painted the sky the trash along the streets was still. They'd remember their guilt for years to come—their impure thoughts, their dirty vagueness, both dissipating cruelly as the conflagration grew and it all made itself clear.

Some—many—thought, Finally something is happening to me.

They were confused by the Truth, every one.

For once they were alone, they quickly settled back into their mobs.

It was chaos and they were a flock of colors and fell back on pride for this was no time for thinking—a shaming catastrophic flailing of devolution to their tribal instincts of defend and feed until they were a race of glass-eyed divorcés staring with chin in hand, starving for touch. All their submerged lost desires finally allowed rampant because no one was standing guard. It was psychological anarchy as temporarily society's strict dress code was suspended and the big trampled the small and all were allowed to go naked. And they knew at the second moment of impact that there was now a line of mattering that exposed the meaning of being a human among idle pick-about. What mattered and what was of worth? And what would this change and would they be remembered?

The Truth came on a Tuesday that nobody wanted to wake up for because it was a Tuesday. The Truth was for reasons no one but they would really ever understand. And so many mommies and daddies and babies died in the Truth that years later those who watched still had to stop and remind themselves of exactly what happened.

Because it was what happened.

What people who were watching the Truth were conscious of was only that they were people watching tragedy happening to people.

They were already sinking into grief as it quickly consumed the dead and traveled on to the living. It inflated the living into giants incapable of remembering the end of humans' lives, only where they themselves were and how they felt watching it, so that they could tell one another where they were and how they felt watching the Truth and this carried over for years until what happened to the people who died happened to those who were in charge of co-opting what happened to those who died and selling what happened back to those who didn't die.

The Truth, as all truths, became a cool reality that transformed and morphed into other Truths and slid through your skin and lived inside you.

Brianne woke Gilbert up mildly hysterical. It was morning, the day's first purple light merging over the hills, and for a brief moment he was confused as to where he was. He said in a creaky voice, —What time is it?

—Like six o'clock. But look.

She went to the forty-seven-inch flat-screen plasma HDTV installed on the wall like a piece of artwork and turned it on as the second plane hit the World Trade Center and they watched it and he said, —What are you doing up so early?

She didn't answer. He had to be at the gym to run sprints at 6:37 before his System of Bravery class, and then a meeting at the Four Seasons that afternoon with Ben Jermaine who lived in L.A. too for his own endorsement season and Ben's lawyers and the Lonestars' front office who were flying in from Dallas, presumably to discuss the growing rift that had appeared in the last month between the two stars, so he got out of the bed and got dressed, saying, —Damn that's fucking crazy.

He went downstairs. Every flat screen plasma HDTV in the house was on. He shook his head and turned them all off on his way out to the garage. He went to his gym and his conditioning coach wasn't there. The gym was locked, so he called Ryan, the conditioning coach, who didn't answer, left a message apologizing for being late, saying it was car trouble, ran suicides in the underground VIP parking lot which stayed empty for the entire twenty-eight minutes of his exercise. He realized when he was done that he hadn't brought water and panicked thinking about all the damage not rehydrating was doing to his body. He went to a 7-Eleven for a Perrier but all they had was Evian which annoyed him but there was nothing he could do about it because now he was almost late for his System of Bravery class at the Star Quarters so he brought the Evian up to the register but the Middle Eastern cashier was immersed in the little TV he had behind the register his arms crossed and a finger on his lips muttering to himself, —Oh God oh God oh God oh God.

—Excuse me, said Gilbert.

He paid for the Evian and got to Star Quarters but his System of Bravery class had been canceled and they were all—John Lui, Mitchel Oliver's assistant, the mononymous R&B singer, Eddie Fulton, Eddie Fulton's wife whose tits seemed to have grown—sitting in the lobby area slack-jawed before the sixty-four-inch flat-screen plasma HDTV normally reserved for showing looped Systemism Joy orientation videos hosted by John Lui for prospective members touring the facilities. Gilbert munched on some walnuts and drank a glass of organic vegetable juice and watched the coverage with them for a little while before losing interest and going to the Four Seasons for the meeting with Papa Bear Ben Jermaine whom he hoped he would manipulate into asking to be traded but the concierge said nobody had yet arrived for the meeting, so Gilbert called Abe Birnbaum on his $732 cell phone with diamonds on it and Abe didn't answer and then he called Ben, cleared his throat, and Ben said, —Garrett.

—No it's me. Gilbert.

And there was a click and the line went dead. Ben'd hung up on him.

Gilbert felt colors rushing up his neck, bordering on rage, called Ben back but it was busy and was still busy twenty minutes later, so he got back in his car, went back to Star Quarters, watched as on the other coast a side of the Pentagon was destroyed, smoke pluming out and flames reaching up and husbands dying and daughters burning and the people here ate homemade nondairy yogurt and said between spoonfuls, —Holy shit.

He didn't know what the Pentagon was exactly but he watched footage of people jumping out from World Trade Center windows and he thought, They'll cancel the season. I won't get a Threepeat. It's all over. He said out loud to no one, —I need to go home and check on my wife. Make sure she's okay. But, man, I just don't know if I feel safe driving right now.

And the others nodded and said, —Yeah.

They were already collecting money for a donation to the victims and organizing a blood-donation drive and they were going to charge the donation to the members' American Express Black Cards which they already had the numbers of on file and so would just charge them directly.

On the road he tried to make eye contact with the other drivers to show how much this tragedy was affecting Gilbert Marcus. He wanted them to see how he was one of them now but all the windows were up and, eerily, nobody seemed to be reacting one way or the other. He turned on the radio but all the DJs had broken character and were somber and unprofessional. He got home and Brianne had already hung up an enormous U.S. flag in the front bay window. It made him think maybe there'd be a draft, he'd have to join the army. Abe Birnbaum would get him out of that. If not he'd run to Canada. He imagined crossing the border at night in a rowboat.

He stayed inside with Brianne for three days watching TV because this was important and you had to watch.

He told the maids they still had to come in and he and Brianne went down to donate blood. Gilbert said on the way down there, —But I mean I was just there. Like, down the road. I *saw* the World Trade Center. What if I had gone to New York just a few months after I did? What if they decided to do this just a few months before?

And Brianne nodded and said nothing because he'd been saying this for three days and the noncelebrities in line pretended not to notice Gilbert Marcus and Brianne Marcus and the day before he talked to Coach and learned the season would definitely go on and as he wrote a check for the Red Cross on the way out he said to Brianne, —What's another couple thousand?

He wasn't sure why she'd been so quiet the last couple days, not laughing at his jokes, shut off in herself in a way that made him nervous but she said to him on the way to the silver Audi parked in the public parking lot with everyone else's cars which unsettled him, —I'm so glad I have you, baby.

He put his arm around her and said, —Yeah I'm glad I have you too.

—We'll be okay, she said, —because they'll find who did it and we'll come together maybe as a country and we'll get married and we'll have a baby.

—What's the matter, baby? You seem like something's been bothering you lately. I mean besides all this.

—I don't know. I've been having these dreams.

—Hey, you want to stop and get a manicure or something?

—They're terrible.

—Manicures?

—No, she said, —the dreams I've been having. I can't even sleep. They're so bad.

—Tell me. What kind of dreams.

—All I see are like burned people. Babies.

—Jesus.

They hadn't eaten a single walnut in three days.

—Their skin is peeling and they're bloody. And they have no parents. And no one is doing anything about it.

—Whoa. That's horrible.

—Yeah, but when I wake up I'm happy. Not really happy but relieved. Because I know you're there and that being with you is one thing I can count on.

—Of course, babe. Did these just start?

—Yeah. Ever since. Because I mean look at the *world*.

—People see how we live here and get pissed.

—Look at what people *do* to each other. If I didn't have you and how good you are to me I'd probably—I don't know what I'd do.

—But, yeah, at least we have each other. And you can always trust in that.

His palms were sweating so much he had to let go of her hand and he looked down at her snuggled against him in the way she liked to walk with him but which made it difficult for him to walk and he saw her eyes looking back at him and they hadn't been to the Star Quarters in three days but they would definitely get back into it once things settled down and life was back to normal. Brianne turned her face toward his for a kiss and he kissed her and he said, —I love you.

But he had to turn away pretending to not be able to get his keys out of his pocket.

Brianne hadn't had more than an hour or two of sleep a night for four nights when she shook him awake early on a Tuesday morning in September and he rolled over and looked at her with eyes that were blank like he didn't recognize her. Briefly it gave her alarm. *Like this is a different person.*

Before waking him up she had been downstairs with the TV on low and unable to look at the newscasters whose off-air lives took place when all others were asleep and this exhausted her. She was holding out for the sun to rise so maybe she could see it and lose herself in its basic awe and feel beautiful. It was five in the morning and she was fighting back tears. She couldn't place them and was ashamed that her new religion had an answer for them no doubt but she didn't know what it was. Coffee gurgled that she wouldn't drink and didn't know why she made it. She hadn't worked in more than two years. There was still no definite wedding plan. Two weeks earlier she had been dropped from her modeling agency. She was twenty-one and washed up. Girls she used to know were becoming megastars and no longer returned her phone calls. She was seriously considering doing a reality show on the USA network that she was offered. A paring knife from the Shun Pro series six-piece set in the kitchen was in her hand and she idly pushed it into the fleshy underside of her wrist considering the thin distance between being alive and not being alive. But she wouldn't really do it.

She was seriously considering moving to Austria and opening a dog-grooming salon there.

This was what she did at night now.

He must never know, even if she'd never broken skin. There was reassurance in metal on flesh. When the sun rose she would take a shower and put on her makeup and smile as he came down the stairs. But that's when the news broke—word that something had happened, in New York. And she dropped the knife and sat up, wiped her nose with the back of her hand, turned the TV up, went to the TV in the kitchen, turned it on, watched, then to the bathroom, turned that TV on, upstairs to the guest bedroom, then the empty one that might one day be a nursery, then both the upstairs bathrooms, every room, every TV, until you couldn't escape.

He was having nightmares too but his were slow and steady and came in the daytime and were dreams of fear and a rampaging disturbance though he wasn't somebody who could remember his dreams and normally placed little importance in them.

His instincts told him as he witnessed what they had already given a catchy name, logo, and theme song that this would make sports and entertainment disposable or at least demoted to the margins as artifacts of a time with no worries, a time spoiled bored and nosy, the future, mere games to stimulate competitive instincts in idle times when disgusting human acts happened elsewhere outside this country cushioned by safety and wealth and food in which importance and emotional energy and testosteronic battling had to be obsessively placed in SOMETHING, but now the competition would not have to be charaded. He thought that because of this it would mean that he might be shoved back into the general mass, his time over, stripped of his medals to become just another citizen. A terrible fear: being average. His championships, his four consecutive scoring titles, and his life would overnight come to signify nothing. All the idols he worshipped would be proved false because people were dead and children were buried and the earth had become twisted in sin, and all fabrics were unraveling and there was no time anymore for games.

But I won't go lightly, he thought. He went to Dallas and worked out alone in the dark in the new arena called the Heffington Financial Palace in which he had a private suite. All night, alone, running suicides, puking his guts out, shooting eight hundred shots in the morning then eight hundred at night, etc., and when the season began in November once again his motivation was his life. And winning was life again and losing was death. And he wrote checks to charities and that trip to the Star Quarters was his last. He ignored threatening phone calls from John Lui and Mitchel Oliver. He had to pull all cylinders and let the excess fall overboard for now was a time for the strong. A time for mattering among a swirl of ambiguity. Focus on his life to do all he could to see to it that he wasn't lost in the smoke but held tight and remained to be remembered.

When they're asleep, I'll be working. When they're putting things in perspective, I'll be here.

It was because when he stopped he found himself thinking of the bartender from New York and what he had done to her and her neck and if she was alive or not and the possibility that she could no longer be breathing and her bruised beautiful body dead after he had been inside her feeling her heartbeat.

When he was in New York the people he had seen from behind the tinted glass of his limo crossing the streets and blowing into their coffee—some, if not many, could very well be dead.

This put things back to the beginning. Back to basics.

People will need to believe in something, he thought, so they will believe in The Athlete. As they always have. For whatever reason.

The season resumed in November, and Gilbert stood in the doorway of the state-of-the-art Heffington Financial Palace high-fiving the Dallas Lonestars as they arrived for the first game against San Antonio, slapping them on the ass, getting in their face and grabbing them by the collar, saying, —We got to let them know we're here! And they assumed he was talking about the other teams in the league, and fed off his passion, and there was a new spirit of fight in the air with the country humming for blood and Gilbert snatched this and carried it, the Lonestars saw the fury in his eyes for a Threepeat and had to keep up with his intensity on the court or he would be on them for it. They were led easily with an unspoken gratitude. They were relieved they could forget about the Truth having already worn themselves limp via mourning and news coverage. Ben Jermaine stepped aside too letting Gilbert take charge (for now), seeing the same thing in Gilbert the other guys saw. Ben Jermaine smelled victory and his spine buzzed with the thought of a Threepeat. He clamored for what was hanging within reach: greatness.

Gilbert hired a documentary film crew to follow him around throughout the season to make a movie about Gilbert Marcus's pursuit of glory in the aftermath of 9/11. Though he had one of the greatest personal seasons in Association history, the movie was abysmal and fizzled due to lack of interest from the studios and never got released. Nonetheless, he set the league record for assists in a game with thirty-one and went seven games with over ten rebounds per game.

Despite a possible officiating conspiracy and many key injuries, the Dallas Lonestars led by Gilbert Marcus had one of the greatest seasons ever in Association history, winning thirty-three straight games and finishing with seventy-two wins in all, tying the record. They were 38-3 at the All-Star Break. In the playoffs they lost a total of just four games in four series. Gilbert played in all eighty-two games and averaged 31.1 points, 6.1 rebounds, and 6.3 assists, and 40.4 minutes per game. He shattered seven different regular-season club records, most of which had been set by him the previous two years—free-throw attempts, field goals made, points scored, minutes per game, field goals attempted in the championship. Another record he set was for most game-winning shots, with eight, not counting game-winning free throws, of which he had three. He had three more buzzer beaters in the postseason. He put in one of the greatest postseason performances anyone had ever seen, in any sport. He was a unanimous choice for league MVP. He was featured on *SportsCenter* nearly one thousand times and won an Espy for Sportsman of the Year. He was on the cover of *Time* magazine and secretly came in at a close second for Man of the Year. *People* named him one of its Sexiest Men Alive. On the social front, when a seventeen-year-old kid in Newark was shot to death over his Gilbert Marcus Dallas Lonestars jersey, Gilbert paid for the funeral. And in the Association Championship when Dallas swept Atlanta in Atlanta in four games they were too tired to celebrate but fell into one another, the stadium silent and emptying quickly. They trudged their way to center court to get their trophy and pose for the pictures. Gilbert Marcus was named Championship MVP. They muttered into microphones in postgame interviews how it felt to win three championships in a row. Then they went home so they could think about how they felt. And what had happened. What it meant to be great.

17

S HE OPENED HER EYES TO GILBERT putting on a tie in the mirror over the dresser and she stretched and rolled onto her back and said, —What are you doing baby?

—Get up. We're getting married.

—Today? Now? What?

—Yup. In two hours.

—But I don't have a dress.

—You're not going to have a dress. You don't need a dress.

—But the dress is what I've looked forward to though. Since I was a little girl. It's what every little girl dreams of. Wearing the dress and being beautiful and everyone being there and—

—We talked about this.

—I know we did. But. I don't know. I can't even call my mom and my dad?

—Why? *I* don't need anyone there. *I* don't need a dress. Why do you?

—Because.

—I just need you. I don't need anybody at our wedding but you. It's nobody's business but ours. It's about you and me. Nobody else. I just need you. Aren't you happy with just me?

— . . .

—Come on. Get dressed. We're late.

—But you said we have two hours.

She took a shower—shaving quickly—and went into the closet which was the size of some people's bedrooms and found a pink dress and held it up in front of her and smiled, cheeks rosy, because this was a dress she'd forgotten she had but it would be the perfect dress, aside from an actual wedding gown. Sometimes she surprised herself at how attractive she was in expensive clothes. Yes, this dress would make everything okay. Getting married like this was a much more acceptable idea in a good dress—really, what was a wedding dress anyway? Some of them could be quite unflattering. And didn't love conquer a silly childhood dream of, what, a garment? A piece of cloth? Childhood dreams were shed all the time—like the one she had about wanting nothing more in her life than a pony—so what was another one? It was part of being a grown woman, and she was to be married, which made her an adult now.

She carried the dress out of the closet and said, —How about this one?

He looked up, picking his lip, with the face of a man waiting for a woman, looked her over, and said, —Yeah fine. Whatever, you know? Then went back to picking his lip and studying the carpet.

FOREVER.

Her shoulders dropped and what was rosy in her cheeks drained, her eyes dulled over, let the dress drag on the floor as she went to the other side of the bed where, with her back to the man she was dressing to marry, who wasn't aware of her, she let the towel drop and bent over a little to conceal her nakedness, stepped awkwardly into the stupid dress, which when she came to think of it made her look fat and even a little slutty, how low the neck was, and made her legs look stumpy. So quiet she thought she'd vomit, her body unfit for the world's eyes, not like trees or swans floating on a lake, which must be seen to be beautiful, but rather like feces or fungal infections, which must be hidden out of public sight because they make people sick and uncomfortable and dislike you, thinking in words so clear like she was whispering into her own ear, —I am not basketball, so I don't exist. I am periphery, surface. An inconvenience. I don't matter and none of this does. Not to him.

FOREVER.

Drove fast to the courthouse, cursing the red lights under his breath and honking at slow drivers, compulsively changing the radio station, wiping his nose with the back of his hand, pulling at his tie and reaching for the AC knob even though it was already maxed out, saying over and over, —Jesus it's *hot.*

Brianne wasn't hot. Actually she was cold because the air vent was blowing right on her, and something about the smell of the car made her a bit carsick. It was a brand-new yellow Hummer H2 that got eight highway miles a gallon and his uncomfortable fidgeting made her quiet and self-conscious. Was she sitting wrong? Did he not like her hair? Perhaps he was noticing finally the slight bump on the bridge of her nose? He was sitting up in his seat, hugging the wheel, cursing and sort of laughing incredulously.

—It's okay, she said, —we have time.

—No, baby, we actually don't. There's *no* time actually. It's fifteen minutes to the 10 alone and then eleven more minutes on that and then thirteen minutes once we exit. And that's not taking into account traffic or breakdowns. Plus parking, which there will be *none* of course. Because there are so many fucking *people* in this city. Plus walking from the parking lot to the actual courthouse. They should have an underground garage but who knows if they actually do or if it's under construction maybe. Since our government is so inept when it comes to things like that. Plus finding where we need to be, which will be impossible because nobody ever tells you where to be. Like you're supposed to *know* somehow. God forbid one of the drooling dropouts paid to sit around there actually helps you. Like if you weren't born with the inherent knowledge of where to go in the courthouse to get married then screw you. *Plus,* then we have to check in with the lady once we finally do find it. It'll no doubt be a lady. It's always a lady. A fat lady. With an attitude, no less. Like with seven kids with no father. A black woman with clown makeup on acting like *I'm* inconveniencing *her* by making her do what I as a tax-paying citizen pay her to do. *Plus—*

—It'll be fine, she said. —It'll be okay. It's our wedding day. Let's try to enjoy it a little bit.

—But they said to be there an hour before. That's RIGHT NOW! Jesus it's hot. And why do radio stations insist on all playing the same *shit* over and over? I mean, *Christ*! Is everyone retarded today?

The sky was blue and they both wore sunglasses and Gilbert had a mammoth hand on the small of her back as he pushed her across the courthouse parking lot. She was tall but next to him she was elbow height, the kind of girl whose body most expensive clothes were designed to fit, as often complained about by shorter wider girls taking things off the rack and holding them up to their imperfect frames and sighing.

—Gogogogo, he said, hustling her past two black kids crouched down next to the door throwing small rocks at a public metal trash can with various *pings* and *thuds* who looked up to see the incoming shadows of the well-dressed healthy good-looking couple—their presence immediately rendered yours invalid. They jolted upright as the couple jogged up the stone steps and the boys turned to each other and whispered, —Oh my God! Oh my God!

—Is that . . . ?

Gilbert groaned audibly. Brianne melted for them, their innocence. She envied them. But so careful not to be the nagging girlfriend— WIFE! FINALLY!—though she wanted to stop, crouch down to them and brush their cheeks with the back of her finger, and say, —Hey guys. And they'd be enchanted by her beauty and Gilbert would stay standing, smiling like he did on TV, and say, —How you guys doing? How about an autograph?

They'd find a basketball, drive down to a court, Gilbert'd let them win. Go home and tell all their friends but no one would believe them until they showed them the basketball, autographed personally to Kyle and Mike. They would be inspired, grow up, become lawyers.

Watching the kids over her shoulder, looking at Gilbert with eyes wide as planets, mouths open, one saying shyly, —Are you Gilbert Marcus?

—Of course he is, stupid, said the other one.

—Why's he here though?

—DUI I bet. Or domestic battery.

As Gilbert pulled her through the door by the hand—oblivious, not caring—he had a goal to accomplish right now and it was to get married, not to sign autographs or parent the youth of America. Brianne realized then that she didn't want to get married to Gilbert Marcus. The boys would remember this moment the rest of their lives, never fading in its picture-perfect clarity—the temperature, the wind, what shoes their hero was wearing, what shape rock they held in their palms as their idol blew them off on a beautiful Southern California summer afternoon when their parents were in court answering for possession and domestic abuse charges—while Gilbert Marcus forgot it as soon as the door closed behind him.

Brianne had been exceptionally pretty ever since she was a very small girl and so strangers' eyes drew to her like a shiny object in the grass. She was never alone. And so, afraid of ever being alone, she married Gilbert Marcus. She could compare the dire contrast between her life before and her life after the velvet ropes, comped tequila, personal bodyguards, party invites, anonymous flashbulbs of paparazzi in the corner of her eye, cash up the wazoo, attractive and important people at exclusive parties—movie stars and wealthy directors, intelligent executives, popular musicians—and when she remembered her life before becoming a model—the popular girl, New Jersey, suburban basements with friends, cold shopping malls, driving around bored on Friday nights, the sterile carpeting and dull bells of high school, homework, a part-time job folding shirts she'd never wear at a store where she told unsexy housewives they looked good in those jeans, ignoring the indiscreet leers from her male teachers—she could never go back. Knowing deep in her heart where the ugliest truths lie that the *Sports Illustrated* swimsuit issue had been her pinnacle as a model (unless she accepted the offer to do *Playboy*, which would only delay the inevitable) and that she would never be an actor like she thought she would be after she was dropped by her agency. She thought of all the auditions she'd gone on in the past four months, the unimpressed eyes of casting directors who smiled like midwestern church wives and thanked her for coming in and the condescending acting coaches who were failed commercial actors if anything who rolled their eyes and said something cruel to her because they knew they could never have her.

The main thing about pledging eternal devotion to someone who she might not be all that devoted to was that she didn't feel too great doing it. A chilly panic quickly set in. She was ashamed of herself, unable to say much, despairing because she was pretty and nobody was stepping in to save her. She was surprised to say the least at the forceful plainness of the act, unreal that it was happening—first she was not getting married and then she was getting married. Like a roller coaster creeping up its first incline and she was already nauseous and then it rises over the hill and WHOOSH! The judge sitting at his desk and putting on little glasses at the end of his nose which thin dark hairs stuck out of, peering down like at the edge of a cliff at the valley below, red-rimmed eyes watery and veiny and voice tired because he'd seen it all and didn't care. He met them, shook their hands, made distracted chitchat about where he ate lunch as he sat and invited them to do the same and he began reading something out loud in an office that could have been the storage room in the back of a DMV and she was unsure of what to do with her hands and suddenly it occurred to her that my God this was it, he was reading marriage stuff, this was the wedding, they were being married. The witness as required by law was a pudgy white girl who looked annoyed or just not very nice with stockings Brianne would never wear and a black skirt that was way too long but, Brianne supposed, was appropriate for a working environment. The annoyed witness must have been a secretary or summer intern. The annoyed witness stood with fingers interlocked over her puffy crotch beside the judge, idly looking over his shoulder at what he was reading aloud, of which Brianne understood nothing and trying to understand it gave her the same headache she got trying to read *Newsweek* which she had subscribed to after 9/11. The judge was reading like someone reading you an article and trying to get through to the important part they want you to hear. These people, she didn't know them, nor would she ever see them again, and their names she didn't recall though they introduced themselves on the way in and Gilbert didn't seem to be sharing the same intense experience she was having and was actually seeming to not only understand it but enjoy it as well. And Brianne was very afraid and alone chewing her lip and wanting this to be over. Which is when the judge stopped reading and Brianne was given a pen and she signed something and she was now somebody's wife forever. And then Gilbert and Brianne Marcus walked out the same door they came in and the sun the sidewalk and everything.

* * *

They got home and parked the Hummer in the sixteen-car garage beneath their house next to the Rolls-Royce with a sheet over it and got out of the car so that they could go inside the house and have sex. He walked ahead of her to the door and disabled the infrared alarm that notified the police in the event of a break-in by tapping the code on the illuminated keypad and opened the door and they went inside and he closed the door behind her and reactivated the security system, not looking at her, and she was so hungry she was grumpy but was able to hide it because this was her wedding day, and he put the keys on the hook by the door where the keys went when not being used, went through the living room and up the stairs with her following him with her arms crossed, and she stood in the doorway of the bedroom watching him remove his $310 gazelle-skin wallet from his back pocket and place it on the spot on top of the dresser where the $310 gazelle-skin wallet went when not being used, and then he removed his loose change from his pockets and dropped it in the Dean & Deluca coffee cup on the dresser where loose change went. The bed was perfectly made with the comforter pulled down, as he ordered the housekeeper Malea to do it, and Brianne watched him sit on his side of it and remove his dark brown custom-crafted Italian leather square-toed shoes and carry them into the closet and place them third from the left in the row of thirty-five similar pairs of shoes organized by color from black to brown, darkest to lightest. She was unsure of how to stand and imagined her parents watching this in metal folding chairs. She felt like a virgin. He took off his shirt and spread it out on the bed and smoothed out the wrinkles with his hand then fetched a wood hanger from the closet to put it on and hung it up. Then he undid his belt which matched the shoes and draped it over the imported rocking chair in the corner which Brianne had never noticed before. He shrugged at her as he draped his belt over the rocking chair as if to say, What the hell, live dangerously, eh? Then he removed his pants which he folded over his arms like a waiter's towel and then placed them on their designated wood clip hanger in their proper location (organized the same way the shoes were—darkest to lightest) in the pants section of the closet. He came out, literally skipping, his erection bobbing from behind his red silk boxers, staring directly at her breasts and breathing through his nose in a relentless grunt as he enveloped her body and kissed her, suffocating her with his sloppy tongue, squeezing her breasts, and she said,—Slow down, slow down. He couldn't hear her. It was more of the body that he needed—her bones, the tissue beneath, something sweet and squishy that he knew dwelled down deep—but no matter how fast he pulled her dress over her head, catching her ponytail and messing up her hair, making her more self-conscious, or how fast he yanked down her thong, making her brace herself against the wall and stand on one foot in order to allow him to TAKE HER PANTIES OFF NOW nearly losing her balance and for-getting about any hope of feeling sexy, or how fast he turned her around and bent her over the rocking chair, snorting as he pushed himself up against her and kneading the meat of her butt like he needed to tear off chunks for consumption, no matter how hard he forced himself into the unaroused vagina, hurting her, which she was used to by now, and no matter if he choked her until she saw little black spots with yellow rings that melted into red, he would never get past her flesh. And he was realizing this in a fast shameful irritation that turned to something more extreme as he muttered, —*Bend . . . over!* and pushed her face into the seat of the chair, smearing mascara all over the white fabric. He sodomized her, thinking about Ben, imag-ining him here, taking his place. She tried not to cry and was thinking about the judge, imagining him here, cross-legged and studious with a cocktail in a clear plastic cup and a paper napkin beneath it. She thought, One minute we can be in public wearing clothes careful not to curse or flatuate and the next minute we can be naked and the parts we wear clothes to conceal engorged, doing *this*.

She thought, All that makes this reasonable is a thin sheet of wood called a door and processed sand called glass combined to form a structure called a house. And then we put our clothes back on and go outside our house and pose for photographs and shake hands and smile, married. And they adore us. And they wish they were us. I'll call my mom and my sister and they'll be so happy for us.

If not for the pain shooting through her like she was being sliced in half, she would have laughed.

Later that night. On the balcony overlooking the Pacific Ocean. Feel-ing better because the air was breezy and salty, the first gasp of breath from sea travel, a perpetual twisting of new that brought in fresh smells from the middle of the ocean where sharks and snakes were and blind spongy things were roaming the floor, sucking the dirt of fungus and mildew—

not to mention the stars, as they had arrived in an expansive blanket spelling constellations and the impossible forever—

Brianne liked the way being small felt, if only for a little while. Fuzzy blue bathrobe wrapped around her and coming down over her hands, feet in white flip-flops, makeup removed in the shower so her face had the polished sheen of cleanliness—fresh, newborn, a perfect way to restart her life. She felt dread when she heard the sliding door open behind her and HER HUSBAND stepped out onto the balcony with her.

Because she wanted to be alone.

She wanted to tell him about the stars, and what they meant to her, and that she imagined the floor of the ocean way out thousands of miles from shore as the happiest place on earth where the animals lived free and got along and how she bet it's like another planet, with creatures no one even knew existed. Aliens, almost. And she wanted to tell her husband about everything else in a rambling tongue with no regard for sense and therefore covering all truths, coming out in one frantic overpowering splash as fast as her lungs could push it. Which, she thought as another gust blew off the beach and through her hair, her husband breathing into her neck, is love.

That's all we have here at the end of the world.

She said, —What were you doing inside?

He exhaled and stiffened and went, —Well I *was* getting dressed. Until I reached up for a shirt and realized one of the housekeepers, the new one probably—

—Elvira.

—*Elvira?* That's her *name?*

—She's from Latvia. It's in Russia I'm pretty sure.

—Russia? Maids don't come from Mexico anymore? Mexicans are too good to be maids nowadays? That's hilarious. But listen to this. She hung a *collared* shirt with the *T-shirts.* I don't know. I don't know what to do.

Brianne said, —So? Who cares. Just put it with the other shirts with collars on them.

—I don't know. He was rubbing his forehead. —I just don't know how to handle this. I'm thinking about firing her. I'll most likely fire her.

—Gilbert, look at the stars. They're beautiful.

—But I mean. Seriously. That's just totally not professional at all. Is it? It's not the professional thing to do. I might fire Malea too since she should have been supervising.

—So mention it to her tomorrow then. It was probably just a mistake.

I don't know. I have a feeling it wasn't a mistake.

Well just mention it to Malea in the morning. But the stars though. They're really beautiful tonight, aren't they? And look at the moon. It's our wedding night.

—Yeah. You're right. You're right.

They were quiet for four seconds then he said: —Maybe just suspend her. Malea I mean. Because maybe it wasn't totally her fault. Maybe what's-her-name tricked her. Like Malea checked on her and saw that the order of the closet was perfect and then went off to do something else, then what's-her-name deliberately took a collared shirt and misplaced it in with the T-shirts and proceeded to act like everything was normal. In fact I bet Malea probably even asked her at the end of the day how everything was and if she hung up the shirts properly like she'd been told and what's-her-name I bet LIED to her and said YES. Yeah, what's-her-name is terminated. I'll call Malea when I go back inside and tell her. I just can't have that kind of person in my house. I mean, who knows what else she's capable of, you know?

—They really make you feel tiny though, don't they? Insignificant. The stars I mean. Think about how far away they are right now.

—I can't have disorder running rampant in my home. We might be starting a family soon, for fuck's sake. And training camp is starting soon too.

—Not for two months though.

—I'm just so stressed out. I mean, I only ran three times last week because of getting ready for the wedding. And I ate a couple potato chips the other night too because of the anxiety. I'm a mess right now. I need to get my life in order. I need to see a therapist maybe. I can't have these kinds of mistakes to distract me. That's what a housekeeper does, right? They KEEP the HOUSE so busy people like me don't have to worry about it. So I can maximize my productivity. Why are they doing this to me?

—It'll be fine.

—I have a meeting with Adidas tomorrow and now I won't sleep tonight. Great. Thank you, Russia. Thanks a lot.

—Gilbert.

—They're on their ass. All of them. I'll find someone who actually takes a little pride in their work. There are a kajillion Mexicans in this city dying to be housekeepers. Literally dying, Brianne. Malea too. She's gone. Call immigration on all of them.

—Gilbert, the stars though.

—I don't *like* looking at stars, Brianne.

That first summer of their marriage he tried hard to be The Husband. It was a tough goal to obtain. He put his drive and work ethic into it, believing that if you work hard enough you can be the best. His time away from off-season training was spent in her company, shopping for new blinds, ordering new china sets from London. He bought her clothes, food. But in the mornings he had to be gone in a private gym or locked away in the basement gym lifting weights with Ralph, one of his personal trainers, consulting with his nutritionist at her office in Sherman Oaks regarding which kind of muffin was ideal for his body temperature, hanging out with up-and-coming rappers in the basement of the pool house, which he'd had converted into an extravagant recording studio with paneled wood walls and a pool table and video games and DVD players by John Sanchez, who did Dr. Dre's home studio and was more than a bit overrated in Gilbert's opinion.

Brianne shopped and wandered around the house sipping cranberry juice and wading in the pool, flipping through *In Touch* and *The National Enquirer* secretly hoping to find herself mentioned, rearranging throw pillows on the beds in guest bedrooms, working with her own personal trainer—a black woman named Vulu—with a focus on obtaining a body identical to that of Jennifer Lopez especially in a particular video she'd seen on MTV which she'd recorded and played for Vulu three times. She tanned with her cousins who visited from Austria for three weeks and stayed in the guesthouse and didn't like Gilbert but one of them slept with one of Gilbert's rapper friends. She had a personal waxing specialist come to the house to rip hair off her upper lip that the specialist—a young Korean or Vietnamese girl with breast implants around Brianne's age who she worried was prettier than she was—swore didn't even exist but slapped on the goo and ripped it off anyway. An intestinal expert came to the house to administer to Gilbert and—at Gilbert's strong goading—Brianne one colonic a month, though Gilbert wanted it more often, but the specialist told him any more often than once a month could potentially harm the intestine by removing beneficial enzymes, a fact Gilbert had a hard time believing and almost called his father to verify but stopped himself.

There was a Tuesday when Brianne stayed home talking to her ex-boyfriend who she was dating when Gilbert Marcus began pursuing her and who she lost her virginity to which was a moment she secretly held close to her heart but swore to Gilbert was something she was pressured into while drunk and didn't enjoy at all and totally regretted. The old boyfriend—Joel, a dancer she met at Fashion Week—wanted to know if they could meet for lunch to catch up since he was at home in Newport Beach from NYU for the summer and they had once been so close and wasn't it stupid to not even talk to each other anymore? Gilbert went with his rapper friends who were from Compton to get a tattoo on his bicep, declining when they suggested going down to Venice Beach afterward for some pickup games. Brianne still had feelings for Joel, who choreographed off-Broadway shows, but didn't know if the feelings were nostalgia or actual attraction. She met him at the Saddle Ranch the next day while Gilbert was meeting with his financial adviser who'd flown in from New York and Joel confessed after three Pilsner Urquells that he hadn't been with any other girl since he and Brianne had broken up and that he still thought of Brianne every day and still loved her and still—he admitted after two more beers—masturbated to memories of making love with her which they did many many times. Gilbert and Brianne met with a private shopper in the living room—her name was Velise and was some sort of Caribbean and had permanent makeup and bare midriff with very admirable abdominals even though she was well into her forties—to pick from the assortment of athletic clothes and linen suits and socks that she'd found in the storerooms of various exclusive designers' studios and boutiques, access to which the general public was systematically denied. Brianne called her older sister in New Jersey after the lunch with Joel and told her that she still loved Joel and that she had kissed him as they said good-bye in the parking lot and didn't know what to do. Gilbert watched the gardener Fernando mow the lawn from the bay window in the kitchen, holding a Perrier and watching the sprinklers catch the sun out in the backyard, the water droplets perfect crystals mystifying in a precision so professional that it made him smile, descending onto the admirable grass whose order calmed him, a rich and thick three-quarters of an inch all around—he went out there with a ruler once and while Fernando watched walked around measuring the blades. Brianne found herself thinking about

Joel as she made love with Gilbert and felt a stinging raw guilt. Gilbert bought Brianne a kitten that was the wrong color and she named it Applesauce because it was the color of applesauce, though he argued that a better name would be Gilbert or Animal. The evening he came home with the kitten, picked up by one of Abe Birnbaum's assistants, they sat on the couch and watched it scurry around and bat around the plastic jingly ball he bought for it, his arm around Brianne's shoulders and socked feet up on the coffee table, laughing with marvel at the pleasing domesticity that a fuzzy creature breathing in their home brought to their new marriage. It scratched at the upholstery of a love seat and Gilbert leaped off the couch and snatched it by the scruff of its neck and made his way to the garage to take it back to the store or, if the store was closed, drive it somewhere remote and set it loose. But Brianne cried and threw herself between him and the doorway until he put Applesauce down and said, —Fine, but train it not to scratch the furniture, okay?

Brianne fed Applesauce candy and ice cream and when Gilbert saw her feeding Applesauce candy and ice cream he said, —Baby, I'm not so sure that's good for it. Its intestine is going to be blocked or at least develop parasites which can cause illness for us if it craps in the house. Or worse, it'll get fat and its coat will be matty and greasy. Do you want that? Do you want a hideous cat?

—Well then what should I feed it? You didn't buy cat food.

—I don't know. Tofu it'll probably like. There's some romaine lettuce in the fridge that's still fresh. Or if not then there are some organic grapes and seaweed.

They filled its bowl with Perrier and watched it in focused silence as it lapped it up and that night it tried to sleep in their bed purring audibly and nudging Gilbert's foot and Gilbert kicked it off saying, —Get the fuck off.

—Gilbert, Brianne said.

—What? It might have rabies or fleas.

—It doesn't have rabies.

—It might. You don't know that. Prove it.

And in the morning Brianne had an acting class and then a Hawaiian massage and Gilbert had to fly to Dallas for a meeting with the Lonestars' front office to tell them that he felt as though one of the guards, Brian Dennis, a ten-year veteran, should be traded or else asked to retire because he wasn't producing up to expectations. And then a colonic and then an appointment with a hairstylist, who actually was the same person. When he came home Applesauce was vomiting and moping around because Brianne, in a woozy daze from acupuncture, gave the cat two Advil for a headache.

—Why would a cat have a headache? he said in a controlled rage as he stared down at a yellowish splotch of bile soaking into his once-white carpet.

—I don't know, she said. —It looked stressed out. It was just sitting there staring out the window like it wanted to go outside and play with other cats.

—Yeah and go into sewers and get covered in filth then track it back inside and all over the house, he said, dialing his head personal assistant, Kathie, a middle-aged white woman on vacation in the Hamptons, to tell her to please call a vet to come to the house and a carpet-cleaning place or on second thought to order a new carpet for the living room and the rest of the house too.

Joel called when Gilbert was in the room one day and Brianne had to hang up on him and tell Gilbert wrong number.

Gilbert—already on human growth hormone for more than three years—began using a steroid produced by a privately owned laboratory in the San Francisco Bay Area that the Association's drug tests didn't pick up.

They went water skiing in Miami on a private section of South Beach. Brianne at Gilbert's forceful urging removed her top and Gilbert dug for seashells. He flew in his personal chef, Jasper, to bake them Maine lobsters and Ipswich clams on the beach. When Jasper arrived from the airport Brianne was still topless and she saw him padding down the beach and reached for her bikini top but Gilbert smiled and snatched it from her and said, —No, wait a second. And she panicked behind her sunglasses as Jasper stopped in the sand, sweating mercilessly, and dropped the two heavy grocery bags he carried in each hand and backpack full of chef's tools, averting his eyes from the horror of his boss's wife's bare breasts, saying to his sand-filled shoes, —I got everything.

Gilbert stood amused with his hands on his hips, smiling, watching both of them squirm, until he said, —Did you remember the tits? Er, I mean *chips*?

He laughed uproariously, doubling over and slapping his knee until Brianne sighed and rummaged through her Kate Spade bag for a T-shirt and Jasper turned away to begin the meal. Gilbert sent Jasper to locate and purchase tiki torches to set up around them. But once the meal was ready they hardly ate the seafood as Gilbert could see only the parasites and bacteria crawling all over it.

Back in Pacific Palisades they played soccer in the backyard, Brianne pouting as Gilbert kept the ball from her, sprinklers coming on per timer and spraying them, but they didn't care because she finally got her arms around him and leaped onto his back, and they both went tumbling down on top of the ball laughing.

They went to Iraq to meet wounded soldiers.

Applesauce sat in the corner of the bedroom curled around itself as Gilbert kissed Brianne awake and rolled her onto her back. The cat witnessed him turn her onto her knees and move behind her with his you-know-what engorged with urine, move her legs apart with his hands to get her at the right angle, push down on the small of her back to make her butt stick out more, pull her hair firmly toward him to make her arch her back so that she'd resemble more closely the girls in the videos he often ordered in his hotel room on the road after night games when nobody was going out. The cat watched The Athlete looking at himself in the mirrors on the wall and over the dresser as he did it, smiling at what he saw, flexing a bit, and taking his wife's face in his hands and forcing her to look too, saying, —Watch. And making her put her hands on her butt and pull the cheeks apart, and reaching under the bed for the vibrator he'd been using on her lately, then after getting bored of the vibrator pulling her on top of him and posing her like a girl in Boston after Game 2 of the championship—Spanish of some sort with nipple rings and sexily snotty-young and who let him sodomize her—but Brianne wasn't sure what Gilbert was doing or what he wanted her to do and she felt foolish so she laughed and he got mad and pushed her off and flipped her onto her back again and finished begrudgingly on her face and she stared up blankly watching it drip onto her and then he lay beside her and fell silent.

He turned down *Late Night with Conan O'Brien* which had been calling Abe Birnbaum every day. Brianne went a week without eating solid food. Gilbert went bowling in a private bowling alley located in the home of a Coppola. Brianne dyed her hair blond then brunette then black then blond. They made an appearance at the Nickelodeon Kids' Choice Awards at which he won Best Athlete. He hiked in the Utah desert, alone. He bought a second sensory deprivation chamber because his old one didn't seem to be working properly and almost rejoined the Systemism Joy Church. They spent their final nights of summer watching movies on one of the six DVD players in the

house—action thrillers, explosions, his face absorbed and eyes un-
blinking. They attended the Country Music Association Awards in
Nashville. He bought Brianne a Mercedes and he had his personal
shopper pick out a few things for Brianne and three times came home
with a box of Tiffany jewelry that shimmered against her spray-
tanned flesh and sparkled her eyes which had been enhanced with the
help of her beautician to closely resemble the eyes of Jennifer Lopez
who Brianne decided she looked like even though she'd met Jennifer
Lopez at the MTV Movie Awards and said that Jennifer Lopez wasn't
nearly as pretty in person. Brianne's fake lashes fluttered as Gilbert
stood behind her in the mirror and buckled the clasp of an $86,000 di-
amond necklace. He smiled and said, —Like it?

—It's beautiful, Gilbert. How much was it?

—Don't worry about it. You deserve it.

Her heart fluttered and she was happy. By now Applesauce wasn't
important anymore and might have run away and then one day in the
first week of September when she was on the phone with a producer
who might have had a part for her in a project which a very well-
known director was salivating over, Gilbert came home with a brand-
new black Porsche wrapped in an enormous pink bow. He found her
inside and covered her eyes with another piece of pink ribbon and led
her outside and before he removed it he said, —I'm so sorry for being
a jerk last night, baby. Forgive me? She didn't know what he was talking about because she had been in New York last night for a benefit
for her charity organization Slam Dunk for Parkinson's but when she
saw the car she gasped and hugged him and he went inside for scissors,
cut the bow, held the door for her as she crawled inside, even though
he had already bought her the exact same Porsche in the exact same
color, and the next day she called Joel and told him that what they
once had would never be again and Joel went back to New York and
Brianne and Gilbert went to Dallas.

Summer.

Brianne said, —That's all you ever want to do is do it.

It was his sixth season, it was his seventh season, it was his
eighth season. The Lonestars hadn't won a championship in five
years. Gilbert Marcus was wondering if maybe his career was on the
decline. If his life was over. He thought about boxers who don't know

when to hang it up. Who hold on and on. Shameful. You have to know when to quit. Maybe it was time for him to hang it up. He was twenty-seven years old. The ankle injury that he sustained in the championship his rookie season had never completely healed. But he hadn't told the trainers that. He hadn't told Coach that. He hadn't told his parents that when he called them on Christmas. He hadn't told Brianne that. He had simply played through the pain. Every time he stepped on his right foot he felt pain. When he ran, he ran with pain. He experienced pain more or less constantly at all times except when he was asleep. His ankle made a strange clicking sound when he walked that you could only hear if it was absolutely silent. Still he was the second-highest scorer in the league. Ron Harrington was first. In third place—behind Gilbert Marcus—was Papa Bear Jermaine. Brianne had become pregnant and had a baby. Gilbert was in bed with Brianne after coming home from practice and even though it depressed him that she was twenty-five years old, slobbering on her neck and ears grunting like a short-snouted canine and shoving a hand into her tank top, the baby being watched by the nanny at the other end of the penthouse.

—I know. It's because I love you. You're so beautiful and I love you so much that I can't help myself and have to do these things.

—Stop.

—I just want to get you naked when I see you and do dirty things to you.

She pulled his hand out of her tank top and said, —I *hate* when you talk like that. It sounds so *awful*. It makes me think of . . . I don't know. I mean why can't it be sweet? Or, like, sensual? Gilbert, *stop.*

—Why?

—Because I'm on my period if you have to know.

—So.

—No, that's gross. I don't like doing it on my period.

It was February and the Lonestars were four games out of first place.

—That's not what I meant. I meant there are other things we can do.

—Me being on my period doesn't mean I'm going to give you a you-know-what. You're not entitled to *that.* Don't look at me like that.

—*What?* I didn't say anything.

—Sometimes I don't feel like it. Is that so horrible? Just because I don't want to do it twenty-four hours a day. Just because sometimes I'm asexual.

He said,   Fine, if I repulse you so much. If I'm so disgusting, then forget it.

—You don't repulse me, Gilbert.

—Well you *make* me feel repulsive. It makes me very insecure, Brianne.

—Well that's your issue then that you need to work out yourself.

He wanted to say, What do you mean, *Just because I don't want it twenty-four hours a day?* You hardly want it once a *week*. I have to about rape you and shame you into doing it *once a week*.

But he got quiet and she let him sulk for a few minutes then said, —You know, sometimes I feel like I'm just your, like, *thing* or something. Like, when you say you want to make love because I'm so beautiful and you can't help yourself and blah blah blah.

—I *do*. That's the *truth*.

—I don't know. It just feels like you just want to screw something. You're horny and I'm here, the right gender and with the right parts.

—No, baby.

—Well. Okay. To be honest? It feels sometimes like when we're doing it you're not doing it to me.

He snorted and started to make a joke about size but she said, —I mean it. It feels like you're not there or something. Or like I'm not there. One of us is not there. Will you roll over and face me please?

—I *am*. I'm *facing* you. What?

—I get the feeling sometimes that . . . I don't know. This is insane but, like, I don't know, just that you're like . . . *you know*.

—Know what, Brianne? I don't know, baby. I do *not* know. I don't have the *faintest* fucking idea what the *shit* you're talking about.

—Like you're *masturbating*.

—Oh my God.

—But instead of your hand you're using my vagina.

—Oh my God.

—That's what it just feels like sometimes. You don't look at me. You don't talk to me. How you like it from behind so much. And always like sort of choking me. It just feels weird. I don't mind it now and then but. Like doing it face-to-face is a chore. Just flattering me for a few minutes so you can do it from behind while sort of choking me like you really want.

—That's just the way I like it is all. I can't do anything I like?

Everything has to be what you like and I can't do anything that I like ever?

—But it's not that. It's how you sound when you do it. You're breathing and grunting. It sounds like . . . It reminds me of somebody chopping up a pig or something. It's horrible, to be honest.

—I'm sorry having sex with me is so *horrible* for you, Brianne. I'm sorry I fucking suck so *fucking* bad. I'll try not to fucking suck so *fucking* bad from now on.

—Just how eager you are to . . . *you know*. I don't know. And speaking of that, the place where you like to, you know, *finish* every time. It just feels like you're using my body and my vagina.

—Stop saying that.

—What?

—That word.

—Why? It's just a part of my body.

—Yeah but *Jesus*. Look, I'm sorry I'm not good enough for you in bed. But I don't know what to tell you. Sorry you feel that way. If I don't fuck you good enough then, I don't know, I guess go find someone who can fuck you the way you want to be fucked.

—Gilbert. Stop.

—You know, maybe it's not my problem after all that you feel this way. Maybe it's you. Maybe it's *your* problem. Ever hear of projection? Coach says that people sometimes project their own failings onto other people. Because they're in denial. They blame other people so they don't have to blame themselves. So maybe did you ever think if maybe if—

—Oh my God, Gilbert. The fact is you treat me like an *animal* sometimes. You make love to my body and not me. There's more to making love than putting your penis inside my vagina.

—*Ack*. Stop saying that. Stop, he said, sitting up, covering his ears.
—Make love. Make love. Vagina this, vagina that.

—Why? Because it puts too much responsibility on you? To think of me as a person and—

—No. It just sounds fucking *retarded*. I don't know. I *hate* it. I picture long-haired guys with beards and girls with hairy armpits all high on pot and listening to hippie music and—

—Okay. Well. I'm done with this conversation. You can go *make love* to yourself. In the *bathroom*. Where you *always do it anyway*!

—Baby. Come on. Look, I don't mean to be cranky, it's just that men have needs though, you know? We have to have sex. It's in our

DNA. And we need to feel wanted just like women do. We need to feel attractive too. When we have to practically rape you to get you to have sex with us, we don't feel too good about ourselves.

—Gilbert, I don't mind having sex with you.

—Oh good. She doesn't mind. She puts up with it. Fantastic.

—No I mean I like it. A lot. But only when I feel like it's, I don't know, *real* I guess. Not you mounting me with your *you-know-what* poking out and tearing my clothes off like I'm in your way and rolling off me afterward and laying there staring at the ceiling while I clean up and want to cuddle and maybe talk. Plus you get all grouchy and irritated afterwards.

—What. I get hot. I can't breathe.

—How do you think that makes *me* feel?

—Afterwards I need to breathe. I get very into it and afterwards I need to catch my breath. If I don't breathe properly it's not good for the heart, not to mention the lymph nodes. You can get cancer if you don't breathe right. Did you know that? You can.

—Yeah but it's always the same though. Sunday night. Nine-thirty. Brush our teeth and change and get into bed and turn off the lights and here we go. Time to you-know-what.

—Well yeah but because with my schedule and the baby it's hard for us to be home at the same time, so. We're both running around and busy so much. Plus I don't know when you're going to push me off and say you don't feel like it. So I don't try any other time. Don't want to take the risk of rejection. Get all worked up for nothing.

—The way you *talk* about it. Gilbert, I like spontaneity. You say you have needs, so do I. I need *spontaneity. Passion.*

—Yeah. Me too. I need passion too.

—That's what turns me on.

—Yeah that's exactly what turns me on too. Exactly.

—Like if you see me carrying in groceries and you're opening a can of pickles or something and see me and just can't help yourself and pin me against the wall. Something like that.

—I don't eat pickles.

—That way it feels like it's really *me* you want. That's what I like.

—It's not like I *plan* it, baby. I don't know. Look, I don't know what you want. I don't know the right way to be. It's like everyone has this secret information and I don't and so everyone hates me.

—No one hates you.

—You do. You hate me because I don't fuck you right.

—I don't hate you.

—Yes, you do. Everyone hates me in the whole world.

—Gilbert.

—Can we not have this conversation anymore? Can we just stop?

Next day he called a divorce attorney and told the divorce attorney that he'd made a mistake and married someone who didn't know who he was and was now trying to change him into something else.

He hated himself for being so obsessed with IT. He'd step out of the bathroom after jerking off over the toilet and as he'd close the door behind him he would hate himself. He'd had to stop taking the steroid made by the San Francisco laboratory because the FBI was investigating the amateur chemists who had manufactured it. The United States Senate was gearing up for a hearing regarding its use in Major League Baseball. His scoring average was the lowest it had been in his entire career. His streak of six consecutive scoring titles was most likely over. Papa Bear Ben Jermaine was demanding to be traded. There were rumors that the front office was going to clean house. Gilbert was increasing his use of human growth hormone and had a good lead on a newer, better steroid but still there was a good possibility that Gilbert Marcus's Dallas Lonestars would not only fail to win the championship yet again, but would fail to even make the playoffs for the first time ever.

As the divorce attorney and he discussed over the phone the first step toward divorcing Brianne he heard Brianne downstairs singing to the baby and he stopped what he was doing and pictured his baby while the lawyer who sounded self-satisfied to the point of sounding almost asleep rattled on about what a busy schedule he had to The Athlete who when he heard people complain about being busy thought it meant they were less important than they wanted you to think they were. The smugness in the divorce attorney's voice drove Gilbert to think of his baby. He became overwhelmed with the urge to hold it, kiss it, tell it he loved it. Or rather HIM, because he needed to start referring to it as HIM, since the baby was a person after all—Gilbert's reason for living. One day his reason for living would grow up and have his own failings and tastes independent of Gilbert and Brianne and maybe do something extraordinary like cure AIDS or something, who knew, anything was possible, especially in America.

He teared up, a man locked in a bedroom conspiring to terminate the family.

He teared up, speaking in hushed tones to a stranger about his baby and his wife downstairs on the couch loving each other and oblivious.

He teared up, imagining his son growing up without a father, becoming gay and letting scummy fags pass him around and videotaping it and he'd get HIV and die alone because his father divorced his mother.

Hung up on the lawyer, thought of his wife's smile as he went downstairs, how she'd call him a jerk when he'd tease her, how she slept on her belly with her hands in fists. Sat down next to her, on the couch, leaned over and kissed his son, kissed his wife, laughed and said to his wife, —Look at his eyes.

—They're beautiful eyes.

—Whose eyes did he get? Yours?

—I'd say yours. You have pretty eyes like that.

—You know, I think I spend too much time away from him. Makes me feel terrible. I get so caught up in things and when I don't spend enough time with him I feel bad.

—Oh he loves his daddy. Doesn't he. *Doesn't he.* Yesh she dush!

—I don't know. It really tears me apart, Brianne. I just want him to have a good life. A perfect and happy life with no worries and no problems. Once the season's over I'm going to spend more time with him. All day every day. I want him to be loved. It's very important that a baby know it's loved.

—Of course. But he already has a good life, Gilbert. And a loving daddy.

—I want him to be a happy person though.

—He is happy.

—And you too. I want you to be happy.

—I am.

—After the season I want to take you on a trip. Anywhere. Wherever you want to go, we'll go. Anywhere in the world this summer after my meetings.

—Ooo! Italy!

—Italy?

—I did a shoot in Milan once and it was so beautiful there. And the Greek isles too. I just fit in there, you know? Everyone always tells me that I have a very Italian sort of sensibility, you know?

—So we'll all go. The three of us. Yeah. That sounds good. I've never been to Italy. I've never even left the country actually, except when we went to Iraq and then I went to Africa to help children with AIDS.

—I just think that with the dancing and the music and the culture I've always felt like maybe part of me was Italian, she said. —I think maybe in another life I was Italian.

—It'll be good to get away from all this craziness. Get out of the country. Take a deep breath, get some perspective. Disappear for a while. Be happy for once.

—I *am* happy though.

—No, me too. But I mean *really* happy.

18

THE PROFESSIONAL ATHLETE EXITS the plane and goes through the terminal and here he is now, standing on the sidewalk in the year 2007 on the outskirts of Las Vegas, moths the size of small birds hovering around the lights and his bag at his feet and retractable handle extended, listening as Sheldon Washington first looks up local limousine companies on his minuscule cell phone with a camera and Internet access on it then dials the number of a local limousine company, seemingly hundreds of taxis—orange and red and green, etc.—lined up before them along the curb, their tired drivers inside. And the driver of the first taxi is leaning over from the driver's seat, rolling down the passenger window, and waving at them and speaking in a heavy accent, and though Gilbert knows that he wants them to get in he also knows that the bodyguards don't see the cabdriver who stares back at him expressing nothing until he kind of throws up his hands and rolls the window back up. Gilbert wonders vaguely how the cop over there knows for sure that none of these cab drivers is a terrorist. This is without a doubt the most unhappy he has

ever been in his life. But he remembers from Systemism Joy that perception is reality and it's your responsibility to will yourself out of unhappiness. He wonders beyond the darkness where the lights of the
airport doors end if there are coyotes out there, because what else
would be in Nevada, and what do coyotes do when they're not killing
things? Do they just run around? Do they fight? Do they mate then
die? Where do they live? Do they bark?

Sheldon hangs up and slips his phone—which by the way has the
capability to store and play two hundred MP3s—into his pocket and
the other three look at him out of the corners of their eyes and he
says, —They're coming.

Gilbert checks the time on his own minuscule cell phone and Will
says, —I'm hungry.

—Don't have time, says Sheldon.

Their voices are low and soft, those of intruders. —Yeah but still
though, man. Starving.

And Sheldon says, —What time is it? Gilbert has a meeting early.

—Go to a casino or a titty bar or something. Put Gilbert to bed
and go find some fucking sluts. There's probably a bar in the hotel.

Gilbert looks at him and says, —No, because you guys are on restriction.

—Tuck you in. Sing you a lullaby. Go find a bar.

Gilbert says, —What kind did you get? What kind of limo?

—All they had was six-person, Sheldon says.

—No, yeah, but I mean is it a Hummer one or does it have a TV in
it at least?

—I don't know. They're sending what they have.

—You told them who it was for though, right?

Will goes, —Hope it has something to eat in there. Some chips or
something at least.

The perception thing isn't working and Gilbert tries to remember
if Brianne packed him a sweatshirt because he always finds hotels too
cold and Sheldon has his arms crossed and an expression like he's in a
crowded elevator and Gilbert feels the unquenchable need to be cool
around Sheldon, to impress him. Will talks too much and has a childish incessant sense of humor and obviously gets on Sheldon's nerves,
and Gilbert is a bit comforted by the fact that Sheldon is dressed only
in shin-length denim shorts and his size XXXL T-shirt and looks suburban. Will stands on one leg and farts and Larry (the white one)
laughs and Will says, —Is there a duck?

There are more stars than you can count. There is no moon. And there are little tufts of green shrubbery, characterless sprouts of desert spruce, and there is a purple toy truck upside down in the one-way street where taxis and cars slug by to pick up and drop off. Gilbert is still wearing his sunglasses and he found his security detail through a friend of his, a singer named Ethan McCready, who he's posed for many photographs with, and is also not a bad basketball player for an amateur though Gilbert suspects he's secretly attracted to Brianne and would be the type to pursue his friend's wife or at least not be very apologetic about it if it were to transpire. The cop, in a thin cop jacket that looks too small for him, is a middle-aged guy who is clean-shaven and big and his eyes are in a frozen sun-wince, and he comes over with a pen and blank parking ticket and says as he hands the pen and blank parking ticket to Gilbert, —Hope you don't mind. My daughter's a big fan of yours.

Gilbert takes it and laughs as he removes the pen cap and says, —Uh-oh. Hope I'm not signing my name to a ticket here.

—Oh no no, the cop says, arms crossed, his voice raspy, —you will not be penalized with a violation.

The cop says it *pee-nalized.*

—Yeah I know. That was a joke.

—It's the only slip of paper I have over there in my car. If you have something better on you—

—No I was just joking. It's cool.

—To give you peace of mind.

Gilbert signs it, gives it back, cop goes, —Well I appreciate it. My daughter's a huge fan of yours.

—No problem at all.

And the cop tips his hat and says, —You guys have a good night.

When he goes, Gilbert turns to them and says, —Wonder what his daughter's doing tonight. Sheldon doesn't laugh, Will does, Larry (the white one) mutters something, and the No Parking sign they stand by is faded and rusting a bit, and beneath it are two cabdrivers of indiscernible Middle Eastern descent who have gotten out of their cabs and are leaning against the trunk of one and sipping plastic-lid coffee out of paper cups with what look like little multicolored firework explosions on them, chatting in their native tongue over the cackle of their radios, one of them with a folded-up newspaper under his arm, the distant sounds of a plane taking off in a whispery scream from way off behind them as farther out, on the highway, cars whoosh by every couple seconds, and the two cabdrivers look serious in their conversation, staring out not looking at each other, nodding, intelligent. Two short hefty white women come out preceded by laughter, wearing white-shirt-dark-blue-pants airline-employee uniforms—ticket takers or check-in people. The laughter is not of amusement or joy but of being tired at fate. They have short brown hair and vague chins and disproportionately large derrieres with low maternal breasts, and they separate at the mouth of the parking lot and one says, —Bye Leslie . . . as she sighs the end of her laugh, in an unsentimental nearly dismissive way, because they will see each other again in the morning, the type of women who have teenage sons and roll their eyes at their husbands' friends who work as finish carpenters, women who know how to properly train big dogs and keep sliced deli meat in the fridge.

Exactly one-half of the men have reproduced, and those men are Gilbert Animal Marcus and Sheldon Christopher Washington, who has a son, six, with a girl he went to high school with, and she was his girlfriend, and he grew up with her in Nickerson Gardens, a housing project in Watts. She had the baby when Sheldon was nineteen and she was seventeen, which wasn't unusual in her community as most girls expected little more from life than that. But now they both live with other people not far from the old neighborhood and Sheldon gets his son, David, every other weekend, which necessitates a handoff at either of their doorsteps, meaning four times a month the new girlfriend must see and converse with the old girlfriend, and the old boyfriend must see and converse with the new boyfriend, but they are all cordial enough to one another, able to put the past behind them and enjoy the baby it has brought them, though Sheldon secretly thinks his baby's mother's current boyfriend is a douche bag, having grown up with him and remembering doing acid on a playground with the guy when they were both fourteen and the dude took a tab and started running around screaming and rolled laughing in the dirt, kicking like an animal, yelling, —Daddy! and eventually urinating in his pants (Sheldon was aware, watching Gilbert urinate in his own pants on TV at home, of the similarity, which may have meant something about Sheldon or about Gilbert, or Sheldon's ex's boyfriend), and Sheldon and his friends had to drag his limp body home and leave him in his front yard, limbs spread out and convulsing, not having the heart to tell him that the acid was fake and he'd eaten construction paper. Sheldon doesn't want to work this weekend, even if it is Gilbert Marcus, which doesn't impress him like it did once, because he works with a lot

of celebrities. The reason he doesn't want to work this weekend is this
is his weekend with David. David needs a new bike and his ex and her
skinny boyfriend don't want to pay for the bike even though he and
his current girlfriend end up invariably paying for the clothes, school
supplies, and babysitter, but it's his son and he needs a bike, so here
Sheldon is. He was a good football player in high school and had an
offer to play offensive tackle at Wake Forest but the full-ride scholarship was rescinded due to his grades being too low and SAT scores
laughable, because it's hard to put much stock in algebra and English
when your girlfriend is pregnant and you have a job making sand-
wiches at SUBWAY to pay for her doctor and the baby supplies. He
has a tattoo of what could be spilled coffee on his left calf-meat and his
son's name in cursive on the right side of his neck, and Tupac Shakur
on the right bicep that he got when Tupac was killed and a Bible quote
in fancy script on his left forearm, and his older brother's name on the
other forearm that he got when his brother got shot and died when
police stopped him for stealing a car and thought he had a gun but it
turned out to be his wallet. Will has a tribal band on his right bicep
and a skeletal dragon on his left and the word MADE in Old English
script on the back of his neck, with a fish-flame thing going from his
right shoulder to his right pectoral. Larry (the white one) has no tattoos and has his facial hair shaved to look like a chin strap. Gilbert
Marcus has the word ANIMAL in Celtic lettering on his back going
from shoulder to shoulder and on his right pec is his son's name. Sheldon's and Gilbert's children have never met.

One good thing though about the outskirts of Las Vegas is that
there's no media, a relief considering the great effort they took to keep
this trip under wraps. Gilbert has developed a sixth sense for media
and can now literally smell the media coming (the media smells like
coffee and red meat) and often he does this thing where he pretends
that the journalists are smirking detectives prowling around getting
their noses dirty and he's the untouchable gangster, and they know his
crimes but can't prove them, and he knows they're out to get him, so
they lie to each other, maintaining the façade of politeness, and when
it's over the detective/journalist lights a cigarette and puts the fedora
back on and skulks back into the rain, frustrated, having wasted time.

There are fluorescent lights above their heads in the little awning
that comes out two feet or so where the tremendous moths are and
beneath the lights a lizard is frozen so still you have to stop and stare
to understand that what you're seeing is not part of the wall. One of

the two cabdrivers leaning against the cab, in a gray nylon jacket, coughs into his fist, and Gilbert stretches by reaching his arms to the side and then up and back, groaning, swatting at a moth, as Will plays with his cell phone that also has universal television remote-control capabilities, the sidewalk more than seven feet wide at this point though it narrows eventually to five feet if you go in either direction. The cabbie in the front of the line now is white and heavy and grumpy, wearing a flannel shirt with the sleeves cut off over an old tan T-shirt, bearded, and his late twenties or early thirties, right-wing talk radio on loudly, window open and an upper arm that has tiny raised red bumps on the bottom of it resting on the windowsill, fingers drumming the roof, and he knows that it is Gilbert Marcus standing right there but after the initial surprise wore off he doesn't give a damn because he doesn't like black people and is a dues-paying member of an organization based in Baker called Operation: Shit for Brains that he found on the Internet whose sole objective is to be proponents of the idea of gathering all the African-Americans together and shipping them either by boat or by plane (they haven't quite got all the logistics hammered out just yet) back to the continent their ancestors originated from and he uses the word *nigger* in casual conversation or whenever a nigger runs out in the street and he has to slam his brakes. Gilbert Marcus is very close to being broke, according to his financial adviser who he flew to New York to meet with last month and who sat him down and swallowed and said Gilbert's spending way more money than is coming in and the oxygen bar called GoGoGo he co-owns with Wilmer Valderrama is going down the tubes (his financial adviser apologized for the pun), but, his financial adviser told him, there is another quote avenue to explore end quote, thanks to the financial adviser's personal connections—meaning his second cousin who founded ValueVacate.com and sold out for millions right before the bubble burst in the '90s and also owns every possible misspelling of google.com, yahoo.com, myspace.com, washingtonpost.com (to name a few) that those companies don't already own themselves and he charges outlandish prices if those companies wish to buy these misspelled domains from him or else he sells advertising space on them, ensuring a steady typo-driven stream of revenue either way. He's made maybe the most money off typos than anyone in the history of the world. And now he is opening a casino in Vegas as his latest hobby but needs some A-list celebrities such as Gilbert Marcus to invest in the casino and to be on the board of directors to help get the word of the casino off the ground and for marketing purposes, etc. Gilbert told his financial adviser—a half-Greek half-French young man who laughed in a wheeze, like a heavy smoker—that he can go in with the casino but will have to do it anonymously, as a pro athlete, and the financial adviser called him back on his cell phone a few days later and said his second cousin wanted to meet with him in person to talk about what they can do. The idea of getting back on track financially without Brianne knowing they were in—in the financial adviser's words—serious trouble and going beyond the law of the Association, mixed with thinking about the flight attendant, puts him in a weird excited mood, and he flicks the back of Will's ear which makes Will go, —Shit!

And Larry (the white one) chuckles and Sheldon sort of smiles and Gilbert pokes Will's gut with his pointer finger and says, —You do a lot of sit-ups, don't ya.

Will does a sort of sarcastic laugh and goes, —Yeah well you take it up the tailpipe, don't ya.

Though they've worked for Gilbert Marcus on numerous occasions in the past none of the guards can say that he knows him. They've watched him pick his wife up and twirl her around in the air and bottle-feed his baby and they've been in the next room playing video games with the sound maxed out as Gilbert's fornicated with juvenile-looking girls. They have—giving in to Brianne's persistence—walked into the room where Gilbert was anally copulating with a young nude yelping female and handed the phone to him mid-pump saying, —It's your wife. And he has taken the phone and put the phone to his ear and carried out an entire conversation with her, even ejaculating onto the girl's fake tits while explaining to his wife where extra lightbulbs would be. They have avoided looking Brianne in the eye and acted polite not letting on what they know about her life, how it's nothing like she thinks, or that they—Sheldon especially—don't like her that much and are secretly a little glad she is so oblivious, because she obviously thinks of herself as some sort of supermodel who should have her ass kissed even though she's a washed-up has-been third-rate model whose biggest accomplishment was having a quarter-page photo in what was widely regarded as the worst *Sports Illustrated* swimsuit issue ever. She speaks to them like children. Their place however is their place and they have a job that pays four hundred dollars per day and offering their moral advice is not in that job's description.

On Gilbert's mind now is the fear that his bodyguards secretly hate him. Will is wearing sandals and his toenails are in dire need of cutting. The baby was born five months ago and Gilbert Marcus often jumps when it cries because he sometimes forgets that Gilbert Marcus has a baby. He often realizes that he is very alone. He thinks, No, I've *succeeded* in becoming alone. I have *produced* being alone. It's his thinking that makes him great. His thinking is his greatest strength. You have to train yourself to think this way. The turning of a missed shot into the making of a miss, the losing of a game into succeeding in losing. His thinking has made him invincible. He says to his bodyguards, —I have to go take a piss. And he leaves his bag with them and walks through the automatic sliding door not making eye contact with the police officer who watches him still holding the autograph and inside he sees a small black woman with heavy makeup shuffling things around behind an Enterprise counter and he says, —Excuse me, is there a bathroom in here?

The small black woman who works at Enterprise makes a face and shifts her weight onto one leg, her hand on her big hip, wrist jewelry rattling, cocks her head and looks at him sideways, her nose somewhat piggish, and says, —Don't EVEN try to tell me you're not him!

He chuckles softly and she says, louder, —I said don't you DARE! DO NOT TELL ME! DON'T DO IT!

—Okay, he says, really having to piss but trying to be black enough for her, handsome and manly enough, better, —I'm him. I'm me.

And she scurries out from behind her counter and clacks her way toward him, big butt and employee ID flying around from her neck, and he notices the huge tits and though there are people he knows who would, he would never in a million years—well if he was stuck with her on a deserted island and she promised to die right after then *maybe*. And she takes his hand and she smells like church, comes up to his stomach, reminds him of a hobbit, holds his one hand with the two of hers and looks up at him with her fake eyelashes and says, —Look at you. Gilbert Marcus. Let me feel on your stomach, you big old ethnic *man*. Look at you, all *sculpted*.

—Thank you very much but listen. I'm looking for the—

—Now what are you doing down here in Vegas, Gilbert Marcus? Looking for a healthy round black girl to take home and treat you right?

—Ha. Well. Actually I'm looking for a bathroom.

—Listen Gilbert Marcus. My name is Sofia. I watch you on TV and I think to myself, He's a nice fine man. He knows how to treat a woman for sure. So smart and well-spoken.

—I treat everyone with respect. Especially women.

—I know just by looking at you. She reaches up and grabs his arm. She's stronger than she looks, which he finds a little frightening. She says, —Go on and flex for Sofia. Let Sofia feel on them big old sculpted *muscles*. Now what's all this? Why'd you go and get all these tattoos and ruin your beautiful tapioca skin? Who did this to you? Your momma know they did this to you?

And he smiles and chuckles, but she's fanning herself with her jingly long-fingernailed hand, stomping away from him and spasming around, hollering, —Lordy lordy LORDY! I can't take it! I'm DONE. Sofia is DONE! Lordy lordy. Oooh LORDY LORDY LORDY!

—Ha ha, yeah, hey, I need to know where the bathroom is real quick. Know what I'm saying? I have to catch my ride and—

—I bet you got a limo don't you. A great big Hummer limo. With a hot tub and a TV and some champagne. I know you do, Gilbert Marcus. I know how you do. I'll show you where the bathroom is, you cute sculpted *man*.

And she leads him down the hall and then a right and there are the bathrooms, men's and women's, and he thanks her and she says, —Gilbert Marcus, anything you NEED. Remember. Come see Sofia at Enterprise. Anything for my Gilbert Marcus.

And he goes inside, shaking his head, chuckling to himself, catches his reflection in the spotted mirror above the sink, admires it, hears Sofia outside shouting to somebody, —Anita! Anita! You are NOT going to believe this. Come here!

And he hears another female voice approaching, saying, —What.

And Sofia's yelling through the door to him, —Come out here, Gilbert Marcus!

—Gilbert Marcus is in there? the other voice says.

Sofia goes, —He's peeing. Gilbert Marcus is peeing.

He rolls his eyes groans under his breath, —Fuck off . . . and aims for the urinal cake, hits it, and says, —Hold on a second please, ladies. He finishes, shakes, flushes, hears Sheldon's deep voice saying, —You all can't be here please.

Sofia says, —Who can't? Excuse me. I WORK here. Okay?

—You can't stand here.

—I work at Enterprise okay? My name is Sofia Mitchell and I
work at Enterprise. Don't tell me where I can stand.

The door opens and Sheldon says, —Gilbert, let's go.

Washes his hands and dries them with the brown paper towels
and leaves, says to Sofia and the other woman who looks exactly like
Sofia but fatter, —Okay, ladies, okay now . . .

And as Sheldon and Gilbert walk back outside, Sofia and Fatter
Sofia are yelling, —Don't tell me okay ladies! Don't tell me okay!
Okay? Okay? Don't tell me okay, Gilbert Marcus! Don't act like you
don't know where you come from, Gilbert Marcus!

At first it's hard to get a good look at it because of the headlights and
the darkness, but the limo is disappointingly small and at least four
years old and Sheldon is making no effort to hide being annoyed at
Gilbert for going off alone and engaging the public, which is what the
industry term is for outsiders, and Gilbert knows this and is minutely
sorry even though it wasn't his fault, fears what Sheldon is thinking
about him, wants to apologize, doesn't, and they climb in and are starting to pull away when Sheldon says, —Bags.

The driver glances back and goes, —What?

And Gilbert leans forward and says to him, —Our bags are still on
the curb.

—Huh? Bags? the driver says, looking out the window.

—Our *bags*. Our *suitcases*. They're still on the curb. *You failed to
put them in the trunk.*

—You want me to put your *bags* in the *trunk*?

Gilbert laughs and says, —Um yeah. That would be nice.

The driver stops the car and shakes his head and gets out, the
door squeaking deeply, and Gilbert looks at Larry (the white one) and
Will and says, —Can you believe this? We going to have to drive it
too? Neither laughs. There is no TV and the limo seats six normal-
sized bodies comfortably and evidently four big bodies not so comfortably. Gilbert is squeezed against the window with his hands
between his knees, Will breathing too heavily, the upholstery smells
like vacuum cleaner, and Gilbert fumbles around the inside of the
door, saying, —How do you open these goddamn windows? Do they
open?

—Manual maybe, Will says.

—You need an *instruction manual* to open the fucking *windows*? Gilbert says.

—No. *Manual.* As in you have to do it by *hand.*

—Yeah but look there's no knob even. Why would they have a limo without power windows anyway? What would be the point of that?

—I don't know.

Gilbert says, —I am never coming back here. Fucking Las Vegas. Who lives here? Why would you *live* in Las *Vegas*?

—If you're a whore.

—Unless you're a whore, yeah.

The driver comes back in sighing as he sits and puts on his seat belt, the only one wearing one, and they start to go and Will says, —Hey is there a McDonald's on the way or anything?

And Gilbert says, —No way. We're not stopping at McDonald's.

—Come on.

—No. We're going right to the hotel so I can get to bed. I have to wake up early.

—Yeah but so do we. We're starving. I'm light-headed. I'm gonna faint.

—Go to McDonald's on your own time. You're on the clock right now.

—There's no clock.

—I say no. I'm in charge and I say no. We're not making a detour for fast food. That stuff is terrible for your digestive system. I just want to get there and go to bed.

—It'll take two seconds.

—No.

—Is there anywhere else open? Will says to the driver.

—Everything's open this time of night, the driver says.

There's no response for a few seconds and Gilbert laughs and says, —This time of night? It's like nine. This time of night. Hey your windows are broken by the way. Is there anything in this town that works? Is there anything from this century?

Driver says, —You want the windows down?

Gilbert says, —What did I just say.

There's a mechanical whirr and Gilbert's window opens about an inch and Gilbert says, —That's all?

—Huh?

—*More . . . than . . . that.*

It opens all the way and Gilbert puts his elbow on the sill, wind blowing into his face, says, —What hotel are we staying at anyway? The Motel 8? I bet we're staying at the Motel 8. We're eating at Denny's I bet and staying at Motel 8. Great. Are there phones there even?

Someone, it doesn't matter who, says, —There's Motel 6. There's Super 8. But there's no Motel 8.

—Whatever. Gilbert slouches down in his seat with his legs spread moderately apart, his right knee a half inch from Will's, and watching the scenery pass outside makes Gilbert feel better. His ankle is starting to hurt. It's a quick sharp jolt of pain that stings once then leaves. He's tried to ignore this for what seems like his whole life. And that is why he has flown his personal motivational consultant to Vegas to help him develop the proper mental image of the injury, and the motivational consultant is in fact already checked in and waiting at the hotel, having flown in on an earlier flight from New York where the motivation consultant was leading his weekend firewalk seminar in Union Square and the meeting with him is scheduled for eight AM tomorrow in the motivational consultant's room which Gilbert is paying for which means Gilbert has to be up and ready by seven-thirty which shouldn't be a problem, and though he too is hungry he is fasting except for water and his supplement and vitamin regimen that consists of twenty-eight different pills and is conscious then of his low blood sugar which is making him cranky and negative even though he's trying to visualize his blood and shrink down the image of the low blood sugar and push it away out of sight, a technique his motivational consultant stresses, along with sense-memory muscle-triggering reaction and that's why Gilbert's taken to listening to "No Ordinary Love" by Sade before every game.

The limo has four wheels and an engine and tinted windows and no rear radio controls and no minibar which is okay because his security guards aren't allowed to drink anyway on the job but it's nice to know it's there, and he wishes now that Will had worn long pants and a suit too or at least a tie, considers making this a rule from now on, and the name of the limo driver is Jason and he wears a white button-down wrinkle-free cotton shirt with a black tie knotted neatly and hair trimmed in a basic fashion, peppery-colored, and a chin like the villain in action flicks, his eyes perpetually puffy and down-drooped, a recovering alcoholic who quit drinking when his brother one night driving home from the Orleans Hotel and Casino drunk—Jason in the car with him—went through a red light at Decatur and Tropicana and crashed into a Jeep Cherokee and died and the woman driving the Jeep was paralyzed from the waist down and Jason got a concussion and a broken nose and three ribs so severely broken that to this day make it painful sometimes to take deep breaths but he still despite the concussion remembers shaking his brother's body and lifting his head off the horn and seeing the blood and his brother's eyes open but lifeless and easing his brother's head back down and undoing his seat belt, stepping out of the car and seeing the woman hanging out her open window then collapsing to the pavement and losing consciousness. Jason is a homosexual who was once married to a woman for ten years and is thirty-seven and has a daughter and has no alcoholism in his family. He developed his alcoholism during ten years of living the life of a heterosexual family man. One night he called his brother and told him to meet him at the Orleans in the bowling alley bar to talk about something. His brother didn't drink but Jason convinced him to have just one beer and the bartender knew Jason and let him not pay sometimes and Jason worked up the courage to tell his brother, a fireman with a wife and three kids, that night five years ago, that he was divorcing his wife and leaving his family because he was a homosexual, and his brother got quiet and started drinking, got drunk, started yelling, came after Jason with a dart, the bartender wrestled him out and told Jason to take him home, but his brother was already climbing into his car and backing out but Jason was able to hop in before he could pull away and so his brother floored it and went over the curb, swerved into the road and he didn't stop for the red light and skidded through the intersection at full speed and crashed into a Jeep Cherokee and died. And Jason who taught seventh-grade English and loved it lost his job when him being gay came out after the accident but life keeps being lived and so now he has a job driving limos and in fact he is at this moment driving his current clients through Decatur and Tropicana and as always he tenses and swallows. He's seen Gilbert Marcus numerous times on the muted TVs with the subtitles on in the bars he would sneak off to to get drunk and meet men, though he doesn't realize this and figures Gilbert Marcus is a rapper or something. As he now goes through Decatur and Tropicana

Gilbert calls to him from the back, —Turn the radio on, man. He does, hand shaking, but able to keep himself composed, then goes back to what he thinks about when he'd rather not think about his brother, which is the children's book he's been working on. He's worried the children's book he has been working on is too obviously ripped off from Shel Silverstein to be published, but mostly it's for his daughter and that's what he tells himself when he starts worrying too much about whether or not it's too obviously ripped off from Shel Silverstein to get published. He's relying on the children's book to make him the money he needs to tell his boss at Party Ride Limousines, Inc., to take this job and shove it. His boss is a greedy man who is fat and also owns a low-income apartment complex and routinely screws his tenants by charging them bogus maintenance fees. Jason had an especially strong urge to tell his boss to take this job and shove it tonight—his one night off. He was drawing a picture of a dog smashing an alarm clock for page twenty, finally getting it right after a week of messing it up, happy, peaceful, and his boss called and told him to come in right now and drive someone from the airport to a resort hotel and spa, afraid to say no knowing his boss would not hesitate to fire him, and, because of the recession, hire the next guy in line to fill his spot, and he'd have to find another job doing who knows what—delivering mail or stocking shelves or even fast food if he had to—to pay the child support and his rent. Now Gilbert is going, —Hey, turn this country shit off.

—What's that? Jason says.

—This country shit. Turn it off. Find some R&B or hip-hop or something. This shit's terrible.

Jason changes it, scans the dial, Gilbert says, —Is that what you people listen to around here? Do you actually listen to that shit?

—I don't know, Jason says.

—You don't know? How do you not know?

—I'll find something else. Tell me when to stop.

Gilbert starts singing, hiccuping and twanging, —My wife left me! My dog died! I got drunk! Because I'm a redneck! I like my pickup truck! Jason isn't too interested in pop music and stops on a station that sounds like something they'd like but Gilbert's still laughing at himself and saying, —Las Vegas, man. Fucking bumfuck. The sticks.

—This good? Jason says. Gilbert doesn't answer so Jason assumes it is, reaches for the button he never thought he'd be so fond of, and as the tinted glass raises behind him, shutting him away from his clients, he cannot hear Gilbert laughing at him, going, —Awww, come on! I want to talk about *drinkin* and *huntin* and *fightin*!

They get on Town Center Drive then take a left on 159. The floor of the limousine is a stiff blue synthetic carpetlike substance though this is not noticeable in the darkness, but if it were light one would see that though the surface bears the streaks of a hasty fresh vacuuming there are still bits of lint and trash including a straw wrapper and the back of an earring and it is fortunate that this is not noticed because Gilbert Marcus has no tolerance for this type of thing and would demand a refund or at least a discount and Gilbert gets excited as he wonders how many people have fornicated in here—teenage strippers, their skirts pulled up. He is afraid that the driver has been insulted and will want to seek revenge by selling his story of what being a limo driver for Gilbert Marcus is like to the tabloids and even, knowing the media won't see much of a story in that alone, embellish and make up details, possibly about Gilbert Marcus smoking crack in the limo or buying HGH, or he'll say that Gilbert Marcus made phone calls to place bets on his own games and is part owner of a casino and the story will run and his image will be tainted and he will have NOTHING. The fear goes from hypothetical to very real, until the driver is no doubt out to get him and might even be an undercover reporter with a microphone and hidden video cameras—which would explain his incompetence. No, something must be done, he must be quelled and bought over, and so he gets up and goes to the tinted panel, nearly falling on a turn, and knocks on it, and when there's no answer he taps harder incessantly until the glass lowers and the driver glances back and Gilbert says, —Hey man how's it going? Hey you want an autograph or something? I can sign something real quick. You have something up there? A pen and paper or anything?

—No I don't think.

—Will you look a little? Actually you know maybe I have something in my bag. It's in the trunk though right now. Actually I'm pretty sure I have some pictures in there I think. My publicist always puts them in there just in case. You know how publicists are.

—What would I do with an autograph?

—Give them to your kids or something. I don't know. You know who I am, don't you?

—Look I'm working here, okay? I don't know who you are or what you're talking about. We're almost there so just sit down please.

Gilbert stares at the back of his head, his goofy ears, and smiles, laughs, says, —Guess you must be a Papa Bear fan, huh? Heh heh.

—Mind sitting down please? Anything happens I lose my job. Insurance reasons.

Gilbert's unaware of this but Jason the driver is attracted to him physically—the smell of him, the aura of his fit and imposing physique—feels an unmistakable intimidation, for he is the kind of man who is quiet and tends to take the feminine role in his relationships and is uncomfortable then around big jockish manly types if they aren't gay, especially those who single him out and pick on him. He finds this bully dynamic secretly erotic because it is in a way a verbal symbolization of carnal relations—one dominating the other, one receiving the intrusion, etc. He becomes then even more uncomfortable because he fears this aggressor will pick up on him finding this erotic and he'll be exposed, understanding that these types of guys do not tend to be broad-minded about this kind of thing and could lead to about a dozen different possible scenarios most of which end up with Jason on the ground, covered in blood, picking up his teeth. He'd rather the topic drop and the client sit back down so Jason can do his job and go home and make something to eat and possibly pleasure himself while thinking of this client's abs then work on his children's book but Gilbert says, —How much money do you make doing this? Driving people around. You must make a lot doing it, right?

—I don't know.

—You don't know? How do you not know? Do you know what your name is?

—Jason.

—Jason? Why don't you know how much money you make, Jason?

—I do. I just. It's my business.

—This is your business? Well then listen. You need better limos. This is like ten years old. It sucks. No one wants to ride in this thing.

—No no no.

—You want your business to be the best, right? Get a couple Hummer limos. Those are hot. Put a DVD player in it. A PlayStation 3. Why would you run a business if it doesn't demolish your competition? See, if *I* had a limo company—

—I don't own the company. I meant it's my business how much money I make.

I don't get it.

It's none of your business how much I make. That's what I mean.

—Where's the button for this back there?

—No you can't control that. If you want it up you can ask me.

—Oh I see. You like that. You like having that kind of power, Jason? That kind of control? You do. You like it. You in a bad mood or something?

—No.

—Just not a cheerful person? You bashful?

—Sit down please. In case something happens. You're distracting me.

—What's going to happen? Are you a bad driver? Do you crash a lot? When's the last time you got in an accident?

—Never.

—Then why then?

—Company policy. It's the rules.

—I was just kidding about country music by the way. I was just playing with you. You have to lighten up. It's okay if you like it. I don't care. Do you like it? You do don't you?

—I guess. A little.

—What kind? I mean who's your favorite country singer? Garth Brooks?

—I guess Shania Twain. Patty Loveless. I don't know. Tim Mc-Graw.

—I don't know who those people are. Are they good? Do they sing catchy songs?

—I guess. I don't know.

—Do you have a girlfriend? Do you pick up a lot of girls with this limo?

—That's my business.

—Yeah yeah yeah. You're bashful.

Jason doesn't answer and Gilbert's quiet for a second then goes, —So what do you all do in Las Vegas? Besides gamble and bang hookers I mean. Ride bulls? Watch NASCAR? What.

—Some do I guess. I don't.

—You don't? What do you do then? Like for fun? Do you have fun?

—I don't know. Well. I'm sort of working on this book.

—A *book*? What kind of book?

—A children's book. I don't know.

—Wow man. I could never write a book. I don't read a lot of books. I read magazines though. What's it called?

—I don't know. *The Sandwich and the Bear.*

—The what now?

—*The . . . Sandwich . . . and . . . the . . . Bear.*

—*The Sandwich and the Bear?* What the fuck is *that* about?

—I don't know. It's sort of hard to explain.

—Well how long is it?

—Twenty pages so far.

—Wow that's long. Gilbert turns to the back and says to them, —Hey he's a writer. He's writing a BOOK. It's about a bear who ate a sandwich. It's twenty pages.

Jason says, —It's not really about that though.

—Oh. Right. Yeah, it's hard to explain what it's about, right? He doesn't know what it's about. It's hard to explain. Isn't that kind of weird though? I mean a grown man writing books for kids.

—I don't think so.

—Just seems a little weird.

—I can refuse to drive the client.

—I wasn't making fun of you though.

—For any reason if I don't feel safe I can—

—I wasn't making fun of you though. Your book sounds really good. Very interesting. I want to read it someday. Are you sensitive?

—Last warning.

—I want to read it though. I want to read it while listening to, who'd you say you like? Tom McCall? I want to read it while listening to Tom McCall and chewing tobacco and square dancing. We can go to a rodeo.

Jason reaches for The Button and stabs it with his finger, tears welling up behind his eyes, but he won't let himself cry, and can hear Gilbert duck walking back to his seat singing like a cowboy, —A bear ate my sandwich! A bear ate my sandwich! Then my wife left me! And I got drunk!

Jason will remember this ride for years to come, even when he is finally able to quit driving limos and gets a teaching job because of a severe teacher shortage in North Dakota in which they will hire just about anybody with any sort of degree. He will never watch another professional athletic event again even when it's on the display TVs at electronics stores. He will walk out of the store, having seen the dark truth behind the veil. He will bristle when his students wear these people's jerseys. From here on out Jason will consider professional athletes as fraudulent half-humans who are idolized jerks and, considering the life his culture affords these people, in Jason's opinion, he will find himself even more isolated from a popular culture that rewards the rotten and places its hopes in their reckless hands. He will float lost in his town cut off by the mountains, a man with a job unsure of what matters or what is right, if anything, because the world as he sees it encourages mindlessness and superficiality and goes out of its way to overlook immorality as long as it's done by the wealthy or attractive.

Now feeling sleepy from an oncoming storm of depression resulting from this encounter that will take weeks to work through and thus hinder for a while progress on the book which he will one day finish and read to his daughter Jason eases the limo onto Agaris Road which will take them up to the hotel.

Gilbert is more than a bit bothered by how right now there is no doubt that downtown in places that matter parties are going on and clubs are filling up and girls are blow-drying their hair and studying themselves in mirrors and putting on whatever they put on that makes them smell good and calling taxis to take them to places where he should be because people who are famous and important will be there and music and drinks and bodies and grinding and sex and he's irritated that the driver whose name he can't remember is an ambitionless man with no talent who isn't the best at his job and thus represents the invisible people of this culture who have all found a way to get through life without doing anything with themselves which angers him and makes him feel alone. This is the true nature of financial woe, he's realizing—not the shame or the powerlessness of it but that it has sent him here into this quite insulting automobile that lucky for him no one has seen him in with bodyguards he doesn't like because they most likely see him the way most every other man he meets does which is spoiled and snobbish and he wishes they would disappear. The limo begins to slow and turns into an unmarked road and he sits up from the slouch he's been sitting in with his hand over his mouth and eyes and says to no one, —Is this it? Where the fuck are we going?

No one answers and he wonders if they heard him so he says it again and Sheldon says, annoyed, —I don't know. Sheldon is the type of person who sounds annoyed all the time, even when he's not. This demeans you for speaking to him, especially coupled with the sheer size of the guy which already demeans you enough. Gilbert though when asking a question needs not only a response but one that expresses that him asking the question is reasonable and even appreciated. He thus says, doing his best to throw Sheldon's negative tone back at him so that Sheldon sees how his tone affects people and is sorry, —Well there aren't any signs. I think we're near Red Rock, for Christ's sake. That's almost *Utah*, FYI. Sheldon doesn't answer, bothering him more, now he needs even more validation to overcome his comment not getting a response at all, and unsure of what then to do he gets off his seat, wondering why he's doing it, and goes back to the glass divider panel and knocks twice, then three times, to no answer. Tries calling through it, —Hey is this the hotel? and knocks some more, then laughs at being ignored, making a face, going, —Ooookay, and goes back toward his seat but stops halfway and makes a show of looking out the window trying to figure out where they are, and says to everybody, —Watch he's going to take us into the desert and kill us. Will makes a noise like a grunt and Larry (the white one) and Sheldon say nothing, and Gilbert says, —Because I made fun of him. And then there's an actual moment of fear when after about another mile goes by and there's still no sign of a hotel and Gilbert can envision the limo suddenly stopping and the silence of the desert as the driver comes around and opens the door holding a gun, hair askew, and breathing heavy with a smile and hissing, —Get out of the car, you city fucks. The choice of whether or not to indeed stop on this remote black road and kill them execution style is the driver's and only the driver's. That the driver has this type of power disgusts Gilbert more than the thought of being shot in the back of the head does. But the fear of being homicided is put to rest when a sign that is carved from wood by hand it looks like and is tastefully stained with a fresh-looking finish appears among the rocks and thicket out of the blue with spotlights shining onto it so you can see that it says HUNTINGTON HOTEL AND CASINO and nothing about how accommodating it is or how they are AAA-approved or any features like free cable or pool which soothes Gilbert because that is a sign that it is a good place, his newest

personal assistant, Rhoda, having booked it sight unseen. Around the
next corner there is a small city which turns out to be the Huntington
Hotel and Casino—hundreds of lanterns lined up along either side of
the driveway—and Gilbert is reminded of one of his visits to the Playboy mansion when he got head from a Playmate behind a miniwater-
fall, a tiny brunette with huge tits who he would have slept with if she
hadn't smoked. The grandeur of their lodgings immediately puts him
at ease as the limo courses past the lawn with lights shining on it that
is stunningly well-groomed with a plaid pattern like a baseball field, a
couple man-made ponds with carp in them, up to the horseshoe drive
and coming to a stop at the entrance where two valets await smiling
serenely in tuxedos, hair slicked back and faces smooth and youthful
and revealing nothing about them, and the limo stops and Gilbert ex-
hales and says, —Thank God. He fumbles around for the handle on
the door and when he finds it, it doesn't open, it is locked, and he
fights with it and says, chafing under the pressure of them up on their
seats, ready to get out, waiting for him, —How do you open this piece
of shit?
    —Unlock it.
    —*Where?*
    The driver's waist and crotch appear outside his window and
Gilbert is shocked because he thinks that the driver's wearing jeans,
and the zipper on his fly is open a little. The driver opens the door easily for Gilbert and stands aside as Gilbert gets out, bumping his head
with a thudding pain that he instinctively ignores so no one will know
he bumped his head, not able to look at the driver, who is a foot
shorter than he and waving off the valets even though they make no
effort to approach. Gilbert rolls his neck and stretches and sighs and
goes around to the trunk, tries to open it with no success and says,
—Hey. Trunk. Hey. The driver comes around as the guards squeeze
out in huffs and groans, the limo creaking, and the driver sticks his
key in the trunk and opens it, and Gilbert realizes he's still wearing his
sunglasses and takes them off as the driver makes a halfhearted attempt to reach in and get the bags out but Gilbert stops him and says,
—We got it, man. Driver makes a face like whatever and stands aside
with his hands in his pockets jingling change and Will who is married
and votes Republican reaches in and grabs everyone's suitcases on
wheels as Gilbert takes out his kangaroo-skin wallet which cost $927
and plucks out three startlingly crisp one-hundred-dollar bills (the
new ones) rubbing them between his fingers as he hands them to the

driver and the driver freezes and stares at them not wanting to take
them but he does.

A valet leans on the little counter and crosses one leg over the
other and says something in a foreign language that makes the other
nod, both staring at the new arrivals absently as the new arrivals extend the retractable handles of their suitcases on wheels and begin
making their way up the wheelchair ramp toward the entrance where
the doors part and a guy in a tuxedo jogs out and puts their suitcases
on wheels on a luggage cart that's there and says in a loud energetic
voice, —Welcome to the Huntington Hotel and Casino, come right
this way. He's a white guy, around Gilbert's age, with a big nose and
the dark shading of a heavy beard. He pushes the luggage cart with
enthusiasm through the sliding automatic doors and Gilbert is in a
better mood now because it smells like a candle store and so he allows
himself to say to the guy who is the concierge, though Gilbert thinks
at first he's just a well-dressed fan, —Thanks, buddy . . .

The valets, in red jackets and bow ties, Brazilian, both of them, one
old and one young, watch, working twelve-hour days, sometimes
more, to send money back to their families in Brazil, live in a janitor's closet—both of them—around the back of the hotel next to the
air-conditioning system so they dream of airplanes, tornadoes, loud
things, during their four or so hours of sleep each night. The younger
one is tossing up keys and catching them, thinking about how he will
get to Mass on Sunday because he has to work, the older one, thirty-
seven, behind the stand with a pen, writing a note to one of the
maids, a seventeen-year-old girl named Maria, to meet him in room
239 at eleven o'clock, a vacant room, and that he loves her, folds it
up and slips it inside his jacket and will go inside in a few minutes
under the pretense of using the bathroom and give it to her as she
passes, discreet, sneaking a smile.

The sounds of the jingling keys and luggage cart rolling over the
meticulously swept rug of the foyer, the younger valet clearing his
throat, past the handmade stand-up ashtray that used to be a small
tree trunk, no butts in it, though a hand-painted sign says BUTTS.
Gilbert points to it and says, —I want that sign for over my bed.

The concierge says, —What?

—Nothing.

As they go in, Gilbert says, —This is a nice place, man. Nice and quiet. I feel like I'm in the woods or something.

—It's off-season now, yeah. Most people come here in the winter to rock climb and get away from the cold. The real hard-core gamblers and tourists stay more downtown. In the winter it's a lot busier. More busy? Busier?

The concierge wears glasses. The concierge's name is Kevin. Kevin the Concierge. He speaks and performs his duties with a distant almost condescending expertise like a waiter at one of the restaurants Gilbert goes to, a sort of overprofessionalism. They pass through a vast nearly unoccupied casino with hundreds of slot machines and blackjack dealers standing at attention behind their tables. Kevin the Concierge doesn't eat garlic because it enrages his irritable bowel syndrome and the emptiness of the hotel is good for Gilbert because if it were crowded beyond a guest or two sprinkled here and there he would not be able to enjoy that this is all for him, the night, the confidence of being Someone in Nowhere, and he can then mentally envision himself as larger than all of this, more vibrantly colored, and thus make himself unaffected by the concierge's condescension beyond considering meeting with the owner of the hotel to suggest either firing Kevin the Concierge or giving him a stern talking-to.

And then they go through another set of automatic sliding doors and are suddenly in a hotel lobby. He is not aware of the effort it took to build the Huntington Hotel and Casino, the strained backs and broken smashed bloody fingernails, the arguments among workers, the sweat and waking up early and problems struggled over then solved, impossibilities overcome. Nor is he aware beyond a brief glance of an enormous chandelier hanging down from the ceiling in the middle of the lobby, a dazzling display of crystal and yellow, hundreds of tiny lights, that was custom-made by a borderline schizophrenic local female artist with long dry gray hair who spent four months slaving over it, almost breaking down twice; a stone fireplace in the corner with two overstuffed beaded leather brown chairs and a matching couch, magazines on the oak end tables, a forty-two-inch plasma flat-screen HDTV where traditionally, over the fireplace, an oil landscape might hang, but now there is cable news there, coverage of a roadside bomb blast in Iraq that killed four soldiers and wounded seventeen others; a modest waterfall trickling down behind the concierge desk, a wall of mismatched rocks of earth tones installed by a mason who had previous territorial disputes with the one who did the fireplace but they secretly envied each other's work; oils of moose and ducks and other wildlife scenes bought from a garage sale because someone was getting divorced; and a bearskin rug that Kevin the Concierge points out and says, —It's not real.

Gilbert says, —What's not?

—The bear. It's synthetic.

—Oh.

Larry (the white one) isn't aware that his overweight wife posts lewd pictures of herself on the Internet and is doing so right now, back in California. Kevin the Concierge by habit pats his pizza down with napkins before eating it to soak up the grease.

There are antique objects on the end tables and on the floor along the walls, everywhere, metal things that look like pioneer cooking instruments and gardening tools, to give the ambiance of being hunkered down in a cabin in like 1870s Oklahoma, the horses hitched outside and Ma and Sis making supper, an old-fashioned gun hanging over the check-in desk which you sit down at like you're opening a checking account at a bank, and there is a restaurant adjacent to the lobby but it is closed and a woman, white, late fifties with short gray hair and corduroy pants and a lot of makeup who when you look at her you know that she lives in a spacious house in northern Virginia with a faux-stone façade and was no doubt quite attractive in her younger years and has a college- or postcollege-age daughter who went to a state university and now lives in Arlington and works for Boeing. But this woman sits on the far end of a couch in the fireplace area reading a popular women's fashion magazine and not really watching the news, one hand around the stem of a wineglass, and she looks up and is a friendly-looking woman and stares at the new arrival with her head cocked knowing he must be somebody judging from his size and entourage but she doesn't know who.

Gilbert follows Kevin to the concierge desk and Kevin stops his cart and goes around behind the desk and says good-naturedly to the bellhop leaning against it, —Matt, would you mind taking care of these gentlemen's bags, please?

And the bellhop smiles and says, —*Definitely*. And goes off with the cart somewhere.

At which point there is a clacking behind Gilbert and he smells something unmistakable and he turns to see a girl with decent tits— white, well-bred, the age hard to tell but Gilbert assumes it's around twenty. The face has the chipper glow of college age, red hair in a ponytail and hoop earrings and a white button-down shirt that doesn't need to be tucked in over a white tank top with built-in bra, a black skirt that comes to two inches above the knee, no pantyhose, pale skin, freckles, the fingernails not painted but well-kept, and the smell of the body is good, the eyebrows satisfactorily plucked and shaped into thin arches, the nose small and upturned, makeup, and the first thought Gilbert has after checking the body out is that after a couple of sec-onds the girl is not as hot as you first thought she was. To him, the girl then is worthy of attention but overall is only slightly above average, the type of girl who is attractive only in context—for example, a small town—thus might get a lot of attention from males there who haven't been anywhere else but compared to the kinds of girls he meets, living in L.A.—where all small-town beauties go to die—and as a pro ath-lete, she is not memorable in the least. But here she is the most attrac-tive girl and so must be pleased, won over, which will be easy because he has the power, and he smiles when she says, —Are you, um, Mr. . . .?

He says, —Aw come on. You know who I am.

She's actually a beautiful girl and there are many men who are willing to love her, but you don't always know it, nor do you always want to.

And she laughs at herself and says, —Sorry.

—Don't be sorry.

She wore a skirt today though she normally wears tight black capri pants, and she was late to work and got a pretty stern talking-to from her new boss, Alan Lyson—who owns half of the Huntington Hotel and Casino and who masturbates to fantasies of her some-times—who told her she would be keeping a potential investor com-pany this evening. Before leaving for work this afternoon, while Gilbert was on the way to Vegas, she got caught up standing in her bedroom in her parents' house, where they moved to in seventh grade, with a pool and four-car garage on five acres of mostly useless land that backs eventually into a golf course, where she went back to after she moved out of the apartment downtown she got with two friends from high school but got evicted because they never paid rent, due partly to her not making enough money at her job at the time which was walking around the dance floor at Rain in a bikini with a whistle and squirting tequila shots into people's mouths then making them pay for the tequila shot, turned and angled before her full-length mirror, not liking her legs and wishing they were longer and more muscular, made a vow to start running more, the price tag still on the skirt and she tore it off, unconsciously making a face that her roommates made fun of her for, saying it looks like she's trying to be a model—so serious! _____ has a MySpace profile and drives a 2005 Nissan Altima that her parents bought her and pay the insurance on, is twenty-one years old, turned profile to examine if her boobs were big enough and tummy flat, admiring her butt and thought, He's going to see me and like me and who knows where it could go from there. Not that I expect anything or am even that excited about meeting him. I know he must have all kinds of girls crawling all over him. Girls who have bigger boobs, better asses. Girls without freckles. I'm prettier than most girls, she thought. Despite my freckles. That's not being conceited. It's just that I can say it's a fact that a lot of guys find me attractive. I have friends who no guys ever talk to or look at. She thought, I'll meet him and do my new job, what Alan Lyson will pay me salary with full benefits for if I do well enough at it, which is hanging out with potential investors and making sure they have everything they need for a pleasant stay at the Huntington Hotel and Casino in Las Vegas and are in a good mood when Alan and his partner Ryan Something meet with them to discuss money. And sure we'll probably chat a little and next time he's in Las Vegas he'll remember me and how much he liked talking to me and then who knows. She shaved her legs in the shower before getting dressed, trimmed her pubic hair with her dad's beard trimmer, and put on her favorite thong, sheer blue Victoria's Secret, and a matching push-up bra, underwear she wears when there's a likelihood of somebody seeing her underwear, and she's had sex with a girl, back when she was a stripper for a month the winter after high school. She was drunk and this guy gave them one thousand dollars for them to split. She's not a basketball fan (but she knows who Darren Dickinson is) and wouldn't have known who he is. But four days ago on her first day she was in the lobby waiting for her first client (a Greek guy who was a total fag and paid her four hundred dollars to leave him alone and tell Alan Lyson thanks anyway; which offended the hell out of her but she took the money) and Kevin the Concierge was hovering around her, flirting with her in his own passive-aggressive way, in her opinion, which turned her off, and Kevin was scrolling through the reservations in the computer and he stopped on one and was like, —Whoa is this for real?

—What.

Kevin's older than she is by a couple of years at least, and she doesn't know that he has been in love with her since the moment she first walked into the Huntington Hotel and Casino and has imaginary conversations with her when he's by himself in his bedroom at his parents' house thirty miles away, wants nothing more than her body next to his, but he's not her type, if she has a type, which she doesn't think she does really, even though they made out a little once when he invited her out two nights after the Greek fag, but she was drunk and loopy from not eating, and so in the morning when it was quiet and calm and sober she regretted making out with Kevin.

—Gilbert Marcus is coming here, he said as she waited for the Greek guy on her first day.

—Really?

—Yeah. He has a reservation. Pretty awesome.

—Wow.

—Kevin Costner came here once like two years ago. He was a dick.

—Wait. Gilbert Marcus. Who's he again?

—Plays for Dallas.

—Oh. Right. Plays what for Dallas though?

—He's a basketball player. He's like the *best* basketball player. Produces some pretty good independent movies too and does all sorts of charity work for kids in Third World countries with AIDS. You don't know who he is?

—No I do. I just. I don't really know that much about sports.

—He's more than an athlete though, you know? He's like an icon. His wife is *banging*. He has the fucking *best* life. And he actually brings kids from the poorest parts of Japan to his summer camp in Michigan and teaches them how to play basketball. I bet he's a dick.

They diagnosed her anorexic when she was hospitalized the first time she nearly starved herself to death—when she was sixteen. She did not believe she was anorexic nor does she now. They misunderstood. She was not sick. She was not diseased. According to the scale in her bathroom that she weighs herself on sometimes as often as eleven times a day, she is back up to 103 pounds, 9.4 ounces, which is the most she has weighed in seven weeks. She is supposed to be seeing a counselor. There are days where she skips work and stays in bed. She

does not remember much of her nineteenth year. Hours come out of
the blue where there is a pressure from inside her head, like the world
is sitting on her head and she can feel a strange hot anger surging beneath the bones of her face. Boiling. There are days when she doesn't
go in to work and instead spends the day stomping around her house
scowling, pacing, seething at nothing, snapping at the dog and her
mother. The scale is the second scale she has owned this year because
the first one broke she used it so much. She goes on and off her medication—Zoloft, 80 milligrams a day, plus Ambien to help her sleep—
because she has a hard time admitting she has anything wrong with
her and Zoloft makes her feel worse and like her bones are rattling
and the Ambien doesn't do anything. No one knows she flushes her
medication down the toilet every morning so her mom will see the va-
cancy in the pill-dispenser thing in the kitchen and think she took it.
She feels free and alive when she flushes her medication, uncaring
what might happen to her, of the belief—though not exactly worked
out and thought through—that people with mental illnesses aren't
really mentally ill, just different, and that the culture doesn't understand them and so calls them crazy and drugs them into submission
instead of dealing with them. Calling people like her mentally ill is society's way of defending itself, is her opinion. She's herself now and
pure, the way she sees it, ready for adventure and fun and danger,
even thinks sometimes about being a firefighter or a cop, to see what
that's like. She thinks she has the mentality it would take. That kind of
power. _____ is the kind of girl that other girls don't like. And
she told her friends, in Greg's basement in Henderson, who she went
to high school with, watching *SportsCenter* on the fifty-seven-inch
flat-screen plasma HDTV and drinking Miller Lite cans, Greg's dad
who owns a chain of liquor stores and his own microbrewery playing
online poker in the corner, that that guy on *SportsCenter* (a segment
about the trade rumors in Dallas involving Gilbert Marcus and Ben
Jermaine) (replaying the footage of Gilbert Marcus peeing himself) is
going to invest in the casino where she works, and Chris, who she had
sex with last year when they both had a girlfriend/boyfriend, jumped
up in the easy chair he was reclined in and went, —Gilbert Marcus is?

And Greg said, —No way.

—Really?

—No. Way.

—You serious?

And she said, —I think that's who it is. I'm pretty sure.

—I bet he's a dick, Greg said.

—Dude, said Chris, —you should bring him back here and we'll . . . And he made weed smoking motions.

Greg's dad said, —Fuck I just lost eight thousand dollars.

Greg said, —No. He doesn't do that. They get tested like twice a week.

Chris said, —I bet he does though anyway. How much do you think he pulls in a month?

Greg said, —You should totally get him to hang out though.

Chris said, —Totally. You have to. Dude. You totally have to. I can't believe this. That is so awesome.

Other people were on their way over and she felt regal and wished they would get there now because the first thing Chris and Greg would say would be, —Dude, _____ is going to meet Gilbert Marcus. Gilbert Marcus is going to be _____'s boss. And they all will like her, The Girl Who Works for Gilbert Marcus, and she was aware that she was dealing with something bigger than she and had to then become a part of it somehow. She scheduled a tanning session for the day before The Day even though tanning was a futile endeavor considering her complexion. This was a taste of what she'd been hungry for. She spent so much time daydreaming, watching so much television, listening to so much music, examining her face in the mirror, caring about and studying the personal lives of celebrities on People.com and *The Insider*, feeling so small and undesirable compared to these rich and cool people. But she is special just like them and deserves what they have. She has this thing where whenever she is in a bar or at a party—which is often—she imagines that everyone is looking at her and is infatuated with her because she's famous and she does this whenever she's anywhere public actually—grocery store, pharmacy, etc. She still sleeps with her ex-boyfriend who she went to high school with and who waits tables at Outback and slept with him yesterday in fact, not telling him about the six other guys she's slept with this month, one of which might have been married. She wishes her ex-boyfriend was an actor and if he had more chest hair there's a good chance they'd still be together. There is a whole world beyond the suburbs of Las Vegas and one day she will be a part of it—fame is her destiny, either as a *Playboy* Playmate or as a host for one of the morning talk shows such as *The View* or *Live with Regis and Kelly*. She practices for this at the Huntington Hotel and Casino—meeting people, charming them, talking to them, and keeping the conversation flowing and lively, imagining she's being watched by millions. Making people happy. Making them like her. She will be wealthy and beautiful. She will live forever and have no worries. A summer ago, she auditioned to be the hostess of an exciting new series for a major television network about the world of fashion. She found the ad in the paper. There would be an open audition held at The Mirage. Anyone could go. The ad said the only requirements were you had to be eighteen to thirty-five with a *dynamic personality, outgoing and youthful, with strong ad-lib and interaction skills.* That was her. The ad also warned that the job required an extensive time commitment along with domestic and international travel. So exciting. This was her chance. She could do this. She knew fashion. She designed clothes. She'd even applied to Parsons School of Design, though she didn't get in. She dreamed of being a fashion designer. Or at least starting her own clothing line one day once she was established as a major personality. What would she call it? What would she call her fashion line? She would focus on plus sizes. Not plus sizes, but rather *realistic* sizes. She would coin the term. Clothes for *real* women. With *real* bodies. She would be a hero to everyday women. They would love her. She'd become an icon. Launch her own magazine and book-publishing company. Recommend kinds of soaps and CDs. Her own daytime talk show. Bring on people like racists or homophobes and ask them why they are racists or homophobes. Give beauty tips. Of course *she* would still be beautiful though. But not *too* beautiful. *Real.* That's what she would call her fashion line. *Real.* A perfume called that too. *Real* for women. *Real* for men. Her parents paid for her to get her hair and makeup professionally done and let her use the credit card to buy a new outfit including shoes. She went to the open audition to be the hostess of an exciting new series for a major network which was held at The Mirage. She stood in line for nearly ten hours with seemingly thousands of other people but she didn't get past the first round with producers or whoever it was who was screening the candidates. Outside in the parking lot there was a middle-aged man who was handing out cards to the girls as they came out in tears: MODELING AND ACTING AGENT. She took his card and went with him to his office and took pictures. She took off her clothes and let him take pictures of her with no clothes on. Never saw him again. When weeks went by with no word from the agent, she called the number on the card but it was out of service. That is when she was hospitalized the second time. When she got out of the hospital, her Zoloft prescription doubled, and with a new prescription, this one for Ambien, she moved in with friends.

A part of her considered in the days leading up to His arrival that He, being famous, would know famous producers or other industry people who He could put her into contact with and she'd meet them and they'd SEE that she HAS IT, and her life would change, the big break she one day recounts happily in interviews, smiling with nostalgia at the luck and her own naïveté. She'd be happy. She often feels bigger than her life, gets bored and frustrated looking out her window at her little brother's basketball hoop in the driveway when she wakes in the morning. She's unusually sensitive, as her mother tells her, has the soul of an artist, which is why she has trouble handling life's problems that normal people deal with easily. As an actress, life sometimes can be overwhelming for her and that's why she cries a lot and has trouble dealing with life's problems.

She put on makeup, made a bowel movement, went to work, told Alan Lyson she had car trouble which is why she's late, and she waited alone until Gilbert Marcus came in with His entourage and she watched Him, struck first by His height—a very attractive man, a chiseled face and piercing eyes, muscular and lean, none of which you get nearly the full grasp of watching him on TV. He is the world she wants, the answer—He is a life with no boundaries, wide-open sky, endless air.

But she finds herself not attracted to Him. She tries to be attracted to Him, but she isn't. It's nothing to do with Him being black or whatever He is, having slept with a running back on the football team her senior year of high school and liking it just as much as if he were white. It's just not there. There will be nothing between them, she admits as she shakes His hand, smiling but dejected. But she is also relieved because now He will be choosing to help her not through any impure motive but out of the simple desire to help a friend. She puts on her nicest face, turns on the welcoming eyes and inviting smile— *Wouldn't you like to wake up to her on your television? She's so pretty, she's so nice, she's so smart . . .*

He asks her what her name is and she tells him but he forgets it almost immediately because he doesn't care what her name is and he asks her why she's staying at a place all the way out here but before she can answer he asks her to tuck him in and she laughs and Kevin the Concierge slides the key across the desk—a plastic card in a paper sheath—and he stares at the key and is too tired to think about where the room might be and he is faced now with the future: saying good night to his guards and going down to his own room and closing the door and being alone in a room. He thinks, I'll call my father, my mother. I'll make amends. It'll be something to do too. He can see where she was a little girl once and wants the smell of her near him, a female soft and warm walking beside him in the halls, because if not then he knows he'll be up alone, and that will be a failure.

It's 10:34, and Greg is having people over tonight and they're probably already there. She is becoming increasingly more attracted to Him, much to the same effect of being in a bar, dark lighting, loud music, alcohol, bodies close, and one person who at first you don't have much interest in but whose eyes you keep meeting and you stare at them until they become something else and you must have them.

The woman from northern Virginia by the fireplace which has no fire in it looks up again as her bewildered-looking husband steps out of the elevator and says nothing as he stands beside her looking at the television, shakes his head and sits, reaches for a magazine. Will leafs through some pamphlets and maps in a wooden stand nearby and he is thirty-two and thinking about eight years ago when he was working for a middleweight champ named Bob Johnson when he—Will did—had sex with a twenty-two-year-old Asian girl who talked like she was black and who weighed ninety-seven pounds (he asked) in a Las Vegas hotel hallway, the whole thing watched secretly by two amused hotel security guards via surveillance cameras he'd find out later. Sheldon stands off to the side watching Gilbert check in, arms crossed, consciously breathing the way he read in *Unlimited Power* by Tony Robbins—inhale four beats, hold sixteen beats, exhale eight beats. Larry (the white one) is filling up a paper cone of water from the cooler by the elevator and examining the light fixtures on the ceiling. Gilbert is aware that Sheldon is watching him. The girl agrees to help them find their rooms, pretending to be reluctant and not sure. She is tired of leaving jobs after a couple months and she prides herself in succeeding in this one as in her mind she's a vital and hard-to-replace component of the casino's success and people depend on her for a pleasant business trip, not to mention, she thinks, that if she's ever going to be successful then she must be successful in every aspect of her life leading up to that, no matter what the pay or prestige. Alan Lyson promised that the people she'd be entertaining in her new position would be very, very prestigious which is why she took the job. Before he had offered her the job she was going to quit her

job promoting Bacardi Silver in bars and clubs around Las Vegas anyway. Wearing booty shorts and low-cut T-shirts, going up to people
and smiling and yelling over the music if they would like a free sam
ple of Bacardi Silver. Often having to repeat herself twice, three times.
It could be awkward. The people she approached could be uncomfortable, not understanding why she was approaching them, what she
wanted. She was misheard over the music. Groups of men could be
cruel. Girlfriends gave her dirty looks and snotty attitude. Quote-
unquote movie producers tried to get her to do porn. If she had quit
like she had planned and if Alan Lyson hadn't approached her (such a
change—her being approached for once, rather than hovering among
the atmosphere, being leered at from afar by horny men with self-
esteem issues), then she would be home right now watching TV or
IMing then backing the Altima out on her way to her friends. I will
help him find his room and spend some time with him, she thinks,
but will keep it professional yet friendly, and he will see my talent
and make me famous and can you imagine how it feels to have what
you've prayed for all your life within reach?

Gilbert observes the white body by instinct, the practiced discreet
leer of men, taking it in in its entirety with one flicker of the eyeball,
judging it. If there's anything that turns him off it is the small black
dots of hair follicles on the girl's shin, and she says, mock-formal,
—Right this way, please.

There is a planned way to show guests around the hotel that she
has rehearsed many times usually for older businessmen who might
take pleasure in knowing what kind of wood frames the doorways are
made of and square footage and how the hotel was originally built in
1967 by an orthodontist for a winter weekend getaway home, a skiing
and wildlife enthusiast, and in the early seventies when he died it was
bought and turned into a brothel that burned down in the late 1990s
and was eventually rebuilt by the current owner and expanded into
the hotel you see now, but she knows He is not interested in this kind
of thing (nor does He seem to understand that she is an employee—
He thinks she's a guest) so she saves the spiel until, on the way to the
back elevator, she stops and they all stop too, looking at themselves in
a mirror at the end of the hall, and she goes, —Shhh.

—What? Gilbert says.
—Do you hear that?
—What.
—This place is supposed to be haunted.

—Whoa, that's crazy. Nuh-uh. By what? I mean, what do they say?

—I don't know. This was a whorehouse before it was a hotel and it burned down. The story is a bunch of people died.

—That's crazy.

And they stand there listening, moving their eyeballs at one another, and she says, —Yeah. I don't believe in ghosts though. Do you?

She comes up to his elbow, and he doesn't look at her, and the guards say nothing and don't look out the window and look bored but she still likes them. Like three big bears! She likes big men, puffy overgrown boys. So cute! Gilbert knows he could sleep with her if he wants to, the way she keeps glancing at him and how her voice is small, the arm brushing his, pretending it's accidental, and he glances at her and their eyes meet, and there is electricity pulling him in, something that is praying that he decides to make a move, encouraging him to figure out how to get to her, and his knees start to buzz so much they must visibly vibrate (his ankle no longer hurting and he is happy). Truthfully he wouldn't mind sending his security guards off to their room and getting rid of the girl and staying here in the hallway all night, waiting for a ghost to come up, alone, just him and the ghost nose-to-nose trying to figure each other out. Or letting the girl stay might be okay too. She'd scream, he'd hold her, they'd laugh.

There's a door there next to the window with the ghosts and she opens the door and hot air rushes in as they stand there, looking out at a little brick path that leads to a wooden houselike structure, and she goes, —I think that's where the pool is. Do you want to go in the pool?

He doesn't know I am an employee and that is what he is supposed to think.

—Where's there a pool? Gilbert says.

—In that house.

—There's a pool in there?

—It's heated. I think they said it's heated. Want to go in?

—You go first.

—No, she says, smiling a little, —go ahead.

—I'm not going out there by myself. Are you crazy? You just said there's ghosts. I'm not going anywhere around here by myself.

Will goes, —Go on, Gilbert. We'll be watching to make sure nothing happens.

—Fuck you, he laughs.

And the girl says, —It's not very far. Just right down there. In that little house thing.

You all are crazy. No way in hell. There's ghosts out there, man. You all are fucking crazy. You guys want to go?

Sheldon shrugs and pokes his head out the door and looks at the house where the pool is and Will says, —Yeah I wouldn't mind going for a dip. But hey is there food in our room though? One of those what do you call them. With the food in it. Because I'm starving, man.

Gilbert says to the girl, —I'll only go in if you go in.

And the girl's quiet and says, —Okay, maybe. But I have to go to the bathroom first. Then I'll come.

—Then you'll come? He laughs, and she slaps him on the arm and says, —That's not what I meant! And he laughs and she calls him a pervert and he sort of tries to push her outside and she screams and resists, and he picks her up (thumb touching the side of tit) and drops her outside with the ghosts and before she can get back in he closes the door on her, but she gets her foot in just in time and they are both laughing and after pretending not to let her in he does and she says, —Jerk, and he says, —Do you have a bathing suit?

—No.

—Uh-oh. You'll have to go in naked.

—Won't be the first time, she says.

—Yeah?

—Mm-hmm. Maybe. Shhh. It's a secret.

In the elevator, they must hear her heart thumping. Her extremities tremble, the power emanating from Him, and His mighty hand is on her lower back, touching so brisk, her flesh goose-bumping and a warm shiver scurrying up her spine, it could crumple her up and squeeze. It could control her, make her do whatever He wished. Someone clears his throat and something must be said, her lungs swollen with air but can't think of anything. This is my moment, she thinks, and I am failing.

He touches her tentatively at first but she lets him, and he sees how relaxed she is, cool, and he gets an erection that he puts his other hand into his pocket to hold down, pushing aside his phone, searching frantically for something to say. She is thinking about her ex-boyfriend and Gilbert is thinking about if this girl is attracted to his bodyguards and Will is thinking about swimming and eating at the same time and if it could be done and Sheldon is thinking about is she of age and Larry (the white one) about why don't girls respond to him like this.

And—now that it has presented itself as a feasible option to Gilbert—there is no choice and sex must be obtained.

She is deciding that she will most likely not have sex with Him. She hopes He will notice her necklace. She wants Him to see her necklace. Her necklace is silver. She loves her necklace, the silver pendant hanging from it. That her mom bought her for her birthday almost four years ago. The silver pendant is what looks like an asterisk, or like a backwards *k*. The Chinese character for *talent*. The Chinese are ancient and she tends to believe in things that are ancient. She finds the more different something is from America, the more faith she has in it. She wants Him to notice her necklace so that He will ask her what her necklace is so that she can tell Him that it means *talent*. So in turn He will ask her if she has talent. But she won't answer that. A trap. She'll look away. Blush a little bit. Look down and say, No. I don't know. Sometimes I don't know. Sometimes I'm not so sure. And He'll lift her head up by the chin gently and He'll say, No, don't think like that. You can't think like that. You do. You do have talent. I can see it. I can tell. I know just from looking at you. You can tell from looking at people who has *it* and who doesn't. And you have it. You do. I can see it in your eyes. She wants to tell Him her favorite quote: *Live as if you will die tomorrow. Learn as if you will live forever.* Which she thinks she made up herself. And tries to live by. Also, *Everything happens for a reason.* Which she did not make up herself but still tries to live by. He'll say those are great quotes and He'll then ask, What's your talent? Do you play an instrument? Or sing? And she'll say, No, but I act. And I write. Mostly poetry and some screenplays. Also I model. And design clothes. I'm interested in politics as well and in forensic science like on *CSI*. I am also considering doing some open mike stand-up comedy. Ellen and Rosie started out that way. I can do what they do but do it better. I know I can. But I don't know. I guess I have stage fright a little. She won't tell him about the audition—a bad memory, a severe mix of shame and unexplained guilt. She was nervous and panicked and screwed it up. So unprofessional. The industry term for it was *green*. She froze and forgot how to talk. Went blank. Started giggling. Went from giggling to cackling. Couldn't stop laughing. And the silence and the cameras and the lights, the producers staring at her from the other side of the room, rubbing their foreheads as somebody said thank you and pushed her away. There she was, in all her wretched mess, displayed to the core. She still wakes up from nightmares of the rejection. Sudden panic attacks when in the car or at a small party with a group of people she doesn't really know gathered around a coffee table playing drinking games: What if one of them was somehow there? What if one of them saw? What if someone KNOWS? She thinks, He will ask me to give Him an example of my talent and I will give Him one. Though I will be shy and laugh and say no at first. I will blush and try to change the subject. I'll put my face in my hands—mortified from my embarrassment—but He will gently pull them away and make me laugh and we will be sitting on the edge of the bed, alone, knees touching, elbows almost touching, faces close, and I will take a deep breath and give Him an example of my talent, and He'll be blown away, genuinely moved, looking at me like He can't believe it, and I will say, That wasn't really anything. I can do much better. If I have time to prepare. And I'll say, Everybody has underestimated me my whole life. And I'll say, Nobody has known that I am special. They have treated me so badly. Life has been so hard on me. He will tell me that He has a feeling that that's about to change. And the next time He is in L.A. He will be at a party and a producer will be casually mentioning to a director and an agent and George Clooney that he is having such a tough time these days finding any fresh, *real* talent, and He will overhear this and will go over and tell them all about this girl He met who is pretty hot, by the way, it just so happens. Not that it matters, though, because this girl, she is like Oprah, where it doesn't matter what she looks like. Because she is beautiful anyway. And He will tell them about how she is a diamond in the rough and how it is incredible that nobody has discovered her yet. He will say it's a shame. The producer will express interest and ask how to reach her. And she thinks, I'll get a phone call at work one day out of the blue from a bored-sounding assistant and I'll fly out the next day to L.A. first class and a limo will pick me up and take me to a very expensive restaurant to meet the producer. I'll tell him about myself and he'll say at one point that he knew right away when he saw me walk in the door that I had *it*. That I didn't have to say a word. That he hasn't had this feeling about someone since the first time he laid eyes on Tyra Banks. And I will be *so so happy*. Because it will feel *so so good*. He'll say, I hope you enjoyed the meal because it was the last one you'll have be able to enjoy as an anonymous person. I will

cry a little from joy. The buzz about me will spread so fast and I'll cancel my return flight home and sign a production deal with a major
studio and buy a gorgeous but small house with a pool and a little
puppy and will go to parties and have a personal trainer and personal
makeup artist and hair stylists and I will do interviews and be beautiful and I will get my photo taken for magazines and I will be so happy
knowing that I have arrived, and I will never have to go back to the
Huntington Hotel and Casino with its stench of sex and drugs and
cheesy carpet and human monkeys at the slot machines and the girls
out-prettying one another, loud married men looking for discreet head
exhaling cigarette smoke and ogling me and everyone who works here
knows thanks to Courtney—a cocktail waitress who hates me—about
how I almost died in January because I had not eaten in four days and
weighed 92 pounds, 7.13 ounces, but my friend Cara, a fairly heavy
girl who never went out or did anything and who was my best friend
since second grade and dressed like she was depressed all the time,
found me unconscious in my bedroom when she happened to come
over to confront me about how skinny I was getting and how I had
changed so much recently and called 911 and I went to the hospital for
the third time.

It's your life you want, the More that makes you want Him to see
your skin, though you can feel yourself watching, calling to yourself,
No don't do that.

No one, you think, deserves to be normal.

Larry (the white one) does not look at her but he is wondering
what she looks like in the prime moments of unbridled coitus. He has
never seen a girl like her without clothes on in person. What he would
never admit is that he wouldn't mind watching while she and Gilbert
do what it's impossibly clear they are going to do. Larry (the white
one) holds out hope that she secretly finds quiet men attractive and
finds something mysteriously alluring about him. They can see themselves in the reflection on the inside of the door. They are people
standing in an elevator. They are four who know one another and a
stranger they have just met, four humans with penises and testos-
terone and one human with a vagina and estrogen, grown from the
same zygote and similar in birth, but from there they split into drasti-
cally alternate universes, contradictory worlds, and they are going up.
It dings, doors open, a new floor, and they step out, _____ first,
and Gilbert is thinking himself lucky that these things happen to him
and that this is what it means to live his life, though is not overjoyed

in the least and even a bit bored, his mental mood that of finding a five-dollar bill on the sidewalk when you already have a hundred more in your wallet. What it is, it's not clear, if anything is, and if it will make him happy, he is certain it won't, but why not. What's there to lose? Nothing.

Downstairs Kevin the Concierge rearranges the magazines on the end tables, waiting to ask _____ about Gilbert Marcus so he can have something to say to her and as usual he's thinking about when he and _____ kissed, her lips so soft, her eyes closed when he pulled away and her smile slight and mindless under the glow of the bar lights, both of them coked to hell and the spark the kiss sent through him and how he could have stayed forever in the moment, everything outside of it and before stripped to black and white and cold, the devastation when she got a call on her phone and said she had to go meet her friends and said good-bye to him, getting into her car and zooming off with music cranked, the distant good-bye you give someone you work with, like none of it ever happened, and he was confused, but knew she deserved a good life, and thought of her all the next day and hoped she was safe, holding his breath all shift and counting the minutes until, staring at the front door hoping for them to part and then her hair and heels as she arrived, her smile and her scent filling the lobby.

They get to the guards' room and the casino is paying for the rooms which cost $919 a night each and the way Gilbert is paying for the private jet which costs $2,250 an hour is because he convinced the Lonestars' front office to pay for it along with his security detail by letting them think he is using both the jet and the security detail to meet with Kofi Annan in Washington, D.C., to talk about what can be done in Africa regarding the AIDS epidemic—using as additional leverage that they paid for all of Papa Bear Ben's plane and security detail when he flew to Puerto Rico for his stint in a mental-health facility when he got addicted to sleep medication—and when the Lonestars balked Gilbert threatened to have Abe Birnbaum demand a trade so they gave in. You have to go after what you want. The guards go into their three-room suite and Will goes straight for the minibar and unwraps a Snickers and sits on the bed and crosses his feet. Gilbert and the girl leave them and go back out into the hall. He decides to put off the phone call to his father until tomorrow after the meeting when he's in the airport with nothing else to do. What's another day? Everything else can wait. They hold hands as they go down the hall and hers is clammy and little and Coach tried to have Jeffrey trade Gilbert to Washington in May because Coach was tired of what Coach calls—to his personal Systemism Joy consultant who Coach began seeing on Gilbert's increasingly intense recommendation— Gilbert's emotional warfare, that Gilbert is ultimately untouchable and has no desire other than the desire to be liked and to be seen as superhuman, that winning doesn't matter to Gilbert if it gets in the way of Gilbert Marcus being liked and being seen as superhuman. Everyone else on Dallas with the exclusion of Papa Bear had given up hope before the season started because of Gilbert and played the schedule in a pretty dark existential despair. Any victories were hollow. They'd rather have lost every game because they knew there was no hope of winning when it wasn't a team and they never knew what Gilbert was thinking or what he wanted. He was a childish mystery to them. He was disgruntled and fragile. He doesn't know that he has already been a destructive force in the lives of so many and that he should have stopped long ago.

She reminds you of Brianne in the days of picking her up from her photo shoots, before her beautiful body was stretched and desecrated by the baby—a trap no one warned you about. And she has no clue about the depths of your clean insulated selfism, and none of your teammates or other members of the Association are here to tell her, for they would not be shocked if they could see what is transpiring, that its hunger always ravages blindly and with no remorse sweeps clear the building blocks precisely stacked by others. There is no limit, there is no hope. The hand is clammy in yours and she is speaking, and the words go, — . . . this hallway totally reminds me of the hallway in my elementary school which was when I first started understanding that I totally have, like, a flair for, like, the dramatic because that was the year I realized the simple but really understated joy of responding to the teacher, like, do you remember how the teacher would ask the class a question and sort of look around waiting for someone to raise their hand, and if no one did then she would call on somebody who would then be mortified? Well one day I asked myself why I was holding myself *in*, you know, and I took a chance and raised my hand and my teacher, Ms. Woodson, called on me, and though I got the answer wrong, I felt as though I were *contributing*, you know, as opposed to just sucking up air and taking up space on this earth . . .

But you are saying nothing, smiling a little because she's terrified, and the reason as you see it for her agreeing to show you to your room, 237, so far down the hall from your guards, is that she did it on purpose, she found out you were coming here and planted herself there to meet you, planning this far in advance with a conniving calculation that is strictly female. She—you understand—is just like you and prides herself on being relentlessly self-serving. She zeros in on what she wants and makes no apologies for it, no matter how off-putting it is to others. You like that.

That the lights in the hall give things a brown-orange tint.

That Jason the limo driver is stepping through the front door of his one-bedroom apartment, crisp and stale from years of other alone men groping for their lives moving in and moving out, taking off the jacket he is required to wear and happily draping it over the chair, off work and with the night in all its brilliant eternity to himself. Time to be alive. Washing his hands and face and pouring a glass of diet soda from a fresh two-liter bottle and sitting down at the kitchen table to his thickening stack of drawings and rhymes, a world of whimsy and perfection, imagination a drug of possibility and disdain, and exhaling.

That Papa Bear Ben Jermaine is on the phone with his ghost-writer—a columnist for the *Washington Post*—regarding his autobiography (tentatively titled *It's Big Ben Time!*) telling the ghostwriter that if he was allowed to pick one person on earth to kill and not be put in jail for it or suffer any other consequence for it such as guilt or going to hell or anything, the one person he would choose to kill would without a doubt be Gilbert Marcus and not only that but he'd do it as slowly and painfully as possible and derive great pleasure from doing so.

That—three hours later in the East—Mervin Marcus is unable to sleep, his face old and body fat and tired, woken by a panic that was as real as two hands shaking him. Gilbert's father—body still, tense, sheets tangled around his ankles—thinks, He is my son and I should have done more. I was wrong. I don't know what about though. Something along the way. Something fundamental. Maybe we all have been wrong. That Mervin Marcus is unaware that the other half of the bed is empty and a light creeps out from beneath the closed bathroom door, and Sue Marcus watches the rain from the window of the bathroom, her knuckles chapped and veins swelling up as thick as rope, trembling even when she clenches her wrist. That the air has a smell to it, though Sue can't say what it is, but it's discomforting and suffocating. That she pulls down a row of the blinds and watches the neighbor's yard, big drops hitting the broken lining of the empty pool, a foot of water gathered at the bottom, drowned bloated chipmunks floating sprawled on the surface, puke-green from chemicals and guts, a swing set in grass deep green and the sound of pummeled siding. That she pulls the loosening strands from her head and counts the boards of her neighbor's fence.

That the airport cop whose name is Tim Mayhew is heading back to the station in the solitude of his cruiser for the last half of his shift, remembering playing football in junior college and he swings home on the way to drop off the autograph for his daughter who is seven and loves it and loves Gilbert Marcus and stares at the autograph with her mouth open, going, breathless, —Oh my God Daddy this is so awesome! Tim hopes nothing comes up, that Las Vegas sleeps soundly for once, so he can get off early and go home and kiss his wife and wake her up and talk about her day, his family peaceful and safe, rub his daughter's back as she sleeps, clutching in one small hand the parking ticket blessed by the scribble of The Athlete.

They go inside Gilbert's room and he puts his bag in the corner and _____ says, —Oh. I don't know if this is like weird or anything but, I mean, I was wondering if . . . My friends who are mostly guys are, like, huge fans of yours and they would absolutely love some autographs if it's possible?

—No, sure, he says.

—Cool. I just I'm not trying to be like That Girl or anything but I mean if it's not too much trouble. They'd love it. They're huge fans. They'd really appreciate it. They watch your games all the time.

—No problem.

They're standing at opposite sides of the room, facing each other, eyes darting into each other's then away, a small room, and she goes, —I actually—

And she reaches into her purse, pulls out a couple blank index cards and a pen, and waves them around and goes, —I have these. Yeah. Here you go. You can use these.

—Okay. Who should I make them out to?

—Um, Greg and Chris and Fucker and . . .

—You have a friend named Fucker?

—Yeah. He's kind of crazy.

—He certainly sounds like a character.

—No, no, it's not his real name.

—What about you? he says. —Don't you want one?

—What am I going to do with an autograph?

—I don't know. Show it to your kids one day.

And she laughs and he smiles and he says, —So who should I make it out to? What's your name?

—Um, _____.

—_____. You're the first _____ I've met I think.

He signs the cards and the room is cozy and to the point, familiar, like the room you stay in when you visit Grandma, a place you could live in if you wanted to, the smell of coffee cooked into the walls and a rotary phone and a claw-foot tub and more framed local art, modest and tasteful, windows that open like miniature doors, a lock safe in the closet, a chair and a desk that look handmade, a nice change from the heartless mass-production wood-finish decor of rooms he's used to, fake furniture, like it could vanish at any time. —This place is cool. I like it. I feel like I'm in the fifties or something, you know?

—Yeah, she says, looking around.

He says, —It's weird. You know? It's not like a hotel room. It's more dirty. But not like that though I mean. Not in a bad way. I like it, you know? A little dirty is okay sometimes. I don't know why I just thought of it or why I'm bringing it up, but growing up my mom had to have everything clean all the time. She was always cleaning. I can't remember her doing anything else. When I think of her I see her cleaning. And we'd have to clean too for like five hours every Sunday night. It was like supposed to be family time. I like this though. People aren't perfectly clean, you know? Too clean isn't comfortable. I don't know.

But inevitably you're going to run out of things to say.

She's sitting on the bed, leaning back on her hands, and he sits down beside her and both their chests are tight and breath short, and he wonders how many people the girl has slept with in her life. He doesn't want to touch the girl and there is nothing asking him to, would rather not see the girl naked and bending over to fumble with the shoes and wishes she would leave, and that he had never met the girl, and that he had never entered the Association and never played basketball and never been born. He knows this will serve no purpose to him beyond an immediate physical gratification which really he can take care of by himself once the girl leaves. He knows any desire for the body will flush right down the toilet along with it. This is not real. But what will happen must happen. And his erection is making a damp spot on his boxer-briefs and he discreetly rubs his hands on his thighs to dry his palms and they stare at their feet then look at each other and she laughs—sweetly he thinks—and he looks at the mouth and the thighs that the girl doesn't tug on the skirt to cover anymore and licks his lips and his mouth is dry so he tries to work up saliva with his tongue for when he will place his tongue into the mouth but doesn't know that she's also working up saliva with her tongue in her mouth and the eyes search his, curious about what he will choose, and after a minute he takes a deep breath and laughs, rubs his forehead, and the girl laughs too and the soft voice frail as the girl says, —What are you thinking about? He shakes his head and thinks, in a very clear internal voice, FUCK IT. Puts his hand on the back of the head and holds it gently there as he leans in, kisses the mouth, puts his tongue into the mouth.

Something changes in the girl immediately. The girl becomes very aggressive. The girl kisses frantically, grabbing handfuls of his hair, fumbling at his zipper. He gets the image of a puppy fighting through the litter half-crazed for its mother's nipple. But rather than becoming taken aback he feels as though he must keep up with the pace the girl has set so he not only matches the girl's aggression but overtakes it. A man must dominate, he thinks. And he gropes the body, pulling the hair a little and sucking the earlobe, squeezing the tits through the tank top, looking into the closed eyes and trying to wonder what's going on in the head but quickly finding that he doesn't care. He tries to pull the tank top down so he can see the tits but it's too tight and so he shoves his hand in there, the built-in bra is like a suction cup and makes it tough, while at the same time the girl is trying to unzip his pants but can't do it because of the angle, so he has to do it, and the girl puts the hand in and runs the hand along the inside of his thigh looking for his horny but it's the wrong thigh and he quickly loses his patience and yanks the hand away and gets his horny out himself and the girl wraps the small white fingers around his horny and pulls so hard it hurts, so he squeezes the wrist and stops the girl, glances down to see his horny sticking out of his fly so sudden and extreme it's nearly comical—The Penis of Gilbert Marcus. He sucks on the neck and the girl whimpers—frantically jerking away—huffing and puffing through the nose and he thinks, The girl really wants Gilbert Marcus and wants to be penetrated by Gilbert Marcus and likes it rough and fast and if Gilbert Marcus doesn't do it like how the girl expects then the girl will be disappointed and look down on Gilbert Marcus for being a pussy and the girl will tell all her friends that Gilbert Marcus couldn't fuck well and they'll laugh, make it an inside joke. He places his hand between the legs, gripping the crotch, and he says, —Give me a blow job. And without hesitation the girl drops to the knees. He holds the red hair back with one hand as the girl blows him, staring up at him with the eyes wide which disturbs him to no end and so he puts his hand on the side of the face and tries to cover the eyes with his thumb under the pretense of stroking the head, but the girl's not moving and only has him an inch or two deep, disgusting him, and so he tries thrusting from his sitting position but can't feel anything and the girl keeps making choking noises and flinching back and taking his horny out, frustrating him even more, and the teeth keep dragging and now he has lost all patience and is embarrassed seeing the girl try so hard and this is just not worth it and the phone rings on the nightstand and he wants to answer it but the girl doesn't seem to be going anywhere but after trying to ignore it and closing his eyes and putting himself into the Systemism Joy mental state of someone enjoying fellatio he says, —Okay, uh . . . He puts his hands on either side of her head, tries to gently pull her up, but she doesn't get the hint so he sort of knocks on the top of her head and says, —Hello? Stop.

And the girl looks up at him, wiping the mouth, saliva all over the chin, breathing hard, and the girl looks so young and helpless that it turns him off and the phone stops ringing and the girl stands up and starts to straddle him and he thinks, Fine. He pushes the girl off and forces the girl around, and the girl resists and he thinks, Must please her, must fuck good. And so he twists the body around harder, and the body stumbles a little and he bends the body over and reaches under the skirt and takes the ass in his hands, squeezes, inspects, spanks, pulls the thong down, never fast enough, hypnotized by his craving and frantic with unbridled fiending, unaware in his extreme focus how loud his breathing has become—a grunting, from the back of his throat.

Out in the hall, two people, a male and female, both Brazilian, sneak through the door of the service staircase and creep along the wall like thieves up to the door of room 239, the male groping the female, and the female teasingly slapping the male's hands away as she unlocks the door. They slither inside and they are both wearing Huntington Hotel and Casino employee uniforms and the male stifles the female's giggles by kissing her and pulls her uniform—a one-piece beige maid's outfit—over her head and in her bra and underwear she wraps her arms around him and in the silence they can hear a muffled woman's voice on the other side of the wall and the muffled woman's voice says quite clearly, —No. The male (thirty-seven) and the female (seventeen) stop and look at each other and the female says in Portuguese, —What was that?

—Nothing probably, the male says, also in Portuguese, trying to unhook her bra.

—Sounded weird.

—It was nothing.

—Think maybe we should do something? Call security? Or the police?

But the male says no because he is working under a false name and doesn't have legitimate papers. The female forgets about the muffled woman's voice and lets the male do what he will because the male is older, loves her, is trusted.

Gilbert remembers another girl, another room, saying the same thing. But where? And what was her name?

This is just what girls say sometimes, he thinks. They have a lot at stake—reputations, conscience. Society doesn't let them indulge themselves sexually like it does men and so girls are forced to say no if they want to maintain any self-respect. This rationalization is what allows him to cover the mouth and pose the body so he can get in, a hand on the back of the neck holding the girl still because the girl is writhing, and he can't get in on the first try, and he finds this confounding and since it makes no sense it must be that the vagina is unusually small so he pushes himself in, biting his lower lip and pulling the ass open with his free hand and with the other pulling the body back toward him to facilitate, firming the grip on the neck, since the body is so much smaller and weaker than he that the body is nearly shoved over with his every thrust. He gets the head in, but it feels stuck, and he grunts and the girl says again, muffled by his hand but still quite clear, —No.

It's a whisper, a gasp, what could be replaced with the word *oh* or *yes*, not argumentative or irritable in the least, certainly not protestant. Like the girl is *pretending* to say no. The *no* isn't a *no*. The *no* is not him but the girl, and so he has no responsibility toward it.

And reinforcing this is how the girl is submissive and not clawing or scratching or screaming for help, which, he thinks, wouldn't you do if you were getting raped? Thinking that word alarms him. It is the first time he has actually considered it. He pushes in as hard as he can, tearing tissue in the vagina and causing a bit of blood to appear on the inner walls, which of course hurts her in a tearing ripping sensation and she makes the appropriate noise, but it doesn't distinguish itself from the other noises she is making, and he wonders—as he now penetrates the body fully—if he is indeed raping somebody right now.

No, he thinks. I'm not. Because if I am raping her—or rather if someone were being raped—wouldn't the act be more violent? Wouldn't she do all she could do to resist? If rape is the terrible thing they say it is then wouldn't the victim be horrified of life after rape and the hell of the act and thus do all she could do to not be raped? It seems like something as huge as rape would be impossible to mistake. And so rape, he concludes, is not happening because rape is not this easy.

But then he is trained, with regard to his high profile and financial status, to always wonder during every sexual act with a girl not his wife if it could be considered rape or not—the possibility that it is a crime comes with the flirting and undressing and cleaning up. It manifests itself always at some point during the encounter at least as a vague and mostly far-fetched concept. It has to. A man must always wonder what is rape, because rape is trouble, death. Rape is destroying Gilbert Marcus and all he has, tearing out the heart of The Athlete and all he's based upon, every twinkle of light on earth.

Rape, he decides, happily fucking the girl, is not this. This is pas-

sionate and raunchy adulterous sex in a hotel room. This is me getting
off. This is me enjoying one of the luxuries my life affords me. This is
me taking care of a basic masculine need. This is me and whatever her
name is, sharing an understanding. The girl knows the way things are.
The girl is cool. The girl knows Gilbert Marcus, is a servant of him,
and God bless the girl for it.

The ass though is a bit disappointing. Too flat, pasty, freckles. He
doesn't like freckles on asses, he decides. He feels cheated. It's simply
a white girl's freckly ass, although nothing compared to Brianne's
white girl ass before the baby when she was faithful to her Pilates
classes. And though normally such a disappointing revelation would
diminish the pleasure of this, he is surprised to find that it has the
reverse effect and turns him on way more than he ever expected. He
finds himself putting his hands around the neck, to maximize this
pleasure but for some reason putting his hands around the neck
doesn't do for him what it normally does for him, so he stops for a
second and reaches down and picks up the thong off the floor and
he puts it around the neck and twists it once or twice but not very
tight and resumes. This works. This does it. This is exciting, sexy. The
girl likes it too, he can tell. He knows he will not last much longer
which is good but the girl is pretending to be trying to pull away,
playing along, and so he tightens the thong, twisting the ends in his
hands a couple more times around the neck, and the body really pretends to be struggling now.

Everything loses itself as the earth pinpoints into a precise focus
on his orgasm, the girl's screams now a sick cough, and there becomes
nothing else and he wants nothing now but to see his semen on the
face and though he knows this is pushing it he wants to see where the
line of the understanding lies. And after two minutes and forty nine
seconds of intercourse he pulls out of it, forces the body—the thong
still around the throat, slightly annoyed at how silent she is being, but
whatever—back down to the knees and she is his zombie and doing
whatever she must to give Gilbert Marcus pleasure and he laughs,
can't help it. The eyes not seeing, opaque, and rolling into the back of
the head. The body floppy like a rag doll. And he rubs his horny with
his hand while keeping his other hand around the neck holding his
breath and grinding his teeth and seeing himself like out-of-body and
Leo is there behind him in his tighty-whities and Mervin his father
and Sandy is there and Colleen is there and Gilbert's legs below the
knees numbing and fury and losing sight and sense of time or place

and bodiless and afterward he lets go of the body and the girl collapses to the floor and doesn't answer when he tries to wake her up.

It is morning and Gilbert is in Los Angeles, in his home. Brianne has locked herself in the master bathroom with the water running and has or has not swallowed a bottle of prescription painkillers from the tackle box full of various medications and nutritional supplements that Gilbert keeps under the sink. She has or has not slit her wrists with the Shun Pro series paring knife that Gilbert noticed is missing from the six-piece set in the kitchen. She may or may not be hanging herself from one of the dual shower heads in the mega-capacity shower, or trying to figure out the best, most secure place to hang herself without running the risk of damaging the bathroom that was customed designed and cost in total hundreds of thousands of dollars. She has not taken one of his twenty-seven guns from the gunsafe in the bedroom because he has checked. But she may or may not have bought a gun herself and hidden it from him specifically for this purpose, having foreseen a situation like this occurring. He bangs on the door and says, —Brianne, don't be so dramatic. I mean, what kind of illusion were you living under? She was a *prostitute*. I didn't *kill* her. She had a *seizure* or something. She's not *dead*. She'll be *fine*.

But Brianne's quiet and Gilbert looks out between the shades but doesn't see them yet, goes back to the bathroom door, says, more softly this time, —Brianne. Brianne? I'm sorry, okay? But right now I need you to help me.

—Fuck you let me die.

—Brianne. Open the door. Come on. Let's talk about it.

—No.

—Open the door.

—I'm taking a shower.

—No you're not.

—I'm washing my hair.

—Brianne.

—Go away.

They are gathering with cameras, laptops, cell phones. They must know by now. He imagines what Sheldon and Larry (the white one) and Will are doing, what is happening to the girl in the hospital, all the way in Las Vegas, another world . . .

—Brianne. What did you take? Did you take anything? Do you have any alcohol?

She doesn't answer, and he listens, head to the door, the baby—Gilbert's reason for living—crying down the hall, and he is nearly delusional from lack of sleep and can feel the sadness of the world drifting through his core, he can hear Brianne muttering softly beneath the sound of rushing water, the bathtub, —I just wanted a baby . . .

—I'm admitting to you here, with the hope of us putting it behind us, that I had an extramarital affair.

— . . . and . . . a husband . . .

—We'll work on it, our marriage can overcome this and become stronger from it. Besides, look, you knew what you were getting into with me.

— . . . and . . . to be happy . . .

—I need you to listen to me though baby.

— . . . and . . . beautiful . . .

—There's been a, well, a pretty substantial confusion and there's going to be a bit of a legal thing here for a little while. But you have to believe me when I say I did not do what they're going to say I did.

— . . . and . . . good . . .

And Gilbert says, —This is nothing, Brianne. This is an obstacle and. Look. Yeah. Real responsible, Brianne. Yeah. Real good. What about the baby? Have you thought about your *son* before you commit suicide? You're being very selfish.

She doesn't answer so he kicks in the door, breaks it down, finds her naked in the tub, hair soaked and clinging to her skull, water running over her bare feet and up between her legs, arms spread out and eyes closed, mouth parted, looking pale and weak. But there is no blood. There is no gun. There is no empty bottle of prescription painkillers and the cabinet under the sink where he keeps his tackle box full of prescription medications and supplements is closed. But everything else except for this cabinet and except for the Archeo copper bathtub with rotary massage jets, inline water heater, pillow, mood light and chromotherapy, and automatic low-water-level sensor (starting at $54,925)—including the floors, the crown molding, the titanium towel racks, the antique flower vases from Malawi from when they went there to consider adopting a Malawian child, the thirty-seven-inch flat-screen plasma TV, the Xbox, the four-foot-tall candles, the original contemporary artwork including the black-and-white photograph of a nude pregnant Brianne taken by Annie Leibovitz (the only copy in existence—Brianne insisted the negatives be destroyed), the Hammacher Schlemmer bath mats, the matching his and hers terrycloth bathrobes with monogrammed initials that they have never worn—*everything, all of it, the entire thing* is torn up, smashed, ripped out, bent, mangled, ruined, cut into thin strips, burned, chewed on, broken, destroyed. Even, to Gilbert's horror, the dual shower heads.

—Brianne what the fuck?

There is a hammer and a crowbar and the paring knife is in the toilet along with some hand towels and some of Gilbert's white dress shirts and there are huge holes in the walls. The powder from smashed drywall is everywhere. Brianne is lying there in the Archeo copper bathtub and she is trying to be dead. She is trying to drown herself. She is allowing the water to fill up the copper bathtub past her knees and up over her thighs and up to her neck and into her ears and nostrils and throat and down into her lungs so that the water in turn will not allow her to breathe anymore. That is how she deals with this obstacle. He stops because she looks exactly like the girl did after he came out of the shower and saw her still on the floor and took the thong, thinking for some reason that it was important to hide the thong. Like remembering a vivid dream you forgot you had.

But the drain's unplugged. She forgets the drain, is how she deals with this obstacle.

He slaps her face a little, she doesn't open her eyes, he turns the water off and tries to pull her out of the tub but she's dead weight, drapes a towel over her and thinks, Don't move the victim until paramedics arrive.

—Did you really take something? Brianne? You didn't did you.

Then there are sirens and he looks outside to see dozens of cop cars, helicopters circling overhead, news vans, and cops dressed in black SWAT gear holding machine guns are ringing the doorbell, and he lets them in laughing because is the fucking *SWAT team* really necessary? And they have their guns out and point those guns at him and throw him on the floor and scream things and put the guns against his head and handcuff him. Brianne wanders downstairs naked and soaking wet and wearing a cowboy hat and she walks through the scene toward the kitchen smiling horrifically and shouting, —Hey y'all! Glad ya'll could make it! Anybody want some cottage cheese? Because I'm having some . . . And before anyone can put a towel over her they—the twenty, thirty cops dressed in SWAT gear and holding pistols and shotguns, and Gilbert, facedown on the floor declaring his innocence into the floor with his hands cuffed behind his back and four or five more cops kneeling on his back and head, holding him down—they all stop what they're doing to watch her. Someone, one of the cops, lets out a long, slow whistle.

They put Gilbert in the back of a cop car and he tries to tell them about the baby upstairs crying but there is a man in the front yard in a cop uniform who isn't Gilbert holding Gilbert's reason for living. And for a moment, he considers breaking the windows with his feet, worming his way out of the handcuffs like a superhero, snatching his reason for living and tearing off in a cop car; or taking a cop's gun and before anyone can stop him putting the gun in his mouth and pulling the trigger. He has to call Abe Birnbaum, he has to call everyone he knows and explain what happened and they'll post bail and take him in and hide him, sneak him out of the country, appear at the end of a driveway before reporters to read a statement from Mr. Marcus.

Then to the station where they put him in jail and tell him the girl died two hours ago and ask him why he fled and he calls Abe Birnbaum and signs autographs for the cops, repeats what happened six or seven more times, starting to wonder if he has it right or if he actually did what they say he did. He could be changing his story inadvertently. They make him tell the part about the blow job again and again and want to know what the vagina felt like, what kind of tits the girl had, the thin line between porn and justice. They laugh with him, give him water, sit with their feet on the table, hands behind their heads, smoking cigarettes as he describes her asshole. They ask how much Ben Jermaine pays to take care of these kinds of things, not that he's ever been in *this* kind of mix-up, but you know what we mean, and he tells them what he knows—somewhere around a couple million dollars total altogether over the years—and they let out long, slow whistles and shake their heads, raising their eyebrows at one another.

These kinds of things.

That is what it is. It is one of these kinds of things. A case of miscommunication. He said, she said. A situation of fucking the wrong girl. It happens all the time to athletes and to men in general and now it is happening to you except a million times worse because how were you supposed to know she would die? This is her problem, not yours, and you are among men who understand. And the autopsy report will come back and clear everything up, the Association has people to take care of it, and you have the money and lawyers to fight back—thank Jesus for the law, which has little regard for right or wrong, only itself. The detectives offer to call you at a private number so your wife won't know they're calling. They say if you cooperate they'll make it easy and won't tell the press. But they can't promise the press won't find out on its own. Especially those things—whattya call them—the blogs. And the short detective, whose name is Rogers, has a thick nose and a wrinkled forehead and stirs his Styrofoam coffee and taps a cigarette on the table and says, —You know the noble thing to do here, Gilbert. You're an adult. I can't tell you whether you need to tell us the truth or not but that's a decision you're going to have to make.

And Gilbert leans back in his chair and everyone's quiet.

PART THREE
Untitled

19

IN THE COURTROOM THERE IS THE sensation of ending. In the courtroom he has lost again but there is no headache.

And that day The Athlete was in Nevada on trial for murder. During a recess he stood with a hand in his pocket on the back steps of the courthouse in the hot dry heat— unknown to the media waiting in bored ambush out front—talking on the phone to Abe Birnbaum.

—Your sweetheart's gone, Abe said, —Shipped him off to New York.

—Who.

—Who. Who do you think. Ben.

—Yeah?

—Yep. Told management it's either you or him. Made them choose. Ben Jermaine or Gilbert Marcus. They chose Gilbert Marcus.

—But it's always been sort of like that though hasn't it. Me or him. Him or me. Like we were kids groveling for our parents' love.

—Think they love you? They don't love you, Gilbert. Jeffrey

doesn't love you. Coach doesn't love you. They were ready to ship you off. Still might, if they get a good enough offer. The Harpoons want you. Which is a joke. Brian's gone. Dave. Nate. Tim. Coach. Everybody. Now Papa Bear Ben. Except for you, it's near total turnover. They want to rebuild. If they can get a good enough offer for you, they'll sell you off like a car.

—I don't know who the parents would be though. Whose love were we groveling for, do you think? The fans maybe? The owner? The game?

—I don't know, son. Reason I called is Ben's gone. Out of your hair. One more thing out of your hair. Lord knows you could use it. They couldn't afford both of you anymore, not to mention you couldn't stand each other. So be it. Had to get rid of one of you. Ben's older, on the decline. New York came up with an offer for him. So be it. The end of an era, as they say. But time for new beginnings, right, Gilbert?

—Sure, The Athlete said.

—Dallas is used to being on top. Time to change some things. Everyone's bored, giving up, going home. How's that trial going?

—Fine. I don't know. Good, I think.

—That lawyer good as I remember?

—He seems to know what he's doing.

—He's a motherfucker, isn't he? You know he used to represent mob guys? In Boston. Whitey Bulger's boys, I think. Do they call them boys? You wouldn't believe the kinds of guys he's gotten off. I don't mean that sexually. I mean that legally. He's tough. Tearing that poor girl to shreds. It makes you feel almost sorry for her and her family.

—Yeah I guess sometimes I feel sorry for them too but it just doesn't make sense. I mean why'd they get rid of Ben and not me? He's not the one going to jail.

—You're not going to jail. Guys like you don't go to jail. Think the Association is going to let you go to jail? After all you've done for them? So knock it off and stay in shape. You're not going to jail. You're playing this season so get in shape.

The Athlete said, —I do stay in shape. Have I ever not stayed in shape? I *am* staying in shape. I run every morning before court. I'm in the gym straight after I get out. There's no Athlete if I get out of shape. I have to work out or I'll lose my mind.

—Who now, son?

—I'll lose my mind. I'll go nuts. Throw my chair at the judge. Break his face. Jump over the table and run across the room before they can stop me and throttle him. Whatever his name is. Fat fuck.

—I think it's best if you should probably keep that to yourself.

—Scream at the prosecutor, What the fuck are you doing to me?! WHY THE FUCK ARE YOU DOING THIS TO ME?! I AM NOT A MURDERER!

—There's probably all kinds of people around with invested interest in this thing and you're yelling, Gilbert.

—In the middle of when they're talking just start screaming, you know? If I take the judge hostage and make them listen to me that I didn't kill this girl so they know how serious I am. Steal the bailiff's gun and turn it on him and say, Get on your knees, jerk. He's really a jerk by the way. It's like he thinks he's the most important person in the world because he's a bailiff. Couldn't even be a real cop but thinks he's tough shit.

—Gilb—

—And take the judge in a choke hold and hold him like in the movies with the gun to his head and say if anyone tries anything I'll do it. I swear to God.

—Gilb—

—I'll have sweat dripping down my face and maybe be almost crying, I'll be so emotional and passionate. And I'll say, I did not murder that girl, I swear to God.

—Gil—

—This is my life, I'll say. I'll scream it. THIS IS MY LIFE!

—Gilbert, shut the fuck up and listen. That's enough right there. There is press around no doubt. You hear me? I understand you're in a tense situation, son, but first of all, you're not *on* trial for murder. It's *manslaughter*. No one worth a damn goes to jail for fucking *manslaughter*. Look at Karl Babcock. He shot a guy point-blank in the side of the fucking head, high as a kite, and not only did he not get charged with murder but he got *probation*. And Karl Babcock's nobody. He'd been out of the league for years at that point. He's shit compared to Gilbert Marcus and *still*. But listen. Press could be undercover or hiding behind something. A tree or—

—I don't care anymore, Abe.

—Tomorrow morning I'm going to read GILBERT MARCUS THREATENS TO KILL JUDGE IN MANSLAUGHTER TRIAL. My God. Where are my Tums.

—Shoot the prosecutor that ugly bitch and say, Now tell them the truth! Tell them she had a hole in her heart!

—Fucking crazy, this kid. Stupid.

—It's true. And the judge will see how serious I am and how much sense it makes and maybe, I don't know, dismiss the case.

—Gilbert just sit there and be cooperative and the truth will come out on its own. Hear me? That's the justice system. Okay? You're stressed, this trial and having to mortgage your own house for bail. You have a beautiful house and get paid a tremendous salary and it's a shame you had to do something like that. Your wife is upset and should be but I don't blame you for getting a little stressed, but, son, you have to take it easy. One thing at a time.

—I'll say yes I made a mistake by cheating on my wife but that's between us and we settled that. And besides, adultery isn't a crime. Is it?

—No. I don't think. Maybe in some states. Like Utah maybe. Texas. Everything's illegal in Texas.

—Yeah but I'm saying though I'll just make her say that there is a possibility, a chance, a pretty large chance, but just a chance that why the girl died is, A, the heart condition she had and the asthma, and B, the drugs she was on for being bulimic or whatever and thus sexually a whore as is a symptom of having a poor body image, which caused some sort of fatal reaction. They are not *looking at that* as a possible avenue to explore even though I tell my fucking lawyer every *day* . . .

—Gilbert, shut up and calm down, Abe said. —Shut up and get a grip or I'll call the team right now and tell them you're retiring for good. Hear me? I will tell them Gilbert is quitting professional basketball so he can get his life and his mind and his soul straightened out. Jennie, call Jeffrey and tell him Gilbert Marcus is done.

—No, Abe. Jesus.

—Go back inside and take a deep breath. Relax a little bit. You're losing it. Focus on one thing at a time. Listen, you want everyone to worship you and think how amazing you are? Well guess what, son. Forget that. That's all over. You're just another black athlete in trouble with the law now. And I don't care what the fuck you are racially you're still a black athlete to the eyes of Joe America Six-Pack who buys tickets. Another nigger who we gave too much money and power to and now he's raping white girls then strangling them. Just another fake black millionaire athlete who has to screw all the time and cheats on his wife and uses human beings as objects for his gratification then disposes of them, literally. Talented and fun to watch, even more fun to hate, reliable in the clutch. Sure. One of the best out there if not the best and you want your team to beat him but they never do. But listen to me now, son. You are not nor will you ever be Darren Dickinson. Never. Dickinson never did this kind of shit. The girls Dickinson was with, they kept quiet. And even when they didn't and went to the press, no one gave a damn. Some glassy-eyed stripper slut in St. Louis goes on TV and proves through DNA testing that her baby is Darren Dickinson's? Didn't matter. Know why? Because he's Darren Dickinson and you're not. Know why? Because look where you're presently located talking to me on the phone. In *court* defending your *life*.

—I'm not *inside* the court actually.

—Shut the fuck up and listen to me very carefully. The golden boy is dead. The dream is over. You lost Reebok and Super H20 dropped you and Nestlé dropped you and Pepsi dropped you and that AIDS charity for fuck's sake is returning every cent you ever gave them, which is more or less their entire resources and is going to have to fold, unless fucking Bono or Angelina Jolie steps in and saves the day. And those are only the ones who are actually returning my phone calls. So forget it. You're something people joke about now. You're a shitty Leno joke is what you are now. You're fooling nobody, Gilbert. You hear me?

— . . .

—It's over. The dream is over. So knock it off. Knock . . . it . . . OFF.

—Abe, I was only—

—You're normal, son.

—Abe.

—You're a normal person. You're a goddamn normal person, Gilbert. That's all you are. That's all you're ever going to be. Get used to it and get comfortable. And welcome to the real world, son. Because guess what? You're just a goddamn PERSON.

The object in the courtroom was The Athlete—bones and flesh in a handsome expensive suit propped up in a chair. These tedious days zoomed by thus. His lawyer reminded The Athlete of Donald Trump. His voice. He wondered if his lawyer thought he was guilty. He wondered if his lawyer thought he was tough. He wondered if his lawyer liked his suit. He found it important that his lawyer who used to defend mob guys thought he was cool.

His job as a defendant was to show up and to be wearing the suit and look like he was listening. But it was summer and Dallas had finished dead last in the Southwestern Division and he thought, at that moment, waiting for the judge, The best athlete forgets. The best athlete is he who endures humiliation.

He thought, It's good that they're trading Ben. They'll never say Gilbert Marcus needs Papa Bear Ben Jermaine to win again. That he can't do it without Papa Bear. That he's not The Athlete without The Behemoth. Starting next year, I'll start winning again and I'll win without Ben. I'll do it alone, the only way I know. Because as long as there was a Papa Bear Ben Jermaine there was Darren Dickinson and if you're not in the footprints of the greatest then what are you, if anything?

Nearly every night since he was sixteen years old he has made a habit—after brushing his teeth, trimming his nose hairs, and plucking his eyebrows—of examining his fair face in the bathroom mirror. He has the habit of regretting that he doesn't have a lot of facial hair. When he tries to grow a goatee—which takes as long as three weeks—it looks like the hair's been drawn onto his face with a pen. He fantasizes of waking one day to a manly thick growth of hair that he'd have to shave twice a day. He fantasizes about being able to grow a beard.

And how many times, how many ghost-town nights, have been marked by the reflection in the bathroom mirror of a man moving the skin of his face, pulling it tight, making faces at himself, pursing the lips, changing angles, looking for a sign of the beard that will one day come but ultimately finding nothing? This sometimes with a beautiful girl dressing on the other side of the door, then the sound of the door brushing against the carpet, clicking shut without a word, everyone leaving without farewell. Then the change in the air, the vacant rush of something gone, her breezy scent on the pillow the only proof she was there at all.